Ralph Y

Dear Caroline...

outskirts
press

PROLOGUE

Weddings and honeymoons are supposed to be joyous occasions. Typically, they are, but something was lacking from this one. A pall of sadness hung over what should have been the happiest days of Caroline's relatively short life. Something was missing. Someone was missing.

Two months had passed since he took that fall. The doctors said it was an inoperable brain aneurism that ruptured. He died instantly. He knew about the aneurism. So did her mom. The doctors knew about it. Caroline did not. They didn't want to spoil her moment. They wanted her to be happy. They were also hoping against reality that her dad might somehow hang on for another six months, a year, or more. That was not to be, and now the happiest days of her life were filled with pangs of emptiness and sorrow.

Feigning joy might be difficult at times, but she knew it was necessary. Richard truly was the man of her dreams. Their honeymoon would be filled with passion, romance, and laughter. If a few moments of sadness crept in, they would somehow manage.

Honeymoon in Key West. That would make it even more difficult. That was her Mom and Dad's place. No, really it was just Dad's. Mom enjoyed her time there but he reveled in it. Dad knew every street, restaurant and bar on the island and could list them all in order of preference. He even knew many of the shop owners, merchants and local politicians by name. Key West was his place and so it was no surprise that he agreed to pay for a week on the island as part of their wedding present. Caroline had been there four times. Three family vacations and one Spring Break getaway. The honeymoon would be her fifth. It would be Richard's second. It was on that Spring Break four years ago that the two had met.

Their plane landed in Fort Lauderdale shortly before noon on the morning of November 16. By 1pm they were heading south, in a bright orange Camaro with a black convertible top. She released her hair and let it fly back in the warm tropical breeze. Warm air, blue skies and palm trees. Maybe she could forgo the sadness. Maybe Key West was the perfect answer. There would be moments, to be sure, but it was time to celebrate her new life, not mourn the life that was lost.

Memories flooded by her as Caroline remembered the routine their family had followed. They usually rented minivan from Budget or Alamo, but on one trip, after some spirited haggling, Dad negotiated his way into a bright red Mustang convertible. The drive typically took an hour on the highway, then thirty minutes through the reeds and sawgrass along the southernmost tip of the Florida mainland. All at once a pastel colored bridge would rise before them like the Yellow Brick Road on the way to Oz. They would drive high above that narrow channel as yachts, fishing boats and assorted sailing vessels were afforded room to pass safely beneath them. Mom would turn to him and smile as watched days and years of stress simply wash off of her dad's face. He was going home. Three hours and forty-two bridges later, there would be a large, multi-colored sign portraying a scarlet sunset. The sign said "Welcome to Paradise."

Caroline and Richard had already established their own Key West memories. During late March of her junior year at

Northeastern, she and four other girls had crammed into her roommate's old Chevy Blazer and drove for nearly thirty hours. It was 30 degrees when they left Boston and 85 by the time they passed the Paradise sign. The ride was dreadfully long, but the prospect of escaping for a full week of beach parties made the trip almost bearable. They were staying in a two-bedroom timeshare that one of the girl's parents owned. Plenty of room and a full kitchen. It was luxury accommodations, just a block or two from the bars of Duval Street.

Richard and two fraternity brothers had also driven down from Beantown. The three were seniors at Boston College. It took them 26 hours to get there, cramped in a beat-up Honda Civic, stopping only for gas, a bathroom and a few burgers to go. Upon arrival, they all shared a small room with two beds and a cot at the Econo-Lodge on North Roosevelt Boulevard. They didn't care. It was Key West. It was Spring Break and they were away from the cold and crowded streets of New England.

Both groups arrived on the same day, exhausted and elated. After hitting a few bars, they chose to make it an early night, vowing to party hard and strong for the remainder of their stay. On the morning of their first full day, Richard and Caroline had risen early, both starting their day with a vigorous run through the streets of the island. Neither had played college sports, but both were fitness enthusiasts. Their paths had crossed when, simultaneously, they stopped suddenly about midway down Duval Street. Their focus had been diverted by a Starbucks sign outside the La Concha Hotel. The morning run was soon abandoned, as they shared coffee, conversation and cell phone numbers over the course of an hour. Later that day, the two groups merged, forming their own communal dance party. Some of their cohorts would splinter off from time to time, but from that point on Richard and Caroline were inseparable.

After graduation, Richard landed a job with an accounting firm in Boston. Caroline moved in with him, taking the train to Northeastern University each day for classes. Her parents neither approved nor disapproved. They liked him but were a little concerned that it was still too early in the relationship for such a big move. Their fears quickly proved to be unfounded, as the couple continued to grow and flourish. Upon graduation, Caroline went to work as a nurse at Mass General. With both of them gainfully employed and somewhat settled, a wedding date was set.

Dad booked them a week at the La Concha. Even if he hadn't heard the Starbucks story a dozen or more times, that would have been his choice for them. First opened in 1926, it was widely considered to be one of the most luxurious haunts on the island. Haunts is an appropriate description, since the hotel, along with the rest of Key West is rumored to be haunted. Local legend has it that Ernest Hemingway kept a mistress at the La Concha where his ghost has long been reported to appear. Another popular tale is of a New Year's Eve party some years ago, when a waiter mistakenly backed his cart into an empty elevator shaft that was under repair on the fifth floor. The waiter fell to his death, but his spirit continues to visit that floor, pushing his cart and roaming the hallways late at night.

Caroline and Richard had room 606, facing eastward to the Atlantic Ocean. It was a much different perspective for them to enter the hotel as welcome guests, rather than as two starving college students in search of a cup of coffee. They felt both comfortable and worthy of the marble floors, crystal lamps and mahogany furnishings that appointed the lobby. They weren't kids anymore, but they were young, energetic and about to make a new beginning. The ebony skinned Bahamian woman at the front desk welcomed the couple with a warm smile.

While the bellman brought their bags upstairs, the two

stopped at the restaurant bar for a celebratory drink. Richard ordered Glenlivet to honor his dad, while Caroline asked for a mojito, which was her mother's adult beverage of choice. A nearby couple from Missouri overheard them say something about a honeymoon and congratulated them. They were older but visiting the island for similar reasons. This was their fifteenth anniversary. There was little doubt that the two newlyweds would be returning for anniversaries as well.

It was once customary for the groom, on his wedding night to carry the bride across the doorway threshold, to symbolize the passing from one stage of life to another. With a dearth of virgin brides, this tradition had pretty much slipped by the wayside. On their wedding night, the two had stayed at the Marriott near the airport. The wedding parties ran late and by the time they got to their room, both were slightly drunk and very tired. They stumbled through the door, set the alarm for five o'clock and fell asleep on the bed, with their clothes on and the marriage unconsummated.

As Richard deftly unlocked the door to room 606, it suddenly occurred to Caroline that this was something she wanted to do. Ever accommodating, he propped the door open and swooped her from her feet

The room was magnificent. The king size bed had a brass headboard, polished to a mirror finish. The bathroom was covered in white and grey marble. The view overlooked the tops of the buildings and palm trees as they could see the ocean just beyond the Key West Lighthouse. On the mahogany dresser was a dozen roses and a bottle of champagne on ice. It was a wedding gift from the hotel staff. They quickly popped the cork and each drew a long guzzle, nearly choking on the bubbles.

With love, laughter, and passion in the air, the couple spontaneously combusted as they began tearing at each other's clothes.

Intertwined, they found their way into the shower while not yet fully disrobed. The two then passed, soaking wet, from the shower to the bed, where they tangled their bodies in a rhythmic dance of thrusts and gentle caresses for what seemed like an eternity. Finally, they drifted into a deep sleep, with their warm, naked bodies still wrapped together in a lover's knot.

It was Caroline who awoke first. By now it was past sunset and the two needed to consider what to do for dinner. Many hotel restaurants, including the one downstairs, were open late, but perhaps room service would be the better option. Either way, she would allow Richard to sleep as late as he wished. While he rested, she could shower again, slip into a summer dress and begin unpacking. Slowly, she hoisted the suitcases off the floor and on to the two chairs near the window. As she did, a melancholy began to emerge from within, rising outward from the depths of her stomach and into her chest. Her heart felt contracted, as though a large hand had gently squeezed around it. Her breathing began to take on a measured, but barely audible heaving. The suitcases were heavy, she thought. She must have strained herself lifting them to the chairs.

That is what she chose to think, but Caroline knew otherwise. There was a presence in the room that she could neither ignore nor deny. Her father had indeed followed her to Key West, if only in spirit. She felt him in every fiber of her being and yet she knew it was impossible. If truth be told, she hardly knew him when he was alive. Now he is dead and dead means dead. Gone forever. Religion or belief in an afterlife was never a strong inclination to her. "Don't be a fool," she thought. "You're just missing him. That's all." She looked to the bed and smiled as Richard lay there, naked and beautiful. This is life. Everything else is history or an anticipated future. We have this moment. That is enough.

Unzipping the suitcases, she began to fill the large dresser and armoire with their clothes. Silently she prayed to whatever essence of spirituality might be out there. What she really prayed for was that her honeymoon would not be spoiled by her sadness and loss. She quickly convinced herself, by sheer will, that her father would not deprive her of her honeymoon. A subtle anger grew. This is no time for grief, dammit. Dancing, laughter, sleep, sex and sun would fill the days and melt the nights. It had to be that way. It would be that way. Then she saw the envelope.

There were two small nightstands; one on each side of the bed. A brass reading lamp and a small alarm clock adorned the table on the right. Below was a single drawer and two empty shelves. On the left side sat the same brass lamp and a telephone. On the shelf below there was a phone book and several tourism guides. The left side would belong to Caroline. She opened the drawer on her side of the bed intending to place a tube of suntan lotion, a small bottle of hand sanitizer and a bottle or two of water.

When she slid the drawer open, she had expected to see the customary Gideon's Bible, with its standard black cover and gold lettering. There was a bible but had been concealed by an oversized manila envelope. The yellow folder had been clasped but unsealed. There was no writing on either side. Caroline lifted and opened it, expecting to find a more extensive collection of coupons and guidebooks. It seemed too thick and too heavy for brochures. Inside was some sort of manuscript. It was hole-punched and inserted into a cheap vinyl binder. The manuscript was easily 200 pages long. Perhaps it had been left behind by the room's previous occupants. No doubt the front desk could return it to the rightful owner.

Caroline turned back the cover, intending to read the first page or two, on the chance that there was a name or return address to the binder. Key West had long been a haven for writers, so she wondered if it was someone's unfinished novel. When she flipped the cover, a single handwritten page fell to the floor, landing gently near her foot. The page had not been hole-punched and therefore was not likely a part of the manuscript. She moved the suitcase, now emptied, off the chair to the closet near the door. Then, after placing the vinyl binder on the nightstand, she plopped herself into the chair by the window and began reading the handwritten note. All the while, Richard slept peacefully.

One sentence into the handwritten page, Caroline's eyes welled up with tears. Her hands trembled almost violently, causing the lamp's reflection on her diamond wedding ring to shine off the windows and back onto the paper. The note was addressed to her. It was from her father. At first, she assumed he had written it prior to his death, then arranged for its placement. That assumption was incorrect. The letter read as follows:

My dear Caroline---

If you are reading this, then you will know I am well. My sudden passing was admittedly a major inconvenience to everyone, including myself, but these things are sometimes unavoidable. Very few of us get to choose our appointed hour. I know you are mourning. As incomprehensible as all of this may be, I too have mourned our loss at great length. The pain I felt was not unlike yours. The afterlife does indeed include grief. Time and space do not translate well on this side of mortality, but rest assured that life does go on. I hope and believe that we will one day be reunited, but hopefully not too soon. You and Richard deserve a long, healthy and joyous life. Now is your time. I had my time, and what a time it was. When the days in your current life are done, I expect to be here to greet you.

Where am I and what is it like? That's a very difficult question;

one that I am not yet capable of answering. It would be foolish to try explaining my current circumstances when I do not yet understand it myself. Instead it seems more appropriate if I could tell you a little bit about this book and why I am asking you to read it.

Every life is filled with episodes of triumph and tragedy, regret and remorse. No one is immune to this. I have made my share of foolish mistakes. We all make them. But the greatest sins are ones of omission. Not telling others that you love them. Not letting them feel needed or wanted. Not letting them get close enough to really understand the person that you are, and how it is that you arrived at this place. Those have been my greatest sins.

If you choose to read on--and you do have a choice--you will be reading the story of a man that you thought you knew, but in many ways did not. I have always loved you, always tried to make time for you, and always did my best to be the kind of person you could be proud of. I tried, but effort does not always equal results. Often, I failed. On the pages that follow you will hopefully begin to understand who this person is. During my fifty plus years I endured great hardships and tragedies that shaped my youth. I never spoke of these events to anyone, not even to your mother, but they need to be told. As an adult I made horrendous blunders. There were times when I hurt people badly, especially those who I loved the most. Those stories and the lessons they taught must also be told. There were also many good times. Moments of magic and miracles and redemption. These are tales that you need to hear. As you read on, you will meet my father as well. As odd as this may sound, I never really knew my own father until after he died. Regrettably, in some ways, I have followed a similar path.

Finally, as is often the case, my greatest regret, both in life and in death is that I never got to say good-bye. Yet before a person says good-bye they must first say hello. On these pages are the stories that I never told you. It is the story of my life. Who I am and how I got to be that person. The events recounted are one hundred percent true as told through my eyes. Others who were there might recount them differently. It is my intention to lay it all out there, naked and unapologetic. I cannot undo the mistakes of my past, nor can I relive the triumphs, but perhaps I can at least explain how they came to be. I'm not asking for praise or forgiveness, only understanding. Most of all, I am asking that you read on.

Richard awoke to the sound of his new bride sobbing. It took a while for Caroline to gather herself. Without a word, she handed him the envelop and letter. Both were bewildered but not disbelieving. Caroline wanted to believe. Richard was perplexed, open-minded, but mostly he just wanted his wife to be happy. He called down to room service and ordered a platter of nachos, a basket of conch fritters and a pitcher of margaritas. Then, together they sat on the edge of the bed and began to take turns reading aloud. Richard went first. In a clear voice he declared, "Chapter One…"

CHAPTER ONE

Dear Caroline-The famed author and satirist Kurt Vonnegut Jr. was known to begin conversations with complete strangers by asking, "Tell me how your parents died?" This was not done out of some cruel desire to torment others. Rather, Vonnegut reasoned that if you want to get to know someone, it is best to begin on a deeply personal level and fill in the superfluous information later. While I don't agree with his reasoning, I understand it. It has long been assessed that the death of a parent, spouse or child is the single most traumatic event in a person's life. These are life altering experiences. My mother died a few days before Christmas, when I was eight years old. My father died a few days after Easter, when I was thirty-one. Both events changed my world forever. Neither change was for the better.

a seven or eight-year-old kid can be fragile, yet resilient. Tell them they can't have a cookie or go outside to play and they burst into hysterics, as though their whole world has collapsed. Yet if they get hit in the head with a rock while they are busy having a good time, the injury becomes of little consequence. In the Spring and Summer before my mother passed, I was a typical kid having the time of my life. When I got hit with the biggest rock of all, I was so wrapped up in my own little world that it really didn't faze me much at the time.

What really matters to a young boy? Going to school. Hanging out with your friends. Cars, cowboys and baseball. Knowing that you are safe and you are loved. That last one is a really big deal, but if you ask a hundred kids what is most important to them, it may not be mentioned at all. That's because it is one of those things that we generally take for granted. It's not until you get hit with the rock that you realize the importance of safety and nurturing.

I was born on June 11th in Bayonne, New Jersey as the second child and only son of Angelo and Camille Campbell. My father worked as a painter for the Jersey Central Railroad. My mother was a stay at home mom, back at a time when that was exactly what was expected of her. Shortly after my birth Dad was laid off from the railroad. He bounced around from job to job until his cousin Peter helped him get hired as a baggage handler for American Airlines. He stayed at that job until his death. My big sister Martha was born two years before me and younger sister Catherine two years after. Martha soon became Marty and Catherine was Catty or Cat. I had no nickname.

Bayonne at that time was not exactly a diverse city. You were either Italian or Polish, with the two nationalities living apart in separate neighborhoods divided quite literally by the railroad tracks. Which group lived on the wrong side of the tracks was a matter of conjecture. It seldom mattered. Both ethnicities usually got along just fine.

I was named Ralph Campbell after my grandfather Raffaello Campobasso, who came from a small village northeast of Naples in the Italian region of Abruzzi. Upon his arrival at Ellis Island in the early twentieth century, an immigration official checked his papers and asked him his name. It was promptly Americanized when the man in the grey uniform wrote down Ralph Campbell. It remained Ralph Campbell until his death, many years later. My mother's family, meanwhile, came from Reggio di Calabria, on the southern shores of the Italian mainland. Her father, Carlo Barretta, came to this country around the same time as Raffaello, when he was just ten years old. My mother was born Camille Maria Barretta. My father was baptized Angelino Luigi Campobasso, but city hall registered it as Angelo Campbell.

Angelo and Camille were both twenty-one years old when they married. They had been childless for more than seven years, when Martha was born. I came along two years later. Catherine finished the trio as a welcome, but unexpected surprise. While I have never been particularly fond of the name Ralph, I have always taken great pride in its heritage and origin. Since my grandfather did not have a middle name, I too was deprived of one. This was unfortunate for two reasons. First, it denied me the chance to have an alternative to the name Ralph. At times I had considered using my Catholic confirmation name, Chris or Christopher, but never really felt comfortable doing so. Second, in later years, the name on my military record would be recorded as Ralph NMN Campbell. I spent the better part of four years explaining that I did not have three middle names. NMN simply meant "no middle name."

Bayonne may have been bi-national when I was born, but it was rapidly becoming more of an urban, ethnic melting pot. As the sons and daughters of European immigrants began moving out of the city and into the suburbs, they were frequently replaced by blacks and Hispanics from nearby Newark and the Bronx. The migration of Italians, Poles, and Slavs to the Central Jersey suburbs was especially prevalent in cities like Bayonne, Elizabeth, and Patterson. Our family moved from Bayonne to the quiet suburban community of Castlebrook, New Jersey as a means of fleeing the influx of blacks and Puerto Ricans. It's not that my father had anything against these groups, he just didn't want to look at them, talk to them and least of all, live among them.

In Castlebrook, Angelo Campbell found his own version of the American dream. After years of saving and sacrifice, he was able to afford a down payment on a small, but newly built home, near the highway. The house, which looked like every other house on the street, was a three-bedroom, 1300 square foot split level, with a third of an acre of land and a one-car garage. Schools were good and the neighbors were friendly. Since it was a new community we all had something in common. Everyone here was fleeing from somewhere else. The Schultz family, our neighbors to the right, were originally from Yonkers, while the Hastings to our left were from Camden. A mortgage, a lawn, two cars, three kids and a dog named Roscoe. What more could anyone wish for? We soon would find out.

Ray Kowalski lived across the street and was my best friend. Ironically, he was from one of those Polish families on the other side of Bayonne's railroad tracks. Along with Ray, there was Tony Berube from Brooklyn. The three of us were inseparable. In the winter we built snow forts, snowmen and had snowball fights. Summer was spent playing ball, climbing trees, or just running around acting like kids. Since the town was still under development, we would frequently go down to one of the construction sites on Sunday after church and hope that no one would catch us climbing all over the abandoned bulldozers and backhoes. Usually, this would end with a police cruiser driving by to politely chase us away. Other times a dirt-bomb fight would erupt and continue unabated until someone caught sand in the eye and went running home crying.

Sometime shortly after arriving in Castlebrook, Mom began working nights part-time as a cashier at the local Acme supermarket. Whatever money she made was put aside for a vacation. With the help of her savings, we spent an entire week at Disneyland, Knott's Berry Farm, and assorted other attractions. It would be the only vacation the five of us ever took together. In November of that year, the Acme store burned to the ground. It would be a portent of disasters to come. For a short while, Mom simply went back to the business of being a housewife and mother.

Mom was a small, frail woman, lacking the stout and hearty stock that her sister and two brothers possessed. Cigarettes and coffee were her weakness. Strong black coffee and unfiltered Chesterfields. She smoked three packs a day and there was always a pot of Maxwell House percolating on the stove. My father too was a three pack a day smoker, usually Lucky Strikes. The white ceilings and painted walls of our house quickly developed a faint yellow tint; the result of a constant cloud of burnt tobacco that hung in each room. There were two or three ashtrays in every room. The smoke and the smell were ubiquitous.

Gradually, Mom began to develop what has been called a "smoker's cough." No one thought much of it at the time. Finally, after developing fairly severe chest pains, she went to see a doctor. A month later, for reasons not yet known to me, my grandfather Carlo abruptly decided to move in with us. Grandpa Barretta had been living with Mom's sister Josie and her husband Uncle Mike ever since the death of his wife Martha, two years earlier. Uncle Mike and Aunt Josie had also fled from the blacks and Puerto Ricans of Bayonne and now lived in the suburban town of Addenboro. Grandpa Carlo would stay with us for less than a year.

I first learned something was amiss completely by accident. Well, not completely. I "accidentally" seized the opportunity to eavesdrop on a phone call. It is important to remember that in those days we lived in a low-tech world. Telephones had rotary dials with short cords that tangled easily. Most homes had only one or two phones. In our house there were three. One in the kitchen, one in my parent's bedroom and one in the downstairs family room. All three were on the same line, so if you picked up each phone, multiple people could join in on the conversation. Around ten o'clock, on a Saturday morning, I was waiting to hear from Ray to find out if he could come over to play for a while. I was downstairs watching cartoons on our brand new nineteen inch black and white RCA television. Mom was upstairs in her room. It was an accident of split-second precision. When the phone rang, Mom and I picked up the receiver at the exact same moment. I immediately realized that she didn't know I was on the line. I also could hear that she was crying.

I was never a sneaky kid, but I was curious. Rather than speak, I held my hand over the mouthpiece and listened. It was Aunt Josie on the line. I don't remember much of the conversation and most of what I heard made no sense to me. I was only seven years old but I do recall hearing Mom say that they got the test results and it was cancer. The word cancer meant nothing to me, but it clearly had serious meaning to my mother and aunt. "Oh Cammie, I am so sorry" Aunt Josie said. "What are you going to do?" Mom's voice was starting to crack. "I don't know." she said. There was a long pause. "It doesn't sound good. I mean, they told me it's really serious, whatever that means. I'm not sure what they can do for me. It sounds like they're not sure either. It hurts so bad Jo, and what are Angelo and the kids going to do?" As her last words trailed off the only sound on the phone was my mother crying. I had never heard her cry before. I was scared. Very scared.

Gently, very gently, I put the receiver back onto the phone. Then I too began to cry. What I didn't know was that as soon as the receiver touched the buttons on the top of the cradle, a loud clicking sound came over the line. From several rooms away, I heard my mother's panicked voice. "Oh shit Jo, I think Ralphie was on the other line. I got to go." When Mom burst into the room downstairs she wasn't crying; she was furious. "Were you listening on the phone? Were you? Answer me!" Her thin bony fingers grabbed my shoulders and shook me with the strength and force of a woman twice her size. Her clasp was soon released as her arms wrapped around my small frame. The violent outburst turned into a hug, with both of us sobbing.

When she released me, I sat curled up on the sofa, more scared than I had ever been. "I'm sorry Mom. I'm sorry. I heard you were sick. I don't want you to be sick. I'm sorry." She sat down on the couch next to me and again wrapped her arms around my shoulders. "It's okay. Everything is going to be alright," she said, although she had to have known it was a lie. "I'm going to have some more doctor's appointments and I may even have to go into the hospital for a few days, but everything is going to be fine. Meanwhile, you and Daddy are the men in the house, so you are going to have to be really strong. Can you do that? Can you be really strong for me?"

I rubbed my eyes until they were red and burning. Still crying I wiped my snotty nose against my sleeve and nodded yes. Somehow, I would be strong. Then she made me promise that I wouldn't say anything to my sisters. They would find out, but she wanted to be the one to tell them. Again, I agreed. Why wouldn't I? How could I possibly explain something to them when it made no sense at all to me?

Things started to change around the house almost immediately. Aunts, uncles and cousins who I usually only saw around birthdays and holidays began showing up on a daily basis. Often, they brought food. This probably worried me more than anything. Mom loved to cook. If she was too sick to cook, then she must really be sick. Marty, who was nine going on ten, tried to help as much as she could. The two of us would meet regularly before bedtime to talk about what was going on, comparing our thoughts and observations. Collectively we concluded that while nobody was lying to us, they definitely weren't giving us the full story. One day Marty saw Mom sitting alone in the living room, just staring blankly out the window. "Mom? Are you going to die?" she asked. "I don't know" came the soft, unemotional answer. At last we knew the truth. Mom was dying.

Dad, for his part, did his best to be stoic around us. Sure, he was a little grouchier than usual, but we just figured he was tired of eating other people's food. Mom was a much better cook than what was in the aluminum trays that seemed to arrive daily. We thought Dad was the lucky one. He got to go to work and hang around airplanes all day. Grandpa Carlo had the tough job. He would drive Mom back and forth to all of her doctor's appointments. That couldn't have been much fun. The only two in the house that went unfazed by all of the turmoil was Catherine, and our dog Roscoe. Since Cat was only five years old, she was generally kept out of the loop. As for Roscoe, well, he was just stupid. Mom, Dad, Grandpa, and just about everyone else called him "that shithead dog". Roscoe didn't care. He got to eat all the leftover food that nobody wanted.

As summer approached, things took a turn for the worse. The cancer was spreading rapidly, so the doctors began taking a more aggressive treatment approach. Meanwhile, school let out for the summer, and Marty and I both had birthdays. I don't remember much about either birthday, but I do remember that we celebrated July 4th with my Aunt Christina and Uncle Raymond at their summer cottage on Barnegat Bay. Christy was my dad's older sister. Her husband, Raymond Stanik was a highly decorated World War II veteran, who was injured during a battle in central Italy.

He was also Hungarian, which must have caused quite a stir in our Italian family. Uncle Ray was my favorite uncle. He was a funny and unpredictable sort of guy who all the kids loved. He would do magic tricks, like pulling a quarter out of your ear, and he would even let you have ice cream and soda for breakfast.

On this particular Fourth of July, he taught me how to fish for crabs off the dock, using a chicken neck, a piece of twine and a net. Ray must have known that this would keep me busy all day. It did, and before long I had caught over a dozen blue crabs that we boiled and ate along with the usual hot dogs and hamburgers. Meanwhile the grown-ups were sitting around the picnic tables discussing more serious matters. When the sun went down and the mosquitoes swarmed in, we all went inside for cake and ice cream.

Once settled in and stuffed with sweets, Aunt Christy asked me if any of my friends were going away to summer camp. I said yes, a few, but wondered what that had to with me. Uncle Ray then asked "Well instead of going to summer camp, would you want to stay here for a couple of weeks? You could fish and crab every day. Maybe go to the beach a few times, and if it's raining we could go to the movies." It sounded too good to be true. What kid would pass up the opportunity to do all that? Suddenly I had forgotten all about Mom dying and everybody being sad or grouchy all of the time. Two weeks of doing nothing but fun stuff. I slept there that night. The following morning Dad brought my clothes, a few of my toys and even my bicycle. Meanwhile, Chris and Ray's eighteen-year-old son, cousin Ricky, brought a huge stack of comic books into the spare bedroom where I was staying. Life was suddenly good again.

With ignorance and innocence on my side, the two weeks spent on Barnegat Bay were about as much fun as any eight-year-old kid could possibly have. Uncle Raymond taught me how to use a seine to catch bait fish. Then he showed me how to bait a hook. I was out on the dock by six o'clock every morning. I caught crabs, white perch, baby bluefish, and eels. The eels were really fun because they were long and slimy and once they were dead we got to clean them by nailing the head to a tree, then skinning them and hosing out all of the guts. I couldn't wait to tell Ray and Tony about that. Cousin Ricky wasn't around much during those two weeks because he worked at a nearby gas station. When he was home, he taught me some fun stuff too, like how to adjust a carburetor. I even got to play on the drum set he had in the garage. I wasn't very good at either of these things but I tried real hard to get Rick to like me. He was different from anyone else I knew. Rick had long hair and used words like "cool" and "far out." Most of the time I didn't know what he was talking about, but I wanted to be just like him. My favorite cousin was also a drummer in a local garage band, so he knew a lot about music. I liked the Beatles and the Monkees. Rick taught me about the Hollies, the Animals and the Dave Clark Five.

When the two weeks were over I was ready to go home. It was a lot of fun, but I missed my family, my friends and Roscoe the shithead dog. Meanwhile I learned that while I was at camp with Aunt Christy and Uncle Ray, my two sisters had a camp of their own. They were in Bayonne, staying with Dad's sister, Rose, her husband, Uncle Joe and their sixteen-year-old daughter, cousin Jean. They got to go to New York three times, mostly shopping at Macy's and Woolworth's. Cousin Jean was just like Ricky except she did girl things. Martha said she had a great time, except she kept getting really sad because she was afraid that Mom would die while she was away and she wouldn't be there to say good bye. Even as a ten-year-old Marty was the smart, sensitive one.

While the three of us were away having fun, Mom spent two weeks in the hospital. They tried radiation, chemotherapy, and a few experimental drugs in the hope that it might destroy enough of the cancer to save or at least extend her life. It didn't. At best, they made her weaker and less able to fight off the disease. At worst the treatments harmed good tissue, poisoned her, and left her with a diminishing will to live. In the end, the treatments may have killed my mother as much as the cancer did. The only good thing that came from this episode was that my sisters and I had two weeks of fun before being stripped of our childhood.

Mom would make several more overnight stays to the hospital, but mostly they let her stay home. By September the doctors told my dad that there was nothing more they could do except for pain pills to keep her comfortable. When the doctors gave up hope so did she. On December 1st, Mom went into the hospital one last time. She never came home. As the cancer progressed, she stopped eating. She was always thin, but she went from 110 pounds when she was healthy, to quite literally skin and bones. When she died on the night of December 21st, Camille Campbell weighed just sixty-eight pounds.

What do I remember about those days leading up to December 21st? Not too much. Mostly I remember not wanting to talk about it. I remember trying to pretend that it wasn't happening, and trying to keep any knowledge or information from my friends. It wasn't necessary. They already knew. Dad had told their parents and their parents told them. They were instructed to be very careful about what they said around me and my sisters so as to not upset us. I just wanted to feel normal. Instead everyone made me feel different.

On December 16th, Martha, Catherine and I were brought to my mother's hospital room to visit. She was very weak and heavily medicated. I remember Marty wiped her forehead and told her she was praying for her every night. I held her hand and said that everything was going to be alright. It seemed like the right thing to say. After all, wasn't that the same lie that everyone else was telling me? Maybe it would work. Maybe God would listen and make everything better. Dad picked up Cat and held her over the bed so Mom could see her one last time. We didn't know that it would be the last time we would see her alive, but it was. On the ride home no one said a word. Once inside Dad put Catty to bed then asked us to come into his room. It was then that he told Martha and me what we already knew. Mom was going to die soon. When we left the room, he asked us to close the door. I went straight to bed. Marty sat by the door and listened. She told me later that she heard Dad crying.

December 21st was a Thursday. That night, Dad had a babysitter come over. Since Grandpa Carlo was staying with us, he would usually go to the hospital in the morning while we were at school, then sit for us at night while Dad went. Instead Dad came home from work early on Thursday and Lorraine, our teenage neighbor, came to stay with us. This was not a good sign. Dad had stayed at the hospital much later than usual the night before. I heard him come in around midnight. Still, he managed to get up at five o'clock the next morning to go to work. Catty was in kindergarten, so she was only in school until one o'clock. When Marty and I got home at three, Lorraine was there and Grandpa was still at the hospital. Dad was rushing out the door as the school bus was dropping us off. He looked panicked and scared. All he said was. "I'll be home later. Be good for Lorraine. I'll call if anything happens." I'll call if anything happens? What did that mean? We may have just been ten and eight, but we both knew exactly what it meant.

Dad didn't get home until two in the morning. I knew the time because I slept with the light on and looked at the clock when he woke us up. I had gone up to bed at nine. Again, he took Martha and me into his room and we sat on the bed. Mom died around seven o'clock. We wouldn't be going to school to-day. Missing the day before Christmas vacation started wouldn't be a problem. I mildly protested because my class was having a party with cupcakes and soda. Marty gave me a look that could burn holes through steel. Dad said he would buy me cupcakes for breakfast. Then I asked about Santa. Christmas was only three days away. Did Santa know that Mom was going to die? If not, he must have already gotten stuff ready for her. Dad said he didn't know but was guessing that Mom's presents were already on their way to heaven for her. Then he asked us not to say anything to Cat. She wouldn't understand. Again, we closed the door and left. Again, he cried.

I don't remember very much about the days that followed. There were too many people around and too much confusion. My three favorite cousins from Mom's family, Lisa, June and Margie were over the house almost the entire time. They were Aunt Josie's daughters. Marge was my age. June and Lisa were just a year or two older than Martha. Their job was to keep us busy.

We still had Christmas. Dad somehow found time to decorate the outside of the house with lights. Our fake plastic tree had lights and ornaments and still adorned the living room. Like all other kids who still had their mothers, we got up very early on Christmas morning to see what was under the tree. Santa must have felt sorry for us because there were more toys and gifts than I had ever seen before in my life. All three of us got bicycles. I was really interested in science, so I got a microscope. Marty liked playing with hair, so she got a couple of different hair dressing kits. She also got this new board game that was advertised on tele-vision called "Mystery Date." I thought that was a little strange because all of the girls I knew hated boys, and Marty wasn't old enough to date yet. Still, they were advertising the heck out of it on TV, so I guess that was enough to make her want it. Martha was also really into music so she got a portable record player and a couple of Beatles albums. Catty got dolls and clothes and whatever other toys you might expect a six-year-old girl to want. Santa didn't get as many things for Dad. He got a Zippo lighter, a new wallet, and the dress shirt and tie that he would be wearing to Mom's funeral.

After we finished opening all of our gifts, Dad told us that Mom had seen all of the stuff we were getting and this made her happy. I didn't understand that comment at all. "Did Santa stop by the hospital and show her," I asked? He said yes. That was good enough for me. As I reveled in the bounty of gifts, I began to say something about what a great Christmas this was. Again, I got the stare from Marty. Even before the words started to come out, Dad corrected me. "This is the worst Christmas ever, but at least you got some nice gifts." His words quickly snapped me back to reality. We all agreed. This was the worst Christmas ever.

Mom's wake was on Tuesday and Wednesday December 26 and 27. She was buried on Thursday the 28th. I remember going to the wake those two nights. Each night I went up to the casket and touched her hand. I didn't do it for sentimental reasons. I just wanted to know what a dead person felt like. I decided they feel fake. The skin was cold and rubbery and covered with so much makeup that it came off on my fingers and made them feel greasy. I knelt in front of the casket and told Mom that I hoped she wasn't sick anymore. Then I got as far away as possible because the whole thing seemed creepy and unreal. Downstairs at the funeral home there was a room where men were smoking cigarettes and cigars. The air was black from the smoke, but it was away from all of the crying people who were closest to the casket. There were cookies and pastries there, and someone made me a cup of hot chocolate.

While I was down there, one of Mom's brothers, Uncle David,

came over and said that he would help to take care of me. He promised to be like a big brother and play catch or take me to the park or the zoo. I didn't know what he was talking about. I didn't need a big brother. I had lots of friends and my dad was always willing to play catch or do fun things. What I didn't understand at the time is that my mom's family didn't like Dad at all. Apparently, they never did. I didn't understand it then, and I don't know all of the reasons now, but I'm sure they had their reasons. As for Uncle David, I suppose it was his way of saying that he didn't trust my dad to take good care of me. I wonder if Aunt Josie had the same kind of conversation with Martha?

On Thursday, December 28th Camille Campbell was buried at Saint Mary's Cemetery in Castlebrook. It was not a good day. Ordinarily I might have thought that it was really fun to ride in the front of a big, black limousine and lead a parade of cars. There was nothing fun about it. I was upset because when I woke up that morning I heard all sorts of noise coming from Grandpa Carlo's room downstairs. Drawers and doors were slamming and he kept muttering under his breath in Italian. Grandpa never got mad. He was mad now. He was also packing. My father had asked him to leave. I asked him why. We didn't need him here anymore, is all I was told. Grandpa didn't ride with us to the funeral or in the limo. Aunt Josie and Uncle Mike came and got him. No one spoke to my dad. I was losing my mother and my grandpa on the same day. They say bad things happen in threes. What could possibly be next? It was Santa.

Shortly after dinner, around eight o'clock, I lost Santa Claus. Once again it was the job of cousins Lisa, June and Margie to keep Martha and me from feeling too sad. They had been at this project for a full week now, and finally couldn't do it anymore. I was grateful, because at last they started acting more naturally around us. They had lots of questions and wanted to talk, not entertain. When did we find out she was sick? What does lung cancer look like? Why is Grandpa moving out of your house and into ours? Why do our parents hate your dad? Does Catty know what's going on yet? Can I borrow your new Beatles album?

We answered all of the questions as best we could. Somewhere in the midst of the chatter, I mentioned that I was confused because Dad had said that Mom had seen all of our Christmas presents. June blurted out that it's because Santa didn't get them for us, our dad did. Lisa quickly clamped a hand over June's mouth, causing June to bite her. Marge meanwhile sat there just as confused as I was. Then Lisa said that what June meant was that my father had helped Santa to make sure we each got just the right gifts. It was a valiant try, but I didn't buy it. Within a few minutes I was able to put the missing pieces together. Santa was a myth. I lost Mom, Grandpa and Santa, all in less than a week. Ever the big sister, Marty quickly dragged me aside and swore she would stab me with a fork if I ever said a word of this Santa stuff to Cat. I swore. And despite the reality that I now knew, I still chose to believe in Santa, at least in theory, for a couple of more years.

Grandpa Carlo died the following year. Whatever happened between my grandfather, the rest of Mom's family, and my dad, became a wound that never healed. When my father remarried the very next year, the wound deepened. Dad was allowed to drop us off in front of Aunt Josie's house but they didn't want to see him ever again. They felt bad for me, Martha and Catherine, but that's just the way it had to be. I never challenged their grudge.

Sometimes you don't get a happy ending, and this episode in my life doesn't have one. I lost part of my childhood when I picked up that phone receiver and learned of my mother's illness. I lost the rest of it after returning home from camp at Uncle Ray's. As I passed through pre-adolescence and into my teen years, I would never again have the joy and innocence of youth. The rest of my childhood would be filled with pain, turmoil and confusion. I survived it and I am stronger for it, but like so many other wounds, sometimes you just have to bury the pain, hide the scars and simply move on.

CHAPTER TWO

Dear Caroline-Why do couples get married? I'm well aware of the historical, religious and anthropological reasons, but in the late 20th and early 21st century, those reasons have lost much of their relevance. So why do it? Why not simply live together as a couple without the ceremony and the legalities? Many do, yet marriage continues to live on as an important institution in our society. And so, the question persists. Does marriage matter?

My father was married three times. Widowed once. Divorced once. The third time he left a widow. I was Best Man at his third wedding. As I prepared to make my obligatory speech, I found myself pondering those questions. It seemed particularly odd to me that a 53-year-old man and a 56-year-old woman, each with grown children of their own, would choose to marry. Why bother? After too much Scotch and few Tony Bennett records, I may have figured it out.

Despite the best of intentions, humans are a flawed species. We want to do the right thing, but our "fight or flight" mechanism gets in the way. We antagonize and embattle when the situation calls for compassion. We run away when the going gets tough. We do this, particularly in our closest and most important relationships. We desperately need each other to share the highs and lows

*that life throws our way, but we do not always act with judg-
ment and reason. Marriage provides a buffer against temporary
insanity. Each couple stands before God and witnesses vowing
that despite the inevitable prolonged periods of adversity and ir-
rational behavior, they will not run away. Marriage strips away
that option. It takes a strong love and a stronger commitment to
make such a stand. And so, I do believe marriage, when done for
that reason, truly does matter.*

*On June 21st, exactly six months after my mother's death, my fa-
ther was married for a second time. His bride's name was Carmen
Rossini. There are many good reasons for marriage, but in this
case, not a single one applied. What followed was an unmitigated
disaster.*

*I*gnorance is bliss. Youthful ignorance is even better.
Psychologists, psychiatrists, and pharmaceutical firms have
created a multibillion dollar industry by convincing us that the
tragedies of childhood have left us irreparably scarred and unable
to function without their help. Bullshit. Kids are made of the
toughest stuff on earth. Their resilience to all that this world can
hurl at them rival's diamonds and cockroaches. Kids live in the
singular moment, while fully understanding that the moment is
about to change. That is how I survived the days that followed
my mother's death.

Life was changing all around me, but the basics remained the
same. Every day I went to school, came home, did my homework and played with my friends. We ate dinner, watched TV
and went to bed. There was a roof over our heads, and food to
eat. Everything was as before, minus Mom, Grandpa Carlo and
my aunts and uncles from Mom's family. Some adjustments were

needed to accommodate the changes that had taken place in our lives, but these were easily adapted to. Dad got us up and dressed in the morning. When he left for work, we went across the street to stay with our neighbor, Mrs. Johnson. Dad paid her to feed us breakfast and get us on and off the bus. After school we usually went to her house, but if the weather was good I would go right outside to spend time with my pals Tony and Ray.

As inappropriate as it may sound, I don't recall missing Mom very much. When you are eight years old a month can seem like a year. Mom had not been home for several months. What I do recall, with some anguish, is not wanting to feel different. Everyone I knew had a mother and a father. In our middle-class blue-collar suburbia, single parent families were relatively rare. I wanted to be treated like everyone else. Once in a while someone would ask me if I missed my mom, or if I was sad or upset about something. Having to answer those questions bothered me more than not having a mother.

One day in early January I was asked by my teacher to skip recess and go down to the principal's office. Someone was there to see me. I got really worried, thinking I had done something wrong. I was introduced to a very tall, thin man with long curly black hair and a graying beard. His name was Doctor Rupert, the school psychologist. The doctor led me to a small room in the back of the library where we could "talk". I could feel everyone looking at me as we walked by the tables and bookshelves along the way. I thought about running away, but there was nowhere to go. Rather, I said that I had to go to the bathroom. I hid in there for as long as I could, figuring he would grow tired of waiting and just go away. After about ten minutes the doctor came in looking for me. I was trapped, so I let him lead me back to the small conference room. Again, we walked by the tables, chairs and students who stared curiously at me.

We sat across from each other at an adult table. The top of the table came halfway up my chest, which made me feel small and inferior to the man with the black suit. Doc Rupert lifted his briefcase and opened it on the table beside him. The top of the case created a wall that was facing me. I imagined that he had all sorts of chemicals and weapons, just like the secret agents from my favorite television shows. But when I leaned forward I saw that it was just full of papers.

"Why did you run and hide from me Ralph?" he began. His voice was dry and mechanical. I imagined that he was a robot and not a person.

"I wasn't hiding. I had to go to the bathroom. I want to go back to my class. I'm missing recess."

"I'm sorry you have to miss recess, but your Dad thought it might be good if we talked."

Dad was behind this? Why? Psychologist? That sounded a lot like "mad scientist". Did he want to suck my brains out? If Dad wanted him to talk to me, what about Martha and Catherine? Were they getting their brains sucked out too?

"I don't have anything to say."

"You lost your Mom recently. How does that make you feel? Do you miss her?"

"I'm okay. Why?"

"Just talking. I lost my mom when I was your age. I know it's difficult. Do you feel angry? Sad? Lonely? How do you feel?"

"I feel angry 'cause I just missed recess, and now the other kids are wondering why I'm not back in class. I have to pee again. Can I go now?"

"Alright." Then he handed me a piece of paper with some numbers on it. "This is my phone number. If you do feel angry or sad or just want to talk about anything, will you call me?" I didn't answer.

When I got back to class, my friend Ray asked me where I had been. I told him I was feeling a little sick and went to the nurse's office. He didn't believe me.

As usual, Mrs. Johnson met us at the bus stop at three o'clock. When I got off the bus I told her I wanted to stop home to get some colored pencils for a project, then I would head back over to her house. That was alright with her. When I walked in the house, I grabbed a few pencils and stuffed them into my pocket. Next, I went down to the basement and grabbed a hammer from Dad's toolbox, before heading straight to the toy chest in my room. I gathered up as many toys as possible from Christmas, put them in the middle of the floor, and began smashing them. Some I crushed with the hammer. Others I jumped up and down on, stomping them as hard as I possibly could. Finally, I took out a picture of Mom that was in my dresser drawer and tore it into little pieces. Then I sat on the floor next to the rubble and cried.

They were tears of anger, not sadness. I wanted my old life back. I didn't want to feel different from anyone else. I wanted people to stop asking stupid questions. I was overcome with intense anger. Anger towards Mom for dying. It was so inconvenient. Dad was acting weird. Other people acted weird around us. I was angry at Dad for fighting with Grandpa Carlo and for making us go to Mrs. Johnson's house. Why couldn't we just stay home and get on and off the bus by ourselves? Marty was ten years old. She could take care of us. More than anything, I was angry at Dad for making me go see Mr. Rupert. What was that all about? Did Dad think I was crazy?

When I got back to Mrs. Johnson's I found Marty and asked her if she had to go to the office today too. She said no, she went yesterday. Maybe it was because she didn't run away, but Marty said that Mr. Rupert was very nice to her. He gave her a glass of juice and asked her a bunch of questions. They talked about flowers and music and a little bit about Mom and Dad, but not too much. She said he just wanted to make sure that we weren't going to start doing badly in school because we were upset about Mom dying.

The three of us were fine. Dad was the one who was unable to cope. A forty-year-old widower with three young children may make for a great TV sitcom, but in the real world, it was immensely difficult. Some people simply do not function well on their own. Dad was one of those people. He wasn't helpless. He could do laundry, cook and clean, but when those tasks, plus a full-time job began to take up all of his time, he buckled under the weight of the load. Dad did his best to stay composed, but Angelo Campbell was never a patient man. He began to slam doors and snap angrily at us for our constant demands on his time.

Mom's family hated Dad, so they were not likely to offer much help. Dad's family lived forty minutes away, so there wasn't much they could do on a daily basis. We were friendly with the neighbors, but he really didn't have any close friends. Angelo's world had become very small and not at all happy.

It is not uncommon for a person on their deathbed to make a final request. Mom made two. It is only now that I can begin to fully understand their long-range implications. They would shape the future lives of me, Dad and my sisters for many years to come. The first was more of a sanction than a request. Mom told Dad that if the right person came along, he should remarry. She loved him very much and knew how difficult it would be for him to live alone. As long as it was someone who treated the kids well, she would offer her blessing. The second request was that he never split up the family. The four of us would always stay together. Dad agreed.

I later learned that those were Mom's final words. As Dad sat next to her hospital bed, she had reached over and he took her hand. With her final breaths on earth she exhaled "Remember Ang, keep the family together." Those words would haunt him for many years to come.

In the days and weeks that followed, there was much debate over that final request. My aunts and uncles all knew that Dad was a good man, but a selfish one. He loved his family more than anything but would not last long without sufficient time for his own amusements. It was immediately suggested that we return to the arrangement of the previous summer. Aunt Rose and Uncle Joe would care for Marty and Cat, while Aunt Christina and Uncle Ray would take care of me. This would be a temporary situation until Dad got settled and readjusted. Then we would all reunite again under one roof.

The logistics of this plan, while a little complicated, actually made sense. Both Aunt Rose and Aunt Chris still lived in Bayonne, just a few blocks apart. There were other relatives, all within walking distance. While Martha, Catty and myself would be sleeping in different houses, we would still attend the same schools and share several meals together. Dad would sell the house in Castlebrook and move into a nearby apartment. This would help him get back on his feet financially as well as emotionally. He would have the support of his family, and we would see him a few nights a week and on weekends. It wouldn't really be splitting us up and the arrangement was only temporary. There wasn't much discussion. Dad nixed the plan.

Dad gave several reasons as to why this was not a good idea. His first reason is that he didn't want to move back to Bayonne, and he certainly didn't want his kids growing up there. Too many blacks and Puerto Ricans. Too crowded. He had moved away for a reason and he wasn't going back. Second, he didn't want to rent and he didn't want his kids growing up in an urban setting. While

Aunt Christina and Aunt Rose had very nice homes, they were your typical brownstone row houses. Aunt Rose's was a multifamily, with boarders above and below. Aunt Chris's was small and had no yard. Kids needed someplace to play. They needed to go outside without leaving the property. Neither home offered that option. Besides, in Dad's mind, this still meant splitting the family. It was Camille's final request and there was no way he would ever waiver from it. He could not and would not compromise her last words by loosening the interpretation. We would stay in Castlebrook and he would find a way to make it work.

Among the many things in life that I will never understand, none will top the events that occurred between January and June of that year. Perhaps it's better that I don't know.

On January 27th, just five weeks after my mother's death, Dad took Marty and me aside and asked how we would feel if he went on a date. Let's try to put that in some sort of perspective. A forty-year-old man, who has been widowed for only thirty-five days is asking his ten-year-old daughter and eight-year-old son if it is okay to go out on a date. This is the same man that two weeks earlier requested that I see the school psychologist.

At eight years old, what would I think? What would I say? I certainly had no concept of romantic love. I remember him saying something about just going out for dinner and a movie. I also remember him trying to reassure us that he was not trying to replace Mom. One of Dad's cousins had called him and said he knew this woman, Carmen Rossini, who was pretty nice. At least that is how the story goes. Had they previously met? I have always wondered. Was Dad cheating on his dying wife, and just now decided to come forward with the relationship? Or was it far less scandalous? It was widely accepted that Dad was incapable of raising three young kids on his own. Yet he was also unmoving with regards to the level of help he would accept. He would not separate us, even for the benefit of all. Mom had given him the green light on remarriage as long as we all stayed together. In my heart I will always believe that there was nothing salacious going on. Simply put, this weak and insecure man had gone shopping for a wife and mother.

And what of Carmen? What could possibly possess a fairly attractive thirty-something single woman to agree to date an older man with three young children, just five weeks after his wife had died? Perhaps she was a victim of the times. Even today, a never married single woman approaching her fortieth birthday is suspected to be either asexual or a lesbian. Carmen was neither. She was a woman of high standards who had never found Mr. Right. By her mid-thirties, her standards were slipping and she was desperate. Both were shopping for a spouse when they collided. I believe this to be true, unless it turns out that the affair theory was correct.

It can be assumed that the date went well. They went out several more times over the next two weeks. We heard a number of small things about Carmen. She was tall and thin, had long black hair, and of course she was Italian. I couldn't imagine Dad going out with someone who wasn't. The thin part was temporary. Her weight would double during the next five years. Carmen worked at a local bakery. Mostly she worked the counter, but over time had learned a bit about making breads and pastries. When we finally met her, on February 12th, she brought us a big box of homemade éclairs and cream puffs. It wasn't a bad way to win over three young kids.

We liked Carmen. She seemed really nice to us. We already had enough toys, so she was smart to bring us sweets. I liked her because she was a Yankee fan, and Joe Pepitone was her favorite player. The Yankees were also my favorite team, but I didn't have a favorite player, so I too picked Joe. Carmen liked him because he was Italian. Dad was a Mets fan. They didn't have any Italians.

Marty said she liked Carmen too. She liked the way she smelled and was impressed with the makeup she wore. According to Marty, most of our aunts stunk. You could smell their perfume the minute they walked in the door. No wonder all of the men smoked cigarettes and cigars. They were trying to kill their wife's odor. A little perfume was fine, but not the whole bottle. Carmen wore Chanel, but not too much. As for makeup, our aunts really caked it on. Carmen used just a little powder and a touch of blue above her eyes. Again, my big sister was impressed. I never learned what Catherine's first impression was. I suspect the cream puffs were good enough to win her over.

I don't know what happened on Valentine's Day, but Dad and Carmen went out early and came home late. Then things started to pick up speed. They were seeing or talking to each other almost every day. Dad stopped talking about Mom and how much he missed her. Instead he just talked about Carmen. By then end of March they had gotten engaged. Again, I must pause and wonder. Who has ever heard of someone getting engaged just three months after the death of their wife? As an adult, it seems unnatural, immoral, scandalous and wrong. A kid's clock and calendar are different. Three months in kid-time seemed long enough to me.

When I heard about the engagement, I thought it was great. Now we would have a "normal" house again. People would stop asking me if I missed my dead mother. We wouldn't have to be shuttled back and forth to Mrs. Johnson's place. A normal life awaited us. Meanwhile, I can just imagine what friends and family members were saying. Worse yet, what did Mom's family think when they found out? They hated Dad before Mom died. This was beyond hate.

The wedding day was set for June 21st, just a few days after school let out. It was also near both my birthday and Martha's. We celebrated my birthday with Marty's because we didn't want it to interfere with the wedding. Instead of helping us celebrate, the two of them talked incessantly about the honeymoon. They were going to San Francisco. They picked San Francisco because Carmen said that Dad reminded her of Tony Bennett, and "I Left My Heart In San Francisco" was her favorite song. It seems like a rather odd reason to me, but after spending some time there myself, I can't argue that it is a very romantic city.

We didn't know much about Carmen, but how much does an eight-year-old need to know? She was the oldest in a family of five girls, each exactly two years apart in age. She was born and raised in Long Branch, New Jersey where her father had run a hardware store for several years until in went out of business as the larger chain stores grew in popularity. Carmen quit high school during her senior to work full-time and help support the family. Her dad eventually found work repairing and installing furnaces and hot water heaters for a local oil company. Carmen worked as a receptionist with the phone company for a few years before her sister Kate got her a job at the bakery. She had been at the bakery for eight years.

We knew that Carmen liked to cook and to play cards, but that was all we were aware of. In later years I would wonder why she had never married. She sometimes made reference to being engaged twice but never discussed why those relationships didn't work out. How did she feel about joining a family with three young kids? Did she like kids? Did she want any of her own? In retrospect it can be amusing to reflect on how different circumstances could have changed the whole dynamic that would follow. What if she had become pregnant, and I wound up with a baby brother? What if we moved to San Francisco to start an entirely new life in a new place? What if the courtship had been spread out over a year or more?

Despite those unanswered questions, Angelo and Carmen were married at Saint Mark's Church, in Long Branch. Ellen Balfour, was maid of honor. Her husband Vincent was Dad's best man. That too seemed odd. Ellen was a natural choice for Carmen. They had been best friends since first grade. Dad knew Vincent for all of four months. They got along, but the term "best friends" would hardly apply. Perhaps no one else approved of the union and he was the only one willing to do the job. Carmen's sisters were all bridesmaids.

It was your typical Catholic ceremony, with none of the personalized vows or tailored invocations that are commonplace today. Carmen's vow to love, honor and obey, in retrospect, seems dubious at best. It may have been my imagination, but I did notice that when the priest asked if anyone knew of any reason why Angelo and Carmen should not be married, there was an extremely long pause and maybe even some impolite whispering before moving on to the rest of the ceremony. In the end, they both got what they thought they wanted. Carmen got a ring, and Dad got a babysitter.

Upon returning from the honeymoon, there was little opportunity to settle into a normal, daily routine. Neither Dad nor Carmen wanted to live in a house that was haunted by the ghost of my mother. The home in Castlebrook was Angelo and Camille's American dream. Angelo and Carmen would have to find someplace else to dream. The house went up for sale in August. It sold in early October.

Our new home was in Eastshore, not far from Long Branch. Eastshore was a predominately white, and increasingly Jewish slice of suburbia. Carmen was a little concerned about living so close to nearby Eastern New Jersey State College. She thought all college kids were spoiled, rich, pot-smoking sex fiends. Still, a nice Jewish community like Eastshore meant doctors, lawyers and accountants. Carmen hoped the sex fiends wouldn't bother us too much.

The house itself was a three-bedroom ranch, slightly smaller than the home in Castlebrook, on a small fenced in lot. Marty and Catherine would share one bedroom, while I had the other. We officially took residency at Eastshore on October 31st. In retrospect, our Halloween arrival seems all too fitting. It would soon become my house of horrors.

CHAPTER 3

Dear Caroline-Ernest Hemmingway once wrote that all great writing is rooted in an unhappy childhood. I only partially agree. If it were indeed true, I should have been the next Shakespeare or Stephen King. I will concede that suffering demands to be expressed and released, but so does joy. Tony Bennett vs. Kurt Cobain. Norman Rockwell vs. Vincent van Gogh. James Thurber vs. John Steinbeck. It is my belief that two things are required to make pain bearable and happiness appreciable. Awareness and contrast. If you are aware of pain, then you are most likely engaged in the pursuit of pain relief. If you are aware of beauty, then you are probably engaged in expressing and sharing that beauty. Neither mean much without contrast. Pain without beauty and beauty without pain is simply the status quo. It is the lukewarm familiar norm. I grew up unhappy, while sensing that happiness was somehow within my reach. I believed that others knew of pleasures that I was not allowed to experience. I wanted to share their experiences, not just vicariously, but by embracing them as my own. Eventually I would, but building a bridge across that chasm would be harder than I ever imagined.

It is a jagged line that separates discipline from abuse. You spare the rod; you spoil the child. Yet perceptions and definitions change. Was I abused or simply kept in check by a strong-willed disciplinarian? Clearly by today's standards there was abuse, but in the context of that time, opinions may vary. Throughout most of my adult years I tried, by various means, to divorce myself from that period of my life. I have buried my emotions with drugs, alcohol, work, sex, and assorted other obsessions. It created a void in my life that was never filled. My adolescence did not exist. I never allowed myself to come to terms with all that happened, however, two defining truths have emerged.

The first truth is that I was indeed abused, both physically and psychologically. I endured unjust and inhumane levels of agony and despair. Thus, the absence of adolescence. The timeframe existed, but my emotional development did not. I endured those years as a confused and largely undefined entity. This was true by the standards of the day and holds equally true today.

The second truth is that Carmen was not a bad person. She was a decent woman possessed by far more demons than angels. Her fragile and addled psyche had found itself in an almost impossible situation for which she was ill-prepared to cope. This brought forth the demons. By the mores of that time, she was probably thought of as an obnoxious and controlling bitch. Present day considerations might be more empathetic. Using clinical terms, she might be called paranoid, obsessive-compulsive, manic-depressive, or perhaps schizophrenic. We are all damaged goods in need of repair. Carmen was more damaged than most.

For a short while after my father married Carmen, a honeymoon existed between the five of us. The pain of my mother's death was quickly replaced by a strong determination to return to being a normal nine-year-old, with normal friends, growing up in a normal neighborhood. Since we again had a mother figure, our family had the appearance that I desired. Carmen seemed to take well to her new role. Changes would inevitably come, but we were all adapting as well as could be expected. Carmen was given the same level of reverence and respect as Dad. I knew she wasn't our Mom, but I pretended she was and tried to make the best impression possible. We were all auditioning for our role. That lasted less than a year.

Despite my youth, I clearly understood why we had to leave Castlebrook. It was my mother's home, and Dad was haunted there. It also was not a part of Carmen's life, so we all had to start over. It was tough leaving our friends, but there would be new friends and new relatives. The new house was small but comfortable. It was also all we could afford. Dad had racked up some serious bills between the hospital, the funeral, wedding and the honeymoon. Add a mortgage to the equation and we were barely getting by. Money problems would be one of the many stresses to plague our restructured family.

My father was not a violent man, but there were many times when stress, frustration or ignorance got the best of him. He smacked me around quite a bit, but it wasn't premeditated, hurtful or hateful. Rather it was more of an abrupt eruption followed by a calm. Whatever caused the outburst of violence was soon forgotten. With Carmen it was different. Her beatings were long and vicious. Often, she would use a wooden or metal spoon, lashing out inexplicably and relentlessly until the utensil broke. Other times she used an open hand or a closed fist. Always it would be accompanied by shoving, hair pulling and an endless stream of vile invectives, designed to create the greatest possible humiliation. Once exhausted from the beating, she would then confine me to my bedroom, sometimes for a day, other times for a week or more. Between fifth and tenth grade I spent more time in my room than I did in the outside world.

The first beating that came ten months after the wedding. Woodrow Wilson Elementary School, where I attended the fourth grade, was a four-block walk from our house. Bus transportation was only available to those children with a walk of more than half a mile. One Friday afternoon in early spring I chose to take a shortcut home, cutting through the back of the school, crossing over a small creek and through an adjacent yard. As I made my way across the creek, I slipped off a rock and stumbled into the water, soaking my feet and legs, while covering my shoes, socks and pants with mud. I entered the house, expecting to be told to quickly change and dry off, lest I catch cold. Instead, Carmen became violently enraged. She lunged at me, pushing my small frame backwards as I stumbled and fell to the floor.

This tall, brawny, red-faced woman loomed over me like a prizefighter trying to deliver a knockout punch. Repeatedly and alternately she slammed the heal of one hand and the back of the other with a flurry of hits to my head and neck. All the while, the venom spewed from her lips.

"How Goddamn stupid can you be. Do you think we're made of money? We can't afford to buy you new shoes and pants just because you are too Goddamn lazy to walk home the right way. What the hell were you doing crossing through someone else's yard? You could have been arrested for trespassing you stupid Goddamn idiot. What the hell were you thinking? Well? Answer me Goddamn it. Your father's always telling me how smart you are and then you do something as stupid as this. How Goddamn stupid can you be? Answer me. You're supposed to be smart, so answer me damn it!"

I was too busy covering my head and trying to protect myself from the next blow to answer. After what seemed like an eternity, Carmen was finally too exhausted to hit any more. I was sent to my room without any supper and ordered to remain there for the remainder of the weekend. I was only allowed to come out for meals and chores. The honeymoon was over. My father stopped by the room briefly to offer a tacit defense of Carmen's actions, but I was in no mood to listen. I turned away and buried my head under a pillow, pretending to be asleep. Later that night from across the hall I could hear them arguing as my father belatedly railed against the cruelty that she had displayed. In truth, he had no idea how hurtful it was. He couldn't see the bruise on my shoulder from where I had fallen, or the scratches on my scalp that were hidden under my thick black hair.

In fifth grade, I made the mistake once of talking out in class. That got me one afternoon of detention and a week of confinement to my room. Before I was done serving that week I made the mistake of bringing home a math test on which I had gotten a "D". Carmen tacked the paper on the refrigerator and another week on my confinement. Before that week was done I neglected to bring the trash to the curb on pickup night, thus earning a third week. Five days later, I somehow managed to add on another month.

There was a residual benefit that emerged from my confinements. While restricted to my room, I could do homework but nothing else. I quickly learned to have an endless supply of homework, usually in the form of reading. Much of what I chose to read was sports. I soon became fascinated with some of the mythic figures of baseball; Lou Gehrig. Babe Ruth. Bob Feller. Rogers Hornsby. Since Dad was a passionate baseball fan as well, he would routinely slip me his copy of The Sporting News. As far as Carmen could tell, I was reading current events from a local newspaper.

I did read more than just sports, taking a liking to science fiction, war stories, and anything where the underdog rose from the depths of despair. During one confinement, I attempted to borrow a copy of the Count of Monte Cristo from the school library. The librarian, an ancient spinster of sorts, refused to loan it, claiming that it was improper for my age and reading level. Mrs. Goldberg, my fifth-grade teacher overheard the conversation and quickly intervened. She rather sternly told the old buzzard that I could indeed borrow it, if I wished to have it for my monthly reading project. I finished the book in four days, thanks to the long Columbus Day weekend and my house arrest. Roughly fifty years later, the Count of Monte Cristo is still among my favorites. With the librarian subdued, I continued to read more advanced books, including most of Jules Verne and several Zane Grey westerns. The room was my prison. Books were the key to my escape.

Meanwhile, hardly a day passed when I was not struck, berated or humiliated. Carmen was not always successful in her caution to not leave any marks. Once, after I accidentally broke a glass tumbler, Carmen beat me so severely that she bruised my right cheek, just below the eye. I was ordered to tell anyone who asked, that I was hit in the face with a baseball while playing catch in the yard with my dad. Carmen swore if I told anyone the truth, the people from social services would take me away and put me into foster care, with a family who would torture and starve me. In retrospect, foster care might not have been so bad.

I don't know if my story is a common one. The outward appearance to our home life was normal. We looked and acted much like any other family. We took yearly vacations, played sports, went to church, and interacted with friends and relatives. The illusion of normalcy was not solely for the protection of my abusers. I needed to feel as though I fit in, although clearly, I did not. I had a few friends at school, but I would always make a point of visiting their homes, rather than allowing them into mine. There was a fear that Carmen might lash out at them or say something embarrassing to humiliate me. If a friend began to pressure me to spend time at my house, I would either make an excuse or simply stop socializing with them. As my few friends were expended, I became reclusive and withdrawn.

Far more painful than the physical abuse or the confinements, was the ability of Carmen to destroy my self-identity and self-esteem. In fifth grade, while the rest of my class took a bus trip to New York to visit the Museum of Natural History, Carmen called the school and said I could not attend. She told my teacher that I was prone to severe carsickness and was afraid I would throw up on the bus. Once over the past summer I had gotten carsick. It was after eating too many hot dogs and spending too much time in the summer heat. Her real motive was to punish me for a mediocre grade I had gotten on my report card. I spent the day at home confined to my room. When I returned the following day, I had to listen to my classmates rave about all the exciting things they saw and did in the city.

Like most young men entering puberty, I soon became obsessively concerned about my physical appearance. Since I wasn't particularly popular, lacked social skills and was constantly being told of my inadequacies, there wasn't much to hang on to. I was not allowed to grow long hair or wear clothing that was in the current styles of that time. According to Carmen, only drug addicts, gang members, or homosexuals wore those styles. I may have been isolated, but I really did not believe that ninety percent of society, including school teachers, doctors and local politicians were all junkies. Furthermore, I failed to understand how people could be corrupted by hair and clothes. Nevertheless, I was restricted to wearing a military style haircut, straight legged dress slacks, a button-down shirts and dress shoes. I was a nerd before nerd was a word.

Height and weight were another concern. I was short and skinny. That is not to say that I was ever deprived of food. Growing up Italian meant that there was a never-ending supply of bread, pasta, fruits and vegetables. Despite a hearty appetite, I remained small. This made me fodder for bullies. Take a small, skinny kid who has no friends and acts a little odd, and you have a kid who will get beat up on the playground with some degree of regularity. I tried to bulk-up. I exercised and lifted weights. Nothing helped. I stayed skinny. I stayed short. I stayed un-athletic. I would learn later in life that none of that matters if you are confident and fearless. Those traits would come later. Given my current situation, confidence was nonexistent and fear was omnipresent. I longed to be big and tall. I clung to the hopes that genetics might look kindly upon me.

There was a chance. My Dad was 6'5" and large. He was neither muscular nor fat. He was simply a big guy. I had one uncle on my mother's side who was six foot six and a couple of older cousins who were over five-ten. That was counterbalanced by other relatives who were five foot four or less. Carmen constantly reminded me of this. She knew I fretted over my size, so she seized every opportunity to assure me that if I made it to five-eight it would be a miracle. As usual, she was wrong. In the summer between 8th grade and the beginning of my first year in high school, I had an abrupt growth spurt, shooting up six inches to the height of five foot six. Hardly basketball material, but it was a start. By the time I graduated high school, I was a six-two.

It is worth noting that it wasn't just Carmen and playground bullies who were knocking me down. Dad was almost as guilty as Carmen when it came to taking matters into his own hands. In retrospect, and perhaps unfairly, I tend to give him a pass on this. I at least want to believe that his outbursts were spontaneous eruptions of pent up anger and frustration, as opposed to Carmen's desire to assert herself as Lord and Master. An ill-advised comment on my part, might result in a swat to the back of the head or a kick to the seat of my pants from Dad, while from Carmen, the same comment would lead to a ten-minute beating and two days in the room. There was, however, one time, when he crossed the line.

The floorplan of our house was such that the garage was attached to a small laundry room which led into the kitchen. The laundry room also acted as a pantry, with several cabinets and a small upright freezer. On Saturday morning, it wasn't uncommon for Dad and I to go to a local flea market. He would shop for used records, and I would get a book or two. The place was as much a farmer's market as a flea market and so we would also buy groceries, such as fresh eggs, fruits and vegetables. One day in late Spring, he went to the pantry to see what we needed to buy in the way of produce. There he found a ten-pound bag of russets stacked on top of a bushel of peaches. The peaches were crushed and rotten, thus leaking all over the potatoes. Both were ruined.

When I heard him yell for me, I knew I was in trouble, but couldn't imagine the reason. He pointed to the bushel and the bag and immediately accused me of stacking the potatoes on the peaches. This was one of those rare times when I was not guilty. I swore I didn't do it. He asked again. I denied again. Carmen came over and smacked me in the head, warning me not to lie. I hadn't lied. She smacked me again, then walked away, telling my father to handle it. He asked again. I denied again. "Then who did?" he screamed as he lifted me up and smashed me into the wall. My head jerked back, leaving a small, round indentation in the wallboard. It didn't hurt, but I was really afraid. "Who did it then?" he shouted and slammed again. This time a small hole had opened in the wall. I could feel the crumbling gypsum in my hair. It mixed with sweat and tears, causing my eyes to sting. "I don't know," I cried.

This went back and forth three or four more times before a

small voice in the doorway answered "Dad. I did it." It was Marty. My father loosened his grip, dropping me to the floor with a thud. I ran to my room and slammed the door. By choice I stayed there for the rest of the day. Marty cleaned up the mess, but suffered no retribution, other than the guilt that came with having to look at the hole in the wall for a couple of weeks whenever she entered the pantry. Eventually the wall was mended and Carmen and my Dad found other ways and reasons to pummel me.

CHAPTER FOUR

*H*igh School. Is there any more stressful, awkward, dis-orientating, emotionally tumultuous time in a person's life? I started high school dazed and confused and stayed that way for four years. It's hard to learn about proper social interaction when you have spent the past five years or more either locked in a room or fearing for your life. I did have a few friends and even one or two girls that I would talk to in study hall, but they had no idea of what my life was like. I didn't tell them. I didn't tell anyone. I wanted so badly to be considered normal, that I built a false world around me so no one would know of my dysfunctional chaos. In doing so, I became an outcast and an oddity. It was better to be considered an oddity than to be pitied or scorned

My high school years were filled with rejection. It was everywhere. The first ten girls that I mustered the nerve to ask out all said no. When I finally did start to date it was always in the company of others. Double dating or triple dating wasn't exactly ideal for a romantic evening, but there was safety in numbers. I would not have my first one-on-one date until I was past my eighteenth birthday and already in the Navy. Then I tried to make up for lost time.

Meanwhile, the physical abuse at home gradually began to subside. After my first growth spurt, I was almost as tall as Carmen. This made it a little more difficult for her to pummel me. It slowed but didn't stop her. Instead of using her fists or household utensils, she resorted to throwing objects at me. Ashtrays, shoes, and assorted hand tools were all fair game. It was generally followed by a verbal tirade and restrictions on my nonexistent social life.

Meanwhile, the psychological torment continued. I was stupid, I was ugly, I was never going to amount to anything. If you hear that long enough, even from someone you despise, you start believing it. Of course, I wasn't really stupid. My grades were quite good. Carmen had dropped out of school in the 10th grade. Her only gauge on stupid was what she saw in the mirror. Nor was I ugly, although I did look out of place, primarily due the short hair and lack of fashionable clothes. Had I been allowed to dress and groom to the style of the day, I might have been considered okay, if not attractive. I was clumsy and unathletic, but at the same time, physically fit. Carmen, meanwhile, had ballooned to nearly a hundred pounds overweight.

As for never amounting to much, on that score I was a victim of circumstance. No one in my family had ever gone to college. We were peasants of a sort. The expectation was that you finished high school and learned a trade. College was for the affluent Jewish kids. I took college prep courses, because they interested me. Amid studying Shakespeare and the American Revolution, I took four years of metalworking. The plan was to become a machinist or a welder. That was my highest aspiration. I would become an articulate and enlightened welder. It was all blue-collar and no blue-blood for me.

What little social life I did have in my middle teen years began to take form when I turned sixteen. I had heard that the local Bullseye Steak House was hiring. McDonald's and Burger King were much closer by, but Bullseye was a modest step up from them on the status scale. It was also a step up from Paramount

Park, the local race track. Some of my friends had gotten jobs cleaning horse stables. Somehow bussing tables and running a dishwasher didn't seem nearly as bad as shoveling horseshit. There was already enough horseshit at home. Starting pay was $1.70 an hour. By the time I left the job, two years later, I was earning a whopping $2.50.

The restaurant was two miles from home. I had to walk. On a warm sunny day that was fine, but there were plenty of cold, rainy nights. Occasionally Dad or Marty would drive me, but most of the time I had to choose between walking along the highway, where I was at risk of getting run over, or taking the dark, scary backroads where strange sounds and shadows terrified me. Most times I chose the shadows, running a good portion of the way. In a typical week, I made between thirty and forty dollars. I got to keep ten dollars and Carmen took the rest. She said it was expensive raising kids, so it was about time I started paying them back. From what I've been told, my father tacitly objected to taking any of my money, but as usual he lacked the spine to hold his ground.

I didn't care. I would gladly walk an hour each way in the cold and rain, then work my ass off for nothing. It got me out of the house. It got me around real people. It even gave me the opportunity to talk with girls and older coworkers who didn't think I was crazy or nerdy or weird.

While Bullseye may have been my sanctuary, it also introduced me to alcohol, barhopping and lying. In retrospect, I'm not sure that this was such a bad thing. At that time, the driving age was seventeen and the drinking age was eighteen. Neither of these facts were relevant because New Jersey had not yet found the wisdom to put photos on driver's licenses. This meant you could simply borrow a license from any eighteen-year-old who fit your general physical description and have immediate access to underage drinking. I was soon doing this with alarming frequency. On any given Friday or Saturday night the restaurant would close at ten. I usually worked until eight and had a curfew of midnight. I would tell Carmen I was working late, then leave Bullseye to go drinking with my coworkers.

While I may have been socially dysfunctional, with a glass of whiskey in front of me I found both confidence and courage. In doing so, I began to create an alternate persona. Among my coworkers I would never discuss my family or anything else about my personal life, and I still was scared to death of girls, but for general conversation I got along fine. One of the cooks at Bullseye, Danny Scavatelli was a freshman at Central Jersey State College. He knew a guy who specialized in fake IDs. As a favor or perhaps out of pity he got me a modified driver's license. All the information was correct, except the birth date which proclaimed me to be of legal age.

Most nights we headed out to a row of clubs near the beach in Asbury Park. It was about a fifteen-minute drive from Bullseye. There was a new club called the Pork Pie. Every Friday and Saturday night a hot new rock and blues band, named Jersey Joe and the Jumping Jives, were playing there. They quickly developed a strong local following. One night, at about eleven o'clock, towards the end of their first set some short, scruffy little guy with greasy hair and a leather jacket walks in with an attractive and much taller blonde on his arm. Everybody went nuts. They were treating this guy like royalty. I turned to Danny and asked what the fuss was. He said the guy was a record producer from New York. I didn't catch his name. Danny said he was from the area and a bit of a local hero. A neighborhood guy who made good. Later that month he signed Jersey Joe. Everyone expected big things from them. They were a bust. Within a year they were back to playing the clubs.

Even though I was still housebound on a regular basis and routinely confined to my room, the one thing I was always allowed to do was work. Since work was my salvation I took on as many hours I could. Eventually Carmen lost track of how many hours I was working or how much money I should be bringing home. Whenever I wanted to go somewhere, even if I was grounded, I simply said I had to work. Shortly after turning seventeen I got my real driver's license. Since work was important, this meant I could sometimes borrow the car. Use of the car meant freedom.

A week before my seventeenth birthday, I approached Carmen and my dad, asking them to renegotiate my contract. I suggested that I pay them a flat thirty dollars a week, regardless of how many hours I worked. I argued that it was a good deal for them, because some weeks I made more and others less, so they could budget more easily if they knew exactly how much money they would be getting. Dad backed me up on this one, and Carmen gave in. It was a great deal for me. Most weeks I pocketed twenty or thirty dollars.

If Carmen had any math skills at all she would have realized that I could not possibly be working fifty hours a week, like I claimed to be. Maybe she knew but didn't care. If I wasn't home I wasn't a burden. Dad knew what I was up to. One night while I was "working" he and Carmen went down to the boardwalk on the beach at Asbury Park. There, he saw me in one of the pinball arcades. When I looked up and saw him my face went white with terror. He put his finger to his lips and made a "shhsssh." Then he quickly redirected Carmen in the opposite direction.

Another time, I stumbled through the door, clearly drunk. I raced to the bathroom and threw up. Along with two coworkers, I had consumed four pitchers of sangria from "Poncho & Pablo," a local Mexican restaurant. Carmen knew I liked to eat there after work. She didn't know I liked to drink there. "It's all that

Goddamn greasy shit you eat from that place," she said. I was sick
for two days. Food poisoning was her diagnosis. Alcohol poisoning was the truth. Carmen called the Poncho's and threatened to
sue them. They probably threw out ton of good food because I
got drunk and Carmen was accusing them of serving rotten meat.
Dad knew the truth, but not a word was spoken.

While I continued to be verbally assaulted at home, incidents
of physical violence became far less common. I suppose one reason the violence subsided was lack of opportunity. I wasn't home
much. This meant my younger sister Catherine became the new
whipping post. In Catherine's case, it got vicious. She fought
back. While I would passively take my beatings, while silently
praying for Carmen to die suddenly from a heart attack or stroke,
Catty fired back with flailing arms and foul mouth invectives that
would add to Carmen's rage. She too spent many days and nights
in confinement.

Carmen's last great assault on me came on my seventeenth
birthday. It arguably could have killed me. They say what doesn't
kill you makes you stronger. This did. On that day, I stopped being afraid.

It is worth noting that while most of my acquaintances came
from Bullseye, I did have one true friend from the neighborhood.
Randy Turner and I had been buddies since fourth grade but
didn't become good friends until our junior year in high school.
Randy was into cars. Classic cars. In his backyard, he was rebuilding a 1929 Model A and a 1936 Packard. To Randy they weren't
machines, they were puzzles. His goal was to reconstruct these
works of art into their original form. Since I had access to the
metal working shop at school, I could help him. We were both
misfits. And while we didn't accept the fact that we were outcasts,
we knew there wasn't much we could do about it. We decided
that the best thing to do would be embrace it.

Randy didn't know how screwed up my life at home was, but he did understand that things were amiss. Out of respect or embarrassment, he chose not to ask. Randy, on the other hand, had a different problem. His dad was Chief of Police. You would think this meant that Randy was kept under his rigid and oppressive thumb. It was quite the opposite. Chief Turner was used to catching kids smoking pot, drag racing, or making out in the back seat along dirt roads. He viewed it as normal. He didn't mind driving home the kid who had too much beer and was puking all over himself, or the girl who wouldn't screw her date, and instead got slapped around and left by the roadside. His kid did none of those things and it worried him. He thought Randy might be gay. It turned out he was right. There were nearly a thousand kids at East Central Regional High School and I was the only one who knew Randy's secret. No one else besides the Chief even suspected. Gay kids didn't work on cars. The Chief didn't care. Randy was his son. I didn't care. Randy was my friend.

One of the ways we embraced our outcast status was to do a sideways variation of whatever the cool kids were doing. While others embraced fast new cars, Randy chose the classic automobile. Others listened to Rock and Roll. We listened to the great jazz artists, like Louis Armstrong, Louis Jordan and Billy Holiday. Everyone else drank beer. We sipped Scotch. Cool kids smoked Marlboros. We smoked cigars.

Chief Turner was the first to catch us. He stopped out back while Randy and I were working on the Packard. We were wrestling with the back bumper that had recently been plated with a fresh layer of chrome. Randy leaned over and a pack of White Owls fell from his jacket. Time stopped for a moment as the three of us stared blankly at the ground. Not only had an open sleeve of cheap cigars fallen out but his Zippo lighter did too. The Chief bent over and snatched up the contraband.

"What the hell is this?"

Randy just shrugged and said "I dunno. Cigars."

"You guys smoke these things?"

"Sometimes."

"I thought I taught you better than that. Stay away from the cheap shit." He laughed and reached into his wallet. Pulling out a five he handed it to Randy. "Go down to Mancuso's News Stand and get some real cigars. Those things you got taste like dog crap."

The Chief was relieved that we actually were doing something semi-rebellious that other kids might be inclined to do. Against his wife's protests we were allowed to smoke in the yard, garage and basement. When he caught us tapping into his Scotch, again he admonished us. This time for not offering to replace the bottle that we were on our way towards killing. The Chief wasn't too fussy when it came to Scotch, so we him got a bottle of Cutty Sark. It came in a dark green bottle with a bright yellow label. Across the label was a clipper ship. Very cool. We didn't know good Scotch from grain alcohol, so the taste didn't matter. Cutty had the best label by far.

I finished my junior year of high school on June 8th. I was looking forward to my birthday in a few days and the opportunity to get my learner's permit. Dad and Marty both promised to give me driving lessons. Our two cars were a Ford Pinto and a Chevy Impala. Marty drove an old VW Beetle. Dad insisted that I learn on the Chevy since it was big sedan. He figured if you can handle a large car there is nothing to a small one. For the past few weeks, things actually seemed okay at home. Marty worked at a local car dealership and was dating the service manager. I was working or hanging out with Randy. Cat had briefly stopped rebelling. The calm would be short lived. The cigar incident from Randy's house was about to be replayed at the Campbell home with a very different result.

That Saturday, I was told to be home for dinner at five. We would be having dinner, along with a few birthday presents. Earlier in the day I had been down by the beach fishing off one of the jetty's. I enjoyed fishing. I could go down to the beach and spend hours alone throwing my line into the surf. Sometimes I would catch a bluefish or flounder. Mostly I got a nice tan, enjoyed the sounds and smells of the water, before returning home empty-handed. In mid-June the bluefish were in near the shore, breaking along the top of the surf. Using a topwater lure with a large treble hook I threw my line directly into the fray. A good a day turned great as I returned home around noon, with seven large bluefish. We would have my catch for dinner. I propped my pole and tackle box in the garage, took a quick shower and went over Randy's for a while. I brought the Chief two fish. Randy and I sat outside for a while, having a smoke and drink, talking about what had to be done next on the Packard. When I got home, my father cautioned "Don't go in the garage." Something was up. I had a momentary fantasy that they had gotten me a car. It was just a fantasy.

There are few meals that I enjoy more than freshly caught bluefish. Carmen, for all her many faults, was an excellent cook. She baked the fish at a low temperature, with garlic and oregano, then smothered it on top with a tomato parmesan puree. The fish oozed with flavor. Italian bread and salad rounded out the perfect meal. Coffee and birthday cake for desert. A good day indeed. Finally, I was allowed to step into the garage.

It wasn't a new car, or even and old one, but I my fantasy wasn't dashed too badly, because leaning up against my old rod and reel was a beautiful new surf casting outfit. I picked up the eleven-foot pole and Shakespeare reel, fondling and admiring it, much in the way an appraiser might review a rare antique. This was no antique. It was state of the art, and it was beautiful. I would now be able to throw my line fifty feet further than ever before, reaching into the deeper waters, where the big fish were.

Dad saw how thrilled I was with it and he smiled with pride. He was the one who picked it out. "Let's take it out back and give it a try." Even Carmen smiled as she looked on. She was hoping, as was I, that there would be plenty more bluefish on our dinner table. Dad stepped back into the house. He wanted to get the camera. I don't know what he thought was so memorable about a seventeen-year-old kid taking practice casts, but for some reason he wanted pictures. He wound up not taking any, although I wish he had. Without thinking, I flipped open the top of my tackle box, figuring I would tie a five-ounce sinker to the end of the line, so I could practice casting in the backyard without using a hook. There, right on top of everything in the box was a small plastic sandwich bag, inside of which were three cigars and a lighter. One of the cigars was half smoked. I grabbed the sinker and quickly flipped the box shut, hoping no one had noticed. It was too late.

"Wait a second. What was that?" Carmen asked.

"What was what?" Playing dumb doesn't usually work, but it was worth a try.

"Open the box again."

I was screwed. I flipped the box open. Carmen quickly swooped down and grabbed the baggy. "This. What the hell is this?"

"Those are cigars." I said rather boldly. "I light one sometimes while I'm fishing to keep the bugs away."

As I turned to face Carmen and gage her response, I leaned directly into the heel of her hand. The blow stunned me, but not before I could see the blind rage in her eyes. "What kind of crock of shit excuse it that? There is bug spray right there next to the cigars. Do you really think I'm that goddamn stupid?" Again, the hand. I tried to duck so it hit me with a glancing blow off the top of my scalp. "You don't think I know what goes on around here? You don't think I can smell that shit on your clothes? You're smoking dope, aren't you? Tell the truth. You're using cigars to hide the smell of dope and you think I'm too goddamn stupid to notice? Well you're the stupid one mister."

I tried to stammer my denials. The honest truth was that I had never smoked pot; at least not yet. Booze and cigars, yes. Pot, no. It was too late. There was no holding her back. Carmen grabbed my old rod and reel and began swinging it wildly. The lower portion of the pole came crashing down on my right shoulder. The pain shot right through to my fingertips. I dodged and missed the second swing, but on backlash the tip of the rod caught me and opened a small cut above my left eyebrow.

Dad had heard the commotion and ran as quickly as he could to the garage. "What's going on?" he demanded. "Your stupid goddamn son is smoking pot and covering it up with cigars," Carmen screamed. Before Dad could reach Carmen, she unloaded one more swing. This time, topwater lure that was still tied to the line, cut loose. The treble hook caught me squarely in the side of the neck and dug in. Carmen pulled back on the pole as though she was trying to land a marlin. The hook dug deeper, but the lure snapped, as the round eyelet that held the treble gave way. The recoil sent her stumbling backwards and onto the floor of the garage. Dad grabbed Carmen, then looked up at me with a combination of disbelief and panic. I stormed out of the garage, walking briskly and purposefully away with the hook still imbedded in my neck. Carmen called back. "Just where the hell do you think you're going? Get back here!" With a firm, clear voice my father asserted, "Shut up. Let him go."

A thin red line of blood streamed from the neck wound, down to my collar, where it was quickly absorbed by the black, sweat soaked tee shirt that I wore. I felt no pain, only purpose. I had to get out of there. I was going to Randy's. If no one was home, I would wait there until someone was. The walk was just over a mile. A tremendous calm came upon me as I walked the streets. Carmen would never again hurt me. I did not have to take it. I would not take it ever again. For a moment during my walk I considered getting a gun from Randy and killing her. There were numerous fantasies about how I could do it and make it look like an accident. They were simply fantasies but comforting just the same. Instead I realized that in one year I would be eighteen, an adult, and a high school graduate. I could get a real job, an apartment and start a life of my own. Meanwhile, for one more year I would survive. I would not take her abuse any longer. I didn't have to. I could simply walk away.

It was a little after seven when I rang the bell. Chief Turner answered the door. The look on his face was one of disbelief and confusion. "Chief, I have a problem. Can we talk?" My heart was racing. Randy heard my voice and came in from another room.

"You're hurt. Come in. Sit down. What's going on?" You could tell that the Chief's heart was racing too. After twenty years of police work, even in a small suburban town, he had seen a lot, but this was different. The Chief's first thought was to get me medical attention. It seemed unbelievable to him that I could walk over a mile down public streets in broad daylight, while bleeding from my neck, and not one passing motorist or resident homeowner stopped to ask what was wrong. I told Mr. Turner that I wasn't going to the hospital. He called to Randy, who quickly retrieved the emergency first aid kit from his police cruiser. Using a pair of needle nosed pliers and a very sharp pen knife, he dislodged the hook. The wound was cleaned with peroxide and gauze. Surprisingly, a little pressure and a small band aid sealed the puncture. It was a damn miracle, proclaimed the Chief.

Those rigs never break, and that hook had to have come within a quarter of an inch of my jugular vein. If my head was turned just slightly to the left I could have bled to death. Randy got me a clean shirt to wear. Meanwhile, I began spilling my guts, telling the Chief of the day's events.

I was too angry to cry. In a tight-lipped, metered diction, I unburdened myself telling my friend's dad one unexaggerated tale after another from my years of abuse. It painted a disturbing picture that neither he nor his son had ever imagined. I could see very clearly that Mr. Turner outraged, however, as Chief Turner he had to remain professional and restrained.

He asked me what I want to do. I could stay with them for a while, if I wanted to. I said no, I just want to erase today and start over tomorrow as if today never existed. We both knew that you cannot undo what has already happened, nor should you try, but the Chief promised he would find a way to help. He sent Randy and me down to the basement and told us to put the television on. He didn't want us to hear what he was doing, or saying, or to whom he was speaking. By now I was too tired or numb to care. As we heading down the steps, he called to us. "No drinking or smoking this time. Got it?"

Randy was in a state of shock. "I thought I knew you. Why didn't you tell me? I mean I always figured your parents were a little weird, but I had no idea. Christ Ralph, you deserve a Best Actor award. How could you live through all that shit and still pretend that everything is okay?"

"I'm sorry, man. I just figured one of us should be normal." Immediately I realized what I had just said. "Shit, I'm sorry Randy. I didn't mean it like that. You're normal and so am I. It's the rest of the world that's so fucked up."

"No offense taken. You've had a bitch of day. Now what? My guess is that my Dad is on the phone with your house by now.

You sure you don't want to stay here? What are they going to do to you if you go home?"

"I don't know man. I just don't know. It all depends on how well the Chief can handle Carmen. She's one tough bitch. She's definitely tougher that my dad."

"Man, this really sucks," we both concurred.

It was after eleven o'clock when Randy and I were called back upstairs. The Chief was standing in one corner of the kitchen. Randy' mom was next to him. Carmen and my dad were sitting at the kitchen table. When we appeared in the doorway Mr. Turner pointed to an empty chair. "Have a seat." In simple show of strength, I replied "No thanks. I'll stand." Randy put his arm on my shoulder. The Chief smiled. Our defiance pleased him.

"It's been a long day for all of you, and it's gotten to be a long night for me. That's okay. Anytime I can help out one of my son's friends, I'm glad to do it. Ralph, your folks and I have been talking here a bit and it seems like things got a bit out of control pretty fast. As a police officer, I see plenty of violence, and I'm not one to condone it, except as a last resort. What happened today wasn't a last resort. What you said has happened in the past doesn't sound like a last resort either. Your stepmother has a temper, and this time it made a bad situation worse. She's sorry about that. Isn't that right Carmen?"

Carmen hated the title stepmother. Rather than speak she just nodded. She wasn't looking at the Chief, or anything else. Her eyes were glazed over and just staring into space. Behind those eyes I saw anger and even hatred. The Chief continued...

"Now I'm not saying you're the perfect kid either. I've been around you enough to know that there are times when you annoy the crap out of me, just like any other kid. So don't be thinking you have a license to do whatever the hell you want. It just ain't so. But this time you get your wish. You said that you just wanted to erase today. We agree. It was a bad day. Go home. Startup fresh tomorrow. Today never existed. Your parents say they can do that. Can you?" I nodded affirmatively, but with obvious apprehension. It was what I wanted, but I did not believe it was going to happen. "Great," said the Chief. "Are you working tomorrow?"

"Noon to six" I answered. "Why?"

"We'll have dinner ready at seven. Come on by. We're having fresh bluefish. If today never happened, you won't know that you are eating it two days in a row". We all laughed except for Carmen. Even my dad let go of a little chuckle. The Chief was trying to be subtle but his intentions were obvious. He insisted that I come over so he could find out if there had been any retribution. The war was almost over.

Not a word was spoken during the ride home. Marty was in the living room watching television. She looked up at me in worried admiration. In unnerving silence, we all went quietly off to bed. I was still afraid, but I don't recall ever sleeping more soundly. When I got up around eight, Dad was already in the kitchen. "I'm going to the bakery" he said. "Want to come?" Statements like that were never meant to be a question. I put on my sneakers and met him in the car. True to his word, the previous day's events were never mentioned. We made small talk about baseball. He asked how things were going at work. By the time we got to Mozzacato's we had already decided what kind of bagels we wanted. That was our conversation.

Before heading to work that day, I stopped in the garage to look at that lure. Divine intervention? There was no logical reason as to why that eye ring didn't hold the hook in place. Meanwhile my old pole and tackle box were exactly where and how I had left them, including the baggie with my cigars. As for the new surf rod and reel, they were nowhere to be found. Along with the rest of the previous day, they never existed.

Carmen didn't speak a word to me for over two weeks. On a few occasions, she would tell Marty or Cat to ask me something. I didn't mind the snub. I found little reason to talk to her as well, but I would not stoop to her condescending levels. If I had something to say, I kept it short and respectful. Eventually, things went back to our own warped version of normal. While there was never again any physical contact, Carmen continued berating me for whatever reason she could find.

One time she told me I was too dumb to go to college. She conceded I might be smart enough, but if I had applied myself in school I could have gotten scholarships. Since I didn't apply myself enough to get a scholarship, that made me dumb. It was pure irony coming from a high school dropout. The insults and criticisms would continue on into my senior year of high school. I was now immune to the abuse. I now lived with a singular purpose. Find a way out. As long as that was my quest, Carmen could no longer hurt me.

After seeing what he believed to be a terrific show of courage on my part, Randy began talking with me about the possibility of telling his dad that he was gay. I could offer no advice, other than to suggest that he would know when the time is right. Deep down, we both knew that this wasn't the time. Chief Turner was a wonderful man, but he was from a time that was not yet comfortable with homosexuality.

The physical abuse that routinely had accented the past eight years ended with my seventeenth birthday. It was a day that by order of the Chief of Police, did not exist. My childhood was almost over. I had somehow survived.

Richard looked up from the pages and gave Caroline a rather quizzical look.

"Did your dad ever talk about his stepmother?"

"No," she replied. "In fact, I never heard him talk about anything

that happened before he joined the Navy. I never heard about his mother, or her illness, or his stepmother. I didn't even know her name. Either of their names. It was as though the first seventeen years of his life never existed. I don't even think my mom knew about it. He never said a word."

Richard mused. "This reads like Charles Dickens meets Stephen King. Do you think it's all true? Could it really have been that bad?"

"Yeah, I think so. It certainly would explain a lot." Caroline stood up, turned to the window, and began to speak reflectively. "Dad was a good man; a loving man, but he was very hard to get close to. I mean that quite literally. Often, if I put my hand on his shoulder or reached around to give him a hug, his body would literally tense up. Years of abuse, no matter how long ago, can do that to a person. The same is true with animals. As a kid, we had this dog, Lucy. She was a mix-breed rescue from a shelter. Lucy was a great dog, but she had been abused. Any time you reached down to touch her, if you moved too fast, she would recoil in fear. Same thing."

"Dad's father died shortly after I was born, so no, I don't remember him. Once in a while we would cross paths with some cousins or other relatives, but it was rare. These encounters were always treated as obligations rather than happy occasions. I suppose the one saving grace is that he did remain close to his sisters. I can't recall any of the three ever speaking of their childhood, but Dad always seemed very relaxed and comfortable in his interactions with Aunt Martha and Aunt Cat." Caroline smiled. "Anyway, they always doted on me."

Stepping away from the window, Caroline again sat in the chair next to the lamp, putting her feet up onto the bed where Richard sat. "This manuscript," she said, "We are talking as though everything about it is real. Do you think it is?"

Richard hesitated, not wanting to answer too quickly. Finally, he sighed, "I don't know what to think. Let's keep reading. Maybe the answer is a little further along."

CHAPTER FIVE

$\mathcal{M}$y senior year in high school began without much change. The domestic violence that had long plagued our household was now gone. Chief Turner had assured my parents that they would both be arrested if they so much as tapped me on the shoulder. Of course, that didn't stop the verbal assaults and it didn't change my persona at school as a creepy, nerdy, misfit. Randy Turner still hadn't told his dad that he was gay, and I still hadn't had a girlfriend or even a first date. I did have a brief crush on Linda Menkowitz, a short, chubby, but still moderately attractive girl from school. We began walking home together. On several occasions I attempted to ask her out. She said she really enjoyed our walks home but wasn't at all interested in dating anyone. In October I got her a job at Bullseye. Two weeks later she was dating Charlie Hendrickson, a wrestler from nearby Preston Beach High School. Six months later she was pregnant and dropped out of school. I would go 0 for 4 years on the high school dating scene.

But some things had changed. Since the incident in June, I no longer lived in fear. Fear had transformed itself into anger and a resolve to do something about it. I knew I wasn't going to college. No one in my family ever had, and we simply could not afford it on my father's mediocre pay. College was for rich kids. The children of doctors and lawyers and accountants went to college.

Jewish kids went to college. Italians and Polish kids learned a trade. If you have a blue-collar skill, you always have something to fall back on. That's what they repeatedly told me. I have no idea what they meant by "fall back on" but I knew that I had few options. I needed to learn a skill. My interest and my ability led me into the metalworking trades.

For four years in high school I took all college prep courses, because that's what interested me. I also took metal shop. I learned to weld. I bent sheet metal. I even did some blacksmithing. Mostly, I ran engine lathes and milling machines. American literature was my first love, but machinist work was a close second. I wasn't very good at it, but for what it was worth, I was the best in the school. Dennis Carlson, the industrial arts teacher took a special interest in me, allowing me to mentor others who were struggling. I did two independent study classes where I built engine parts for the auto shop. On graduation day, I received a one-hundred-dollar savings bond and the school's Industrial Arts Award for the best craftsman. My dad was proud. Carmen was unmoved.

Shortly after being jilted by Linda, I began devoting all my free time to finding a way out. I wanted to leave town and preferably go as far away as possible. Since college wasn't an option I had to consider other possibilities. Maybe I could work full time and go to a trade school at night. Every big city had trade schools. I knew New York would be too expensive and too dangerous, but Philadelphia was a possibility. A few places sent some nice brochures, but they were all exceedingly expensive. For me to get any kind of financial aid, my dad would have to sign for a loan. That was out of the question. His credit wasn't very good and even if it was, Carmen would never allow it.

I wasn't panicked yet. I still had a few possibilities. Bullseye was willing to hire me full-time out of high school, and I figured I could find someone to share an apartment. That was one choice. It wouldn't be like moving out of state, but at least I would be out on my own. Another possibility was Civil Service work. I took the Civil Service exam at school and did very well. Once I turned eighteen I could get on the list for a job at the post office or court-house or some other government job. That would be great. Those jobs paid well enough that I might even afford a small apartment all to myself. There was still time for things to work out, and there were probably other choices I hadn't considered. Something would surely turn up.

Good grades were never a problem. While I wasn't particu-larly studious, I had a decent memory which allowed me to ab-sorb enough from my classes to get by. I was also a decent writer, which afforded me the luxury of bullshitting my way through some of the more difficult school assignments. Most of all, I ben-efited from my frequent incarceration to my bedroom. This ex-ile forced me to devote more time to my academics than any ordinary teenager might commit. If I faltered anywhere, it was math. The abstract formulas required for algebra and geometry didn't make much sense to me. I wasn't a numbers guy. Instead, I was driven by words and the escape that came with a good story, both in literature and in history. By the start of my senior year my class rank was 54 out of 288. Top 25%. Not bad. I was the only student in the top quarter who would not be going straight to college.

Most seniors took six classes and a study hall, jockeying the time frame so that it was either first or last period. This would allow them to either arrive at school late or leave early. I took seven classes. Any time away from home was time well spent. Two of the classes were metalworking, while the remaining five were college-prep. The first quarter ended on the last Friday in October. Report cards arrived by mail the following Thursday.

On that day, I wasn't working at the steakhouse and there wasn't any important place that I had to be.

When I arrived at home around three, Carmen was on the sofa watching soap operas. That was how she spent most of her afternoons. I called out a hello and started back to my room. I wasn't serving another sentence there, I just figured I would do my homework first, then head over to Randy's. Carmen called back that there was something on the kitchen table for me to look at. Puzzled, I backtracked into the room and picked up the small manila envelope. I knew what it was, but I didn't expect anything unusual beyond a balanced assortment of A's and B's. What I saw made me smile. Six A's and a B+. The low grade came in Honors English. It was a pretty fair accomplishment for someone who was working 25 hours a week, while going to school and avoiding his family.

It was my best report card ever and I was proud. This was an accomplishment that deserved recognition. With a strut and a swagger, I strolled into the living room tapping the envelop against the palm of my left hand. Politely, I waited for a commercial break, then interrupted Carmen's afternoon ritual with a simple "Pretty good grades, huh?" For once, just this once, she would have to concede that I had done well. Just this once. Was that too much to ask?

Like a mountain lion waiting to leap onto its unsuspecting prey, I had fallen into the trap. Carmen leapt. "Pretty good? You think you're hot shit, don't you? You should be embarrassed. You couldn't get an extra two points in English? Isn't that what we speak around here? Aren't you always reading something? How could you not get an A in English? You might think you're smart, but if you ask me you're pretty goddamn stupid."

First, I was crushed; then my blood began to boil. My lip nearly bled as I held back the tears and the vile words that I wished to return. "When the fuck did you ever get an A? What have you ever accomplished in your fat, worthless life? You're a fat, ugly, loser. You're a high school dropout, a child abuser, and one poor motherfucking excuse for a human being. You're a waste of space, air, water and food." That is what I thought to say. Instead I simply shut my mouth and turned away without a word, retreating to my room.

I didn't eat dinner. "Not hungry," I said. I didn't go to Randy's. Why keep burdening him? Instead I sat in the dark for about an hour, thinking that nothing would ever change. Later, after turning the light back on, I found myself reading "Of Mice and Men". I knew that George and Lenny, the book's two main characters, would understand. At about eight o'clock Dad stuck his head in my room.

"Hey pal, I saw your report card. Nice job."

"Fuck you. Tell that to your wife. She doesn't think so"

Dad was startled but not offended. He was used to being cursed at. "Don't sweat it." He was trying to console but the undertone was patronizing. "We know you're smart. We just want you to live up to your ability."

"Too bad. That is the best of my ability. In fact, that's beyond my ability, so don't count on ever seeing it again."

With that he looked down and closed the door. He was the henpecked husband and I was the rebellious teenager. Those two ingredients don't mix very well. There was no sense in stirring things up. He would try to talk again tomorrow or the next day when I cooled down. The problem is that I didn't cool down. Not for many years. This was the last straw. Now, more than ever before, I knew I had to escape.

Redemption came unexpectedly, in the hallway outside of the high school cafeteria. Lunch was over and I was standing next to Bobby Statler. Bobby was one of the few black kids who attended our school. It's not that there was anything segregated about East Central High School, but if I had to guess I would say that a third of the students were Jewish, a third were all or part Italian, and a third were everything else. Bobby was simply part of everything else. As I stood by him in the hallway, I notice that he was holding a U.S. Army notebook and an information guide. This did not seem unusual. His dad was a Warrant Officer and a career soldier stationed at the base nearby. When I asked Bobby about the book. He told me he was signing up.

My heart leapt. It was an instant epiphany. My quest had ended. What better way to escape? Let Uncle Sam pave the way. I would learn my trade, travel the world, and get as far away from Carmen as possible. Jackpot. Sure, there were concerns. There was always some sort of saber rattling somewhere around the globe, so the risk of finding myself in harm's way was certainly possible. And while travel seemed like fun, I could easily be sent to Greenland, Guam, or some other remote outpost. None of that mattered. The gates of freedom were about to swing wide open and I would proudly march on through.

The rest of the day was a preoccupied blur. I ran home from school, quickly changing into a modest, but neatly pressed pair of slacks and a shirt. No sneakers and jeans for this. I wanted to make sure they would have me. Bursting out of my room I grabbed the keys to the car and without asking said "I have to run an important errand. I'll be back in an hour." Three hours later, I arrived home with a new life and a whole lot of explaining to do.

The nearest armed forces recruiting station was in Littleton, about five miles down the road. I knew the place well. It was the red brick building on Main Street, located next to Sal's Tavern. A popular local landmark, Sal's was one of the best Italian restaurants in the state. It had been there forever, and despite its rather bland setting, (it didn't even have its name on the building), it did have character. The walls were lined with photographs and signed menus from all the great Italian celebrities that frequented the joint. There was Tony Bennett, Frank Sinatra, Joe DiMaggio, and Yogi Berra to name a few. For a moment I stood outside of the building, seriously debating whether I should join the Army, or duck into Sal's for a plate of linguini with clams. As I entered the recruiting station four men in uniform immediately stood up and offered to help me.

I had already decided that I wanted either the Navy or the Air Force. The Navy was my first choice. There was something both heroic and romantic about the Navy. Crossing the ocean, with the salt air in your face. Men against the sea. It was all the old war movies showing sailors out on the town with a girl on each arm. I soon found out that reality was a little different from what the cinema portrayed, but that was still okay with me. I settled into a cubicle in the far corner of the office, where I spent the next two hours talking with Brian Harrington, a Hull Technician Second Class with just over four years of service. Brian had spent the last three years working on aircraft carriers. His reward for reenlisting was that he got to spend a year in his home town of Littleton.

All recruiters have quotas to meet, but to his credit, Brian was a straight-shooter. Although my mind was made up, I asked him dozens of questions about what opportunities might be available and what military life was really like. He made no attempt to understate the truth. It was a hard, gritty life. The romantic images projected in movies and even history books were not true. What was true is that in exchange for four years of hard work and low pay, there was travel, training, and opportunity. There was the chance to do and see things and be part of something big that relatively few ever get to experience. In just over four years Brian had been to eight countries on three continents. He had served on two ships. He had been shot at. And he met his wife, while serving in the Philippines. His story was not unusual and it could become my story.

His candor earned my trust. I wanted to be a machinist. He initially offered Machinist Mate's school, until upon further review we figured out that what I called a machinist was actually a Machinery Repairman. More conversations followed. Where might I be stationed? What types of ships could I serve on? How long was the training? I left with almost a dozen brochures to review. He told me to give it some serious thought. My mind was made up, but I wanted all questions answered before I signed anything.

Was it odd that in the span of a few minutes, I could decide what I would be doing with the next four years of my life? No, because the specifics didn't matter. It was simply a way out. A good way out. Of all the options that I had already explored, only this one gave me food, clothing, shelter, a job and an education, --all guaranteed. The only other thing I knew that promised all those things would be a long prison term, and that wasn't in the plans. At once the matter was settled. I was joining the Navy.

Some things they could guarantee and some they could not. If it could be put in writing, it was a sure thing. What wasn't a sure thing was that my parents would sign for me. That was always a risk with recruits coming from high school. I could enlist now, and take active duty following graduation, but since I was only seventeen, a parent or legal guardian would have to cosign all papers. If I had to wait until I turned eighteen I could do it myself, but by then the offer might change.

One prospect that was particularly appealing was the chance to go to college after four years. Money for tuition. College was not in my immediate picture, but Brian kept pushing that point. If I went to school full-time I would get a monthly check for several hundred dollars a month to assist with tuition and expenses.

I knew I was smart enough for college, so in the back of my mind it was worth considering.

When I walked through the door at six-thirty, I was promptly greeted by both Carmen and my Dad with an unfriendly chorus of "Where the hell have you been?" I answered the chorus by throwing the pile of books and papers on the kitchen table. The thud and the splash of loose pages spilling over the edge and onto the floor was greeted with long deadly silence. The top booklet was entitled. "Your Navy: Benefits and Privileges for Enlisted Personnel". They both stared down at the title. It was like watching a car accident progress before your eyes. You see what is happening, but the mind does not yet comprehend what any of it means. The trance was finally broken when I firmly declared "I'm joining the Navy."

On the drive home from Littleton I had decided that the best approach would be to discuss my plans as though they had already come to fruition. This is what I am doing. This is what must be done now. These are the papers you need to sign. Don't give them the chance to second-guess anything. My plan worked. They complied without debate.

I had missed dinner, but there was sandwich meat in the refrigerator. I threw together a ham and cheese sandwich, and then started talking. A half hour later the sandwich was still there, but the first few rounds of papers were signed. They were both stunned numb. Carmen was elated. My father looked like he might throw up. This was not something that I had ever discussed with either of them. I lied and assured them that I had been exploring the possibility for a very long time. That was bullshit, but they bought it. Much of the rest of the night was spent answering their questions. I didn't have many answers, so I just made stuff up. Some of their concerns were valid, so I scribbled down a few questions to ask Brian when I saw him again on Friday.

What began as an uneventful Tuesday, turned out to be the most important day of my life. It has often been said that you don't realize the most significant moments when you are in the midst of experiencing them. That may be true some of the time, but I knew this was big.

Ironically, from that point on, Carmen began treating me a bit better. She knew I would be leaving, and that clearly made her happy. Sure, it was done under the façade of being proud of me for deciding to serve the country and learn a skill. Other times she was typically blunt, saying how she wished we still had a draft because it would force other useless kids like me into the service, where we would have to grow up. Those words meant nothing to me. I was pleased just to know that she was not going to be an obstruction to my departure.

Dad couldn't sleep that night, and when he saw the light on in my room, he knew that I couldn't either. He stopped in around midnight to talk.

"I think I know why you're doing this." he said.

"There ain't a lot of jobs out there right now. I don't have any skills. I'm not going to college. You want me to learn a trade. This is my best bet."

"That's not what I'm talking about."

"Anything else is a bonus."

"Carmen is thrilled. I'm not."

"Carmen has been trying to get rid of me since the day you two got married."

"That's not true."

"Yeah. If you say so."

Dad pretended to know something about being in the Navy. He had joined the Naval Reserve when the Korean War broke out. His draft number was low, so he wanted to make sure that he didn't wind up in the Army. He did his basic training at

Bainbridge, Maryland, and then wound up getting stationed in Brooklyn, twenty minutes from home. Somehow, he had lucked into serving as a driver for the Commanding Officer of the Brooklyn Naval Shipyard. For almost two years his contribution to the war effort consisted of commuting to work each day for the easiest job he ever had. He wore the uniform but he was never in my Navy.

After Friday's meeting with Brian, the wheels were in motion. There would be more papers to sign. Then the ASVAB tests. Those are the military's equivalent to the SATs. They would determine which schools I qualified for. I took the exam with a few dozen other recruits at nearby Fort Dix. I damn near aced it, thus qualifying for virtually any service school that was offered. I still wanted Machinery Repair. One of the final steps was a complete physical, which was done at the Veteran's Hospital in Newark. This was a bit stressful, not because of all the poking and prodding, but because this was one thing that could disqualify you immediately. Flat feet. An irregular heartbeat. Diabetes. Any one of these things could keep you out. I sailed through. The final stop was to see the psychiatrist. The entire evaluation lasted less than a minute.

"Do you like girls?"

"Yes."

"Do you hate your mother and father?"

"My mother's dead. I don't hate my father"

"Do you ever think about killing yourself?"

"No."

"Why are you joining the Navy?"

"To get trained as a machinist."

"Any other reasons?"

"Yeah. I don't like New Jersey."

"I don't either. Congratulations young man. You are sane."

With all formalities out of the way, Brian made the final preparations. The earliest they could get me into basic training, followed by MR school would be some time in August. That was fine with me. Boot Camp would be in Great Lakes, Illinois, just north of Chicago on the shores of Lake Michigan. A week off would follow, then MR School in San Diego, beginning in early November.

On Tuesday December 7th, on the anniversary of the Japanese attack on Pearl Harbor, I took the Oath of the United States Armed forces, along with eleven other individuals, at a small ceremony held at Fort Dix. It wasn't much of a ceremony. Neither Carmen nor my Dad attended. I just showed up, raised my right hand, repeated the words, and was officially inducted. From there I went to Randy's house. His dad had been in the "real navy," serving as a boatswain on a Destroyer in the North Atlantic. We each lit a cigar, raised a glass of Scotch, and toasted the seven seas. Then I went to work cleaning tables and dishes at Bullseye.

For the next eight months I pretty much went about my business. I went to school, went to work or pretended to, and went out from time to time at night after work. Randy found himself a "friend", so the three of us would sometimes go to Sal's Tavern for pasta and wine. Other times I would go with the Bullseye crowd to the boardwalk at Long Branch or Asbury Park. There was both excitement and fear in knowing that my days here were numbered. Mostly it was a feeling of relief. I had begun to break the chains that bind. August 10th was to be my own personal Independence Day.

I really didn't know what to expect of military life, or specifically of Basic Training. I expected it to be tough, but what could possibly be tougher than living with Carmen? Randy's dad told me what basic was like for him, and even gave me his old Blue Jacket's Manual. That was enough to make me more than a little nervous. It wasn't the discipline that worried me, it was the actual training and physical hardships. How could I ever learn all of those rules and regulations? Chief Turner talked about having to know how to tie about a dozen different knots and know what each were used for. There were other doubts. Could I pass the swimming qualifications? How well would I interact with other recruits?

The fear and uncertainty motivated me. Beginning in early March, I put myself on a strict training program. I would get up with my dad around 5am and run down to the beach. That was about two miles away. Next, I would do fifty pushups and one hundred sit ups, then run back home. There was just enough time to shower, dress, have a bowl of cereal, and make it to school before the 8am bell. I did this five days a week, taking the weekends off so I could go out drinking at night if I wanted to. The first month was brutal. I developed blisters on my feet and cramps up and down my legs. My hips and ass hurt. I felt the pain of muscles I never knew existed.

The fear of failure was relentless but the progress empowered me. I started timing myself, marking off the Broad Street Diner as the first mile of my daily run. My first attempt at a timed mile was on April 14th. Seven minutes and forty-five seconds. By June 1st I had shaved a full minute off that time. I began running in the sand for a length of beach, picking an area where the sand was soft and loose, so my feet would sink in. In doing so I found other unused muscles to strain. As pushups became easier, I added pullups to the regimen, lifting myself from a beam on the lower facing of the boardwalk. More than once I pulled up too hard, clipping the bridge of my nose or the crest of my forehead on the lower edge of the beam. The pain didn't bother me. I had to be ready. In a few months I would be entering the abyss that was my future.

I maintained that regimen until August 3rd. During that span I gained twenty pounds of lean muscle and trimmed my mile down to six minutes and five seconds. Physically I was ready. Mentally, I was terrified. Most young men entering the military have worries about adapting to the discipline, the physical demands, and even the potential of going off to war. I had none of those concerns. My fears were more abstract. They say if you live your entire life with the weight of someone's foot on your neck, then the lifting of that weight can be a terrifying experience. When old norms no longer exist, there is the potential for chaos.

I was about to be thrust into a situation where I was the sole person responsible for my existence. The navy, and my future shipmates, did not care about my disjointed family life or my lack of experience with social interactions. In the months leading up to my departure, I would lay awake at night thinking about who I wanted to become and wondering if I could ever be that person. Where I was going, nobody knew me. It was a blank slate.

Meanwhile, Spring rolled into Summer. Prom came and went without me. I didn't have a date and I didn't see any reason to find one. That rite of passage held no meaning to me. Not surprisingly, Randy didn't go either. Likewise, graduation came and went. It was all so anticlimactic. There would be no parties on my behalf. I didn't ask and none were offered.

The week prior to my departure felt surreal. Secretly, I hoped there would be a moment of reconciliation between Carmen, my dad and me. That never happened. I knew I made the right decision. Dad and I did attend a Sunday afternoon game in New York, where I watched the Cincinnati Reds beat his beloved Mets. It was a bus trip from his job. I spent the entire game enduring endless tales from his coworkers who wanted to tell me about their own experiences in World War II, Korea and Vietnam. Mostly I nodded politely and pretended to listen. Whenever possible, I tried to change the subject to my Yankees, who were well on their way to winning the division. The Mets would finish last.

The day before leaving, Brian gave me and four other recruit's a ride to the Federal Building in Newark. It was there that we got our final physical, were handed train tickets and again took the oath. We were now on active duty and official property of the United States Navy. It was then that it began to feel real. The following day I would share the train ride with three other guys from surrounding towns. Ben, Steve, Matt and I would not only share the twenty-four-hour trip to the Naval Recruit Training Center in Great Lakes Illinois, but we would also be in the same unit for the eight weeks of basic training.

My final day at home was awkward. Randy stopped by to share a beer and a cigar and to say good bye. We did it right in front of Carmen. What could she say or do now? To her credit, Carmen was civil. She asked what I wanted dinner. I suggested we all go to Bullseye, and so we did. I had worked there right up until the Mets game. Ray, the manager, let the restaurant pay for our meals. Ray was a good man, who had lost his best friend in Viet Nam. He didn't want me to go. There wasn't much dinner conversation beyond the constant interruption of former coworkers who stopped by to wish me well. Afterward we went down to the beach for ice cream.

As we strolled down the boardwalk, Dad and Carmen lagged behind while Marty, Cat and I walked further ahead. It was then that Marty started to cry. Carmen started to walk towards us, but Dad pulled her back. "Let them be." he said. "They need this time."

I put my arm around Marty and assured her that I would be fine.

"I'm not worried about you," she sniffled. "I'm worried about us. You took the brunt of everything, and now that just leaves me and Cat. You found a way out. I don't have one."

"I spent almost every waking hour of the past year looking for the best way out. You can do the same. Can't you get a place with Barb or Denise?"

"Hey wait you guys," Catherine chimed in. "You both can't leave me here alone."

"You'll be fine. Marty will still look after you, and now you have a map to show you how to get out when it's your turn."

I handed Marty my handkerchief, and after a moment of composing we rejoined the other two. We all walked silently before Carmen broke the still air by saying. "It sure will be quiet not having you around."

Marty and I both gave her our best "Please drop dead" stare before I laughed out loud. Carmen didn't get the joke.

I went to bed around ten and spent the next three hours staring at the ceiling. I finally dozed off about 1am and got up at five. Dad was taking me to the train station on his way to work. Carmen, Martha and Catherine all got up to say good bye. I hugged my sisters. Then, turning to Carmen, I forced a smile and said "See you in a couple of months."

Dad and I always had our best conversations when the two of us were alone together in the car. Now there was nothing to say.

"You sure you want to do this?"

"Yeah. There's no future for me here."

"There are other ways."

"Other ways for other people. This is my way."

"I understand."

I knew he didn't.

Dad double-parked in front of the train station. We shook hands as I climbed from the car. Then I walked away without looking back. It was my Independence Day. With nothing but the clothes on my back and fifty dollars in my wallet, I stepped onto that train and into oblivion.

CHAPTER SIX

Dear Caroline- One of the great misconceptions about those who join the military is that patriotism is a driving force. After the September 11, 2001 terrorist attacks that may have become a consideration, but it certainly wasn't true during the Vietnam War or in the twenty or more years that followed. There were thousands of other misfits just like me. Some were running away from home. Many were fleeing the inner cities and an economy that lacked opportunities. Some were the children of servicemen, continuing the family legacy. There were even a few courtroom enlistments. Every now and then someone would find themselves before a judge and be given a choice. Jail or the military. Four months or four years. Four years was probably the right choice.

Basic Training was neither difficult nor overly unpleasant. Conversely, I cannot say it was easy or enjoyable. What is to be enjoyed about waking up at 5am every day, marching everywhere and getting incessantly screamed at? In some ways it was strikingly similar to the lifestyle I had left behind.

The purpose of boot camp is quite simple. It turns a civilian into a sailor. The process takes eight weeks to complete. For four weeks, we were berated, humiliated, shoved and shamed. We were told how worthless we were and how quickly we would die at sea if we didn't get our heads out of our asses. We were pushed to the edge of breaking, then pushed just a little more. For four weeks we were stripped of any sense of individual self-worth. By the end of the fourth week we had lost all that had defined our past lives. We were soft clay, ready to be molded.

The last four weeks was the molding period. It was there that who we were and who we would become began to take shape. We weren't really worthless scum, as we had been previously told. We were former scum on the verge of becoming something great. Little by little we started to show the qualities that would forever separate us from the civilian world. We had strength, speed, and quick, instinctive reflexes. We learned the Navy's culture and adopted it as our own. Most importantly we shed our individuality to become a part of something much greater than ourselves.

I had a few advantages over many of my fellow recruits. The abuse that I had endured at the hands of Carmen was as bad as anything Uncle Sam would throw my way. My personal sense of self-worth had already been minimized. Discipline had been necessary for me to survive adolescence, so the structure and regimens of the military were no challenge. As for the physical demands, again, it was not difficult. I had been correct to assume that the training would be arduous, so my routine of running and calisthenics paid off. I entered basic training in the best shape of my life and left it in even leaner and stronger than when I began.

The four of us had arrived at the Great Lakes Training Center at about three in the afternoon. After checking our names on a roster, we were led to a large classroom where we were instructed to sit and wait, but otherwise were told nothing. There was to be no smoking, eating or drinking. We were told we could talk, but only in a whisper. Gradually, as more busses and trains pulled up, other recruits were led to the room. By six o'clock, the room was filled with seventy would-be sailors. At that point a very large, muscle-bound black man in full military dress stepped into the room.

"Good afternoon gentlemen. I am Chief Petty Officer Peter J. Marshall. For the next eight weeks you will address me as 'Sir'. In conversation with others, you will refer to me only as Chief Marshall. Take a good look at this pathetic bunch around you. For the duration of Basic Training, these are your shipmates and I am your Company Commander. I can be your best friend or your worst nightmare. At times I will be both. If you do exactly as I say your problems will be few. Cross me and you will regret the day you were born."

"By now I would assume that you are all tired, hungry and confused. Good. That is the way it should be. If you do as you are told, it will get easier and it will get better. If you do not, it will get worse. Much worse. Here is what you can expect from the next twenty-four hours. In a moment you will walk single file to the mess hall for dinner. Next you will be led to the laundry, where you will receive your bedding. Then we go to Barracks 209. This is your new home. Tomorrow you will be processed for training. You will be issued a uniform and a duffel bag. All civilian items will be shipped home at that time. You will then receive the fastest haircut of your life." Chief Marshall pointed to one young man whose long blonde hair nearly reached his waist. "Goldie Locks over here will be getting special treatment. I'm doing your haircut myself." Everyone smiled sheepishly except for the young man who looked down at the table with a pained and unamused expression on his face.

I doubt that any of us slept well that evening. What had we gotten ourselves into? This was going to be like an eight-week prison sentence; maybe worse. The following morning came early and erupted violently. At precisely 3am the lights were turned on and the long room, lined with rows of double bunks, awoke to the thunderous crash of Chief Marshall hurling a half a dozen large galvanized trash cans across the room.

"Wake up motherfuckers! Quit jerking off and get your asses up and ready to serve your country. You're in the fucking Navy now. This is my fucking Navy and don't ever forget that. Do anything to disgrace my fucking Navy and I will tear you apart with my bare hands. What a sorry-ass bunch of pretty-boys you all are. Is this the best we can do? You boys are going to be one hell of a project. I told the C.O. that I loved a challenge and he gave me one with this group. Yes indeed. You over there…What's your name? Simpson? Give me twenty pushups. Every time you screw up, Simpson, you'll be doing pushups. You are going to be one physically fit motherfucker. What's your name? Rosenberg? Got a girlfriend Jew-boy? Yeah? Forget her. She's fucking someone else now. And you? Campbell? Where are you from Campbell? New Jersey? Got a sister? Do you know what the difference is between a pile of garbage and a girl from New Jersey? The garbage smells better and gets picked up faster." And so it went. The Chief went right down the line, tearing into every single person in our group. If you could get past the cruelty of it all, it was a fairly impressive tirade. Some of his insults were worn out cliché's. Some were quite original. No one was spared.

The mess hall opened at five-thirty. Chief Marshall woke us up early because he wanted to get a head start on our training. He took us out to a remote drill field where we were taught how to march. It took fifteen minutes to teach us the basics and two hours of practice before we were allowed to march down to the mess hall for breakfast. From that point on, we marched everywhere we went. Our feet went from blistered to calloused. At the end of basic training, it was estimated that we had marched more than five hundred miles.

For some, the most memorable part of boot camp was the gas chamber. Early in the second week we spent two hours learning to don and properly use a Mark V gas mask. Once our instructor, Petty Officer Lansing, was convinced that we had mastered the basics, we were marched down to see Bessie. Bessie was an enclosed air-tight chamber located at the far end of one of the drill halls. The metal box was rounded on the edges, with a single hatchway door on the middle of the starboard side. Despite appearing vaguely similar to a roadside diner, there would be no eating. Puking, yes. Eating, no.

Our unit was divided into thirds. Each group would get their turn entering the chamber wearing the Mark V. I was in the first group. We entered with Lansing, who had us line up evenly around the perimeter of the room. He stood in the middle barking orders. Bessie was then filled with tear gas. Once a series of dials and meters showed that the room was thoroughly saturated, our group was ordered to walk single file, twice around the chamber. Then, while keeping his own mask on, we were commanded to take ours off.

Less than twenty minutes earlier we had been sitting in a classroom, getting step by step instructions regarding what to do if you are ever confronted with tear gas or other types of chemical weaponry. It soon became obvious who among us was not paying attention. As our eyes welled up, and our lungs began to fill with an intense burning sensation, all hell broke loose. The two guys in front of me raced for the door. The hatchway had been firmly secured from the outside. The two pounded violently and began screaming to be released. The exertion caused them to take larger gasps of air, which in turn caused greater agony. While one guy clung to the hatchway puking, the other slumped to the floor, sobbing like an infant. They were not the only ones who panicked. After seeing that we were trapped, one large Hispanic guy charged the instructor. That was not a smart move. He was greeted with a hard fist to the center of his chest. Lansing then held him in check with a boot on his neck, while the brawny Latino lay writhing on the deck, gasping and wheezing. Several guys had tried holding their breath. That didn't work either. To hold your breath successfully, you must first fill your lungs with air. They filled their lungs with tear gas and began choking immediately.

While it may not have been pleasant, the majority of us were paying attention during class and did the right thing. We covered our faces as best we could, and began taking short, shallow breaths. As we walked our two laps we tried to refrain from exerting too much energy or do anything that would compel us to take deeper breaths. It's easy to say this now, but it really wasn't that bad. We had the advantage of being treated to the sideshow that our less disciplined mates put on for us. That made the exercise seem to pass more quickly. It also reminded us that these lessons were not purely sadistic. They could save lives. Once our allotted time was completed, the room was flushed with fresh air and water from an overhead sprinkler system. As we exited, we were escorted away from the other two groups and firmly ordered not to say anything about the drill until all three groups were through. I later learned that the other two groups had very similar experiences to ours.

By the seventh week we were a nothing like the group of kids that had just stepped off the train. Our number had been reduced from seventy to fifty-eight. We lost a handful of guys for medical reasons. A couple couldn't swim, and after two days of one-on-one instruction were deemed unfit for sea duty. There was Ray Crawford, who caught pneumonia, and had to be hospitalized for ten days. He later became my shipmate on the USS Havasu. Paul Pennington broke his leg when he fell from the ropes during a climbing exercise. Some say he jumped. Paul was a bit of a loose cannon, so the Navy was probably better off without him. Along with Paul there was maybe a half-dozen others who were deemed to be unfit for military life. They were given a General Discharge and a train ticket home.

As for the remaining fifty-eight, we had evolved rather nicely. While cliques and friendships existed, we were essentially a single unit. Some guys I liked and some I didn't but those feelings didn't matter when it came to getting through the final twelve days. Together we had already been through a lot. There was the marching, the gas chamber, swimming instruction, life saving techniques, firefighting, combat readiness, military protocol, military law, and shipboard training (including three days of knot tying). With each level of instruction, there were no guarantees. You had to do more than just show up to pass. If you didn't pass, you had just one chance at a retest before you faced the risk of being held back and forced to repeat a week. None of us wanted to see that happen. If we saw someone was struggling, we stepped in to help. That was the ultimate goal of our basic training experience. It was a single unit, single team mentality.

Physical training, however, was another story. Three days a week we were marched down to the gym for a one-hour workout. We ran for miles. We did pushups, sit ups, chin ups, crunches, stretches, windmills, and an incredibly painful exercise called butterfly kicks. You lay flat on the floor with your legs straight and your arms overhead as though you were going off a high dive. Then, without bending elbows or knees, you bow your body upward so that your midsection is the only part in contact with the floor. From that position you wave your arms and kick your legs in a swimming motion. Butterfly kicks are painful as hell.

Our unit had several guys who were prominent athletes on their high school teams. Ray Stevens was a state champion on his swim team in Michigan. Glenn Forman, from Delaware, ran marathons. There were other standouts. Unfortunately, not everyone took it quite so seriously. We had some fat guys.

As a group, we weathered every challenge thrown our way. We passed every exam and every inspection. One test remained. The final test, before we were all assured to graduate, was for physical training. Chief Marshall told us that this would be a timed run in the gym. We had to do two miles in eighteen minutes. No problem. I could do that without breaking a sweat. The fat guys were in trouble. Then he told us that we would be timed as a unit. Everyone passes or everyone fails. Now we all were in trouble. The logic was sound. In combat, if one guy screws up, everyone in the unit suffers or gets injured or killed. I understood the logic and I even agreed with it, but what could be done about the four fat guys who stood no chance whatsoever?

Glenn Forman and I were the best runners in our unit. Glenn came to me and suggested that we meet in private, along with a few others, to figure out a plan. Two nights before the run, right after the lights went out in the barracks, Glenn, Ray and myself met in the showers, along with Don Nelson, Bill Conway, and Rocky Martinelli. For nearly an hour, we brainstormed for ideas.

One idea that received serious consideration was that we injure the four guys so they would be unable to participate. Nothing too traumatic; a broken toe or a sprained ankle should do the trick. It would be unfortunate that the portly four would not graduate with us, but that was better than holding everyone else back.

Several other possibilities were proposed before Glenn came up with a plan that might actually work. It was decided that when the run began we would break off into two groups of three. Each trio would hook up with two of the slow guys and lock arms. We would then run with the fat guys, dragging them along as quickly as possible.

My group consisted of me, Rocky and Bill. We had to drag

Andre Popodoulis, and Wally Johnson. Andre was large rather than fat. As a civilian he had worked as a bricklayer with his father's masonry business. He was tall and muscular, but slow. Wally, meanwhile, looked as though he had never walked past a cheeseburger without lunging for it. According to plan, the line would consist of me on the outside, then Andre with Rocky in the middle, followed by Wally and Bill. As for Ray, Don and Glenn, they lined up with Larry Young and Steve McGraw.

We kept the plan a secret right up until the time of the race. As we were gathering in the locker room, the six of us informed our four understudies that they were being abducted. No one objected. Despite our secrecy, Chief Marshall soon realized that something was up. The six speedsters, who competed against each other whenever we were allowed to run freely, were missing from the front line. When he finally spotted us in the back of the group, locked arm in arm, he knew.

Once the whistle blew and the run began, I immediately had some doubts. That big Greek was one slow and heavy piece of meat. The primary problem was the footing. We all had to run with the same cadence, otherwise someone's feet would get tangled. After a clumsy start, Rocky, Bill and I all got on the same pace, the other two followed reasonably well. They didn't actually run. Mostly we ran and they scrambled their feet to keep up with us. When necessary, we dragged them. From what I could tell, Glenn's group had the same problem.

At the one-mile mark, Chief Marshall told us our time was at just under nine minutes. Allowing for fatigue, we had hoped for an eight and a half minute first mile and a nine and a half minute second. We had lost time getting our footing and cadence straightened out. Now we would have to pick up the pace.

With half a mile to go, Wally stepped on Rocky's foot, stumbled and fell. As we pulled him up Glenn quickly moved his group forward and locked arms with ours. We had a ten-person whip going as six runners dragged four fat guys to make a final desperate sprint. For no particular reason, I began singing "Anchors Aweigh". The other nine followed. Soon all fifty-eight were singing. It helped us keep cadence. As we completed the last verse, ten very sore and off-key sailors stumbled across the finish line. Our time? Seventeen minutes and fifty-two seconds. Eight seconds to spare. Although I will never know, I strongly suspect the stopwatch had malfunctioned in our favor.

Later that afternoon, when we returned to the barracks, Chief Marshall gathered us all together to discuss the upcoming schedule. Graduation was a week away. Much of the final week would be devoted to rehearsing for the upcoming ceremony. Meanwhile to celebrate our successful PT exam, the Chief obtained a temporary pass for our entire unit. Following the evening meal, we would be permitted to march down to the base recreation center. There we could bowl, play pinball, play basketball; you name it. They also had a large bank of phones, which meant that we would have a chance to call home. As a small cheer went up throughout the unit the Chief, almost as an afterthought, said "And I need to see Forman and Campbell in my office."

As Glenn and I nervously approached the door, the Chief waved us in. "Close the door. Sit down men." There was no urgency in his voice and no cause for apprehension. Although this big black man posed a figure of intimidation, we had grown comfortable and comforted with his presence. If we messed up, we knew we would hear about it in high volume and colorful language. Likewise, we understood just how difficult his job was and we respected him for the dedication and compassion with which he went about his business.

Marshall stood up behind the desk, and taking is cap off, began rubbing the top of his shiny bald head. As his head tilted downward a wide white-toothed grin emerged and he began to laugh. "Shit. I have been in this man's Navy for eighteen years, and I have seen plenty of crazy shit go down, but I ain't ever seen anything that comes close to the shit you two boys pulled off today." The Chief then picked up his cap and looked at the insignia. "You know, it took me sixteen years to make CPO, and when I did I swore it was the proudest moment of my career. It still is. But what you guys did today was out-fucking-standing! For the last few days I have been losing sleep, worried about how we were going to handle those four guys. They could run that course every day for a year and there ain't no way that they could make time. It turns out you guys had it under control the whole time."

"Chief it wasn't just us. Four other guys helped."

"I know that. I asked around. I also know that you two were the ringleaders. No way I could have seen that coming. Forman, when you got here, you reminded me so much of those spoiled-ass rich kids, with a silver spoon in your mouth and a bug up your ass, like the fucking world owes you something. Then I hear your Daddy's an airline pilot, and I'm thinking all sorts of bad things. Son, I apologize for that."

"Campbell, I never knew what to make of you. I do know that for the first three weeks here you were just another screw-up. But something kicked in. Of the fifty-eight guys in this unit, you have improved the most. I'll go to sea with both of you, any day, any ship, anywhere. This is my sixth unit of recruits. We try to teach one thing and one thing only. How to succeed as a team. You guys got it right. You cannot believe how goddamn proud I am right now.

You two earned that rec pass for everyone here and they all know it. Oh, by the way, don't tell the other guys this, but if we had flunked the PT exam, you would still be graduating on time. We throw that threat in, just to add some extra pressure.

On the other hand, by passing the test, we picked up enough points to ensure that we will finish as the top unit graduating next Saturday. What it means to you is that we get the front row. We march first, and we are recognized by the Commanding Officer. What it means to me is that on my sixth and final batch of recruits, the last group is the only one to finish first. Thank you, men. Thank you.

That's it. Now get out. Go. We'll be heading out to the mess hall in ten minutes."

"Yes sir. Uh, Chief?"

"What Foreman?"

"When you get a chance, could you at least say something to the other four? This wouldn't have happened without them."

"Consider it done."

Dad and Carmen flew out for the graduation, then I flew home with them for a week of vacation time before heading out to Machinery Repairman School in San Diego. I had been gone for two months but it may just as well have been a lifetime. It sounds cliché to say that I left home a boy and returned a man. Cliché, but true.

I was supposed to be home a week, but after four days I was ready to leave. I hopped a flight on standby and reported to the training center in San Diego three days early. It was good to be back among my people. It would be another six months before I returned to New Jersey. By then it would be my hometown, but no longer my home.

When the final separation came, I was stationed aboard the USS Havasu, a repair ship ported in Norfolk, Virginia. In late September we had cruised north to Newport, Rhode Island to work on several training ships that were docked there. I hadn't received or sent a letter or phoned home in at least two months. I had been thinking about it, but simply chose not to. Small talk is fine, but I didn't have much to say. I had my own life now. It was sad, but I accepted it. Besides, they could just as easily have reached out to me but chose not to. When the call finally came, it became clear that a tempest had been brewing ever since I left.

Bear in mind that back then, we did not have cell phones. A ship at sea had a radio to communicate with, and not much else. Most ships, like the Havasu, had a small switchboard on the quarterdeck that could handle about a dozen calls at a time. There was also a bank of four pay phones in the common area by the mess hall. When a ship pulled up to the pier, water, electricity, sewage and telephone lines had to be connected.

We had been in port for just a day when the call came. As luck would have it, I was standing watch on the quarterdeck at the time. Aboard a ship, sailors serve what is called a "duty rotation". Once every few days you have to spend the entire twenty-four-hour period confined to the ship. Rotations vary depending on the vessel and the circumstances. While on duty you are expected to stand watch, work late, and take part in various training exercises. In Newport we were on a four-day rotation. Guys would regularly swap days or pay other shipmates to take their duty for them. Some would arrange it so they stayed on board for four straight days, then had the next eight or nine days duty free. Others would simply do it for the money, earning an extra forty to eighty dollars a week, at a time when most of us were only making four or five hundred dollars a month.

Standing watch on the quarterdeck was quite simple. The quarterdeck is like the front door to the ship. On duty at any given time, was an officer who stood watch in four-hour shifts, along with a petty officer and a seaman who did two-hour watches. Anyone arriving or departing the ship was checked for identification. Any object being brought on or off the ship was subject to inspection. Outside visitors had to sign the log book and be accompanied by a crewmember. The quarterdeck was also where the switchboard was located. It was a pretty good gig. A seaman could just as easily wind up with parking lot duty during a rainstorm, or in the engine room, watching gages and pumping the bilges. On deck you spent most of your time working the switchboard and saluting people on and off the ship. You were sheltered from the elements and had people to talk to.

It was about 5pm on a Thursday afternoon when Petty Officer Carrigan picked up an outside call. The voice on the other end asked for a sailor named Campbell. I was standing right next to him. The voice on the phone was my dad. There was obvious distress in his voice, but I was not in a position where I could stop what I was doing and hold a conversation. Dad was always a talker, and what should be a three-minute conversation routinely lasted an hour. This time I got him to cut to the quick. There were problems at home. How soon could I get to New Jersey?

I already had the upcoming weekend off, so I quickly put in for an additional two-day pass for family reasons. Much to my surprise it was approved without question. It would cost me eight dollars each way to catch a bus from Newport to New York, and then another two dollars for the train ride into Littleton. The bus left at five, so I got there around noon on Saturday.

They say a chain is only as strong as its weakest link. Remove that link and the chain is broken. It soon became apparent that without my link in the Campbell household, the chain had disintegrated. The crisis was threefold. First, Catherine turned Dad in for child abuse. Next, Carmen kicked Marty out of the house. Finally, Dad had a big fight with Carmen and she moved back to her parent's house.

Marty picked me up at the train station. Rather than heading home we went straight to Sal's Tavern for lunch and several drinks. There she briefed me.

Things had deteriorated rapidly over the past year. Cat had assumed my role as the family punching bag. It didn't help that she had a flash temper and a knack for saying the wrong thing at the wrong time. As a high school sophomore, she began dating a twenty-one-year-old and was regularly skipping class. One morning in late May, Carmen received a call from the Vice-Principal stating that Catty was missing again. He went on to inform her that she currently had failing grades in three subjects and D's in the remaining two. Rather than assault Cat herself, Carmen called my father at work and demanded he come home immediately to deal with the problem.

Dad returned home, furious that he had to leave work to address a situation that could have easily waited until after his shift. Rather than refusing to leave, or taking issue with Carmen, he unleashed his rage on Catherine. When he confronted his wayward daughter, Cat told him to fuck-off. He exploded with a backhand across the face that bruised her cheek and split her upper lip. The following day, she made a point of going to school, to show off her battle scars. Whenever anyone asked what had happened, she simply responded, "My father hit me."

Carmen didn't call him at work this time, but when Dad got home that day, Chief Turner and a representative from Youth and Family Services were waiting for him. Dad had to go down to the station, where he was booked and given a court date. Catherine was assigned a family counselor, and everyone was subject to random spot-checks.

Marty, meanwhile, had been working as a legal secretary for Charlie Wallace, a criminal defense lawyer. Carmen knew of this lawyer and didn't like him. She liked him even less because he was thirty-one years old and divorced with two kids. Marty was twenty-one. They began dating. Dad didn't seem to care. Carmen thought it created a scandal, as if our family didn't already have enough mud on its name.

One afternoon Marty made the mistake of leaving her purse on the kitchen table while she was taking a shower and getting ready to go out. Carmen took the opportunity to inspect its contents. Amid the makeup, keys and wallet, she found a packet of birth control pills and a joint. When Marty returned to the kitchen to recover the purse, Carmen pounced. Suddenly my sister was a drug addicted whore, who along with that scumbag lawyer was responsible for the overall decline of western civilization.

As a shouting match ensued, the scumbag lawyer arrived to pick her up. Carmen was going to have him disbarred. That was her first threat. Soon it got a little more personal. She was going to cut his nuts off. Then she started throwing things. He threatened to have her arrested for assault. How dare he threaten her, while he makes his living getting drug addicts, murderers and rapists, out of jail. (In truth, the criminals he defended were usually white-collar businessmen who were charged with drunk driving or some other misdemeanor). Dad tried desperately to calm everyone down. It didn't work. Carmen told Marty to pack her shit and get out. She had three days to find a place to live. Marty threw a few things in a bag and left with Charlie.

She couldn't stay with Charlie. He didn't want her to spend the night while his two young boys were at home. He paid for a week's stay at the local Travelodge, so she could gather her things and move out immediately. It took her just two days to find a new home. She ran into Denise, an old friend from high school, who was sharing a four-bedroom beach house with two other girls. They were looking for a fourth person to lower the rent. The place was beautiful, and the price was good. The two other girls seemed nice enough.

Marty didn't suffer from the move. That ticked off Carmen more than anything. She had expected her to come crawling back, begging for forgiveness. Instead Marty earned her own Independence Day.

For Martha it was a personal victory. For Dad it was the final straw. Ten years of subservience had exacted too great a toll. On Thursday night, they had the fight to end all fights. He accused her of driving both me and Marty out of the house. She countered by saying that Marty created her own situation and denied having anything to do with my joining the Navy. "Ask him" was Dad's reply.

That was just the beginning. She called him a pathetic loser. He called her a fat cow. She slapped him in the face. He poured a pitcher of ice tea over her head and told her to cool off. She started throwing things again. Two end tables and a widow were broken as these two pugilists aired out their differences. Catty, the not so innocent bystander, decided to call the police. Dad was handcuffed and spent the night in jail. When he got out the next day, Carmen was packing her bags and moving back home to her parents. For the price of a night in jail, Dad too would get his Independence Day.

For all the invectives and accusations that were tossed in the heat of battle, only one comment seemed to cut deep. Carmen could not believe that I had joined the Navy to get away from her. She wanted to ask me herself. I was eager to comply.

After hearing Marty tell me all that had transpired, I knew I would have to visit Carmen. I also knew I had to be prepared for what I might hear, so it was imperative that I spend some time with Cat and Dad before I go see her. Meanwhile, I kept in mind that regardless of the near hatred that I held towards Carmen, a modicum of restraint would be required out of respect to her parents. Her mother and father had always shown me the kindness and compassion that their daughter seemed incapable of.

What could I possibly say to Carmen? No doubt she would attack me over the accusation that she had driven me away. How should I respond? Confrontation and open hostility would serve no useful purpose. I tried to anticipate every question, comment and answer. The Navy had taught me the importance of preparation. I had to be prepared. I needed to choreograph and control the situation. That was the task at hand. I spent a sleepless night rehearsing scenarios and memorizing responses.

On Sunday afternoon I donned my uniform, borrowed Dad's car and drove to her parents' house. Her mother greeted me warmly with a hug and a kiss. Her father got me a beer and beckoned that I sit down. For about fifteen minutes we sat in the living room exchanging small talk. Yes, I gained a few pounds since I joined the Navy. I showed them pictures of my ship and told them of the places I had been. Yes, I am glad I enlisted. Then, as if on cue, Carmen's parents departed the room, leaving the two of us to tend to our unfinished business. Despite a palpable tension in the air, the conversation began in a calm and civil manner.

"You know your father and I are separated. I plan to file for divorce in a few weeks. How do you feel about that?"

My initial thought was, "Since when do you give a damn about how I feel?" Instead I shrugged and calmly responded "I guess I'm not surprised."

"What do you mean?"

"I mean you were always battling. The whole damn house was always battling."

"Your father said I drove you out. Is that true?"

"True. You drove me out. You drove Marty out, and now you drove yourself out."

Emotions began to rise. "How can you say that. You think it's easy raising someone else's kids? I raised you as though you were my own."

There was no way I would let her get away with playing the guilt and pity game. I quickly fired back, "Then I guess it's a good thing you didn't have any kids of your own, because you would have driven them out too." My voice was calm and metered. This intimidated her.

"You think you had it tough? You don't know tough."

My words dug deeper. "Oh, I know tough alright. I'm in the U.S. Navy, and you know what? It's a piece of cake compared to living with you. Do you really think you gave me a normal childhood? You think it's normal to beat the shit out of a kid on a daily basis? You think it's normal that I was locked in my room for months at a time? Normal for a prison maybe, and that's what it felt like. It felt like a prison. Funny thing is, I didn't realize it until I escaped."

Despite the open wounds that now laid bare, I never raised my voice. If I lose control, she wins. If she loses control, well, that was to be expected.

"You never gave any indication that you were so unhappy."

"What recourse did I have? I was just a kid. Besides, I didn't want to make it any worse for Dad. If I fought back you would have taken it out on him."

"Make what worse? I loved your father."

"Bullshit. You were thirty-something years old and afraid of never getting married. You loved the idea of a ring and a house. If you had to put up with a husband and three kids to get it, so be it." I was still in control, but my words were turning cruel. I didn't want to be cruel. I wanted to keep my dignity, now that I had some dignity to call my own.

"Look, I'm sorry. I didn't come here to argue. You asked a question. The simple answer is that I was unhappy at home and you were a major part of that unhappiness. That is why I joined the Navy. In the end, I probably owe you a debt of gratitude. If you didn't drive me out, I might be working in some dead-end job right now without a future. You did me a favor."

"Is that right?"

"Yeah, that's right. But here's the thing. I chose to leave. I did I on my own terms. What I find unforgivable is that you threw Marty out. No parent should ever throw their own kid out."

"Did you hear what she did?"

"Yeah I heard. I don't' give a damn what she did. For all I care she could have killed somebody. You don't turn your back on family. Taking birth control doesn't make you a whore. It makes you safer and smarter. How many people in your family got knocked up before getting married?"

"I was a virgin when I married your father."

"That was your choice."

"She was doing drugs."

"How many alcoholics in your family?"

My voice was growing tense, so I sat back in my chair, had a swig of beer and took a deep breath to regain my composure. "The bottom line is that blood is thicker than water. It's thicker than anything. I can take a punch, but don't mess with my family. You don't seem to get that. I'm glad you're getting a divorce. Maybe Dad, Marty and Cat can start having a normal life now. As for me, I'll be fine. Just don't ask to see me again."

Slowly I rose from the chair. Before leaving I stopped briefly by the kitchen to say good bye to her parents. I apologized for causing any imposition. No imposition. They hugged me and wished me well. Nice people. Sadly, I never saw them again.

Upon returning to the ship, I vowed never to return to New Jersey. I only saw Carmen once since that day. She attended my father's funeral. We acknowledged each other's presence but did not speak. Why should we? There was nothing left to say.

Everyone has regrets. I do not regret severing all ties with Carmen. It was necessary for me to heal and grow. My remorse comes from my failure to reconstruct one bridge as I burned another. It was then that I should have begun to renew and repair the relationship with my father. He had a lot to explain and I had the right to know. Why did any of this have to happen? This was the time to demand answers, but I never asked the questions. I was too angry and too bitter to care about answers. It took a long, long time for the anger to subside and the bitterness to wane. When I was finally prepared to reconcile it was already too late.

CHAPTER SEVEN

Dear Caroline-Falling in love is not something I do very easily. Lust. Temporary infatuation. Sure, I'm as likely as anyone to fall victim to these emotions, if in fact they are emotions. My guess is they are more like animal instincts. Like others, I have also been prone to falling in love with the idea of falling in love. That can lead to big trouble. True love is very rare and it scares the hell out of me.

Why is falling in love scary? Let's start with the basics. I'm not very good at it. There is no handbook on how to fall in love, except for those creepy large format paperbacks that you might find in the self-help section of your local bookstore. No offense intended, but only pathetic losers buy these books. I bought plenty. George Carlin used to do a comedy routine about how stupid self-help books are. If you are getting it from a book, then it is an author helping you. If you are getting it from yourself, then it is self-help. Skip the book, help yourself, and save twenty bucks.

The way I see it, for a person to fall in love there has to be three C's: Commitment, Chemistry, and Confidence. It also helps if there is something or someone to fall in love with. As for the three C's, commitment the big one. How hard you are willing to work to make it work? When do you decide that you are in it for the long run and it is not just a moment? Commitment is the dreaded line "for better or worse." When you hear that phrase, you better underline the word worse. When do you pull the plug on commitment? When is it no longer worth it? Big questions. Hard to find answers. Chemistry is the easy one. You either have it or you don't. Love at first sight may actually be lust, but more likely it is chemistry. Things just feel right. They don't have to make sense because you already know what is real. Finding you have Chemistry is one of the best feelings in the world. Confidence for me is the hardest to find. Let's face it, in any relationship the odds are in favor of it blowing up in your face and leaving you a weak, sniveling puddle of your former self. Confidence is the ability to say "I can do this. I want to do this. I am worthy of this." With Confidence you can even ask yourself "Are they worthy of me? Are they good enough? Will they satisfy my needs and desires? Do they have the Commitment required?" If Commitment is the hard part, and Chemistry is the fun part, then Confidence is the deal breaker. Without it, the first two C's will not survive.

I fell in love with New England the moment we sailed into Boston Harbor. On April 6th I reported for duty aboard the USS Havasu, a repair ship home ported in Norfolk, Virginia. On June 15th, we left Norfolk, bound for Boston. We were on an eight-day training exercise. Four days at sea, four days in port. Captain Charles Winthrop Worthington was a native New Englander, so whenever the Navy would allow it, that is where we went. Boston was my first trip out to sea and my first trip to the cradle of American democracy. I loved every minute of it.

One of the great things about visiting a port with the navy is that you have neither the time nor the money to be a tourist. You do the job and when you are able, you leave the ship to roam around and see whatever you can in what little time you have. Most sailors have neither the smarts nor the desire to look for sites and landmarks. Our goals were much simpler. A cheap meal. A cheaper date. A friendly pub. Then it was back to work or on to the next port. In my short time in Boston I saw a ballgame at Fenway Park, hung out with assorted college students near Quincy Market, and visited a half dozen used bookstores not far from the South Street train station. I also had delusions of higher learning, so I made a brief visit to Harvard University, where I pretended to be an actual student.

Boston was love at first sight. The juxtaposition of new and old. The youthful ideals of its many colleges and universities contrast well with the stench of old money. There is beauty in its history and the seductive promise of future histories waiting to be written. Boston is, if nothing else, a romantic contradiction. As our ship left the harbor for its return trip to Virginia, I vowed to return to this wonderful place very soon.

Soon was to be sooner than expected. In mid-September we learned that we would be departing for a second trip north. This time, our destination was Newport, Rhode Island. Four weeks in Newport, followed by a brief visit to Portland, Maine. I was elated. I was going home to a place I had never been. Newport had once been a major outpost for the navy. The Naval War College and Officer Candidate Schools were both there. It had also served as a major summer training locale for Midshipman from the Naval Academy. During more prosperous times Newport had been home to several destroyers, frigates and cruisers from the Sixth Fleet. Gradually, however, the town was abandoned by the military. The War College and assorted training facilities were still there, but most of the ships that once called it home, were now assigned to other ports as a means of consolidation. The Navy's downsizing, coupled with a nationwide recession, drove Newport into hard economic times. An old destroyer, a minesweeper, and a seagoing tugboat, all used solely for training purposes, were all that remained

As a repair ship, our task for the next four weeks was to ensure that those three vessels received whatever basic maintenance they required to stay operable for the next year or two. The work was easy, the town was fun and we were spending fall in New England. I was finally learning to enjoy life.

This had not been the Havasu's first trip to Newport. While not an annual visit, the ship had been there several times in recent years. Some of my shipmates were familiar with the town. While Newport may be best known for its Victorian era mansions, scenic coastal cliffs, and its many fine dining establishments, my comrades had two recommendations: Jai Alai and bowling. I found this to be more than just a little bit odd. I can go bowling anywhere, and what exactly is jai alai?

I soon learned that jai alai is a gambling sport popularized in South and Central America. A series of players are paired against each other on a hardwood court, slinging a small ball against a wall using a large scoop called a cesta. The game is similar to racquetball. Players are eliminated as they miss the return volley or fail to place the ball between the appropriate markings. Eliminations determine who comes in first, second, third, etc. Betting is just like horse racing. There is win, place, show. There are also exactas, daily doubles and other winning combinations. Also, as with horses, you can have a cheap evening, betting the two-dollar minimum; and neither winning or losing much, unless you happen to call a longshot. The game has a reputation of being frequently rigged, so the possibility of a longshot is never so long. Most patrons get caught up in the daily doubles and combination bets that cost more, in the hope of a big payday. In my one and only foray into this sport I won ninety dollars on my first six-dollar bet. Two hours later I was showing a fifty-dollar loss. I never bet on jai alai again.

Bowling was a different story. I have never been a great bowler, but I tend to be better than most. My wrist sometimes runs astray, so I always use the heaviest ball available. With a little luck, I could throw a 150 to 190 most games. Less than a half mile from our pier was a strip mall that had almost everything a sailor could want. There was a small grocery store, a liquor store, a bar, a movie theater, and Mallard Lanes.

Mallard offered this bizarre game called duck pin bowling. I had never seen such a thing. It was like regular bowling but the pins were roughly half the height and the full width of regular bowling pins. The balls were not the standard large variety with finger holes. They were about the same size as bocce balls, only heavier. There were no finger holes. The ball was rolled at the pins in essentially the same way as their larger counterparts. Scoring was the same as in regular bowling, except you had two chances for a spare. A score of 100 is good. 200 is very rare. Despite an obvious lack of skill, I thought this was the greatest game I had ever seen. It was also a cheap night out.

From the moment we arrived in Newport, shipmates Steve Rogers, Jack Santoro, and myself became regulars. Every night, before heading out on the town, we would stop by Mallard's for a couple of games. It didn't take long before we skipped the rest of the town. It was close, it was safe, it was friendly, and it was a place we could call our own. Don, the owner, liked the fact that we were well behaved and didn't upset the locals.

Mallards also had a bar. It was a small room tucked in the front left corner of the building. Ten barstools, four tables, no band, pool tables or pinball. Just a jukebox with maybe forty songs, half of which were Charlie Daniels or Willie Nelson. That little bar became home.

Amy Martin was the twenty-one year old daughter of Mallard's owner, Don Martin. She was also the resident bartender and she was very cute. Her short, wavy, light brown hair and face full of freckles gave her a wholesome look that belied the fact that she was tough, confident and just the right amount of sexy. Amy had tried college for a year, but lacking any real direction, decided it was best to just stay local and work for her Dad while trying to figure things out. As the three of us became familiar faces at the bar, it was not uncommon for Amy to spend much of her time laughing at our silly jokes or listening to tales of insanity from the ship.

Insanity was something we got to see first-hand, after a ship-mate of ours, Frank (Nick) Nichols was taken away in a straight-jacket. How Nick got into the navy I will never know. He was a tall, thin, ruggedly handsome guy with piercing blue eyes that warned of deep emotional problems. When Nick was seven years old, his mother committed suicide. When he was twenty-two, his own young wife did the same. That's when he joined the navy. Prior to enlisting Nick had been a machinist for the Stanley Company in Waterbury, Connecticut. With regards to pure met-alworking talent, Nick was the finest craftsman I have ever seen. With regards to anything else, he was a time-bomb about to go off.

One night, upon returning from Mallard's, we passed through the machine shop on our way to the berthing area. It was there we found Nick, with one wrist cut open, bleeding all over himself. It looked bad, but not life threatening. Meanwhile with his good hand he was smashing whatever equipment he could find using a small four-pound sledge hammer. By the time we got to him he had severely damaged an engine lathe and a milling machine. Steve and I tackled him, while Jack ran and got help. We later learned that he had been tripping on peyote. There was alcohol on his breath. It was the third anniversary of his wife's suicide. Nick was taken to the nearby hospital. Two days later, his locker was cleaned out and we never heard from him again.

It was stories like this that kept Amy amused. Despite the tough exterior that she tried to project, Amy had lived a rather uneventful life. She had grown up in a comfortable suburban home in nearby Middletown. We had tales from a reality she would never know. It didn't take long for the three of us to realize that Amy had taken a personal liking to me. The truth is that I didn't have much competition since Jack was married and Steve was engaged. I knew she liked me, and the feelings were mutual, but I was hesitant to move forward. I never had a real girlfriend. Still, I found it easy to be relaxed around Amy, particularly in the safety of my two companions.

Amy's interest in me became completely obvious one Saturday afternoon. She had told her father she wanted the night off to go out with some friends. Jack, Steve and I stopped in around 2pm for a quick beer. We were planning on seeing a movie a little later. As was customary I put a ten-dollar bill on the counter as Amy poured our first round. She took the bill and replaced it with some change. Two hours and several rounds later we were still drinking on that first ten dollars. We had never been there before on a Saturday so I figured they must have a really good happy hour. Eventually, I had to use the men's room. Beer will do that. Rather than leave cash on the bar, I left a tip while pocketing the change as I walked around the corner to use the facilities. When I went to transfer the change from my pocket to my wallet, I saw there was more money than expected. I had entered the bar with twenty dollars; now there was forty-six.

When I got back to the bar Jack and Steve were gone. Amy said they got tired of waiting and left without me. It was a set-up. I had been gone less than five minutes. Then with a devious smile she snickered "Thanks for the tip. Did you get all of your change?"

We had dinner at Anne's Tavern, a local seafood place just over the line into Middletown. They were reputed to have the best baked, stuffed lobster in the state. The food was great and the conversation even better. Later that night we caught up with the other two guys at the theater. Amy had told them to meet us there for the nine o'clock show. It was a great first date. We walked for an hour or more after the show, simply enjoying each other's company. We knew the relationship, if that's what it was, probably wouldn't last beyond the few weeks I was in town, but we were both okay with that. Until then, we saw each other almost every day. When the ship finally left Newport, we bid each other a fond but permanent farewell.

My relationship with Amy had no effect whatsoever on how much time we spent as customers at Mallard's. Duck-pin bowling was such a novelty to us, we wanted to see how fast we could become good at it. Every time we started to show signs of figuring the game out, immaturity reared its silly head and we began acting like school kids. Once we played the entire game having to toss the balls using a full windup before shooting it between our legs. That was one of my best games, as I scored a 110. Another time we each threw the entire game left handed. None of us were natural lefties. That time I scored a 30. It was fun. Don always treated us well, giving us free games whenever we brought someone new in with us. Always we finished the night talking with Amy at the bar. Most nights there were a handful of others who wandered in and out at any given time. Beyond our little group, only a few seemed to be regulars. One was this grumpy little bastard who liked to sit by himself in the corner of the bar, nearest the cash register.

It is worth noting that there are many misconceptions about

how the different branches of the military feel towards each other. They all have reputations. Members of the Air Force are the consummate professionals. The Army is hard-working and blue-collar. The Marines are the toughest of all. Navy? We work hard and we play hard. Most people know of the Army vs. Navy rivalry. It is also true that when sailors and Marines serve together on a ship, some scuffles will ensue. Yet it was the Air Force that we most disliked. Two reasons. First, we felt that they had it too easy. Sailors went to sea. Soldiers and Marines fought in hand to hand combat. The Air Force fought a sanitized battle, leaving their comfortable barracks to fly planes over targets, then returning home without any direct engagement. They also did not face the perils of life in the trenches or at sea. As far as we were concerned they were nothing more than a bunch of goddamn sissies. That disdain is magnified by the belief that the Navy has better pilots than the Air Force. Let's see an Air Force pilot land a jet on an aircraft carrier in rough seas in the middle of the night. While we didn't always get along with the other branches, they did have our respect. The Air Force never did.

My two cohorts and I entered Mallard's bar at eight o'clock on a cold, rainy Friday. The bar was empty, except for that grumpy little bastard in the corner. Immediately we knew something was up. There was a look of distress on Amy's face. It's nice to feel loved, but she was never so happy to see us. Before we even got to the counter there were three beers waiting for us on the three stools immediately next to the only other patron in the room. Amy leaned over the bar to kiss me, then whispered in my ear that this jerk keeps trying to stuff a dollar bill down her blouse. I nodded and turned to my friends. "Boys, I think we may have a little excitement tonight." I leaned over to Jack and whispered in his ear. Jack leaned over to Steve. Suddenly the small strange man came to life.

"What are you guys faggots?" Then he began sniffing theatrically into the air. "You know, I think it's starting to smell like seafood in here. Yeah, I think I smell some rotten squid." At that time, in military slang, calling a Navy man "squid" was the approximate equivalent to calling a black man a nigger.

Out of respect for Don we exercised great restraint. "Let me see," I replied, speaking with a slow and measured voice. "As I recall, there are three types of seafarers. Squid, sailors and men in the Navy. Since we have never been formally introduced before, I believe 'men in the Navy' is the proper salutation, don't you? The term squid would be generally reserved for a scumbag piece of shit like you." Meanwhile, Amy had moved closer to the bar to listen in, while Don, sensing something might be amiss, watched through the doorway from the bowling alley snack bar.

"Fuck you, Mister Squid. I spent six fucking years in the Air Force during Viet Nam, so you don't know shit." Then he reached across and again tried to stuff a couple of bills into Amy's cleavage. "Here sweetheart, take my money."

It wasn't much of a fight. Before he could reach her blouse, I grabbed my beer mug and smashed it hard against the right side of his face. Perfectly good beer splashed against the walls as the scumbag hit the floor. Steve and Jack looked on as I jumped on top of him and dropped the heel of my right-hand flush against his collarbone. I heard it crack. He responded by spitting in my face. The three of us quickly escorted him outside where we showed his face to the bottom of several street puddles. Don followed us outside and hailed a cab. He gave the driver twenty dollars and told him that the guy was very drunk and kept falling off his bar stool. "Make sure he gets home safely."

Standing outside in the pouring rain I immediately began apologizing. "I am so sorry Don. I know I overreacted. I just lost it. You saw what he tried to do to Amy. But Christ I could have killed him. Shit. I screwed up bad. Now you hate me. Shit, shit, shit."

Don just grabbed the door and yelled "Get inside."

Once back in the bar I couldn't even look at Amy. I figured that was probably over as well. Don meanwhile tried to look angry. It didn't work. Tossing me a towel he burst into laughter. What started as a chortle soon turned to belly laughs. The three of us didn't get the joke, but we started laughing too. "That was beautiful." he said. "You guys are the best." Amy poured a round of Jack Daniels and a beer for everyone including Don and herself.

"But Don," I started again. "I hurt the guy bad. I know I busted something. What if he comes back and tries to sue you? Besides, the guy's a freaking Viet Nam vet. What if he comes back with a bunch of his psycho buddies and lights up the place? We should have just taken him outside. Man, I screwed up. It's all my fault."

Don turned to Steve and Jack. "Will one of you guys shut him up." He shook his head, still laughing. "I've been wanting to get rid of that son of a bitch since the day I opened this place. It's about time somebody took him out. What's he got for witnesses. He's got no friends. Five of us saw him fall off his barstool and hit that table. And he aint a Viet Nam vet. Is that what that asshole tried to tell you? Yeah, he was in the Air Force a few years back, but he never left the base at Westover. That sure aint Saigon. Besides, a buddy of mine grew up with the guy. He was always a jerk."

From that point on we couldn't run a tab in the place. We bowled for free. We drank for free. The only time I paid for anything was when Amy and I hit the town.

Nine days after the incident at Mallards, the USS Havasu left Newport never to return. Amy met me on the pier the morning that we left. It was a clear, cold, blustery day. We swore we would write and I promised to take the bus up from Norfolk to visit, but never did. This wasn't a heated romance. It was a couple of kids having a good time. Before saying our final good-bye, we made several poor attempts at kissing and posing the way they did in that famous photo on the cover of Life magazine at the end of World War II. It must have looked ridiculous. We giggled for a moment like teenagers, then she handed me a brown bag with a bottle in it. She told me to stuff it in my jacket and don't get caught. It was a gift from her father. We hid the bottle of Jack Daniels in the bottom of a large upright drinking fountain in the machine shop. A short while later the Havasu was underway, heading up the rocky New England coastline, bound for Portland, Maine.

During my time in uniform, the U.S. military was not treated with the same level of respect that it now gets. The Viet Nam experience was still a raw and open wound. It would take several more years before pride and honor would be returned to the military. One positive side effect of this lack of patriotism was that it made us a more cohesive unit. The outside world didn't care much for us, so we had to look out for each other. There was one exception. It was the small city of Portland, Maine.

Back before the days of instant communication, the Captain would, from time to time, speak to the crew using a ship wide intercom system called a 1mc. I have no idea what 1mc stands for, but when you spoke into the microphone the entire ship could hear you. Even less frequently there were times when Captain Worthington would address the crew using a closed-circuit television system. We would gather around various sets throughout the ship. This was most commonly done immediately before we left port on an excursion. Available data regarding sea conditions would be passed along, as well as information pertaining to our next port of arrival. At the end of the Captain's talk there would be a brief question and answer session where you could call in and speak directly to the skipper.

A fair number of sailors were upset that we were going to Portland. This wasn't Miami, it was Maine in November. We had been gone for a month and guys with wives, children and girlfriends back in Norfolk just wanted to get home. Two days up the coast, followed by two days in Portland meant more time away. That was not winning the Captain any popularity contests. Just the same, you didn't want to cross the old man.

Despite that caution, several shipmates did call in during the Q & A session of the broadcast. The Captain was brief and to the point. "Portland is a beautiful city. Next to Boston it is the cultural capital of New England. The weather may be cold and windy but the people are warm and friendly. I assure you we will be well received. It is also my home town. Now some of you may not like the idea, but you better get used to it. Last time I checked, there was only one captain on this ship and goddammit that's me. If you want to bitch to me personally, I'll be in my quarters, but I wouldn't recommend it. Any other questions?"

The Havasu pulled into Portland's harbor at 9am on the morning of November 2nd. In a hundred other ports throughout this country, our arrival would have been met with ambivalence, but this was different. Five-hundred people and a high school marching band met us on the pier that morning. A fifty-foot banner hung across the side of an old warehouse building. Spray painted on it were the words "Welcome U.S.S. Havasu. Welcome home C.W.W." The front page of the Portland Herald proudly emblazoned the headline: THE FLEET IS IN. CAPTAIN CHAS. WORTHINGTON BRINGS HIS SHIP HOME!

Sensing a sudden change in climate, we quickly ironed our dress uniforms, and spit-shined our shoes. For two short days we owned the town. As hard as we tried we couldn't spend a dime.

For our first stop, Jack and I had heard of a place called D'Amici's. It was a noted Italian seafood restaurant located just off the end of the pier. Aside from a great menu and a reputation for excellent food D'Amici's stood out because in the lobby was a large tank that held a twenty-pound albino lobster. We swore it was fake. The owner suggested we stick our hand in the water to find out. We didn't take him up on the offer. Once we ordered, the owner came and sat with us for a few minutes, suggesting various shops, theaters and pubs we might want to try. Then he had us sign a copy of the newspaper for him while he tore up our bill. Carlo D'Amici had grown up with the Worthingtons.

It was like being a rock star. Walking down Main Street in Portland, we were stopped every twenty yards by strangers who wanted to shake our hands. "Are you one of C.W's boys?" they would ask. On one corner a cabby quickly double parked and hopped out, handing me and Jack two tickets to that night's hockey game. The Portland Sea Dogs were at home against their rivals from Bangor. After stopping in a bar, we were accompanied by two college girls who joined us in cheering ourselves hoarse for the home team. Portland won the game 3 - 2 in overtime. The four of us then went to the pub across the street, where again our tab was zero. We were driven back to the pier by the same cabby who had given us the tickets.

On November 5th, at 6am, the USS Havasu quietly slipped out of Portland harbor. A few people gathered on the pier, but this time there was no fanfare. There was also no Amy. I left this beautiful port with an empty bottle of whiskey and an abundance of warmth and satisfaction. I swore that someday soon I would return to this special town. Sadly, I never did.

I do not fall in love easily, but I fell madly, deeply and passionately in love with New England in three short excursions. We are still in love. The three C's of commitment, chemistry and confidence were never a problem. They were omnipresent. On November 9th, when the USS Havasu returned to its home in Norfolk, I made a vow that if ever given the opportunity, I would make this wonderful place my home. A few years later I made good on that promise. I became married to the region. I am still married to it. I am married to its diversity, ideals, culture, history, and architecture. I am married to its small hamlets, rocky coastlines and bustling cities. Most of all, I am married to all the other travelers who have been everywhere else and yet choose to call it their home.

CHAPTER EIGHT

Eternal Father, strong to save,
Whose arm hath bound the restless wave,
Who bidd'st the mighty ocean deep, Its own appointed limits keep;
Oh, hear us when we cry to Thee, For those in peril on the sea!

—The Navy Hymn

Dear Caroline-We learned the Navy Hymn in boot camp. To this very day, it is the only song that will always make me cry.

$\mathcal{J}$t's easy to feel bulletproof when you are a nineteen-year-old sailor. The training and the lifestyle makes you hard fisted, hard headed, quick thinking and quick tempered. You own nothing and have nothing much to lose. While there is constant repetition, there is little routine in the course of a sailor's life. It's not like in the movies. It's a job. A tough, dirty job. You sleep on a paper-thin mattress that is set on top of a locker. In Navy jargon, it's called a rack. Racks are stacked four high, with about a foot of headroom. The boatswain's shrill whistle wakes you at 6am and meals are served on a strict schedule. At morning muster, you meet with your coworkers to review the plan of the day. Then it's off to work. Depending on the assignment, the job can be quite dangerous. OSHA does not keep close tabs on the military.

In December we got orders to go overseas. For the next four months, almost everything we did was to ready the ship for our impending trip to the Mediterranean. We were scheduled to depart on April 16th. Preparations included three weeks in January at Guantanamo Bay, Cuba. Gitmo, as it is commonly called, is not the dreadful outpost that is often portrayed in the media. It is a large, self-contained community, set in a tropical paradise. While there, we got to enjoy snorkeling, fishing, sunbathing and drinking. But when it came time to work, we worked our asses off. Most of the time was spent in training exercises, preparing for our extended trip across the Atlantic. There were war games and safety drills. There were refueling exercises and damage control training. We worked hard and played harder.

During an "abandon ship" drill, various groups gathered along the main deck, in preparation to lower the lifeboats. There, the officer in charge, gathered information.

"Longitude?" asked Ensign Burke.

"74 degrees" came the call-back.

"Latitude?"

"20 degrees."

"Windspeed?"

"Five knots from the Northeast."

"Air temperature?"

"92."

"Water temperature?"

"86"

"Nearest land?"

Andy Deforge couldn't help himself. "About a mile straight down!" he yelled. The drill was halted immediately, as the rookie officer chewed out poor Andy. The crew quickly rallied behind their comrade. Even Captain Worthington, who heard the comment, agreed. There was plenty of daily stress. A little humor would hardly erode discipline.

Every pump and valve had to be inspected and repaired. Every inch of the hull had to be checked for cracks and defects, then welded and painted accordingly. Electronics had to be tested. Engines had to be capable of running at top efficiency. Some of that work was tended to in Guantanamo, but most of it was done upon returning to Norfolk.

On April 16, a group of wives, children, family and friends assembled on Pier 11 to watch the USS Havasu slip quietly out to sea, departing Norfolk, bound for Naples. There were tears and cheers as the whistle blew. It would be October before we would return home. I was excited. This was the big adventure I had hoped for. Jack was forlorn and distraught. He had hoped his wife Louise would be there on the pier with their six-month-old son, but they were not. Jack had returned home to Baltimore to be with them the week before. Saturday night he went out with friends and got drunk. Sunday morning, they had a fight and he stormed out. He returned to the ship where he fumed for several days before realizing how much he missed them. His teary phone calls home and pleading apologies must have fallen on deaf ears. He silently wondered if she would be there for him when he finally returned home. Steve and I did our best to console him, but we were hardly authorities on romance. Steve broke up with his fiancé two weeks before we left and I hadn't had a girlfriend since Amy.

It would take us two weeks to get to Naples. We would not see land for ten days. At that point we expected to pass through the Straits of Gibraltar. It would be another four days to Italy. While crossing the Atlantic, we would see whales, dolphins, sea birds. turtles and sharks, along with an occasional passing freighter, but there would be no sign of land. Water, water everywhere. Occasionally we would wander by the chart room and ask Lieutenant Baker to show us where we were. On day six our location showed that we were nearly a thousand miles from any land.

When you consider that the Havasu was just under 500 feet long and had a crew of almost 800 enlisted men and officers, one might think it would feel confining. Put it in perspective. You are a thousand miles from land on a ship that is less than a tenth of a mile long. Yet claustrophobia seldom comes into play. Most crewmembers have been aboard the ship long enough to grow accustomed to its limitations. Furthermore, the many decks and compartments that layer the vessel makes it seem much more spacious than it really is.

There is something truly magical about being out to sea. Without the obstruction of manmade objects and rough terrain, you can actually see the curvature of the earth when you gaze upon the horizon. This is not an illusion. Likewise, without the luminous glare of civilization, the night sky is much brighter than you can ever imagine. A hundred million stars light up the sky, with a spectacular show of constellations and planets. Even the water is alight with phosphorus planktons and algae. When weather intrudes, lightning bolts dance across the water like dueling sabers as the sea rises to meet them. Swells of twenty feet or more toss the sturdy steel hull like a toy boat in the bathwater of a child. In high seas, the ship might pitch and roll such that it seemed easier to walk walls rather than decks. There was never a sense of fear or danger; only awe and wonder.

While at sea, the boilermen, quartermasters, enginemen and boatswains worked long and hard. This was their calling. They keep the ship afloat and running on course. The rest of us were there for support. You can't run a machine shop while pitching port and starboard. Our time was spent mopping up lubricants as it seeped from the lathes and milling machines. We performed routine maintenance checks to ensure our equipment would operate efficiently once we arrived in port. We also trained. There were emergency drills, first aid classes, and cultural sensitivity classes. The cultural classes were designed to acclimate us to the customs of the region. it was done in the hope that once ashore, we wouldn't disgrace our ship, our country, or do anything stupid that might get us thrown in jail. For the most part it worked.

Despite the chores and training, there was plenty of free time. Part of this was spent in covert drinking binges. Prior to our departure, we hid bottles of cheap booze all over the ship. It was inside shop equipment, behind desks, in ceiling tiles and almost anywhere else we thought it might go undetected. We also hid six joints in the light fixture directly above our division officer's office door. We were saving the pot for a special occasion.

If we weren't drinking, we were probably playing cards. Hearts, spades, cribbage, and poker were all popular games. What would start as nickels and dimes, could quickly become dollars. One lucky night I won two hundred dollars off of Tommy Parnell. Rather than try to explain it to his wife, he traded me his Nikon camera along with a flash and two lenses to settle the debt.

Early in the trip I borrowed a Scrabble board from the ship's enlisted lounge and brought it down to the machine shop. Taking on all challengers, I made quick work of my first ten opponents, beating each by several hundred points. That smelled of opportunity. I opened a standing challenge. If I beat you, I get two dollars. If you beat me, you get twenty. It helped pass the hours, and by the time we reached Naples I had an extra hundred and twenty dollars to play with. I never lost.

Ten days after leaving Norfolk we found ourselves preparing to enter the Straits of Gibraltar. This was cause for a party. Jack, Steve and I decided we would stay up all night and celebrate with a joint and a bottle of bourbon. We prowled the ship drunk, stoned and looking for mischief. Shortly after midnight, while suffering from a severe case of marijuana munchies, we decided to break into the ship's bake shop to find something to eat.

The bakery was locked at night, but it was hardly maximum security. A simple hasp and padlock kept the door closed. Four sheet metal screws kept the hasp in place. It took us less than three minutes to get in. Once inside, there were several choices. One refrigerator was lined with cakes and pies, ready to serve the masses on large sheet cake trays. Another had five-gallon cans of peaches, pears and fruit cocktail. We opted for the cherry pie. In the spirit of inebriation, we cut and took only the inside portion of the pie, leaving about three inches around the perimeter. The center portion was then sliced and slid into one-gallon zip lock bags.

Steve insisted we leave a calling card. I found a piece of paper and wrote on it "Needs salt." The note was left in the center of the tray, which was then dutifully returned to the center rack of the refrigerator. We each stuffed two of bags of pie into our shirts and departed the bakery, replacing the hasp and lock to its original status. Later the next day we watched as technicians welded the hasp to the steel wall. If we ever decided to break in again, it wouldn't be so easy.

We ate what we could stand of the pie back at the shop, while deciding what our next course of action should be. One thing we recognized rather quickly was that cherry pie and cheap bourbon are a volatile combination. Jack threw up twice to prove this point. We were sympathetic to his plight, while at the same time ridiculing him without mercy. We were not about to allow our barfing brother to miss out on the evening's festivities. We figured some fresh air would do him well, so we headed up to the ship's bow.

It was a full moon on calm seas, so the night was aglow, as the lunar rays shined across the water. We finished what was left of the joint while watching dolphins leap and play across the hull's leading edge. Up ahead we could see land. Up until now, the Rock of Gibraltar meant nothing more to us than a logo from Prudential Insurance ads. Now we were staring at it. What really blew our minds was that we could also see the shores of Morocco. We were viewing two continents at the exact same time.

Because visibility was so good, there was an anticipation and miscalculation on our part as to how far we were from that land. It was nearly seventy miles away. We were hoping to hang around the bow and watch Gibraltar pass by within the hour. It would be six hours before we had crossed the strait and entered the Mediterranean. By that time, the sun had risen, breakfast had been served, and the three of us were looking for a place to hide so we could sleep off a waking hangover. We found our spot in the safety nets that surrounded the helicopter landing pad above the ship's fantail. Throughout our time on the Havasu this would become a common place for us to catch a quick snooze and hide from the authorities.

Once past Gibraltar, we entered the confines of the Mediterranean Sea, just four days from Naples. Our trip across the sea had been calm and peaceful. That calm was about to be shattered by chaos and tragedy.

On the morning of April 28th, we were two days past Gibraltar. Steve, Jack and I had just finished breakfast and were killing time waiting near the pump and valve repair section of the machine shop. Morning muster would begin in about fifteen minutes. Steve had a book of magic tricks that he was trying out on us. We pretended to be amused. His sleight of hand was less than smooth. Jack took great pleasure in ridiculing him for his ineptness. I tried to pay attention but found myself distracted.

Something wasn't right. There is sullen and constant background hum that permeates a ship when it is underway at sea. I couldn't exactly place it, but the pitch was wrong. Call it intuition, but I began to feel anxious. As usual, my comrades thought I was nuts.

"Shhhhhhsh. Listen up guys. Hear that?"

"Hear what"

"The engine noise. It sounds funny. Different."

"That's just shit between your ears."

"I'm serious Jack, listen up."

"I think I get what you mean," Steve agreed. "It's kind of a higher pitch."

"Yeah, something aint right."

"Maybe. Maybe they're just working on something."

"I guess."

Exactly four seconds later there was a loud repetitive thumping noise, followed by a momentary dimming of the lights, then silence.

"What the fuck was that?"

More strange noises were followed by the sound of screams coming from the passageway just beyond the machine shop. The machine shop was located on the same deck as the mess hall, with the two compartments separated on each side of the hull by a narrow passageway. Between the two passageways there was a hatchway on each side which led to the inner skeleton of the ship. This was the engine room. A series of metal ladders and walkways created a maze that tangled through several large compartments within the hull. At the bottom were three turbine generators and two immense diesel engines. The three of us sprung from our perch and looked down the portside passageway. The hatchway door was open as the first signs of smoke began to emerge.

"The fucking engine room is on fire!"

In all of the old World War II movies there is a scene at the start of a naval battle where the officer on deck calls over the loudspeaker "General quarters. General quarters. All hands man your battle stations." That isn't just Hollywood. It happens, and when it does it is no joke. Translation: All hell is breaking loose and if everyone is not where they are supposed to be, people will probably die. Several times each month, we would practice this routine. This time it was real.

"This is not a drill! Fire, fire, fire! Fire in the engine room. I repeat, this is not a drill! All hands to your assigned stations. Fire team One and Two report to repair lockers three and four to respond. Medical response team at the ready. This is not a drill."

Every person on the ship is trained and retrained in firefighting. In port and at sea, drills are conducted. Everyone knows exactly where they are supposed to be and what they are supposed to be doing, but until you hear those words and you know that it's for real, there is no telling how everyone will respond. Not everyone is responsible for fighting the fires. Some are assigned to emergency repairs. Others act as medics. Some keep the lines of communication flowing. Everyone has a job. Jack, Steve and I were part of Fire Team Two. Repair locker three was in the machine shop, about fifteen feet from where we stood when we noticed the first signs of trouble.

Even before we knew what had happened, the three of us, along with two other shipmates opened the locker and began donning gloves and an OBA. The OBA is an Oxygen Breathing Apparatus. It is a canister about the size of a canteen that, when activated, creates oxygen so you can breathe while in an otherwise unbreathable environment. The canister clips into a harness and the chemically generated air is fed through a gas mask. The compact size and light weight of the unit makes it ideal for firefighting.

Less than a minute after the alarm went off, Hull Technician

First Class Wes Robertson arrived, already shouting orders. "It's a lube oil fire. Grab the foam. Let's go!" Steve and I hooked up the nozzles, as Jack and fellow shipmate Raymond Morse began rolling out and straightening the hoses. Wes connected the foam siphons. Then we headed for the hatchway. Ray and I went in as nozzlemen, while Steve and Jack were ordered to stand back and feed the hoses.

One of the basic tenets of firefighting is to know what kind of fire you are dealing with. You never use water on an electrical fire. A fire that has grease, oil or fuel as a component is never fought with any high degree of pressure. To do so would spread the oil and spread the fire. Instead, you cover the surface with foam and deprive the fire of oxygen. The primary goal in extinguishing any blaze is to eliminate its source of oxygen.

My first step into the engine room was almost my last. I slid on the metal grating, and fell down five steps, hitting my head as I landed. Luckily adrenaline was high and I only suffered a bump and a few scrapes. Visibility was almost zero and the sounds of choking and screams permeated the thick, black air. It was blind chaos. Out of the murk I saw a shoulder pass near my face. With the hose tucked under one arm and the nozzle grasped firmly in my right hand I waved into oblivion and grabbed part of a shirt. The dazed shipmate followed towards me and was guided back along the hose line. That was how it would be. Fight the fire with one hand and lead people to safety with the other.

That was the plan, but fires are not inclined to play by the rules. As we descended further down towards the bowels of the ship I again attempted to reach a landing. As I came off the last step my boot came in contact with a large uneven surface that sent me sprawling. Through the smoke I saw the body of Boiler Technician Hector Montinez, crumpled, semiconscious, and covered in his own vomit. His tan Hispanic complexion was a sickening grey. I froze, completely paralyzed and unaware of what I should do. Ray saw me lock up. He began screaming "Medic!" and ordered me to move on. Morse began shouting in my ear "Stay focused. Keep your head in the fucking game! Don't think. Just keep going. You know what we got to do. If you think about it you're going to fuck up and then we're all going to die." It was what I needed to hear at that moment. Regaining my footing, I trudged forward.

Finally, we reached the bottom level where the engines and generators all work in tandem to drive the ships propellers. By now everything was covered with foam. Slowly, a black cloud began to ascend from the lower levels of the hull. Portable ventilation equipment was pumping smoke from the chamber out through several portholes and into the bright blue Mediterranean sky.

We never actually saw flames, because there were none. Had we not gotten there as quickly as we did, we almost certainly would have hit flashpoint. That was small consolation. There was plenty of carnage to deal with. We met the other primary hose, manned by a couple of hull technicians, near the number two generator. Through the oil smeared gas masks our faces were unrecognizable, but someone screamed to us that a lube oil line going into the main engine sprung a leak and sprayed across the hot casing of the generator. Instantly the entire compartment turned to smoke. We got there in record time, but there were still shipmates in trouble. We continued to layer the bilges in foam. Through the haze I could see several comrades being helped to safety.

Everyone had to be evacuated and the air cleared before they could send in a crew to assess the damage. A fresh crew of emergency workers in OBAs found their way to the foggy bottom and began pumping out the bilges. Finally, we switched from foam to water. Once convinced the danger had been minimized, we were ordered to slowly retreat. Ever so cautiously, we retraced our steps. The hoses remained charged, with nozzle and foam at the ready. All I could think of was daylight. I needed to see the open sky. Most of all I needed to peel this goddamn mask off my face and suck in some real air.

Over my shoulder I could finally see the hatchway again. It was going to be okay. I never really doubted that. Adrenaline may be the result of fear, but fear was not the driving force. Intensity was. It was a complete heightening of all senses. Even when there was no visibility my eyesight never seemed so sharp. A hundred sounds and voices pierced the air. All were heard, processed and comprehended. I could feel my body move within my own skin, orchestrating each motion with purposeful intent. Ray was right. This was not the place for thinking. There is no thinking in Hell.

We were only down there for about twenty minutes. It could have been a second or a lifetime. Reaching the doorway, it was my turn to be pulled to safety. A sturdy brown arm grabbed my blouse near the waste and guided me through to daylight. It was Wes Robertson. He had remained topside at the hatch, sending information and relaying orders. He kept us alive and enabled us to save others.

I yanked the mask off and took a deep full breath. This was immediately followed by a gag reflex that doubled me over, spitting cluster balls of slimy green phlegm onto the deck. Wes shouted over and pointed to a nearby bucket of water. I unscrewed the canister from the OBA and dropped it into the waiting pail. It erupted into a turgid boil. The byproduct of the chemical reaction which enables the canister to create oxygen, is heat. The OBA harness was backed with a thin sheath of asbestos to shield the body. Despite this protection, a light pink contact burn swelled across my abdominal region.

Once the waves of nausea had subsided, I removed the rest of my equipment and with a heaving sigh of exhaustion slumped down to the deck, with my back resting against the cool metal bulkhead. My body tingled with the sensation of a thousand muscles suddenly being released from their contracted state. Physical exhaustion, however, did not abate mental acuity. My mind raced, knowing that at any moment I might have to call on those muscles to once again spring into action.

The deck was a flurry of activity, with sailors running in every direction, each with a clear sense of purpose. A few feet away I spotted Jack and Steve being relieved of their duty. They came over to share my wall. For a while no one said a word. We just decompressed. Wes stopped by just long enough to hand us each a Coke. "Hell of job you guys did." His large brown hand gave a firm, comforting squeeze to my shoulder. "Rest up. I may need you in a few." A couple of guys from the shop saw us and asked what it was like down there. I couldn't answer. The truth is I didn't remember much. It all happened so fast. Then we got word that Montinez didn't make it.

I forced myself to my feet, climbed the ladder and flung myself outside. Leaning across the railing I began to vomit over and over in long heaving waves. When the nausea subsided, I just hung there, face down, staring at the water. I remained motionless in that position for several minutes, unaware that Steve and Jack had been there at my side. With strong yet gentle arms they grabbed me by the side and lifted me up away from the rail. We took three steps backwards and sat on an equipment locker, as I continued to stare into space. They didn't know what to say and I didn't want to tell them. They didn't know. They weren't down there. The silence was uncomfortable. They deserved to know.

"I stepped on Montinez on my way down. My boot hit his shoulder and I went flying. Goddamn it. I saw him and I froze. I knew he was bad, but I had no idea how bad. Goddamn it. Ray called for a medic and then kicked me in the ass to keep moving."

"You couldn't have done anything. You didn't do anything wrong."

"It's not that I did anything wrong, but I was there. I saw him begging for his last breath." By now I was sobbing. "What the fuck happened down there? How could something like this happen? There were a lot of people down there. Is there anyone else?"

"Maybe O'Neill. We heard he's in bad shape. They'll airlift him out, but word is he might not make it. A few others are in sickbay, but he's the only one who's critical."

"Fuck. Goddamn it."

I told the other two to get up for a moment, which they did without questioning, except for a brief quizzical look. I opened the equipment locker and reaching below a couple of first aid kits and blankets, I pulled out a bottle of tequila which I had hidden there before we left for the Mediterranean. Not caring who saw me, I opened the bottle and took two long pulls. When Steve and Jack refused my offer for a drink, I let out a primal scream and hurled the bottle overboard before quietly returning to my perch.

We were roughly thirty-six hours outside of Naples, and word began trickling in that we might have to make an emergency stop in Valencia. Captain Worthington quickly squashed that rumor and began giving hourly updates over the ship's intercom. Amazingly, the only quantifiable damage to the ship was the blown lube oil line. Assorted fans and pumps would soon have the grease, foam and water removed. It would take a few days to clean up the mess, but the ship was otherwise operable. What Havasu lacked in physical damage was more than made up for by a collapse in morale. A different flashpoint was approaching.

After a brief stop at the galley, Steve and I made our way along the portside deck and headed back to the shop. Our trip was promptly detoured when we saw almost the entire engine room crew clustered along the deck. Their faces dripped with a black sweat, that did nothing to camouflage a seething anger. Mutiny is too strong of a word. This was not mutiny. This was a spontaneous protest and a show of unity. Machines fail, emergencies happen, mistakes are made, but long prior to that fateful morning, conditions in the engine room had deteriorated to a dangerous level. There had been other lube oil leaks. They were patched but never repaired. At sea, the engine room temperature routinely topped one hundred. The fumes were nauseating. The men had complained. Their complaints had fallen on deaf ears. The men demanded to be heard. They would not return to work without assurances that changes were forthcoming.

It was not until Captain Worthington came down and met with them, that some level of harmony was restored. He heard their grievances and did his best to understand their frustrations. He apologized, with some embarrassment, for being unaware of past problems. With that he shot a stern look towards Lieutenant Drexel and Chief Ferguson who oversaw the department. Ever the politician, he reminded the men that above all, the needs of the ship and the Navy had to be met, however, those demands must be met with minimal human toll. After meeting with the engine room crew, he then met privately with Drexel and Ferguson. Worthington was less diplomatic in that conversation. Fifteen minutes later, the three men emerged, seemingly united. The crew's concerns would be promptly addressed. Fatigue was identified as a major problem. There would be changes in scheduling. Other crewmembers from outside of the engine room would be brought in to assist during peak times. Once we reached Naples, certain equipment upgrades would be requisitioned. Again, Worthington apologized.

Reluctantly, the men returned to the ship's bowels. Their

voice had been heard, but it should never have come that far. It should never take an act of defiance to accomplish what common sense and human decency expects all along. On the morning of April 30, the USS Havasu limped into the Bay of Naples. What should have been a joyous moment, filled with anticipation and excitement, was instead an exhausted sigh of relief. No spit shine smiles. No gunpowder salutes. Just a few hundred weary sailors hoping for better days ahead.

Better days would come. Over the next six months we would visit six ports in Italy and four in Spain. Despite growing up in an ethnic Italian family, I found Spain more interesting and exciting than Italy. We toured Majorca on motorcycles, saw a bullfight in Valencia, and spent eight drunken nights in Barcelona. Our final stop was in the Spanish town of Rota, to pick up supplies before heading home.

We returned to Norfolk on October 25th to a packed pier, filled with wives, parents, friends and girlfriends. We brought photographs, gifts and mementos. There were many stories to tell, but the tale no one told was of our baptism by fire in that smoke-filled engine room.

One month after returning from the Mediterranean, the USS Havasu was dealt a final blow. The Navy had decided to remove her from the fleet. She was to be decommissioned on April 1st. We were her final crew. She was old and tired and had served her country well, but it was her time to go. I was among the first to depart; taking my transfer to the USS Mohegan, a submarine repair ship ported in Groton, Connecticut. Steve was heading to an aircraft carrier out of Pearl Harbor. We stayed in touch over the next few years. Along the way, he got a college degree and became an officer. Jack's wife filed for divorce, so he stayed in Norfolk, taking duty on an amphibious ship that was docked in Oyster Creek. I heard from him once, thirty years later, when he found my name on a website for old Navy veterans. We exchanged pleasantries, but soon realized that our time had passed.

The Havasu was my mistress. She had a seductive charm beneath her grey skirting. She held many secrets that will never be told. She was a deep, intense and passionate lover. Is it possible to love an inanimate object like a woman? Not really, but the Havasu was no inanimate object. Yes, she was old and weary, but when blessed with that final crew, no object has ever been more alive. It was a singular, magical moment in time. And after all this time, I find I still miss her. Damn, I still miss her.

The two newlyweds finished off their third margarita and paused for a break. Richard emptied his bladder, while Caroline washed her face and brushed her hair. Her makeup was smudged from tears, sweat and the reassuring caresses from her husband.

"It's funny," she said. "I've heard him tell a thousand Navy stories, but never once did he mention the fire."

"Your father liked to tell jokes," Richard offered. "That story has no punch-line."

"True, but it has plenty of punch."

"If the story is true, then what your dad did was nothing short of heroic. Do you think he ever thought of himself that way?" Richard asked.

Caroline shook her head. "Dad swore that he was a lousy machinist and a mediocre sailor. That's not to say that he wasn't proud of his service. Veteran's Day in our house ranked right up there with Thanksgiving and Christmas in its importance. Dad loved the navy. He always said that the navy did far more for him than he ever did for it. He also liked to say that he learned more in five minutes in the navy than he did in four years of college. No, he never had any ego when it came to his service, but he definitely had plenty of pride."

"Did he stay in touch with any of his shipmates?" Richard mused.

"Not when I was young," she replied. "Later, when everyone be-gan flocking to Facebook, he got reacquainted with a couple of them. Wes Robertson was one. There were others, but Wes is the only name I remember."

"And what of Jack and Steve?"

Caroline touched her hand gently to her chin and mused. "Good question. I don't know. Dad talked of them often in his navy stories but it was always in the past tense. My guess is that after he left the Havasu they all went their separate ways."

CHAPTER NINE

*T*he last eighteen months of my naval service passed with little fanfare. Like the Havasu, the USS Mohegan, or "Big Mo" was an older ship, whose sole purpose was to service and repair submarines. It was interesting work, but both the ship and crew lacked the character of Havasu. I guess it's true that you never forget your first love. Just the same, it was a good ship, in a good port. We seldom traveled and so I enrolled in several evening classes at nearby Connecticut College. I knew I would never make a career of being a machinist. The Navy had filled me with stories and I was now convinced that my true destiny was to become a writer.

The time had come to bid a fond farewell to my military career and become a full-time student at the University of Connecticut. It was the early 1980s and I knew nothing of college life. The navy prepared me in many ways for many things, but institutionalized academia was more foreign to me than a month in Guantanamo. I had a little money saved, but it was far too little. I needed a place to live, a job, and a girlfriend. If I could somehow acquire those three things, everything else would be fine.

Finding a job came first. I simply stopped by the Student Labor office on campus. There were more minimum wage jobs available than students who would take them. Since I had background as a machinist, they asked if I wanted to work in the locksmith shop. They mistakenly thought I had mechanical ability. It didn't matter. I took the job and would soon begin working there twenty-five hours a week. Rick Carson ran the shop. He had been there for over twenty years and when it came to students, he had seen it all. He too was ex-Navy, so right from the start we got along.

Finding a place to live was what had me most worried. Living in a dorm on campus was never an option. Connecticut would be my home for at least the next four years. I had to have a permanent address if I was to qualify for in-state tuition. Besides, where would I go when the dorms closed for winter and summer breaks? I could go to New Jersey and move in with my Dad, but that was never really an option. I was too busy being bitter about my rotten childhood to ever consider the possibility. I needed a cheap apartment near campus. Since I couldn't afford a place on my own, I would have to share a rent. That scared me. Almost everyone has heard horror stories about bad roommates.

Those fears were unfounded. The campus newspaper was flooded with requests for roommates looking to share an apartment. In responding to one ad, I found a place called Husky Estates, about two miles from school. The name sounded far more romantic than reality. It was a small, two-bedroom town house style complex, with walls so thin that you could hold a conversation with your next-door neighbor without ever raising your voice. Even worse was the fact that your neighbors knew exactly how often you showered, flushed the toilet, or had sex. I took the place because it was cheap and because my would-be roommate Jim seemed like a good guy. I signed the lease for a year. I stayed for five.

Jim Resnick was a twenty-year-old sophomore and an anthropology major. A couple of his friends gave up the apartment after final exams, so he lived there alone for the summer while looking for a permanent roommate for the fall. Despite the thin walls, I liked the apartment, I liked the price, and most of all I liked Jim. We immediately became friends.

On the surface, we were the oddest of couples. I was a relatively clean cut, military disciplined, politically moderate, stereotypical navy veteran. Jim was the poster child for extremism. As the son of a wealthy insurance executive, he rebelled against everything his privileged lifestyle afforded him. Jim was an avowed socialist, peace activist, and John Lennon fanatic who could charm a crowd with all the skill of a spiritually possessed televangelist. He was at the helm or in the forefront of almost every radical group on campus. I never joined the ranks of his true believers, but as an aspiring journalist, I found Jim to be an endless source of ideas.

There was a lot to like about Jim. He was charismatic, energetic and fun. I also liked the fact that he made it possible for me to meet girls. Jim always had an entourage. It was through Jim that I met Jennifer Katz. She was a twenty-one-year-old undergrad majoring in Communications. She was also program director for the campus radio station. She shadowed Jim, knowing that he was always good for an interview, an editorial, or for having his thumb on the pulse of the campus. Jen was short, athletic, and had wavy red hair that she usually kept tied back. She wasn't my usual type, but then again, I'm not sure that I have a type. We dated for two years. It was more friendship than courtship. I think we both knew that there was little long-term potential, but the affection was mutual and real.

With my basic needs met, I could now settle into my new role as a college student. At first I struggled. I finished my first semester with a 2.3 GPA. One reason I stumbled was that I was required to take various core requirements that were of no interest to me. I was ready to immerse myself in the humanities and social sciences. Hard science and fine arts took me away from my passion. The other obstacle was that there was too much freedom and too little structure. Once I worked my way past the prerequisites and infused some strict scheduling to my routines, it was smooth sailing.

It helped that I cut back on my proclivity for pot and alcohol. I began working out. I had noticed that one of my neighbors, Tom Creighton was out jogging every morning around 7am. Tom and I had shared a few classes. Before long, I joined him on the morning run. This led to a pretty strong friendship. Tom was no health fanatic, but he had played some sports in school and was now involved in intramural soccer. It was a good pairing. I had always enjoyed running and found it nice to get back on the road. Both my stamina and mental acuity improved dramatically. By the start of my junior year, my GPA had soared to 3.4.

Meanwhile, my roommate, Jim Resnick, left the university and joined the Peace Corps. That was good for him but bad for me. While he was preparing to move to the jungles of Ecuador, I was abruptly left without a person to share the rent. To his credit, I wasn't completely abandoned. Daddy Resnick had paid for the apartment in full through August. I knew I would miss Jim. Despite, or maybe because of his eccentricities. I really enjoyed sharing the place with him. Although we never grew to be the best of friends, there was never a harsh word between us.

Finding a good roommate is a lot like applying for a job. Every job and every job hunter sounds great in the interview. By the time you learn the truth, it's too late and you're stuck. I was extremely cautious. My first choice was Tom Creighton. It would have been an easy fit, were it not for the fact that Tom was a senior and would be graduating in May. I was looking for someone who was likely to be a long-term tenant.

In early June I got a call from a girl named Jackie. She was twenty-two and had a two-year-old son. A month earlier she had broken up with her boyfriend. After two weeks of living with her parents in nearby Willimantic it was clear that she had to get out quick. Jackie was friends with Jodie, a friend of mine who worked in the library. Jodie asked if I would consider her as a roomie. As a favor to a friend, we agreed to meet. She liked the place and I liked her. She had grown up in the area and was working in Mansfield at one of the supermarkets. I almost agreed to share the place with her based on looks alone. She was extremely attractive, and since she already had a kid, I assumed she liked sex.

After she saw the place we went for lunch at a local pizza place. An hour in a restaurant with her rotten kid quickly brought me to my senses. The little bastard was climbing all over everything, including the table, knocking over my beer, spraying salt across the table, then using it like finger paint. Unintelligible shrieks echoed throughout the room, followed by various forms of spasmodic tantrums. I knew Fran the waitress, so I excused myself to use the bathroom and then cornered her begging for forgiveness and asking if there was a back door so I could ditch them both and get the hell out of there. Fran insisted that I tough it out. Over lunch I explained to Jackie that I still had a couple of other people who were scheduled to come and look at the place. Jackie said it was no problem and that she also had a few other places to consider. Since it was Monday, we agreed to talk again on Friday when we knew a little bit more. Neither of us ever called, but fate was about to come knocking.

June 20th seemed like most other days. Jen was working at the radio station and I was at the locksmith shop. Later, Jen was coming over for dinner and would probably spend the night. Then, while on my lunch break, I found my future, clipped to a slip of paper on a bulletin board.

Most of what I did at the locksmith's shop consisted of cutting new keys, then delivering them to various locations throughout the campus. Occasionally I would get to go out on repair jobs, which was boring as hell since it generally meant carrying the tool box and holding a flashlight. Around noon, a job came in for the student union. They had a rush order for ten keys. That worked out fine. I cut the keys, then told Ray that I would take lunch at the cafeteria right after I dropped them off.

After my delivery, I grabbed a copy of the Daily Campus and stopped by the cafeteria for a bite. Checking the classifieds, I was dismayed to find that none of the ads from students in search of a rent looked promising. There were only three. All of them were looking for something temporary. As I headed for the left exit on the back side of the building, I had a sudden thought. Instead of going left I turned right and into the stairwell facing the front entrance. It was there I checked out the long bulletin board that listed, among other things, postings for students in search of roommates.

There were more apartments for rent than potential room-mates, and some of the potential roommates were downright scary. One student advertised himself as a Jerry Garcia wannabe. I have nothing against the Grateful Dead, but that seemed like a sure recipe for disaster. Another was from a gay couple looking for a place. I considered that one, but the idea of sharing space with a couple, whether straight, gay, married or otherwise, just didn't feel right. Two ads had potential. One was from a fellow veteran, who was majoring in engineering. The ad didn't say much except that he was looking for a quiet place near campus. I took down the number, along with the name and number from an adjacent ad. The second one was from a student transferring up from the Stamford branch campus. Diane Simmons was a pharmacy stu-dent looking to transfer to the main campus for the Fall semester. She was looking for an "older student" to share an apartment with. I didn't know what "older" meant or if twenty-four quali-fied, but I figured it was worth a call.

When I got home from work I gave them both a ring. Don, the vet, sounded like a great guy, but when he learned where the apartment was he immediately declined. "One thing I know about those apartments," he said, "is that they are anything but quiet." While it is true that the walls were paper thin, we actually were a pretty civil community. No matter. Don was out. I then called Diane. Her voice was so soft, I had to strain to hear her. She was thirty-one years old and living with her parents in Bridgeport. That sounded a little odd to me but I let it go. After two minutes of polite conversation she agreed to check out the place. Diane had to run some errands on campus and was coming up on Friday. She would stop by to see the apartment between 3 and 4pm.

The possibility of sharing an apartment with a woman both intrigued and terrified me. I had a girlfriend, but that was very different from living with someone. Who would protect me from raging hormones? To what extent would I have to watch what I say or do? What if I hated her friends or she hated mine? I had a two-minute phone conversation with Diane, we arranged a meeting, and for the next four days I drove myself into a panic attack. For all I knew she would take one look at the place, hate it and I would never hear from her again.

I cleaned the apartment as best I could. I didn't go to the extreme of scented candles or potpourri, but I did make sure the place didn't smell liked gym socks. What wasn't choreographed, was the album I had playing on the stereo. In order to keep my veteran benefits coming in, I had to take two classes over the summer. I also needed a fine arts credit to graduate and decided to take Music Appreciation: Jazz. It was a pretty easy choice. I grew up listening to Louis Armstrong and Duke Ellington. They were my dad's two favorites. I always enjoyed Armstrong. Duke I thought was kind of boring. No matter. The class seemed interesting, and it served a purpose. For homework, we would have to listen to various pieces and identify specific characteristics. I was doing my homework when Diane Simmons rang my doorbell. The room was filled with the sounds of Billie Holiday. It made for a great first impression.

Diane made an even better first impression. In the Navy we had a variety of sexist comments to describe an attractive woman. A tall woman with great legs was said to have legs that went clear up to her neck. That would have described Diane if it wasn't for fact that those legs didn't have a chance to get that far. Halfway to the neck they were met by a beautiful heart shaped bottom. All of this might have gone unnoticed if she hadn't been wearing a pair if tight fitting, very short, shorts, that highlighted every curve. I opened the door and smiled.

Looks do count. I was showing an apartment, not asking her on a date, but I liked the idea of having an attractive person to share my space with. She was tall and thin, but not too skinny. It was a nice, well-proportioned figure. She had short strawberry blonde hair, neatly cut above the shoulder but below the ears. Aside from those magnificent shorts, there was no immediate re-action, but I definitely liked what I saw.

As for my own looks, I have never been the one to judge. I always assumed my looks were average at best. I was physically fit. Ever since the weather started to turn warm, Tom and I had been working out five days a week. What started out slow had grown to several hundred sit-ups, a hundred pushups, twenty-five pull-ups, and a couple of trips up and down the steps at the football stadium. We would then finish off this routine by feeding our egos with a series of one-armed pull ups and one-armed pushups. At more than six feet tall and one hundred and seventy pounds, I was in the best shape of my life. I didn't know it then, but Diane Simmons really liked what she saw.

As she stepped into the living room we were greeted by the tortured and sultry voice of Billie Holiday crying out "All of me. Why not take all of me…" Diane smiled approvingly.

"Great song. What a voice."

"Yeah, my dad's a Sarah Vaughn guy, but I don't think you can top Billie Holiday." Then I explained about the class I was taking, lest she think I was plotting to seduce her; although the thought may have crossed my mind.

There wasn't much to showing the apartment. Two bedrooms, one bath, a living room and a kitchen. I had the back room, but she could have her choice. The front room got more sun, but the back was quieter. Being from Bridgeport, she was used to street noise, so quiet was not imperative. The place was inhabitable and the price was good. After a quick look around, we sat at the kitchen table and shared a couple of glasses of cheap red wine. I told her my story, she told me hers.

Diane was thirty-one, never married, and a former eighth grade school teacher. She had gotten her teaching degree from Western Connecticut State College ten years earlier, but after five years of teaching in a section of Bridgeport known as The Village, she had completely burned out. The Village was known more as a war zone than a neighborhood. Teaching meant she was a babysitter for addicts, whores and thugs. The final straw came when during a week in November, when one thirteen-year-old student died from a heroin overdose, while another attacked her with a fork from the cafeteria. She was stabbed in the shoulder with a fork. The school gave her a paid leave through the Christmas break, but she never returned. Diane collected unemployment for a while, then bounced from job to job for a while before winding up at a local community pharmacy in the affluent town of Westport.

Working as a technician at West End Pharmacy, Diane developed a new interest. Drugs. The legal kind. Instead of working with future convicts, she worked with doctors and health care professionals. Sick people came in, she gave them medication, and a few days later they returned healthy. It was clean, safe and rewarding. After a year as a tech, Diane decided to take the plunge and go to pharmacy school. Living at home rent-free, while still working at West End, she was able to finish off her pre-pharmacy classes at a nearby branch campus before having to make the move up to the main campus at Storrs.

"I like the place," she commented with nonchalance as she again looked around the apartment. "What are the neighbors like?"

"Mostly students. Some married couples. A bunch of live-in relationships, but mostly roommate situations. Barry and Louise in unit C7 both work on campus. He is in maintenance and she's clerical. Just about everyone else in this row are students. Tom, in C9 is my best friend. If you move in, you'll probably see a lot of him. Great guy. He shares the place with Greg, a grad student. Greg spends most of his time at his girlfriend's place and Tom's girlfriend Gloria spends most nights there. How about you? Got a boyfriend?"

"Yeah, sort of. A construction worker in Bridgeport. I'm a little pissed off at him right now, but Jay's alright. You got a girl-friend? "

"Yeah, I guess. Nothing serious. Jen is okay. She's a couple of years younger than me but way too mature." We both laughed.

The day was unseasonably warm. Probably low 90's. Since we were sitting at the kitchen table, I couldn't ogle her ass as it clung to those cheeky shorts, but I could admire the narrow cleavage and the sleeveless tee shirt that read "Dos Amigos. Two Friends Bar. Key West Florida". I may have been staring a bit too long.

"I like the shirt." I said abruptly. "I've been there. I've been to Key West, and I've been to Two Friends."

"A couple of years ago the ship I was on pulled into Port Everglades. Somehow me and a buddy of mine, managed to get a two-day pass. We decided to rent a car. We drove straight south to Key West. Island hopping down there was one of the most scenic drives I've ever been on. Then we get to Key West and there's this crazy vibe about the place. You've been there. You know. "

Diane smiled and nodded. I wasn't sure if she was nodding and smiling as one who knew, or if she was amused by how animated I had suddenly become. "We spent about ten hours down there," I continued. "We hit five or six bars, including Sloppy Joe's, Skipper's, and Two Friends. Then we watched the sunset from Mallory Square before heading back north. As we left the island I swore I would go back first chance I get. I haven't had the chance yet, but I will. How about you? How long were you down there?"

"Two days. Jay and I went with my parents down to Disney for a week, but we had to get away. My mother was driving us nuts, so we took off and headed to Key West. Jay hated it, but just like you, I fell in love with the place. Yeah," she smiled wistfully, "I'll be back."

We continued to talk for another hour, discussing everything from family histories, to our favorite rock bands. Her family was Polish. The name Simmons was an Americanization of what was originally Szymkowicz. I explained that my name was Italian. Campobasso had been homogenized into Campbell. We laughed at the similarities in our backgrounds.

I was pretty sure Diane would take the place. I was a little nervous about sharing my living space with a mature, attractive woman, but I knew it could work out. If I could live on a ship with 500 sailors, I could handle just about anything. Besides, I could always escape to Tom's if need be. As for Diane, she made it clear that she planned on spending most of her weekends home in Bridgeport. For the rest of the week, pharmacy school and the library would take up all of her time.

Three days later I got her call. "Ralph, if it's still available, I'll take the apartment."

"Great. Are you going to be up at all this summer? I'll make sure the room is cleared out in case you want to start bringing stuff up early"

"I have to be up a couple of times to take care of my financial aid. I may bring a few things up. You already have the place furnished pretty well, so I won't bring much."

A Brief Chronology of an Accelerated Relationship:

August 28: Diane Simmons, aided by her parents and her best friend Dana, moved into my small two-bedroom apartment. I thought it was a bit odd that the boyfriend was nowhere to be found. I soon learned that both Dana and Diane's parents didn't think too highly of Jay, so he stayed away. Come to think of it, my own girlfriend wasn't around either.

September 12: After her first two weeks of classes, Diane returns home to Bridgeport. The first couple of weeks had gone very well. Neither of us got in each other's way. Diane spent much of the time locked in her room studying late into the evening. What little studying I did was usually done in the predawn hours, before my first class. Morning person vs. night person. It worked out fine. Most nights we had dinner together. Conversation flowed very easily. Thursday at dinner, Diane mentioned she had a birthday coming up. September 14th.

With Diane gone for the weekend I was hoping to spend some time with Jen. That didn't happen. She visited a friend at Nichols College, so instead I got a jump on writing a couple of papers. Sunday morning, I went to the mall. I wanted to get a small birthday gift for Diane. Nothing fancy, just a coffee mug and a card. When I went to bed around eleven, she hadn't gotten back yet so I just left them on the kitchen table. Monday night at dinner she told me that her weekend was horrible. Jay got drunk and completely forgot about her birthday. It's no fun growing old. It's even less fun to grow old and forgotten. When she got back to the apartment she was stunned to see that I remembered her while her boyfriend did not. That night we talked for several hours. Nothing too intense. Just good conversation, but a spark was struck.

September 28: Diane and I agreed to have our significant others over for a double-date dinner. I had grown a bumper crop of plum tomatoes just outside the back door and they were ready for harvest. I would make lasagna, using home grown tomato sauce. Things got off to a bad start when I attempted to puree the tomatoes without putting a lid on the blender. Light blue walls and brown cabinets were immediately covered in red. Things went from bad to worse when after spending the entire day slaving over a hot stove, Jen called around 4pm and said she wasn't coming over. She "wasn't feeling well." Worse went to worst when Jay showed up an hour later, very drunk. First, he threw up in the kitchen sink. Then he passed out on the couch. Diane and I spent the night drinking and feeling sorry for each other. On Sunday morning we ended our relationships with Jay and Jen. At that point I don't think either of us had considered a romantic relationship with each other, but the spark was soon a flame.

October 15: It was payday, so a few friends from work, along with Tom and Gloria, all decided to go out for dinner and drinks. Someone suggested the Hawthorne Tavern, in Glastonbury. It was owned by Ellis Templeton, a former pro tennis player. More as a courtesy and almost as an afterthought, I asked Diane if she wanted to join us. She politely declined. After several minutes of cajoling about the need to break away from the books once in a while, she reluctantly agreed. The food was average, but the bar had a DJ and the company of friends made for a good night. After dinner we drank and danced until closing. Mostly 80's pop music, with a little bit of swing thrown in. Lisa, one of the secretaries, started showing some interest in me, while some guy named Fred, who was already there when we arrived, started asking Diane to dance.

Lisa and I danced a bit and shared some laughs. Diane and Fred seemed to get along too, but as the night progressed Lisa got sleepy and Fred got creepy. Lisa left early. Fred began telling Diane stories about his ex-wife and why she was such a bitch. I wasn't monitoring the situation too closely because I actually thought Diane liked this loser. Last call and last dance finally came around and Fred decided to make his move. There was an unmistakable look of panic on Diane's face. After watching her squirm for a second or two I leaned between the two of them and said "Come on honey, we have to dance. They're playing our song."

I had no idea what the DJ was playing. It was simply the first thing that came to mind. Fred stepped aside, stunned and rejected. Before the song was over he stormed out of the place, but not before eliciting a stern threat from Bruno the bouncer. Meanwhile, the song turned out to be "Electric Avenue" by Eddie Grant. It wasn't exactly "As Time Goes By" but for the 1980s it was definitely a classic.

October 28: Shortly before Diane headed home to Bridgeport for the weekend, I asked her if she wanted to go to a Halloween party on Monday at the ROTC building. It was a campus event and it sounded like a lot of fun. She loved the idea. What could we go as? I suggested we could be Rocky and Roxy, a couple of Jersey mobsters. Great. Her mother had a closet full of old clothes, most of which fit her. She could dye her hair black and do it up with bobby pins. Meanwhile I had the stereotypical black shirt and red tie, along with an old pinstriped suit. On Sunday I would go to a local flea market and look for other props. I found a starter pistol and holster that looked frighteningly real. I also found a silver and onyx cigarette holder for Diane.

October 31: Rocky Calamari, and Roxy Scungili, alias Ralph and Diane, stepped out on the town and knocked them dead. Diane had a dress her mother wore in the 1940's, along with a fake mink coat from a local thrift store. She wore stiletto heels and a very old pair of black nylons with a seam running up the back. We each wore a red rose boutonnière. I shaved my moustache to pencil thin and donned a grey fedora. We were stunning. My New Jersey accent was natural and flowed easily. Diane was a little too good in the role of a mobster's bimbo arm candy.

I knew the DJ and I knew one of the judges, so while it wasn't a fix, it was easy for us to garner a little extra attention. I got them to play Roxanne by the Police. They also played the theme from The Godfather. We danced until midnight. In the end we walked away with several door prizes, including "Best Couple." It's funny how quickly things can change. We returned to the apartment gushing over what a wonderful evening it had been. Then, like a chapter in some cheap romance novel, I leaned over and kissed her on the lips. We embraced, then kissed some more. By the time we awoke in my bed the following morning, we really were the best couple.

Two days later: Regrets? None. The big question was, "What do we do now?" We both agreed that we wanted this relationship and should give it a little time to see where it takes us. But should we be roommates and lovers at the same time? Diane suggested she move out. We both thought about it for a couple of days, then decided that her moving wouldn't accomplish anything. We already knew we could live with each other. If the relationship didn't last, then we would just have to figure something else out. Those concerns were unfounded.

November 22: We both went home for Thanksgiving weekend. She went to Bridgeport and I went to New Jersey. We had decided it was time to tell the parents. Since I was in my mid-twenties and she was in her early thirties, it should have been no big deal, but it was. Living together as an unmarried couple was something her Polish-Catholic parents would never approve.

In my case it was easier. I didn't care what my father thought. He said he thought I was making a mistake. I told him it was my mistake to make. Diane, meanwhile, chickened out. She told her brothers, she told her sisters, she told her best friend Dana, but they all agreed that it was probably better if Mom and Dad didn't know just yet. After all, they were still celebrating the fact that she had finally dumped Jay. Diane waited until Christmas before telling her parents that we were a couple. At the same time, she assured them we were still sleeping in separate bedrooms. Fortunately for us they were either naïve or in denial. They liked me, and Diane was happy. That was all that mattered.

January 12: As winter break progressed Diane suggested we take a weekend and visit her sister Karen in Arlington, Virginia. Karen was a successful attorney, who lived in a beautiful home just outside of Washington. She was a gracious host, providing a much-appreciated respite for two starving college students.

January 14: At Porto's Italian restaurant in Arlington, over a plate of linguini with red clam sauce and a bottle of chianti, Diane and I first discussed the possibility of marriage. We both knew it was too sudden, too soon, and very impractical, and yet it seemed inevitable. She then assured me that when the time was right, she would say yes.

October 31. Exactly one year after becoming a couple, we attended a wedding in Bridgeport for one of Diane's old friends.

Jay was there. She spoke briefly to him while I made small talk with a fellow tagalong. Whatever Diane said to Jay didn't go over well because he left without a word. The rest of the wedding was boring beyond belief. We snuck out early, hoping our absence wouldn't be noticed. On the ride back to her parents' house we decided to begin moving forward with our own wedding plans. No formal proposal. We just knew the time was right. Her parents approved. I phoned my dad to tell him. I was surprised by his excitement and approval.

November 24: The day before Thanksgiving. Diane's sister Allison gave birth to her son John. On that same day we became officially engaged as we picked up a ring we had selected from Spirit Jewelers, at the Stamford Mall. This was followed by a long and futile search through the shopping center for a bar where we could toast the event. Whoever heard of a mall without a bar? The best we could do was a small Indian restaurant that served liquor. We ordered two shots of Jack Daniels, then I dropped to one knee, asked her to marry me and placed the ring on her finger. No one noticed.

Saturday, August 10: Diane Simmons married Ralph Campbell in a very small wedding at Saint Michaels Church in Bridgeport, Connecticut. And they lived semi-happily ever after.

Caroline shook her head and exhaled a befuddled sigh. "The things that are written here all ring true. But how? I still have a hard time believing that Dad is talking to us from the dead."

"Talking to you," Richard interjected. "Is it possible he knew he would never live to see our wedding and made the necessary arrangements for you to get this manuscript several months ago."

"Maybe, but I don't see how. Maybe Mom knows. Maybe she is in on it."

"Would she tell us? We could call her?"

"And say what?" Caroline laughed, holding an imaginary phone to her ear. "Hi Mom. Yes, we are fine. Yes, we are still married. No, I'm not pregnant yet. Yeah, I know you want grandchildren. Listen, the reason I'm calling is to see if you know anything about this ghost in our room? You don't? Oh, okay. Just wondering. Gotta go. Love you too. Bye."

They both laughed, then Richard smiled. "True or not, it really is a compelling story, so far. I love the part about how your parents got together. Is that part true?"

Caroline nodded. "Mom loved to tell the story of how they met, but she never told the whole thing straight through. She would start talking and let Dad tell the rest. It was that way with a lot of things. He was always interrupting her. You know, finishing her sentences. It would drive her crazy. Well, sort of. He always was a good storyteller."

"Their first encounter was a little like ours," Richard offered. "An unlikely coincidence and a wonderful piece of serendipity."

The two kissed and then kissed again. Perhaps it was time for a short break. They started to disrobe, but this time, perhaps for the first time ever, it didn't feel right. There would be plenty of opportunities for that. With a gentle touch and a knowing smile, they returned their attention to the pages on the bed.

CHAPTER TEN

*D*rugs are bad. Drugs are what killed Elvis Presley and Janis Joplin. Drugs have killed a lot of people. So, what makes them so appealing? For some, drugs offer an escape from the pain that living brings. For others, it enhances a pleasurable experience, making it better. Many take drugs to fit in. Peer pressure. I drank, smoked, and took drugs for all of those reasons and more. Mostly I wanted new experiences. I wanted to know what it was like. I also wanted to know if the hype lived up to the reality. It did not. Still, any experience that doesn't maim or kill you is a lesson learned. I studied hard and often.

I smoked my first joint at the age of eighteen, in the barracks of the Naval Training Center, in San Diego. Given the circumstances, I'm surprised it wasn't my last.

Following basic training I was sent to San Diego for Machinery Repairman Class A Training. The school shut down from December 22nd until January 5th. Vacation time was granted for anyone who wanted to take it. Those of us who stayed behind had it pretty easy. We would work from 9 to 3 each day, painting, landscaping or performing other mundane tasks around the school. Every fourth day we were required to stay in the barracks to perform various routine duties.

Some stayed because they didn't have the money to go home. Others stayed because they had nowhere to go. I stayed because

I didn't want to go home. We were lonely misfits and we banded together. It wasn't bad, but we all dreaded Christmas Eve and Christmas Day. No family gatherings. No big meals. No tree with neatly wrapped presents. To ease the loneliness, we counted on overindulgences in alcohol or some other drug, to provide euphoric oblivion.

My mental anesthesia of choice was Scotch. One of the guys made a liquor run, so I had him buy me a quart of Cutty Sark. On Christmas Eve night, I stood watch at the barracks front desk. I kept my bottle in a brown bag inside the drawer. The Officer of the Day, Chief Petty Officer Leon Whitney stopped by to check on things. He could smell it on my breath. It didn't matter. He was drunk too. He took a long drag on his Marlboro, blew the smoke in my face and sputtered "What have you been drinking kid?"

I figured since he was obviously intoxicated, it didn't much matter. "Scotch," I replied.

"Good choice," he said. "Scotch doesn't give you a hangover. Next time chew on a mint so it isn't so noticeable." With that he staggered away.

The following afternoon, six of us were sitting around in Curtis Hartley's room. A couple of guys brought in boxes of cookies and candy that they had received from home. I passed around what was left of my bottle. Curt lifted his mattress pad and pulled out a small baggie filled with pungent green buds. "Dessert anyone?" We all smiled and nodded. I had never smoked anything other than cigars before, but it seemed like as good a time as any. Using his Principles of Machine Tool Technology textbook as a desk, Curt deftly rolled two large joints. One for now. One for later.

I was the fourth person to the right of Hartley. I watched as he lit one end and took a long draw. He then inhaled a second time before holding it and exhaling. After a short harsh cough, he began chuckling softly to himself. Passing it to his right, Curt handed it to Tommy Gill, commenting that it was pretty good Mexican shit that he got in Tijuana. I wouldn't know good shit from oregano, but at least by the time the joint made it to me I knew how to smoke it without looking like an idiot. I inhaled deeply then passed it along to Larry Glickman. I smiled and nodded.

The joint made it around our group twice. Only Bernie Agosto abstained. He had the next watch and didn't want to risk it. By the time it got back to Curt again there wasn't much left. Thinking as quickly as a stoned person can, Curtis popped open his tool box. It was standard issue for all Machinery Repairman students. He then pulled out a pair calipers, a tool used for rough measuring the outside diameter of an object. Tightening the calipers around the edge of the joint, it functioned perfectly as a roach clip. We could now finish it off without any waste.

Curt pressed the calipers to his lips and leaned his head back. As he exhaled, he casually commented, "Anyone know who the Officer of the Day is?"

"Nope" replied Glickman. "Who?"

"Look at the door."

The door to Curt's room had been left unlocked and slightly ajar, thereby acting as an open invitation to anyone who wanted to stop in. Now it was wide open. Instructor and Chief Petty Officer Pat Corcoran stood in the doorway shaking his head while trying not to smile.

"You guys are really stupid. Real fucking idiots."

Chief Cork, as he was known, was not just any instructor. Legend was he spent two tours in some of the nastiest shit that Viet Nam had to offer. He wasn't old, but damn he was grizzled. Just twenty-eight years old, he carried more medals than some thirty-year vets. Among his decorations was a scar that ran from his right ear to the base of his chin. He didn't talk about Viet Nam and he definitely didn't talk about the scar. No one else dared to either. We didn't fear him. We simply held him in awe. He had seen a world that none of us, thankfully, would ever know.

"Give me that thing." He barked. Curt complied reaching up and handing him the calipers. Cork held it up, turned it around and studied it as though it was some strange foreign object.

"This is a fine machine tool." Cork rambled. "Do you know what these are?" he asked.

"Uh, a pair of outside calipers?"

"Yes, but it is so much more. This is a precision measuring instrument. This is a fine piece of workmanship that is used to create other fine pieces of workmanship. You boys disappoint me." Suddenly he raised his voice to a loud shrill. "YOU DO NOT, I REPEAT, DO NOT USE A FUCKING PRECISION MEASURING INSTRUMENT FOR A ROACH CLIP. DO I MAKE MYSELF CLEAR!?"

Stunned, terrified and dumbfounded we all looked down and nodded.

Cork lowered his voice to a whisper. "Now. Can any one of you geniuses tell me why you don't use a pair of outside calipers for a roach clip?"

Still looking down, Glickman mumbled "Because it is a precision measuring instrument?"

"NO!" Cork roared, then laughed. Pulling out his Zippo he fired up what was now left of the joint. He smoked the last few remnants and popped the burning ash into his mouth. "You never use outside calipers because it will rip the fucking papers."

Taking close inventory of who was in the room, he then informed us that he would be coming by at midnight with buckets and scrub brushes. We were going to scrub every shower, sink and toilet in the barracks. "Got that, you assholes?" he growled.

"Merry fucking Christmas." With that he closed the door and walked away humming Jingle Bells. Cork wasn't kidding about the latrine duty. From midnight until 4am, using scalding hot water and bleach without the benefit of protective gloves, we scrubbed everything in sight. Our hands were swollen and blistered, but we never for one minute, lost our respect for Cork.

Several people have told me that they didn't get high the first time they smoked. I know I did. Maybe it really was good Mexican shit. I can't say. I knew I was heavily buzzed for a couple of hours and it was different than drinking. My lungs burned. My eyes grew itchy. My tongue felt thick and my mouth was dry. Still, I felt very relaxed and at ease with the world. I didn't care that I was three thousand miles from home. I didn't give a shit about my family or if they gave a shit about me. That's what being high was all about. It meant not giving a shit when you really should.

Within six months of smoking that first joint, I had graduated to trying speed, hashish, and something called Thai stick. I think it was marijuana laced with opium. That shit could paralyze you. By the time I had left the navy I tried just about anything that didn't include needles or LSD. Those two things scared me, but everything else was fair game.

Mostly we smoked pot or hash. Ships were always coming in from overseas, so there was never a supply shortage. Some guys became real head-cases. That was never me. I liked getting high, but I hated being stoned. I just wanted the euphoria. While I am not an advocate of foolish behavior or constant inebriation, it is my belief that getting high taught me how to be myself and relax around girls or anyone else who might otherwise intimidate me. When I was sober, I was shy and nervous. Since getting high made me not care, I could relax and be myself or whomever I wanted to be. Eventually I figured out who that person was and became naturally comfortable around others.

As my junior year of college began, I had finally grown accustomed to academia. I was writing several columns each week for the campus paper and gaining a modest reputation for my editorial skills. Yet even with studies, work, and Diane, I still found time to socialize. Most of that time was spent with my neighbor, Tom Creighton. Tom was smart. He was an English major bound for law school. Success awaited him. He came from a family of lawyers in the Stonington area. As he finished the Fall Semester of his senior year, he had been accepted at the Western New England School of Law. It wasn't Harvard or Yale, but it didn't have to be. All he needed to do was pass the Bar and a job in the family business awaited. Tom was easily my closest friend on campus. We shared the same absurd sense of humor and an unavoidable temptation to test our limits by whatever means possible.

Diane soon became friends with Tom's girl, Gloria, who was majoring in Chemical Engineering. Together we joked about the contrast of the two guys pursuing humanities while the girls opted for the more challenging hard sciences. None of us were hardcore partiers, but because of a few acquaintances, there was always a steady supply of intoxicants at our disposal. It wasn't something we indulged in on a daily basis, but after a stressful exam or a really hard workout it did offer both release and reward.

Tom was more than willing to partake in almost any indulgence. Diane liked smoking pot and drinking rum, but generally avoided other libations. Gloria did nothing stronger than wine, but you could always count her to laugh with great amusement as Tom and I got stoned. Who could blame her? When the two of us got together anything could happen. One night we walked into a bar pretending we were gay and started slow dancing. Other times we would stage a fight. Since neither of us could act, our fake fight usually involved real punches as we beat each other senseless.

One of the nicer things about attending a larger school like the University of Connecticut was that if you didn't go to class, no one really cared. Classes were often so large that professors only knew you as a name on a roster. There were advantages to that. One semester, Tom and I took a Sociology course together. Social Movements and Revolution. The class had been around since the late-1960s, all the while being taught by the same professor. Jerry Rosenberg was a radical socialist who wished the chaos of the sixties had never ended. He spent much of his spare time writing for the remnants of counterculture newspapers, trying to rekindle a flame that had all but burned out.

The Social Movements class had 178 students. Because of the large class size, it was taught in the Fine Arts Auditorium. Tom and I took the class for several reasons. First, we wanted to take a class together. Second, from previous classes and various readings, we both already knew most of the info, so getting a grade would be easy. Third, the class was three hours long and taught one night a week on Wednesdays. It was the perfect choice. We sat in the back row. Sometimes we listened to the professor and sometimes we played cribbage on the empty seat between us. Occasionally only one of us would go to class and then copy any notes for the other. The final exam was held at 8am on Saturday, December 15th. For both Tom and I it would be our last exam for the semester. We figured to have the exam done before 9am and be celebrating by 9:05.

To celebrate the end of finals and the start of the holiday season, we decided to go hiking in a nearby state forest. We would enter the park from the east, off state road 198. There we would park the car and begin hiking along a narrow river bed for as far as we felt like going. Tom packed sandwiches and a bottle of vodka. I brought apples and pears, Gatorade, and a small but potent quantity of hallucinogenic mushrooms. It was a dangerous combination and yet it seemed to make perfectly good sense at the time. As it turned out, Tom was one brain cell smarter than me. He ate a full breakfast before the exam. I overslept and was running late. I guzzled a cup of coffee but was otherwise functioning on an empty stomach.

December 15 turned out to be one of the coldest days of the year. A bitter wind from the north had blown in, first depositing a soft, two-inch layer of dry snow to an already existing sheet of ice. Clear skies quickly dispersed any heat from the sun, leaving us with single digit temperatures. It never got above ten degrees for the day. We dressed appropriately for the frigid climes. Aside from the chill, it was a beautiful day to be hiking, assuming you were not under the influence of anything that might impair your judgment.

We kicked off our celebratory trek with a brief tailgate party. We ate the mushrooms; then washed them down with a couple of slugs of vodka and Gatorade. Our rationale was to get wasted early so by the time we headed home, one of us would be sober enough to drive.

Prior to this hiking excursion, I had only tried hallucinogens twice. Once was when I was stationed on the Havasu. We had been drinking at some bar and were walking back to the base. One of the guys I was with pulled out a joint filled with a grey, pasty substance. He said it was opium. I'll take him at his word. After the second hit, I began watching the red taillights from cars as they drove past. A long stream of neon fluttered behind passing vehicles. Eventually the stream would recede back to the taillight then pop into a white popcorn kernel. It was amusing but not frightening.

My second experience was with my old roommate Jimmy Resnick. This time it was mushrooms. Three things happened. First, I watched an entire episode of "Love Boat" on my old

Sylvania black and white television while completely convinced it was in color. Once it returned to black and white, Jim convinced me to go out and get some fresh air. We each brought a pillow and laid across a large boulder in the far corner of the apartment parking lot. Staring at the stars we both claimed to be watching dueling shooting stars ricocheting across the sky like some out of control video game. It was a shared hallucination. As we returned to the apartment I picked up a stray cat that had wandered near us. Looking into its face, I offered a friendly "Hello kitty." In return the cat looked back and with a Cheshire grin began laughing hysterically. I dropped the cat, ran inside and put on my headphones, listening to Joni Mitchell records in the dark until I finally calmed down.

Given my past experiences, I should have known the mushrooms were a bad idea. But like most bad ideas, I did it anyway. The mushrooms tasted awful. We flushed them down with Gatorade to kill the bitterness. Tom figured that we should go easy on the vodka until we had been outside a bit longer. Besides, the vodka didn't taste much better than the mushrooms, so we decided to wait awhile before we began poisoning ourselves with alcohol. A few hundred feet upstream seemed long enough.

The river ran about thirty feet across at the point where we parked the car. From there it narrowed, as we followed it up the long, gradual hill that we presumed would take us to its source. As a precautionary measure, we made a pact to always keep the river within our view. This would provide us with a foolproof means of finding our way back to the car. But nothing is foolproof.

Despite the Arctic air, the cold was not a major obstacle. Our footwear was warm and waterproof, and the rest of our clothing was appropriately layered to maximize protection from the elements. The bare trees allowed the icy ground to be exposed to gleaming sunlight, creating moments of blinding reflection that penetrated well beyond the polarizing abilities of my cheap, plastic sunglasses. I avoided looking directly at the river, or into the sunlit snow around us. Instead I concentrated on the rhythmic sound of our boots as they crunched through the glazed surface.

It took about twenty minutes for the fungi to start working their magic. A feeling of warm euphoria flushed my face, which by now was adorned with a giddy smile and sense of heightened awareness to all that was around me. Tom was a few feet ahead, having stopped to rest on the trunk of a fallen and uprooted tree. It was time for another break. I tossed him an apple as he passed me the bottle.

"Is it hitting you yet?"

I took a deep, exaggerated breath, filling my lungs with cold dry air, before expelling a cloud of white vapor. "Yeah. Nothing crazy. I just feel really freaking good." I took two gulps from the bottle, winced at the taste, then bit into a pear. "How 'bout you?"

"All is right with the world, my friend. A kick-ass day."

Tom then reached into his backpack and pulled out a small hatchet. He carefully selected two of the long, straight branches from our perch. With short, quick chops, walking sticks were crafted. "Let's stay along the banks of the river," he said. "It's a little loud, but I love the sound of water as it rolls over the rocks."

"Lead on McDuff." I vaguely remember the line from reading Macbeth in high school, but I have no idea who McDuff was, or if he ever led anyone anywhere. I didn't matter. Nothing mattered. Tom led; I followed.

Since the class we had just completed dealt in part with revolutions, Tom and I began talking about the American Revolution and the role that this river and this land might have played. The landscape was littered with stone walls and the fallen remains of crumbling wooden structures. We imagined that New England landowners and their slaves may have perched behind these very walls, musket in hand, fending off attacks from either the British, or maybe the Pequot or Mohegan Indians. The truth is that neither of us knew a damn thing about the history that surrounded the area, so we simply let our chemically enhanced imaginations run wild, oblivious to the facts.

"These stone walls are how landowners used to divide up property," Tom offered. "Ever since the glaciers receded at the end of the Ice Age, these rocks and boulders have littered the terrain. When the colonist cleared the land, they found ways to put the rocks to good use. Stone walls made sense."

"Then how come we don't see any roads in front of the walls, or farmhouses made of stone? Sounds like bullshit to me."

"No really. At least that's what they taught us in high school. I'm guessing since they had to clear trees as well as rocks, they used the trees for log cabins, lumber and firewood. The logs were lighter than the rocks and could be fastened into a more stable structure than stones. Two hundred years of storms, floods, plants, animals, and insects destroyed almost everything but the rocks."

"I'll agree about the glaciers, but I think the walls were used as pens to keep livestock in. I don't know why there aren't any remaining structures. You would think that there would be something left standing. A barn. A dirt road. Something."

"Maybe there is." Tom postulated, stabbing at the icy ground with his stick. "Could be that we are taking a narrow perspective." For two stoned comrades walking through the woods, we were starting to sound very collegiate in our hypotheses. "Maybe this narrow trail that we are on was once a major roadway. Sure, it has been overgrown, but the pathway exists and it seems to be going somewhere. As for structures left standing, I guessed there still are plenty around. Perspective. There is a shitload of land around here, and the population was sparse. For one person to own a thousand acres was probably no big deal. How many eighteenth-century farmhouses are still standing? A ton. Maybe one of those old buildings on the edge of route 198 was the home for the guy who had all of this land. I'm not saying it's so, but it could be."

We had been walking for what I thought was an hour but time-perspectives can get really screwed up when you are stoned. It may have been two hours or ten minutes. It didn't matter. The sun was still high overhead. As long as we got out before sunset, everything would be fine. "Up ahead the river splits into three streams," I offered. "A bridge crosses over the junction. Let's break for a few minutes when we get to the bridge. We can then decide which stream to follow."

The bridge was farther than it looked. By the time we got there, I was breathing heavy. I was clearly feeling the effects of inebriation more than Tom. It was now noon and my food intake for the day had consisted of a cup of coffee, a pear, an apple, a little Gatorade, psychedelic mushrooms and a third of a bottle of vodka. I tried not to let on that I was struggling. By stopping to rest at the bridge I figured I could start to regain myself.

We sat on the bridge with our feet dangling over the icy stream below. Three gulps each and the vodka was gone. I turned to Tom and asked how the 'shrooms were affecting him.

"Pretty cool. I don't know. I think I was expecting more of a trip, but still it's pretty cool. Everything is more brightly colored than ever. It's like somebody shaded everything with a neon high-lighter, then outlined it with a black marker. I like it. What's with you?"

"Kind of like you said. No big trip, just everything is more intense. Sounds and smells in particular. Can you smell the water? I'm used to the smell of salt water, but I never knew a crystal pure river had such a smell, or the snow, or the bark of an oak tree. Pretty wild stuff."

"Yeah. Can't beat the cold air and the great outdoors. Man, every time I take a deep breath I'm getting a lung freeze. You okay? You're looking a little beat."

"Yeah, I'm fine. A little ragged, but good. Just pass me the Gatorade."

We stood for a moment on top of the small bridge taking in a panoramic perspective. A hawk soared overhead. In my heightened sensitivity I could hear the wind passing over its wings. To the right a large rabbit burst across the snow, with no predator in pursuit. Squirrels danced in the trees, foraging for any last-minute provisions that might protect them from even harsher days to come. It was all strikingly beautiful. As I scanned the surrounding landscape my thoughts again turned to the stone walls.

"I remember reading how colonists would use the stone walls as protection from the British and the Indians. Doesn't look like much protection to me. Too low to hide behind don't you think?"

"Not at all," Tom responded. "Watch this." Tucking his walking stick under his arm he burst into a full sprint towards one of the walls. A few feet from the rocks he dove to the ground, crawling on his belly as he approached the low-lying structure. Mimicking a soldier loading a ball and cap musket, Tom then lifted the stick to his shoulder. With a short burst he raised himself up just above that top of the wall and fired. "Take that you red-coat bastard!"

Suddenly all perspective changed. Looking around, I saw British soldiers behind a half dozen walls. We were in trouble. Clearly outnumbered. I had to help my friend. Hurdling over the bridge's rail, I dropped down to the frigid water below. Landing with a splash my feet were wet but not soaked as I sprinted towards Tom's wall, loading my musket as I ran. A shot rang out behind me. I dropped to the ground and turned but saw nothing. "Sonofabitch must have dropped back behind a wall," I muttered. "Hold your ground; I'm on my way."

The exact details of the battle are understandably vague. My first kill was a young kid in a red and gold double breasted uniform. He couldn't have been more than fifteen or sixteen years old. I saw him behind a tree holding a dueling pistol. As his arm came up to aim, I fired. The lead ball shattered his shoulder, separating his arm and pistol from the rest of his body. The arm hit the ground first, then he did, staining the white snow with red. Two soldiers came over the wall and raced towards us. Tom quickly fired on both, hitting one in the chest and another between the legs. Both were killed instantly. How he did that using a ball and cap musket without having to reload is a mystery. Things happen quickly in battle, and you don't have time to ask questions.

For the better part of an hour we held our ground, as each red coat tried but failed to invade our land. The forest was littered with bodies. I counted sixteen in all. My ear had been grazed as a shot whizzed past, but overall, we were fine. Then perspectives changed.

A bomb exploded behind us, creating a shower of snow, rocks and ice. Mixed in with the debris, was a piece of green cloth and a leather boot. The boot contained the remains of a severed foot. I immediately retched and vomited. Several more bombs went off. In the distance I could see a small group of soldiers running towards us wearing metal helmets, while gripping tightly to their bayonet rifles. This wasn't the Revolutionary War any longer. This was trench warfare. France 1918. I got up to run, but a shot rang out. I was hit. I fell forward, but before I could connect with the ground, Tom grabbed hold of me. "Let's get the hell out of here."

The following day I woke up on the sofa in my apartment. Diane was standing over me looking both concerned and amused. "Welcome back soldier." Then she purred, "What a long strange trip it's been."

"Grateful Dead lyrics. I hate the Grateful Dead. And right

now, I feel more dead than grateful. Last thing I remember Tom and I were standing on a bridge talking about the scenery. What happened?"

"Well, I'm sure Tom can tell it better than I will, but according to him you jumped off the bridge and into the river, running upstream while screaming something about being surrounded by British Redcoats. A short while later you abruptly switched wars and found yourself fighting the German Army in World War I France. Shall I send word to General Washington or General Pershing? I'm sure they would love to hear of your heroic deeds. Maybe we can get you a Purple Heart or a Medal of Honor."

"Not funny. That's no way to treat a veteran. I knew I should have stayed in the Navy."

After two days of dry toast and tea, I was sort of back to normal. Tom's tale of carrying me out of the woods, while both of us were hallucinating, would become a permanent part of our collegiate folklore. My loyal friend draped me over his shoulder and plodded downstream until he found his way back to the car. Once there he still had the unenviable task of driving us home while heavily impaired. To hear Tom tell it, the car never moved. He put the transmission into drive and watched the road roll by beneath his stationery vehicle.

Once home he passed me off to Diane. She undressed me, drying my wet legs and feet, before tending to a myriad of cuts and scrapes, some of which were in places that would be hard to explain under any circumstances. She then dropped me on the couch with two blankets and a pillow. That was at three o'clock Saturday afternoon. I returned to the world at ten o'clock Sunday morning. In between, I was prone to suddenly sitting up and yelling "Look out!" or "Find cover!" then returning to sleep.

I have always believed that not enough people know how to experience life to its fullest. I made it my mission to have as many varied experiences as possible. You can be part of the action or part of the scenery. This, however, was one time when it would have been better to learn vicariously from the experiences of others. And so, if you are ever inclined to mix psychedelic mushrooms, cheap vodka and an imaginary Revolutionary War battlefield, don't do it. It might seem like a good idea, but trust me, it isn't.

CHAPTER ELEVEN

Dear Caroline-Sometimes it's better to be lucky than good. Once in a while, you get to be both.

D o you remember as a kid how people would ask "What do you want to be when you grow up? This happened at the start of almost every year in grammar school. When Mrs. Jackson, my second-grade teacher asked this, I replied "A house builder." She responded "Oh, you mean a carpenter. That's good." I had no idea what a carpenter was, so I smiled and agreed. In fourth grade when Miss Jablonski asked me of my career plans I told her I wanted to be a scientist. That idea didn't last long. By sixth grade I finally figured it out. By then, I had begun to display some writing skills. Phil Pepe was a sportswriter covering the Yankees for the New York Daily News. I became as much of a fan of Mr. Pepe's work as I did of the team he covered. The Yankees were my religion and Phil was my priest. He was my favorite Yankee without a uniform.

I wanted to be Phil Pepe. I began attending sporting events at my school, then upon returning home I would practice my journalistic skills by writing articles or editorials from the event. In early April I was sitting in the back of my sixth-grade class, not really caring about how to conjugate a verb, so I began editing my most recent article. It was a piece about the tryouts for our school's baseball team. Ricky McBride, a classmate, hit a ball that was estimated to travel more than three hundred feet. That was unheard of for a twelve-year-old. I described the flight, it's majestic arc, the turn of heads at the crack of the bat, and the gasp of all onlookers as the ball rocketed across the sky. Mr. Harris caught me writing when I should have been conjugating, so he confiscated my paper. He didn't say anything, he just took the paper away. The next day he stopped me before the start of class. Mrs. Grady, an eighth-grade teacher, was with him.

Waving my paper with one hand he began to lecture me. "Ralph, you know I should have given you a detention for this." I hung my head low, in worried shame. Detention would surely get me another beating from Carmen. Silently I prayed as Mr. Harris continued to speak. "We were covering some useful information that will definitely be on the test, and your head was off on some ball field." Then he paused and smiled. "I read what you wrote. It's really very good. More than good. It's excellent. Mrs. Grady agrees. Do you know Mrs. Grady?"

Looking down at my feet, I shrugged and nodded, without any sense of where this was going. "Not really."

"Hello Ralph." This kind old woman, at least forty years old, gently smiled. "You write very well. Would you like to be a sports-writer for our school newspaper?"

I was stunned and elated. Whoever heard of a sixth-grader writing for the school paper? Eighth-graders ran it. Mostly girls. I was being asked to hang out with eighth-grade girls. "Sure," I said with a cool nonchalance. "What do I have to do?"

I very quickly learned that it wasn't nearly as glamorous as I had imagined. There were several problems. The first was that my sister, was an eighth-grader. The girls on the paper knew her or knew of her, but they weren't among her friends. That made things a little awkward. The second problem was that despite my being the best writer on the staff, other reporters treated me like a little kid. The third problem was that I had the bad habit of telling the truth. This was particularly bad when people didn't want to hear the truth. It was a flaw that would continue to haunt me throughout most of my life.

Bear in mind that this was not exactly the New York Times we were printing. It wasn't even the Long Branch Daily Record, although in that comparison our writing may have been on par. Our paper was called The Monthly Reporter. Not the most original name, but what do you expect from five pages of mimeograph paper?

My first article wasn't about sports. It was a revue of the school science fair. This was not the most distinguished group of scientists ever put on public display. There were several electromagnets, and electricity experiments. Others went for biology. One girl grew four different ivy plants, exposing them to the same soil, light and water conditions. Each plant received an hour of music each day. Rock and roll, country, classical and no music. The plant with no music was the healthiest. I still don't know what that proves. My sixth-grade classmate, Fran Evans, took first place for dissecting a large striped bass that her father had caught. Each of the fish's organs, including the eyes, brain, heart and intestines, were put in mason jars containing formaldehyde and labeled with a detailed explanation of their function. My classmates wondered where she got the formaldehyde. We all avoided Franny after that. Preadolescent boys tend to like disgusting things, but this put her in a league of her own. The teachers who were at the science fair all said my reporting was excellent, but they may have just been patronizing me.

My second article was my last. I was told to write a story

about the boy's baseball team. That was exciting. I got to ride on the team bus and go to their first game, which was at rival school, Warren Township. We lost 18-2 in a six-inning game. There was no mercy rule or the game would have been over after one inning. Warren jumped out to a 12-0 lead, then put in all of their back-up players. Ricky McBride hit two homers for our team's only runs. I counted nine errors, three wild pitches and seven walks. Ricky made four errors in left field. The coach was not pleased. Somewhere around the fourth inning Coach Wagner started to lose his composure. He started swearing. He began throwing equipment around. He tried almost every player at pitching. He even asked me to pinch hit. I could not, since I had no uniform and wasn't listed on the roster. I simply sat quietly on the bench taking notes. Then I reported what I saw.

Mrs. Grady was not a big fan of baseball, nor was she a fan of Coach Wagner. She printed my article unedited. I accused the team of being poorly prepared. I also accused Mr. Wagner of throwing a tantrum whenever one of his players would make a miscue. My account was peppered with colorful phrases like "bumbling ineptness" "epic futility" and "an embarrassment to our national pastime." Some of that was plagiarism. I learned such phrasing from my idol Phil Pepe.

Minutes after my article hit the streets I knew I had a problem. Ricky McBride tipped me off that several team members, including Coach Wagner wanted to beat the crap out of me. Wagner called me into his office and demanded that I make a public retraction and apology. Mrs. Grady refused to let me do so. On the playground at recess two players were having a catch. I was nowhere near them but twice the ball whizzed by my head. The second time it happened I was knocked flat as Joey D'Amato retrieved the ball. I got up and dusted myself off just in time to have him hit me again on his way back. I'm not surprised he was mad. He had made two errors and walked six opposing players. Despite Mrs. Grady's objections, I quit the paper the next day and apologized to the team. Staying alive was more important than writing. I would not be published again until college.

After my grammar school foray into writing, I figured I was done. In high school my path was predetermined. Learn a trade. Writing is a skill, not a trade. So how did I go from machinist to journalist? Reality has an ungainly knack for altering plans. I was the best metalworker in my high school and the worst in the navy. What they taught us in school didn't translate so well to the real world of repairing and rebuilding damaged pumps and valves. I proved to be almost completely incompetent as a machinist.

Part of the problem was that my high school instruction was fun but impractical. It may have been impractical, but at least it was interesting. On the ship I had a blue print, a lathe or milling machine, and a cup of coffee. Someone handed you a folder and told you what needed to be done. Some jobs were easy, some were hard, but most were boring. Boredom is a recipe for failure.

Two people got me back into writing. One was my shipmate Donny Owens and the other was Dr. Nelson Pressman. Donny was nearing the end of his enlistment. He had done most of his four years, in the Havasu's machine shop. Donny was incredibly skilled, but not the most literate or articulate of guys. His intention was to stay in the Norfolk area and get a job in one of the local shops that subcontracted to the military. Donny decided he needed a resume'. I knew a little bit about writing résumés from a business class I took in high school. I offered to lend a hand.

It was a simple process. We sat down over a cup of coffee and in about an hour we had a basic document that seemed to work. It was no big deal, just a shipmate helping a shipmate. We fashioned a cover letter to go with the resume'. Next, we found a phone book, gathering the addresses of several local machine shops. Cover letters and resumes were sent out without any real expectations. I suggested he stop by a few of the places or at least follow up with a phone call over the next week or two. It wasn't necessary. Within a week he had five phone calls asking him to come in for an interview. By the end of the third week Donny had three job offers.

A short while later, Johnny Prentice, another short-timer, approached me. "I'll give you ten bucks if you can write me a resume' like you did for Donny." Ten bucks for less than an hour's work sounded great to me. Johnny and I sat down over a beer. Like Donny, he got a resume', a job, and a pretty nice paycheck.

I've never considered myself to be a shrewd businessman, but this was clearly an opportunity. Sailors are a transient group. There are always men leaving the service and returning to work in the private sector. Most who were leaving needed a résumé', but had little experience in writing one. I went down to a local pawn shop and bought a used Smith Corona electric typewriter for fifteen dollars. I then came up with a simple standardized questionnaire that could be filled out in advance, so I didn't have to waste time interviewing the person. I advertised on every bulletin board on the ship. When we were home in Norfolk I averaged five résumé's a week. It was a great way to supplement my meager Navy pay. The writing came easy, and the résumé's continued to get results. At some point I began to wonder if it was possible to make a living doing something like this. I certainly wouldn't make it as a machinist.

The resume' business temporarily came a halt whenever the ship went out to sea. During the six months that we spent in the Mediterranean, I had just four jobs. Yet my reputation as a writer continued to grow. Several of my supervisors asked for assistance in writing performance evaluations. It wasn't Shakespeare, but I enjoyed the writing. More importantly, others appreciated my work.

The Navy, at that time, offered a program in conjunction with Old Dominion University, where they would put a college instructor on a deployed ship to teach a class to anyone who wished to participate. The classes were very basic, but the course credit was real. We were fortunate enough to get two instructors onboard for our Med cruise. They lived on the ship and were afforded all of the status and respect of an officer, minus the military formalities.

David Meyers taught a History of World War II class. It wasn't his normal expertise, nor was it much of stretch. David had a PHD in Russian history. The class was well attended for obvious reasons. Military men like to learn about war. When it comes to war you can't get much better than WWII.

Professor Nelson Pressman was an Ivy Leaguer. He did his undergraduate work at Yale, then got his doctoral degree at Brown University. He had written two novels and was widely published as an expert in American humor. Now, nearing fifty years old, he had just come through a rather messy divorce. His ex-wife, a divorce lawyer by trade, had found out about his affair with another faculty member. It was best that he left town for a while. He joined our crew, agreeing to teach a basic college English class. It was a step down for such an esteemed academic, but it was a way to disappear. Doc Nelson was the man who convinced me that I should go to college to become a writer.

The first part of Nelson's class covered grammar and syntax. I thought I knew how to write grammatically, but soon proved to be mistaken. He made the needed adjustments. The second portion involved basic writing skills. Our first assignment was to write a two or three-page essay on what our career aspirations would be if we weren't in the Navy. To me it sounded a bit like the "What do you want to be when you grow up?" assignments from second grade. I didn't take it seriously. I wrote ten pages about my future as a corrupt politician, culminating in my ascension to the White House. I would then resign several weeks after taking office for "medical reasons." The real reason would be alcoholism, since all politicians, in my mind, were either drunks or prostitutes or both. I was striving for bitter sarcasm. I hit my mark. Professor Nelson found it to be well written and quite humorous.

The professor believed I was already writing at a college level, well above the rest of the group. At his behest, I met with him after class and received personal instruction. I completed the same assignments as the other students and got the same college credit, but I was allowed to work at my own level. Unbeknownst to me, the doc was so impressed with some of my work that he shared it with several officers on the ship, and even forwarded a few pieces back to his colleagues at Old Dominion. One day while walking across the forward deck of the ship I heard the loud, booming voice of authority behind me. It was Captain Worthington.

"Hey Campbell, I hear you want to be President someday. You ought to try being a sailor first."

I was pretty cocky and not easily intimidated, but Worthington scared the hell out me. I stopped dead in my tracks. "Yes sir," I replied while trying not to look him in the eyes.

"Relax son," he laughed. Dr. Pressman has been reading us some of your writings. I'll take you as a drunk President over half the jokers I've served under. Just remember to pull a few strings for me, will you? I'd like to make Admiral someday. Great stuff. You should keep writing. Keep it clean and not too political, and you'll be fine. You have a talent. I'd love to read more."

I walked away with a spring in my step and my head in the clouds. I decided at that exact moment that I would finish my time in the Navy and become a full-time college student, pursuing a career in writing. I chose journalism over English for the same reason I chose machine shop in school. English and writing are skills. Journalism is a trade. It's blue collar writing. Like most trades, it is marketable in the real world. Two years later I was a freshman at the University of Connecticut, majoring in journalism.

In February of my senior year, I began looking for a job. It wasn't so much a job search as it was an exercise in panic and desperation. The economic downturn of the previous year had finally begun to improve, but for a college student of marginal distinction, it didn't improve much. There were plenty of low paying jobs available, all with the promise of advancement, but I needed a living wage.

The job search was further complicated by the fact that Diane and I had gotten engaged in November and set a wedding date for August of that year. She had two years left of pharmacy school. It wouldn't be long before she was in high demand, but in the meantime, we still had to find a way to make ends meet.

This was a tumultuous time for journalism. The electronic media was about to explode, as cable television and computer technology struggled through its infancy. Fledgling networks like CNN, ESPN and MTV offered an exciting alternative to the stagnant mainstream networks. Despite being a forward-thinking individual, I chose to concentrate on print media. I interviewed with almost every major newspaper in Southern New England, as well as several magazines. Twice I was offered minimum wage to work in the mailroom. Two other publications wanted me to sell ad space for commission. I did get offered one writing job; doing obituaries for the New London Day. For that they would pay me $6.50 an hour. It was more than minimum wage, but hardly enough to live on. I declined, but by early April it was my best offer to date.

I went on every interview offered, regardless of the job, pay, or qualifications. Often my meetings were for non-journalistic positions. I figured I could earn a paycheck working forty hours a week while still looking for a job in my chosen field. With that notion in mind, I became an assistant manager for Brigham's Supermarket, earning a hefty $7.90 an hour. That may sound rather pathetic for a college graduate and aspiring writer, but it paid the rent. For now, it was the best I could do.

I knew nothing of retail. I caught on quickly, but any job that is unfamiliar is not easy. The first thing I learned was how to be exhausted all of the time. Fifty hours a week was a short schedule. All of it was spent on my feet, on concrete floors, in uncomfortable shoes. I may have been in the best shape of my life, but my knees, legs and feet experienced adventures in pain that exceeded anything they had previously known. The people there were nice, and I tried to do a good job, but I hated it. I have great respect for anyone who works in the retail profession, but it just wasn't the job for me.

Diane and I were married on August 10th in Bridgeport, Connecticut. We spent the next five days honeymooning in Key West, Florida. We walked the island, spent long hours dancing and drinking and doing pretty much whatever else you might expect newlyweds to be doing. Master Card had been foolish enough to give me a credit card with a two-thousand-dollar limit. By the time we returned home, we were tanned, rested, and completely maxed out on the card. I also returned with the resolve to find a new job. In September Diane returned to pharmacy school, and I began banging on every door, to beg for a writing job. Had the New London Day still needed an obituary writer, I would have gladly taken it.

Sometimes the universe decides to do something weird. You can call it Karma, or divine intervention, or synchronicity. I just call it weird. On September 19th, I came face to face with a heavy dose of cosmic insanity.

For two weeks prior, I had been on the phone, mailing and faxing the Hartford Daily Examiner. It was the second largest newspaper in the state, competing head to head with the Hartford Courant. Earlier in the week, I had met Diane for lunch and ran into one of my former professors, Mark Woodward. He knew people at the Examiner and offered to let me use his name. Mark's friend Larry Bergenstrom was the head of the marketing department at the paper, but he also had close ties with the editors. Larry knew they were looking to take on a couple of cub reporters. I got my resume to Bergenstrom, who in turn passed it on to Fred Vaughn, the Editor in Chief. After several phone calls and a little pleading, I finally landed an interview with Fred.

This was to be my big break and I was determined not to screw it up. Fred had a terrible reputation as a tough, no-nonsense guy, in the tradition of the old-time news editors. He was widely known as a cigar chomping, foul mouth, ass grabbing, bourbon swilling, mean old bastard. At five-foot four and over two hundred pounds, he was a heart attack waiting to happen, but it was believed he might never die because neither heaven nor hell wanted him. Fred had four ex-wives, countless mistresses, and six kids, all of whom hated everything but his wallet. The job always came first. For over forty years the paper had been his life. Fred held the top position for most of that time. The paper was called the Hartford Examiner, but it may just as well have been the Vaughn Times.

The interview was for 7:30am on September 19th. For two days prior, I spent long hours at the library, devouring every morsel of information available about the paper and its notorious editor. I learned that the paper had been founded in 1873 as an alternate bias to the Courant. It was a time of unrest as the post-Civil War Reconstruction was in full swing. The Industrial Revolution was also heating up and immigration was becoming a major political issue. While the Courant embraced social unrest, the Examiner became the voice of commerce. It was Connecticut's answer to the Wall Street Journal. Business filled the front page, but the paper also covered high society along with local happenings.

Since the Courant came out in the morning, the Examiner began as an afternoon edition. In 1901 it switched to a morning paper and a tabloid format, becoming the moral equivalent of the Washington Times as it compares to the Washington Post. Like the Times it never quite reached the readership of its rival, but found a comfortable niche that enabled the paper to be consistently profitable.

As for Fred Vaughn, I learned that he began there, sweeping floors and emptying trash when he was thirteen years old. After high school he entered Trinity College to get his journalism degree, while still working at the paper. Fred got his first reporting gig in 1948, during his senior year at Trinity. President Truman was making an early morning campaign stop on campus. Vaughn not only got a front row seat at the event, but while pretending to be a big-shot reporter, he bribed the head of security who gave him a few moments backstage with the President. By noon he returned to the Examiner bearing photos and an exclusive interview. Two days later Fred dropped out of Trinity and began a full-time job writing political copy.

In the years that followed, his work would earn him enemies and accolades, as well as two Pulitzers. Circulation increased, and for many years the Examiner challenged the Courant for dominance. Meanwhile Fred moved quickly up the ranks through hard work, posturing and backstabbing. It's not that he was dishonest, Fred just out-hustled everyone else. In 1963 it was Fred's work covering the Kennedy assassination that propelled him to Editor in Chief.

The night before my interview, I practiced for several hours in front of the mirror rehearsing answers to every possible question he might ask. I wanted to be confident but not cocky. I gassed the car up, polished my shoes and made a point of getting to bed early so I would be alert and well rested. Sleep didn't come. The alarm was set for five o'clock. I finally dozed off around three. Coffee and nerves would have to get me by. Knowing that Hartford traffic could be brutal, I allowed an hour for what should have been a half hour drive. Thanks to a jack-knifed tractor trailer and a busted water main near Albany Avenue, I arrived at my interview seven minutes late

Since I was late, Fred had Lois, his secretary, move up his eight o'clock appointment. After some pleading I got her to reschedule me for nine o'clock. Waiting outside his office was a little bit like waiting outside a confessional to see a priest, while the person in front of you was being excommunicated. Through the office door I could hear him demanding that God damns everything and everybody within earshot. I counted five times that his fist banged on the desk. Twice the phone slammed onto the receiver, and on four separate occasions he paged Lois, to find this goddamn paper, or get some stupid asshole on the line for him. By the time the door opened and it was my turn, I was cold, sweaty and had to pee very badly from all the coffee I had consumed. Mostly I was wondering what I was doing there and why anyone would ever agree to work for this guy.

I extended my damp, clammy hand and greeted the short fat bastard. Stammering, I blurted out, "Mr. Vaughn, I'm Ralph Campbell. Thanks for taking the time to meet with me."

His short, stubby fingers wrapped halfway around my palm. He quickly pulled away, wiping his hand on his slacks. "Jesus kid, your hand is soaking wet. Where the hell did you have it last? Scratch that. I don't want to know."

"Sorry sir, I know I'm late and I'm a bit nervous. There were a couple of accidents and a water main break."

"You should be nervous goddammit and stop making excuses." Vaughn continued talking as he led me into his office. It was a large corner room with two walls of windows on the eleventh floor of what is commonly referred to as The Gold Building. The other walls were covered with various awards and citations, all centered around his Pulitzers. He didn't tell me to sit, but there was only one chair across from his large oak desk so I helped myself. Something told me I wouldn't be sitting very long. "You've got two strikes against you and you shake hands like you're holding a piece of raw flounder. I'll give you five minutes to change my mind and convince me that you're not a total waste of my time. Why do you want to be in newspapers?"

I had anticipated that question and rehearsed it thoroughly. Silently I smiled. "I enjoy the craft of writing," I replied. "I'm good at it. To me, newspaper journalism is the purest form of writing. The reporter is charged with telling the story truthfully in the fewest words possible while still making it interesting and readable. I want to be a part of that."

"What a pile of horseshit. Is that what they're teaching you college boys? If it is, then you just wasted four years and they're wasting my tax money. Viva the fucking humanities. Viva taxpayer funded higher education. Idealistic bullshit. Now you are down to two minutes. So, tell me mister idealistic college boy, what do you think the most important tools are for a good reporter?"

I hesitated for a moment, not because I was stumped by the question, but because I had rehearsed that one too. If my last response was any indication I had better scrap the rehearsed stuff and wing it. This time I fared a little better.

"Writing skills and time management," I blurted out.

He reached into his humidor, pulled out a Cohiba and bit the end off. Spitting the end at me, Fred Vaughn then rolled the cigar back and forth between those stubby fingers and stuck it in the corner of his mouth. "Half right," he growled. "Writing skills don't mean shit. You have to write like a fifth grader so the idiots who read this crap can understand it. Time management counts. The more you can squeeze into the day the better you can be. The other thing is connections. You have to have contacts everywhere for everything. People you can call to gain access. People you can lean on for a story even when no story exists. Contacts are everything in this business.'

With that comment, Fred Vaughn pressed both hands down hard on the table and stood up. Yanking the cigar from his maw he growled, "Your five minutes are up. I don't hire people who show up late and give rehearsed answers, so get out. Go next door to the Courant. If they hire you it will improve my circulation." With that, he, blew a plume of smoke and turned his back to me, tapping the intercom button as he stepped away from the desk. "Lois, the kid here is done. Who's next?"

I stood for a moment in stunned silence. There was a brief instant when I thought I might burst into tears. Instead, I simply placed my folder of writing samples on his desk, spun around and got out as quickly as I could. In the elevator I had trouble breathing. My face was flushed as I raced outside, gasping for fresh air. Once on the street, I was met with the pungent mixture of urban smells. Trash, urine and bus fumes. Glancing down the street I found a payphone. There was no need to bother. Diane was in classes until late afternoon. Rather than go straight home I walked the streets of downtown Hartford for an hour or more until the emotional kick in the crotch had somewhat subsided.

Diane stopped home for lunch around 1pm. She did her best to console me, but by that time my self-pity had turned to anger. That anger intensified when the mail came, delivering two past due bills. They say two can live as cheaply as one, and that may be true, but one couldn't live on the income I was making. Fred

Vaughn was a bastard and I hated him. I poured myself a shot of cheap vodka and cursed again. Then the phone rang. It was Mark Woodward, the professor who had helped me get the Vaughn interview. When I told him how it went, he didn't seem surprised.

"Look," he offered, "at least you got that far. Most people don't even get into the office. Vaughn was right about one thing. Contacts are everything. I'll tell you what, I'm getting together with a few friends, all in the print business. We're meeting this afternoon at the Pitkin Street Pub, in Manchester. Why don't you meet us there? Do you know where it is?"

"Yeah, I've been there."

"Good. Get there around four-thirty. Just sit at the bar and I'll call you over to the table. You'll have to put up with a bunch of blowhards tell lies to each other, but at least you can make contact with a few more people. Besides, they really aren't a bad group of guys. Oh, and be sure to tell them you're a vet. Two of the guys did stints in Viet Nam."

I couldn't afford the luxury of a bar tab. There was twenty bucks in my wallet and less than two-hundred dollars in checking. The car needed gas and payday was still four days away. Diane gave me a stern look that showed just a small hint of sympathy. "It better be happy hour."

My old Chevy Nova had over 200,000 miles and a V-8 engine that guzzled gas. I put in five dollars knowing that it would barely nudge the needle. The pub was twenty minutes away. I left around four, opting to take I-84 to West Middle Turnpike and then head down Main Street.

As I drove to Manchester my head was still in overload. I couldn't help but to second guess myself for how I had prepared for the morning's interview, for not allowing more time to get there, and for not offering a stronger rebuttal to Fred Vaughn's verbal assaults. I now had to redirect that insecurity and anger, while somehow appearing to be relaxed and glib in this next en-counter. It wasn't an interview, but it was an opportunity.

Turning right from West Middle Turnpike on to North Main Street I considered for a moment that it might not be a bad idea to stop at the 7-11 on the left for a pack of gum or breath mints. Again, I was thinking too much. Those thoughts abruptly ended as I passed through the next intersection, only to have my pas-senger's side door slammed into by a white Lincoln Continental that had burst from the parking lot of the Silk City Tavern. There was the earsplitting sound of metal colliding with metal; then everything stopped. I knew the door was smashed. No glass was broken and it seemed unlikely that anyone was injured. I mo-tioned to the short, fat silhouette in the Lincoln, indicating that we needed to get off the road. The white car retreated back to Silk City's lot. I followed him to the far corner by the dumpster.

This was the crowning jewel on a perfectly screwed up day. I watched with both horror, and disbelief as an obviously drunk little man emerged from the long white car. It was Fred Vaughn. I paused for a moment before stepping out to confront him. First I was angry, then amused. Then I burst into a fit of laughter. That involuntary reaction proved even harder to control when Fred saw me emerge from my vehicle. The cantankerous old man looked perplexed. It took a moment to clear the fog before he finally remembered our previous encounter.

Fred Vaughn looked long and hard at me, pausing to col-lect himself to choose the right words. It wasn't exactly eloquent. "Camby? Ain't you Ralph Camby?" he slurred. "What the hell are you doing in Manchester?"

"Getting my car smashed into by some drunk old bastard who has suddenly found himself in a world of shit." The indignity of our morning meeting came flooding back, enveloping me with rage. "Payback is a bitch, Mr. Vaughn. Let's step inside so I can call the cops. How shitfaced are you, old man? Can you walk or should I just kick your fat ass through the door?"

"Lissen Camby, let's go inside and talk..."

"Campbell you stupid fuck. The name is Campbell."

"Okay, okay. You're pissed off. I get it. I was hard on you this morning. I understand that, but I was just trying to help you. The newspaper business isn't for lightweights. Let's go inside. I'll get a coffee, you get a drink. I'm buying. Let's talk."

"There isn't a goddamn thing that I want to talk to you about. I just want to see your fat ass getting shoved into a cruiser and carted off to jail. That, and I want my car fixed."

"Hey, hey, hey. There's a lot to talk about. Namely your new job. Seriously, I like you. I didn't see it this morning but I sure as hell see it now. You have the fire and the attitude it takes. I was going to call you anyway. I looked at the writing samples you left behind. Not bad. Not bad at all."

"This is bullshit."

As reality set in, the small round man began to sober up. Speaking more articulately than at any other time today, he looked at me with pleading eyes. I was unsympathetic, but I was listening. "Look kid, I can be a mean old son of a bitch. It's just who I am. I was a prick to you this morning and you have every right to be hot. Now you have me by the shorthairs. I have a prior DUI from a few months ago and a suspended license. If you call the cops I'm going to jail. That's a story I don't want to see get written."

"Okay. I'll go inside but you know this is going to cost you."

"Yeah, that's what my ex-wives said and they were right."

When we walked into the bar the owner immediately raced to Fred's side. "What happened Fred? Is everything alright?"

Vaughn quickly waved him away. "Yeah, yeah, everything's fine. I just ran into an old friend. Give the kid a drink will you."

"Cutty on the rocks."

"The usual Fred?"

"Just coffee. I've had enough for one day."

It wasn't much of a negotiation. I didn't know enough about the business to know what to ask for. I also didn't want to find myself in a position where I might fail. Lucky for me, this was one time when the fat, drunk, bastard was sort of reasonable. We settled on a base salary of $22,000 a year with additional payments for special assignments and featured articles. I would get three weeks of training, tailing reporters from various desks at the paper. My first solo assignments would be covering high school and college sports. Lots of nights and weekends, but not the worst gig to have. The truth is, for $22,000 he could have offered me obituaries and I would have taken it. Before we shook on the deal there was still one problem to resolve.

"Uh, Fred?"

"Yeah kid?"

"What about my car?"

"What do you mean?"

"What do you mean what do I mean? You smashed into my car and the passenger side door is caved in. The job is great and we have agreed I won't call the cops, but I still have a smashed-up car that I can't afford to get fixed."

"Isn't handing you the job of your dreams enough?"

"No. It's not a deal until you take care of my car."

Mumbling under his breath, he reached into his wallet and pulled out a bank roll that was twice the thickness of a deck of cards. Peeling off five one-hundred-dollar bills, he said "You better be the best damn reporter I ever hired."

I'm pretty sure I was.

CHAPTER TWELVE

For some couples getting pregnant is easy. Too easy. A flirtatious wink and a wry smile. Before long you are picking out names and coming up with excuses as to how this could have happened.

There seems to be a direct relationship between your desire to get pregnant and your ability to accomplish this feat. If you are a teenager, unemployed, nearing bankruptcy or have just had a one-night stand, your odds of getting knocked up are pretty good. Be on sound financial and emotional footing and you might as well forget about it. There will be more complications than you ever imagined.

Diane always knew she wanted to have kids. By the time we got married she was already well past the point where most of her friends had started their families. A few of her former classmates already had teenagers. Her maternal skills were based on a very simple premise: Don't make the same mistakes that her mother made. Diane always thought her mother was too authoritarian and self-centered. Her dad was everyone's friend. He was a nice guy, who worked hard, while struggling to support his family. Often that meant two or three jobs, but he did it willingly. Mom ran both the house and her father. He was the paycheck, but she was the matriarch. Mary Simmons was essentially a benevolent dictator. She had none of the violent tendencies of Carmen, but when crossed she could become cold and insensitive. Diane felt she had been largely ignored by her mother throughout her teen years. She vowed that if she ever had kids of her own, they would be given an unlimited supply of love and attention.

That is not to say that she didn't have some concerns about starting a family. When she was nineteen, she became unexpectedly pregnant. Her boyfriend disappeared as soon as he got the news. A college friend helped to arrange a backroom abortion by a second-year medical student. It went surprisingly well. She was lucky. There are plenty of stories of rusty knife surgeries leading to infections and hemorrhaging. That was not the case. There was some discomfort, but no long term physical scars. The emotional scars, however, ran deep. Diane would forever be haunted by the potential life she left behind.

We waited two years before trying to get pregnant. Kids are expensive and we wanted to make sure we had some degree of financial stability. By that time, Diane had graduated from pharmacy school and was making fourteen dollars an hour at North End Pharmacy, a small independent drug store in Manchester. I was firmly established at the paper, moving quickly from local to national sports. My next stop was Staff Reporter, where I might be assigned at any time to any story. In two years my salary had risen past $30,000. We were both making good money and things were looking up. The time was right.

While Diane sure, I had strong apprehensions about becoming a parent. Given my past, the idea scared me. What did I know about raising kids? I had no role models. All I had was examples of what not to do. That's a far cry from knowing how to do the right thing. I liked the way our lives were going. We liked our jobs. Financially we were in good shape. In May we decided to indulge ourselves by buying a new Mustang convertible. The next step would be to buy a home. Diane had her eye on a small Cape

Cod style house, on a nicely groomed half acre, in the small town of Bickford. It was an older house, that needed work, but it had potential. With everything starting to go our way, I began to wonder why we should take a chance and maybe screw everything up.

While I may have doubted to myself, I never did so out loud. Outwardly I professed to want children every bit as much as Diane did. I lied. What I really wanted was the status quo. Live comfortably, eat well, party with friends and travel. This sounded great, but the reality was different. We lived comfortably, but often worked long and opposing hours so we didn't see a whole lot of each other. Eating well usually meant that if we were home together we would go out for pizza or get takeout Chinese food. If there was enough time for a nice sit-down dinner, we were too tired to cook. As for our friends, they were all busy having kids. If we were to continue to commiserate with them, we would have to produce some offspring of our own. We tried, but it wasn't easy.

Sex is both natural and fun. Having sex when you are trying to get pregnant takes a bit of the spontaneous joy out of it. I'm not complaining. I have always considered myself a team player. I was more than willing to give it my best effort. In the end, it became questionable as to whether my best effort was good enough. It took far longer than expected. Six years, to be exact.

The first year was more fun than effort. We abandoned all forms of birth control, and simply did what came naturally. It didn't result in a pregnancy, but there was still no cause for alarm. For now, we were leaving it up to chance. If it happened great. Relying upon science, religion, and the paranormal would come later.

By the second year we became more aware of monthly cycles. There was the unmistakable look of disappointment on Diane's face every time she got her period. We calculated when her most fertile time of the month would be and tried to put a little more effort into achieving our goal. By the end of the second year we began to suspect that something may be wrong. Diane had her gynecologist give her a complete physical. Tests were run. Results were all negative. The doctor assured Diane that she was in perfect child bearing health.

By the third year we began to get questions from friends and family. Diane figured if we simply told everyone that we were trying, they would leave us alone. She figured wrong. Instead it opened a floodgate of well-intentioned but completely useless advice. Probably the worst and most often given advice was, "Just relax. You're trying too hard." What the hell is that supposed to mean? Take two Xanax before going to bed? Practice meditation? Could you be a little more specific please? And how do you try too hard? Are these people imagining that we are going at it three times a day seven day a week? Or that we were studying "The Complete Idiots Guide to Getting Pregnant"? Comments like that were well intentioned, incredibly stupid and only added to our stress.

By the fourth year there was real concern and a little bit of panic. We began seeing specialists. Diane had ultrasounds, biopsies and numerous extremely unpleasant exams. I provided so many sperm samples that for the rest of my life the mere sight of a small Tupperware cup was cause for arousal. After months of tests, office visits and exams, we finally got an answer. The problem wasn't Diane; it was me. Low motility, low morphology. In simple terms, I had underachieving sperm. This didn't do much for my manly ego, but at least it was an answer. The doctors assured us that this was not an insurmountable problem. There were procedures they could do. They told us not to worry. Easy for them to say. They weren't the ones who were getting poked, or told they had inferior sperm.

The first option to consider was donor sperm. This had a

fairly high rate of success, but we quickly ruled it out. Any child of ours would be the two of us or none of us. There was no in-between. The second option was a procedure by which I gave a sperm sample. It was then taken to the lab where the most active and healthy little guys were concentrated, and the delinquent sperm were discarded. During ovulation, this sample would be placed in almost direct contact with the egg. Diane, meanwhile, would receive regular shots of a fertility drug that would increase the likelihood of success. It was expensive, and the success rate was around twenty-percent per cycle. Other options were discussed but seemed less promising. We went with option number two. While the hope was that we would get pregnant on the first try, the odds were not in our favor. It was recommended that we take up to six tries, alternating with a month off in-between before giving up or going broke.

Several doctors asked if adoption was a consideration. A few had contacts with various agencies. We had discussed the option but left it as our last resort. We were told that even if adoption was a last resort, we needed to get started immediately. There were a lot of other people in the same predicament. They were all considering adoption. The process could be long, difficult and frustrating. Get on every list possible. If you got pregnant, you could always remove yourself from consideration.

Every week I poked Diane with needles. Next, we would closely monitor her cycles. At the appropriate time we raced to the clinic so I could "produce a specimen." Then without fail and right on schedule Diane would get her period. Usually this would happen when I was away from the office and on assignment. I would come home to find her sobbing hysterically. After the second time I didn't have to ask what was wrong.

That is not to imply that all we ever did was visit doctors and work on getting pregnant. Diane changed jobs and began working at Saint Joseph's Geriatric Hospital in West Hartford. The job was more money and Diane flourished in a clinical setting. Meanwhile, I had written a series of articles about organized crime in Hartford that garnered me a few accolades. The piece was picked up by Connecticut Magazine. In late April with a few extra dollars from the articles, we spent five days in Bermuda.

We took the Bermuda trip shortly after the fifth failed fertilization attempt. It was a much-needed escape. The burden of endless doctor visits, a hectic work schedule and the monthly disappointment made it an absolute necessity. We strolled the pink sand beaches and drank in British pubs. By now we had been together for almost eight years. The relationship was on solid ground, but it was a good time to assess where we were, where we were going, and how we should get there. This was hashed out over a warm Spring evening, at a tavern on the outskirts of Hamilton.

The Dark and Stormy is a wonderful drink that is very popular on the island. It is a simple concoction of Gosling Black Rum and ginger beer. It was over many glasses of this beverage, along with a rack of lamb and roasted red potatoes that we decided to modify our plans. The attempts at artificial insemination had become too stressful. We would give it two more tries. If that failed, we would quit. All efforts would be then devoted towards adoption.

If adoption was the way to go, there had to be some parameters. The first was that we didn't want a black or Asian baby. This decision was not out of any prejudice or malice. We both agreed that it would be easier for all concerned if the adoptive child looked like it could possibly have been conceived by the parents. Since I had a Mediterranean complexion, and Diane was fair skinned, that left us great flexibility. Unfortunately, Asian babies were the most readily available for adoption. There were also poor countries in South and Central America that did adoptions, but they too would probably not look like our own offspring. Our best prospect was Eastern Europe, which was experiencing a great deal of economic turmoil. If an American baby was not available, Europe was the next best bet.

The second parameter was that each agency had to be thoroughly researched and referenced. Religious or political affiliations were not a concern as long as the agency was legitimate. By now we had heard horror stories warning of scams that were long on broken promises. They take advanced deposits and, in some cases, gain access to bank accounts and credit. Then they disappear leaving you penniless and without a baby. Desperate people have always been the most vulnerable to scam artists. The poor, the elderly, the terminally ill, and the childless, are all easy prey to such vermin. I had written several articles on this topic. We would not allow ourselves to be victims.

The third parameter was that the baby should be under a year old. First words, first steps, first teeth, were all signature moments that we did not want to miss out on. A newborn would be ideal, but when dealing with overseas adoptions there was a far greater probability that the baby would be three to nine months old.

We finished off our fifth Dark and Stormy, capped by a dessert of English tea and rice pudding. Pouring ourselves into a cab, we staggered back to the hotel. The following morning, we were hung over, but optimistic and committed to our newly refined plans. A few months later we underwent our final attempt at artificial insemination. Two weeks past the procedure I once again awoke to Diane sobbing in the bathroom. The sixth attempt was our last. We would adopt.

Within three months we were on ten different adoption lists. The wait times were staggering. Catholic Family Services had a waiting list that averaged six years. That seemed odd. I would have thought there would be a lot of promiscuous and careless Catholic girls who didn't believe in abortion. Were they all keeping their kids? A few major hospitals had lists, as did Planned Parenthood. Again, the wait times were long and the prospects unlikely. One social services group offered us a five-year-old black boy. We seriously considered it, but really wanted a baby, so we tabled that offer as a last resort. Rather cruel when you think of it; calling any child a "last resort." Such was our world at that time.

Finally, a friend of a friend of a friend came through. Diane worked with a woman at Saint Joe's who met the daughter of an elderly patient. This daughter's, daughter was adopting a baby from Poland. Recent economic struggles in that nation had left a great many of its citizens facing hard times. Few could afford another mouth to feed.

Poland is over 90% Catholic, and fairly devout at that. Abortion is usually not an option. We learned of an organization in Waterbury that was assisting with adoptions in Poland. They were appropriately called PAL. The Polish-American Adoption League.

The basic requirements were simple but the process was not. One of the would-be parents had to be at least 75% Polish. That was no problem. Diane's immediate family was 100%. Second, one of the adopting parents or one of their parents had to have been born in Poland. Diane's father was, but proving it could be tricky. Jan Szymkowicz Jr. had indeed been born in Poland, but after two world wars, the village of his birth was now part of the Ukraine. Tracking down birth records to prove this might be difficult.

It proved to be less of a problem than we feared. Diane's grandmother came to America to be reunited with her husband, who had arrived several months earlier. He met his wife on the docks. While the baby had no travel papers, she had brought his baptismal records with her from Poland. A sympathetic immigration official created a substitute document and let both mother and child pass through. That baptismal record had been untouched for decades, confined to a desk drawer at Diane's parents' house. Her mother knew exactly where it was. When the time came, we had our proof for the agency.

Proof of ancestry was not the only paper trail. Diane and I each had to write a fifteen-page autobiography, outlining our personal history, courtship and marriage, while further explaining in great detail why we would make good adoptive parents. I wrote extensively about my troubled childhood and how after overcoming those obstacles, I felt it was imperative that I help another child with obstacles of their own. Diane opined on the value of having an ethnic identity, and the joy of passing great customs and traditions along to a future generation.

The authorities were impressed. Kris Sobieski, who ran the Adoption League, told us our autobiographies were the most interesting and moving they had ever read. My tale of tragedy and abuse, coupled with Diane's embracing of all that was Polish pushed us to the top of their list. Things were looking up. The next step consisted of a two-hundred-dollar deposit so they could arrange a face to face interview with officials at the Consulate in New York. This was to gain permission for travel to Poland for the purpose of adoption. P.A.L. would arrange the meeting and notify us of the place, date and time. Kris assured us that this was a legal formality and would not be a problem.

Kris was overoptimistic. There were other worries. Travel to Poland was expensive and difficult. We were also expected to make a five-thousand-dollar donation to the baby's mother. A second trip to Poland might prove to be necessary, because there was always the chance that the birthmother would suddenly back out. The average cost for the whole process would be approximately twelve thousand dollars. Financially we were doing okay, but that was a lot of money. We had a mortgage, a car payment and a fix-er-upper home that was always costing us something. What little money we had saved, went towards failed fertility treatments.

On the afternoon of Wednesday August 18th, I was at my desk finishing off a rather unflattering story about a Connecticut senator, Chris Killian. When you work in the media, you get to rub shoulders with some big-shots. Most are jerks. I never liked Chris, and negative press sold papers. When the phone rang just after 1pm I assumed it was his office, trying to intimidate me. Instead it was Kris from P.A.L. The conversation was short and joyous.

"It's a go. Can you be in New York for 10am on Saturday?"

"One of us or both?"

"Both."

"We'll be there. Where do we go? What do we bring?"

"I have two packets for you. One has instructions, so you will be prepared for the interview. The other has the legal documents they will need. You will also need a two-hundred-dollar bank check for processing fees. Can you stop by my office before Friday?"

"How late will you be there today?"

"I'm here until five."

"I'll see you in forty-five minutes." I dropped everything, stuck my head in Fred's office, and said "I'm gone for the day. Family problem. I'll have the Killian story on your desk by nine tomorrow morning. Lots of dirt. You'll love it." Then I left.

Kris was all smiles. She said the timing might never be better. The recent Warsaw elections played heavily in our favor. More importantly, PAL just got word that there were several prospective birthmothers entering their last trimester. We should plan on going to Poland in late September.

The newspaper business is never nine to five. Some days you work a twelve-hour shift, sometimes it's overnight, other days you get home early. Still, it was rare for me to be home before five. Diane's normal shift at the hospital was either 8 to 4 or 2 to 10. When we both pulled into the driveway at 3:15 there was some concern.

Two questions. Two answers. The same question. The same answer.

"Is everything okay? What are you doing home so early?"

"Everything is fine. I have big news."

"What?"

"We are going to Poland to get a baby"

"I'm pregnant."

"Holy shit," I blurted. "No shit?"

"No shit."

"What do we do now?"

There are two, maybe three plausible theories as to how we got pregnant. All or none of them may be true. The one I'm sticking with is the "Father knows best" theory. As previously mentioned, we were constantly inundated with annoying advice that was of no use to anyone. We didn't need advice. We knew how babies were made, and we knew that fate had given us a few obstacles. These challenges actually solidified our marriage. Overall, we grew closer as we endured our struggles together.

Surprisingly, our infertility also helped mend some fences between myself and my dad.

By now the Carmen era was behind us. Dad had again remarried; this time to a wonderful woman named Beverly. The ice began to melt. Little by little I began to realize that we had more in common than I wished to admit. Infertility was one of them. My father and mother tried for several years to get pregnant before my sister Marty miraculously came along. Dad never talked much about it, not because it was a secret, but because he felt it was a knock on his virility. I harbored no such ego, but it was nice to know he understood my plight.

"Everyone wants to help and everyone's an expert," he would say when we talked by phone. "Be nice, but don't listen to any of them. They're all full of shit."

Those were the words of someone who knew. He never offered advice, because he remembered how sick and tired he was of getting it. The only advice he ever gave proved to be both accurate and prophetic.

On a Saturday night in January, Diane and I met Dad and Beverly at Giordano's, a small Italian restaurant on 14 Street in New York. I was doing some freelance work for a popular monthly magazine. Diane and I spent the day in the city, so I could research a story about changes in Manhattan's ethnic neighborhoods. We had met Dad and Bev at Giordano's before. The food there was amazing. Much of the talk was about the story I was doing, but as you might expect, conversation drifted into other areas, including the forbidden topic of pregnancy and adoption.

Towards the end of the evening Dad leaned across the table to me and said "Let me tell you the truth that no one else will ever tell you. Your problem is simple. You are doing too well. You're not far enough in debt. Everyone knows that kids are expensive. Mortgage yourself to the hilt. Get yourself so goddamn far in hock that you can barely pay your bills. Do that and I guarantee kids will come."

What Dad didn't know was that we were doing just that. First, we bought another new car. A beautiful black Honda Accord. It was fully loaded and looked like a poor man's Mercedes. Then we put the house up for sale. If we were to start a family, we needed a bigger home. The housing market was booming so we decided to sell and trade up. If all went well, we would soon have a big house in a nice neighborhood while more than doubling our mortgage payments. Our jobs were secure, and we were making good money, so in addition to the house and car, we bought everything in sight, stretching our credit and cash flow to the limit.

Dad insisted that the reason my mother got pregnant with Martha was because he got fired from his job as a truck driver. He was doing deliveries for a local oil company in Jersey City but got caught taking side trips on company time. When he smashed the truck while visiting his cousin Tony in Brooklyn, he not only lost his job but got saddled with the cost of repairs.

That was my father's version of how to get pregnant, and given the results, who am I to argue, but there was more to the story than that. My mother's version, as recounted by family lore, was quite different. As a young child, Mom had rheumatic fever. The doctors said that while they couldn't be certain, there was the possibility that she would be infertile. Like most newlyweds, Angelo and Camille didn't think much about the possibility of going childless. They assumed the doctors were wrong. They were young and in love and sure that they would soon start a family. After several years of no children, along with countless annoying questions by family members, they began seeking professional help. Infertility was very primitive as a medical specialty. Options were few and prospects were bleak. There was a distinct possibility that they might never conceive, but no one knew for sure.

The idea that no one knew for sure didn't set well with Camille. As a good Catholic she was confident that God knew. Silently she prayed every night and often throughout the day. Dad would catch her mumbling something to herself. When he asked what she had just said, she simply replied "Oh, nothing. Just thinking out loud." He knew. Every Sunday they went to church and on several occasions stayed afterward to speak with the pastor. Camille asked that he offer up special prayers for her.

Father Raphael was eager to comply, but also asked that they stop by the rectory on Monday night for "couples counseling." Dad balked at this. They didn't need couples counseling. They got along fine. They just couldn't pregnant. He could have argued the point but didn't.

Father Raphael was a short, stout man in his mid-fifties. A kind old gent, he had a booming voice and a distinct Napolitano accent that my parents had no problem understanding. The good priest spent an hour or so discussing the virtues of Saint Gerard Majella. Raphael had several books and pamphlets which he loaned them. Saint Gerard is the patron of mothers, difficult pregnancies, and childless couples. Pray to Saint Gerard he urged. Father Raphael also expressed a mild concern that problems such as infertility could put a strain on a couple's relationship. He suggested they go away for a weekend. He told them of a small shrine to Saint Gerard, just past Cornell University in Ithaca. Enjoy a day or two on the shores of Lake Cayuga, visit the shrine, and just be happy.

It all sounded too easy, but on Labor Day weekend Angelo and Camille drove eight hours to Ithaca. When they returned late Monday night, they were pregnant.

Dad never told me that story, rightfully assuming I would have dismissed it as coincidence or farce. Instead, at a family gathering he told Diane's mother. Mary Simmons immediately went to work. She knew of a priest named Father Walter Kopek who was believed by some to be a healer. His parish was in Queens, but he regularly passed through Bridgeport. After several phone calls, Mary learned that Father Walter would be conducting a healing service in New Haven. She told Diane and they agreed to go. I knew nothing of this. The service was to be held at an auditorium at Yale University on a Saturday night in late July.

Diane was never a good liar and I am not naïve, but when she told me she was meeting her mother in New Haven to go shopping, I thought nothing of it. Since it gave me the night free, I made plans to go to a minor league baseball game in New Britain with a couple of friends. She would stay the night at her parents and return Sunday afternoon.

The service was packed. The two arrived early and sat in the third row. For a small donation to charity, Father Walter would invoke a special prayer on your behalf. Diane put twenty dollars in an envelope that was marked Saint Jude's Hospital. Her mother put in ten. For the better part of an hour, the charismatic pastor spoke of the healing powers of faith. All things are possible through God. He also did his best to offer a simplistic and not too dogmatic explanation as to why bad things happen. Why this disease? Why this accident? Why this personal tragedy? Things happen for a reason. God has a plan. Tonight, he would ask God to remove the suffering of his servants and accept that they have fulfilled their calling.

At the end of the service a line formed for those who wished to have Father Walter touch them as they asked to be healed. The most infirm went first. A parade of wheelchairs rolled past the altar. Diane was among the first group that followed. Upon arriving at the altar Mary addressed the priest. "My daughter can't get pregnant. Her husband can't be here tonight so I am here for him. Please help them Father."

Walter looked kindly on the two and placed his hand on Diane's stomach. He then softly recited a prayer that had something to do with Saint Gerard and the Holy Spirit. Diane fainted, briefly falling to the floor. Walter's assistants helped her back to her feet. She immediately regained her composure, then proceeded on her way.

Three weeks later, Diane and I would return home from work early, meeting each other with incredible news. Diane will always believe that Father Walter made her pregnancy possible. Who am I to say? Strange things happen and they do seem to happen for a reason. As for Dad's recommendation, while Diane was seeing faith-healers, I was hard at work getting us further in debt. We sold our small comfortable home for $120,000 and bought a large four-bedroom colonial in Ellsworth for $220,000. We were broke but happy.

At some point Diane nervously told me of her "shopping trip" to see Father Walter. My first thought was to dismiss it as the power of suggestion. If you believe strongly enough, you then create all the right circumstances to make it so. I believed that then and I believe it now. I also know not to attack anyone for having belief in something greater than themselves. While I did not acknowledge Walter's "powers", I was grateful if, in any way, he contributed to the results.

The pregnancy progressed well and without incident. It was recommended that Diane have an ultrasound and several other tests done. There was no reason to expect complications beyond our difficulty in conceiving. Since we were eager to use whatever tools might be available to us, we readily agreed. The results were all good. We were going to have a healthy baby girl. Caroline Diane Campbell was born at 6am, on April 3rd. Easter Sunday. Do I believe in the power of prayer and an empty bank account? Indeed, I do.

CHAPTER THIRTEEN

Dear Caroline-In times of tragedy and great despair one can either lose faith or take solace in it. There is great comfort in the idea that God has a master plan and that our suffering is part of a greater good. Even when I did hold a fair amount of religious conviction, I never really bought into that notion. Instead I held doubt in the existence of God or at least wrote him off as an absentee landlord. That non-belief caused me greater pain than any tragedy ever could. All too often in life, faith is our only comfort.

On a day to day basis, we go through our lives oblivious to most of what goes on around us. Triumph and tragedy coexist while we move blindly in its midst. Yet, we know that at any minute we might receive a letter, a phone call or a knock on the door that will change our lives forever. I got one such phone call two years after Caroline's birth, on the morning of April 10. There was no foreshadowing. No sense of foreboding. It was a typical Monday morning. At 9:05am I walked over to a nearby cubicle belonging to John MacDonald, our sports editor. With coffee mugs in hand, we talked about baseball and babies. My Yankees versus his Red Sox. My young daughter and his twin boys. At 9:09, copy editor Frank Carlson called over to me. "Ralph, you have a call on 101. She says it's important."

"My wife?"

"Don't think so."

"Got it."

In the split second before lifting the receiver, my mind raced and took inventory. A woman. Says it's important. Did I forget to return a call? A breaking story? A missed dentist appointment? Nothing registered. I picked up the call. It was my sister Marty.

"Did Beverly call you?"

"No, why?"

"Then you don't know?"

"Know what?"

"Dad had a heart attack."

"Oh no. Shit. Hang on. Let me grab a piece of paper." My reporter instincts kicked in as I bombarded her with questions. "When? Where? How's he doing? What hospital? Marty's cracked voice interrupted.

"He didn't make it."

Silence. Stunned silence.

"Shit," I whispered. "Are you still in Florida?"

"Yeah, I'm home. Rick and I have a 12:30 flight to Newark."

"Where are you staying?"

"We got a room at the Holiday Inn in Long Branch. We booked four days. Do you want the number?"

"Yeah. Will four days be enough?"

"I think so. I don't really know much more right now."

"Diane's working at the hospital. I'll track her down. We should be in Jersey by early evening. When you get in, leave a message for me at the desk. If I get there first I'll do the same."

As the line went dead a cold numbness overtook me. For a moment there was a flashback to the fire we had on the Havasu.

One thing the military teaches is that in time of crisis you must put all emotions aside and stay focused. The circumstances demand rational action, not emotional wreckage. I began moving quickly and thinking even faster. First, I burst into Fred Vaughn's office. As usual he was screaming insults into the phone at someone. He put his hand over the receiver.

"What the…"

"Big problem…" I told him of my phone call.

The perpetually cantankerous patriarch was surprisingly empathetic. He had completely alienated whatever family he once had. Let others learn from his mistakes. "Do what you have to do. Take whatever time you need; but call me when you get settled in Jersey. I may need you to run an errand while you are down there." Despite his rare moment of compassion, the job was always there. I didn't mind. I shared Fred's drive for the business. Besides, a side project might provide some needed distraction.

Next was Diane. I had to be careful with this call. We had just seen Dad and Beverly a week ago. They had come up for Caroline's birthday. It was there we announced that Diane was pregnant again. It was a very good day. Now tragedy strikes. Two weeks later it would strike again when Diane miscarried. Life had been going well. It was about to suck for a while.

There was calm in Diane's voice when I told her about Dad. What I heard was an immediate concern for my mental wellbeing. I assured her I was fine, but in truth it was just adrenaline. I booked the room at the Holiday Inn. Caroline would come with us. Diane would have to pick her up at the sitter because the kid seat was in her car. Hopefully we could hit the road by three and miss part of rush hour.

On the way home, I stopped at a Dunkin Donuts and grabbed a cup of coffee. Caffeine was probably the last thing I needed, but the hot bitter taste would do until we got to New Jersey and I could have a drink. I noticed there was sports memorabilia shop next door. Almost instinctively I wandered in and called out to the owner. "I need a Carl Furillo Brooklyn Dodger card and a Gil Hodges Mets manager card. You got any?"

The proprietor wasn't sure, but after some fumbling came up with two 1953 Bowman Series Carl Furillo cards. No luck on Hodges. I bought both cards for thirty dollars. One would go in the casket. The other one I kept. Carl was Dad's favorite player. They called him the Reading Rifle, so dubbed because he hailed from Reading, PA. The rifle was his arm. For nearly twelve years he patrolled right field for the Brooklyn team, then hung on for a couple more after the Dodgers moved to Los Angeles. He was a fan favorite; particularly to those of Italian descent.

Marty and Rick were at the hotel when we arrived around 7pm. Together we drove to Dad's house. Two days of preparation would be followed by an evening wake and a morning funeral. I was not involved in the arrangements. When asked, I ran errands, bought pastries, and entertained nieces and nephews. Otherwise, I tried not to think. There was no attempt to drink my way through the grief because grief had yet to set in. Two years later I would feel the full impact of my loss. This would lead to addictions in alcohol and marijuana. For now, an infrequent beer or Scotch was all that was needed.

There were a few cracks in my armor. On the second day, Mary, Rick, Diane and I, met for breakfast at the nearby Cristo Diner. Dad was a regular there. Somehow, the waitress recognized us, commenting on how much I looked like my father. Later, Martha, Catherine and I went to a local florist to pick out a funeral arrangement from the three of us. It was Dad's florist. Maria, the shopkeeper had seen his name in the paper and cut out the obituary to remind herself to send condolences. It was taped to the wall behind the cash register. Maria spoke affectionately of how, almost every week, he would stop there on his way home from work, to pick up roses or a small bouquet to surprise Beverly.

Often, he would bring Maria a coffee from the bakery next door. A simple act of kindness. Since he was buying himself a coffee, perhaps Maria would want one too. She never told him, but she only drank tea. "A nice man," she said. "Not just a customer, but a friend. I will really miss him." As we began to look at our floral options her words echoed in my head. A nice man. A friend. I will miss him. The room spun and my throat tightened. I raced outside and sat on the stoop, trying to regain my composure. The others let me be. They too would have their moments.

Most of us, by the time we reach our thirties, have had the misfortune of attending several wakes. Usually you try to get in and out as quickly as possible. You stand in line, pause for a moment over the body, then mumble trite condolences to the bereaved. Nobody wants to attend, least of all the corpse, but it is an obligation and we all must play our part.

When you are the bereaved it's a little different. Your first duty is to try and hold your emotions in check. Just as attendees have a duty to show up and express sympathy, you have a duty to remain stoic and respond to their acknowledgements. Often the brief conversation consists of introductions. Old friends, distant relatives, and coworkers make up the majority of the procession. "You must be Ralph. I'm Harold Rosenfeld. I worked with your father for many years. I'm sorry for your loss." In return I would reply "Nice to meet you Harold. Thank you for coming." Then on to the next person. "I'm you father's second cousin Ethel and this is my daughter Joan." And so it goes.

We had to be at the funeral home at least a half hour before the wake started. There were things we had to do. First, we had to make sure everything was in order. Flowers were arranged properly. Sympathy cards would be placed in a basket. Once we were satisfied with the arrangements, we had a "private viewing." If you are going to lose it, this is the time. I was okay. Three shots of Scotch before leaving the hotel helped. Even without liquor I was numb. Military training had kicked in again. Act now, feel later. Do what you have to do to get through it. For a while I distracted myself with thoughts of the paper. What was it that Fred wanted me to check on? I never did find out.

Beverly arranged for one of her neighbors to stay with Caroline. Diane, Marty, Rick and I would take one car. Bev and her two sons took another. Cat and her husband Brad met us there. We were met at the door by John Tortollo, the director who took us through the process. One thing that immediately both-ered me was all of the whispering. Why? Were we going to wake the dead? I opted to break this ritual and talk in a normal voice. Soon everyone else followed. Later it occurred to me that this is exactly what Dad would have wanted. If you want to laugh, then laugh. If you want to cry, that's fine too.

John led us to the casket and we all gathered around as they opened the lid. We would first tend to details. Did everything look as it should? Was the body positioned properly? When the lid opened, Beverly crumbled to her knees. One of her sons caught her and gently helped her back up. It was a painful mo-ment but she soon regained composure. The body was fine, but already I began to view it as just a body. It was not my father. We were each given our own private moment to reflect. I chose not to go it alone. Diane stayed by my side. As we knelt in front of the casket I thought of nothing. No prayer. No memory. Nothing except metering the time to decide how long I should kneel before getting up to walk away. Thirty seconds was plenty. Finally, I reached into my pocket and placed the Carl Furillo card next to his right hand. Some people would find that odd. My father understood.

There seems to be a protocol for everything. Once the wake began, it was my place to stand closest to the casket and acknowledge people as they filed past. As is my nature, I ignored protocol. Beverly came first, then myself, Martha and Catherine. Our spouses along with Bev's children stayed close by for support. After an hour of standing upright, shaking hands, and muttering a trite recognition of condolences, my legs were tired, my throat was dry, and boredom had set in. I excused myself to get some fresh air, never returning to the grief line. I stood near the doorway, making small talk with anyone who would converse about something other than death.

I knew less than a third of the people who attended. There was no ill will towards anyone who chose not to attend. Instead, I was quietly moved by some who did. None surprised me more than when Chief Turner, walked through the door.

Throughout the wake I had held my composure, but at the sight of the old policeman, my eyes welled up. I had not seen the Chief since I left for basic training. Randy and I kept in touch for a few months, but that soon passed. After a long hug and the exchange of platitudes, we took a walk around the building. He lit a cigar and I accepted the one he offered. As we talked, I learned that Randy was now living in Seattle where he was working as an electronics technician for Boeing. He had just recently bought a home in the suburbs with some fellow he met in tech school. There was no sense of judgment as the father spoke of his son. He had known for many years that Randy was different. He loved his son and always would.

We sat for a while on the bench near the side door. The Chief drew deeply from the cigar and we both paused for a moment as the smoke swirled. "How about you?" he asked. "Are you still angry? It's okay if you are."

"A little, but not in the way you might think." I took a short puff, then drew a long breath as the bitter exhaust streamed from my nostrils. "Truth is, I don't remember very much about that time. That's one of the reasons I lost touch with Randy. It was time for me to throw some things away. Sometimes it's easier to forget than forgive." The elder Turner nodded.

"The anger I feel now is not for what I went through, but because I never had the chance to confront him for it. A lot has happened since then; the Navy, marriage, a kid. I've made some stupid decisions. Some really good choices too. I'm older, wiser, but I know more mistakes will follow. If I want other people to forgive me, then I have to be able to forgive them. To do that I have to know why things happened, or at least how. We were getting closer, but now it's over." For a moment I felt as though I was confessing my sins to a priest. After a long pause I stood up. "Diane's probably wondering where I went. Come on. I want you to meet my wife."

From the time I phoned Diane with the news of Dad's death until the wake began, we talked very little. Diane was always perfect that way. She knew when to talk, when to let me talk, and when to be silent. I was trying not to feel. We had driven to New Jersey in almost total silence. A brief sentence here and there, but no distracting small talk. There was too much chaos in my head. Driving the car in quiet distraction was enough. Shortly after crossing the Tappan Zee Bridge, I turned my head slightly and asked myself out loud "I wonder if Carmen will be there?"

This was probably my greatest fear. How would I act? I knew I would someday forgive my father. He deserved absolution. She did not.

"Do you think she will be?"

"Probably. I can't imagine she wouldn't. It's the right thing to do."

"I'm sure you'll do what feels natural at the moment. Be polite. This is not the time for hostility."

I nodded. Of course, she was right. It was an odd moment. We had been together for more than a decade and yet Diane knew almost nothing of Carmen. I had no photos and only when telling an anecdotal family story did I ever make reference to her. What little she knew came from my sister Marty. Diane must have been curious, wondering if they would ever meet.

The opportunity came as we sat near the back row, conversing with Chief Turner. Diane and the Chief had taken an instant liking to each other. He embarrassed me by her telling stories of my awkward teen years. She laughed quietly, gaining insight to a person who she knew so well yet so little of. If Diane had heard a thousand navy stories, there were less than a dozen stories told of my pre-military years. The affable cop welcomed the opportunity to add a few.

As we smiled and laughed, enjoying a happy moment in a somber time, I caught glimpse of a familiar presence kneeling at the casket. As she proceeded down the aisle she spotted me; making and holding eye contact. While instinctively I knew who it was, in many ways she was unrecognizable. Years earlier, when we had last spoken, she was rotund and obese. Dad once mentioned that she was nearing three hundred pounds. Now she was less than half of that. Her jet-black hair was pure white. In a moment I imagined her as an apparition or a witch. Perhaps she was both. Diane was in the end chair, the Chief in the middle and I to their right. Without a word, Carmen reached past the other two and extended a hand. I took the hand, held it for a moment, then gave a polite nod. As I released her grip, she returned the nod then silently moved on. The moment I had so dreaded was over in an instant. Diane, aware of what had just transpired, quickly turned to clutch my hand, as though to exorcise any demons that may have been passed through by the contact. "Are you okay?"

"Yeah. I'm fine." I laughed nervously, reflected for a moment, then returned Carmen to the dumpster of discarded memories. Snapping the spell, I turned my seat to the left. "Chief, I'd love to get in touch with Randy. Can you give me his address?"

The day of the funeral was sunny but unseasonably cold. We were to meet at Tortollo's around 9am, then proceed to a near-by church for a short mass. The final burial would take place at the Old Orchard Cemetery, about two miles from the church. The plots had been taken care of two years earlier, when Dad and Beverly rewrote their wills. Over the course of my lifetime, I probably attended a dozen funerals. I don't recall any of them taking place on a warm, sunny day. Usually it was bitter cold or driving rain. This day was sunny, but windy and cold. Forty degrees tops. My thin black suit provided little protection.

Just prior to leaving for the final proceedings, I felt a need to reconnect with my life back home. I called the paper and asked to talk with Fred. Lois, his secretary, stammered a bit and then cautiously replied, "Fred's not here. Ralph, I don't know how to tell you this, but he's in Saint Frances Hospital. Mr. Vaughn had a heart attack yesterday. He collapsed at his desk. They took him away in an ambulance. They said he should recover, but he's going to be out for a while."

I was stunned. Within four days the two dominant men in my life had been felled by a heart attack. One was dead. The other was uncertain. After recovering from the initial shock, I took a deep breath and asked Lois, "Who's running the paper?"

"Technically it's Alan, but nobody expects that to last very long. You know Mr. Vaughn. As soon as they let him near a phone he'll be handling everything from his hospital bed."

We both laughed. "You got that right. I'll probably be getting home late tonight. Expect me in around noon tomorrow. You need anything from me?"

"A dozen Italian pastries and a Pulitzer Prize would be nice."

"The pastries I can do. Don't expect the Pulitzer anytime soon. Besides, if I got one, Fred would claim it as his own." Again, we both laughed.

A few minutes later I was standing outside of the funeral parlor being told it was time to go in for one final viewing. I firmly but respectfully declined. I had resigned myself to the passing of my father, but the corpse was not the person. There would be plenty of time to say good bye and even hello again, but no dead body was needed. Martha, Catherine, and Beverly went inside. There was no protest or criticism of my decision not to go.

The funeral mass was long and infuriating. In the first line of the sermon the priest admitted he did not know and had never met my father. He then proceeded to blather on for ten minutes about what a good man he must have been and then railed for another forty minutes about the significance of church rituals. By the time he started off about how there can be no questioning of church doctrine, I was so angry that I rose and walked out. Diane quickly followed, assuming I was overcome with grief. She was surprised to learn it was rage not grief that drove me from the building.

I let forth a harsh but muted tirade. "Where the hell did they find this asshole? Would it have been too much freaking effort for him to talk to a couple of family members, perhaps get an anecdotal story or two so he could give a proper sermon? Instead this jackass admits he knows nothing of my father so he fills the air with a bunch of dogmatic bullshit."

Diane did her best to calm me. "It's almost over. I agree with you about the priest, but what can you do? Beverly or someone picked him so we have to accept that. If they're satisfied with his eulogy, then for their sake at least pretend to be. I could see you starting to wear down over the past few days. We need to go home. Right after the reception dinner we can go. Just hang in there a little longer. Go for a walk if you need to. Have a few drinks at the reception. I'll drive."

Since I was one of the pallbearers I had to return inside. I got there just as the ceremony was ending. With a stern glare and a stiff lip, I made it through the rest of the proceedings. Before leaving, I spoke with Beverly, assuring her that that we were still family, and would continue to visit and talk. But for now, it was time to go. Once again, we drove home in silence.

I have heard that people are often unaware of the most significant moments in their lives when they happen. For me this has never been true. Joining the Navy. leaving home, getting married, having children were all life changing experiences. Time hasn't changed the magnitude of those events. What I have sometimes underestimated is the broad and far reaching impact that these experiences have. This was particularly true regarding the death of my father.

On the surface it was a big deal. We had not been very close but were becoming closer. It was unfortunate that our relationship would no longer be able to grow, but I didn't expect to miss what wasn't there. In truth, his passing would alter every other relationship in my life, both past and present. My father's death would decide how I would raise my daughter and what kind of relationship I would have with her. It altered my perspective about the universe and a god I no longer trusted. Worst of all, it planted seeds of fear from which I would never completely recover. For the rest of my life, I lived with the specter of death. Kindness and happiness existed, but they were temporary. Tragedy always loomed close by. I had received the phone call. Other calls would come. One day, someone would receive the call for me.

And yet, despite my loss of faith, I never stopped communicating with Dad. I wasn't sure if he was a living spirit or a pile of rotting bones, but still there was a need to talk. I never again visited his gravesite but I visited with him often. The cemetery was where the body could be found. The person was somewhere else.

There were many conversations. Some were angry but most were friendly words of understanding or advice. Often, he would come to me in a dream. Once, after stacking a load of firewood near the house, he told me to move the stack away from the building and pile it under the steps of the back porch. The directive made no sense, but an hour after awakening, I went outside in the pouring rain and dutifully moved the wood. The meaning of that message is still a mystery to me.

On another occasion, we were returning home from a vacation in South Carolina. Twelve hours into the return trip I was crossing the George Washington Bridge into Manhattan, completely exhausted. I began to fall asleep at the wheel. Suddenly, I felt a strong presence and a burst of energy that I immediately recognized as Dad. While Diane and Caroline slept, I smiled and whispered "I was hoping you would lend a hand." The small SUV glided across the expressway, weaving through traffic as though it was floating on the wings of an angel. Perhaps it was. Other experiences were subtler. With every trip to New York City or to a baseball game, I knew he was there. I enjoyed his company. Dad was not a departed soul looking down from heaven. He was a presence. When he was alive, he was not always there for me. In death he never failed.

Caroline could barely see through the tears, as thoughts of the recent funeral came flooding back. Had she been closer to her father, he might have told her of the aneurism that would suddenly claim his life. If so, she might have been a little more prepared to cope with the loss. Instead, it was a complete shock; not at all unlike the phone call

her dad received when he learned of her grandfather's abrupt demise. We all get the call, but we are never really prepared. We are never completely willing to accept the loss.

There were other similarities, beyond the sudden loss. While most of the funeral was a blur, she too felt a mixture of anger and appreciation. The appreciation came when she encountered others, whom she knew nothing of, but who came to pay their respects, because in some small way he had touched their lives. The anger came from those who showed up, purely out of protocol, or who feigned an attachment that never really existed.

Richard looked at his bride. "You okay? You look exhausted. This is exhausting. It's okay if you want to put it down for a while."

"No!" she proclaimed emphatically. "We can't stop now. I'm okay. Really. This is difficult, but I can't stop now. It's all so overwhelming and yet it all rings true."

"All of it?"

"Yeah, pretty much. Mom liked to tell the story of how Father Walter was responsible for her getting pregnant with me. Dad never endorsed or denied the story. This was one time when he would let her be the storyteller, without comment or interruption. On the other hand, I never heard the part about his father telling him to go for broke. I guess he didn't want to take away from Mom's moment."

"And the funeral?"

"Never heard the story, but I can definitely relate."

CHAPTER FOURTEEN

*T*raditions are important in any culture. They are rituals, and habits that create cohesiveness through repetition. Over time, their origins become clouded and steeped in legend, lies and folklore. Any truth to the legend is far less important than the underlying meaning. Any tradition that brings people together is a tradition worth keeping.

Growing up, we had more traditions surrounding Christmas Eve than any other holiday. Dad would usually get home from work early. Mom and later Carmen would spend the day cooking. Early in the evening we would congregate at one of my aunt's or uncle's home where the rest of the night would be filled with eating, drinking, and telling exaggerated stories of past family gatherings.

There were a great many routines surrounding this event, but the most important was that everyone had to eat seven different kinds of fish or seafood. This was linked to the spiritual significance that Catholics assigned to the number seven. God created the world in seven days. There are seven deadly sins. Whatever. As for the fish, most of Christ's apostles were fishermen. Then there was the story of a few fish and loaves feeding the multitude. Lots of stories. Presumably myths, but you never know. While I suppose any fish would do, we had a pretty set fare. There was dried salted cod, broiled eels, shrimp cocktail, smelts, pickled herring, anchovies, cherrystone clams and flounder. The tradition says seven, but there was always a multitude of choices. This was a good thing because I hated the pickled herring.

After several hours of food and drink, everyone headed off to midnight mass. The younger kids would quietly fall asleep on the pew, while the older ones would be bored and confused since the mass was usually done in Latin. Upon returning home in the early hours of the morning, Marty, Cat and I would race to the tree to see if Santa had arrived while we were gone. For some reason he always got to our house late. He never came before we got home from midnight mass, but invariably would show up somewhere between the time we fell asleep and the time we awoke, three hours later. Every year, Marty and I would make a pact that if either of us woke in time to see Santa, we would wake the other to go meet him. We never did.

Likewise, in Diane's family, Christmas Eve was laden with tradition. They too had a big gathering at her parents' house, along with much drinking and some traditional Polish foods. The event was called "Vigilia. I assume the term means "The Vigil." While the foods were not as exotic as my Italian fare, it was a pretty good feast. The meal was highlighted every few minutes, with shots being poured as we toasted something. I fit right in.

The cornerstone of this ritual was the breaking of bread. Each person gets a piece of flat imprinted wafer that is made from the same dry, tasteless material that Catholics receive during holy Communion. It is a mixture of sugar and corn starch, pressed into the consistency of Styrofoam. One by one everyone greets each other by offering their bread and breaking off a piece that is being offered. It is then followed by a kiss, handshake or hug, along with the exchange of "Merry Christmas." It is always recommended that this ritual be performed before anyone has too much to drink, otherwise kisses get sloppy, handshakes are knuckle-busters, and hugs become two people falling down on top of each other. If done properly, it can be a very warm and charming introduction into the meal.

The Christmas following Caroline's third birthday should have been a joyous occasion. I had a wonderful wife, and an adoring daughter. This was the beginning of her prime Santa years. This energetic little girl knew that pretty soon the fat guy with the red suit and long beard would be showing up to bring her lots of toys. There was never a shortage of toys in our home. Diane had grown up poor, and my family was dysfunctional, so we overcompensated by lavishing her with excess. Spoiled? It's such a negative term. I prefer to think of it as abundantly loved.

Meanwhile, work was going very well. Earlier in the year I had been promoted to Assistant Editor. I still did reporting and editorial work, but now I had writers working for me. More importantly, I had a certain level of control over the paper's content and style. Fred was still the big boss, but he was showing signs of aging and mellowing. He leaned on me with greater frequency to get the difficult jobs done. For that I was well compensated. We lived in a nice house in a nice neighborhood. We had good neighbors and several close friends nearby. It seemed almost perfect.

But things were not as they seemed. I was struggling mightily with my new role as parent. Some men are born to be dads. I was not. The adjustment from childless couple to having a highly dependent child was far greater than I could have ever imagined. Kids cry all of the time. Since her ability to articulate was limited, I struggled to understand what all these tantrums were about. Kids don't sleep when you sleep. It gets better when they become toddlers, but better is still not good. And while a toddler may be portable, they cannot possibly walk at the same pace as I do, so they must be carried everywhere. Carrying includes an additional thirty pounds of accessories that goes wherever they go. Finally, there is the diaper issue. Most kids get potty trained between the ages of two and four. I have been told that Caroline was easier than most. Easier is a relative term.

Work may have been good, but there were problems. As Fred Vaughn aged and developed a few health concerns, he relied heavily on me to carry the weight of his responsibilities. Easier said than done. The paper was his whole life. There was never a moment when Fred wasn't involved in the paper. It was all he had known. He didn't have to work at it. Everyone else did. In most jobs the accumulated knowledge from any given group of employees is far superior to that of any one individual. That didn't apply here. Fred knew more than everyone else combined. The weight of trying to be Fred Vaughn was a daunting task, and I was buckling under that weight. I began working sixty to eighty hours a week. Soon I found myself becoming every bit as much of an asshole as Fred.

With poor parenting skills and long hours at work, my marriage began to falter. I was seldom home, but when I was, Diane and I fought constantly. Our daughter was Diane's whole life. My job had become mine. She was completely devoted to Caroline, which left very little time for me, even when I was home. I was completely devoted to the job. I was always there, regardless of whether I was at home or at work. We both wanted our old lives back. I became resentful of the Caroline. Diane resented the paper.

During this time our sex lives became nonexistent. When we did have the time and opportunity, our daily arguments eliminated the mood for romance. Talk of divorce would soon follow. I suspected she was having an affair with our neighbor Alex. She suspected I was having an affair with his wife, Ellen. They too were having couple's problems. Our marriage would somehow survive. Theirs would not.

Finally, there was the issue of grief. The death of my father had been a crushing blow. In order to survive in a time of crisis one must bury all emotion and simply focus on the unforgiving tasks at hand. The military teaches this well. It is also a lesson that I had to learn from growing up with Carmen. In times of crisis, I am a very good person to have around. Unfortunately, those emotions do not stay buried forever. They resurface and demand to be recognized. That winter, the loss of my father and its unresolved grief got the best of me. On the surface things were under control. It was a façade.

Unhappy at home and overwhelmed at work is a recipe for disaster. Sometimes I worked late because the job was so demanding. Mostly it was because I did not want to go home. When I did go home, I often stopped first at a local pub or liquor store. Three drinks before dinner. Two during. Three after. I knew this was wrong. I knew it made things worse. I didn't care. At least for a little while, it would ease the pain. Call it a midlife crisis, if you will. I was having my first. There would be others. I hated myself and everything around me. Something had to change.

I should have left work around 2pm on Christmas Eve, but I didn't. I didn't have to be there but found plenty of reasons to hang around. In this case it was a breaking story. In East Hartford, some nut with a handgun and a bottle of Jack Daniels had just gotten laid off from his factory job and decided to take it out on his wife and six-year-old son. First, he killed the bottle. Next, he killed the kid, the wife and himself. This happened shortly after noon. Within minutes, I was on the scene.

In the news business there is always a breaking story and this one, while tragic, was hardly worth the extra effort. There were enough cub reporters around to do the job. Besides, nobody reads the paper on Christmas morning. It's the slowest day of the year for readership. Nobody cared about politics, local news, or some psycho. The holidays were tough enough without getting bummed out over a story like that. Just the same, it gave me another reason not to rush home. I called Diane to let her know what was going on. She was already at her parents' house, getting there early to help her mother with whatever needed to be done. I promised to be there by six.

Six was when I left work. With good weather and not much traffic I could make Bridgeport in an hour. Freezing rain, heavy traffic and a couple of minor accidents backed up traffic along I-91 South. By the time I arrived at their house it was nearly eight. I was tired, hungry, aggravated, and in no mood for the argument I was expecting.

Much to my surprise, no one seemed to care. I was warmly greeted by all and promptly handed a beer. "Relax," I was told more than once. "Dinner's ready. We'll eat just as soon as everyone sits down." The tiny kitchen was overflowing with food and family members nudging their way around each other. Diane was grimacing, while shaking her hand. "Shit, shit, shit. I burned my hand on the oven door. Oh, hi Babe. How was traffic? We heard about your story on the news. Dad saw you on TV talking to someone in the background." We craned our necks around two other people to kiss. This is odd, I thought. It almost feels normal

"I got the story, then passed it on to one of the rookies to write it. It will be in tomorrow's paper. Traffic sucked. Let me look at your hand. You alright? Where's Caroline?"

"In the living room with Sophie. Yeah, I'm okay. Get yourself a drink,--oh, never mind, you have one." There was no criticism in her voice.

I pushed my way into the living room. "Excuse me Lynn. Where's Michael? Oh hey, hi Howard, Merry Christmas." I greeted Diane's father. "Merry Christmas," he called back. "Care for a drink?" He was pouring shots of Scotch. As soon as he finished topping off three glasses we shook hands. "Get Michael," he said. "I don't know where he is," I said. "I haven't seen him yet. One of those is mine I hope."

"He's playing the piano," Lynn answered. "You guys better take it easy. You're driving home tonight."

"Relax Lynn, I just got here."

"I know. That's what I'm afraid of."

Michael appeared in the doorway. "Hey bro, Merry Christmas. Glad you made it. Hey Dad are those shots for us? Pour one for Frank." A voice came in from the living room. "I'm good," Frank shouted. "I'm working on a beer. You guys go ahead without me. I'll catch up later." Howard, Michael and myself each downed our shots. Then another. I had been in the house for almost ten minutes and already had two Scotches and a beer without even saying hello to my daughter. I talked with Michael for five minutes while food was being brought out to the table. Diane's mother stuck two fingers in her mouth and let out a shrill whistle. "Everybody sit down!" she shouted. "Let's eat."

The first I had seen of Caroline was when Frank and his new girlfriend Wendy brought her in from the living room. Wendy and Diane set her up at the table using the booster seat we brought from home. Franklin and I shook hands. "Ralph, good to see you. How were the roads? You remember Wendy?"

Yes, I remembered Wendy. At that moment my personal problems seemed small compared to what Franklin had been going through. He was in the midst of a messy divorce and was now living back at home while things sorted themselves out. Frank's soon to be ex-wife, had developed a gambling problem that destroyed their personal finances. He had no savings and his credit cards were maxed out. Frank knew Wendy through work. She handled invoicing at the Audi dealership where Frank was a mechanic. They had been friends for several years. When things were at their worst, it was Wendy who pulled him through. They would be married a few years later while on vacation in Maine.

The couple made an interesting contrast. Frank's ex was bold and loud. She played hard, lived fast, and never met an impulse that she wouldn't succumb to. Wendy didn't drink or smoke and her domestic skills could make Martha Stewart feel inadequate. The only thing we couldn't figure out is what she was doing with a burly, coarse guy like Frank. Diane's brother is a wonderful man, but it seemed like an odd pairing. Somehow it worked.

At the table, we broke bread, ate, drank and told stories. Frank talked about rebuilding his old Harley. Michael and Lynn talked about what colleges their son was applying to. Diane and I bragged about our girl. Mary gushed over the wonderful assortment of deserts that Wendy had made. Howard just sat and smiled. For two hours I was able to relax and enjoy myself. I was in good company. If anyone knew of our problems, they didn't let on. This was not the time or place. As dishes were cleared and coffee was served, Wendy leaned over my shoulder and said "Come on upstairs for a moment. I have something I want to show you."

I followed her up the steps to the back room where Frank had been staying. On the bed lay a mountain of red velvet and white fluff. "Try it on," she said. "It's a Santa suit. I made it for my brother last year but he didn't wear it. He's about your size. If you want, you can surprise Caroline when you get home tonight. Go ahead. Try it on."

The suit fit perfectly. Wendy had thought of everything. Fat padding had been sewn into the waistline. The white hair and beard were meshed from some old wigs she had gotten from the beauty parlor where her sister worked. The red velvet trousers and top were lined and trimmed with fake fur from a coat she bought at a Salvation Army thrift store. Over the right breast she embroidered the name S. Claus. It was magic. When I put the suit on I felt as though I could make reindeer fly. A moment later we heard footsteps coming up the stairs. Wendy peaked around the corner to make sure it wasn't Caroline. It was Diane. She took one look and gasped "Oh my God!" Then we all burst out laughing.

For once, I couldn't wait to get home. Santa was coming! Although we arrived in separate cars, it was decided that we should return home together. I could bring Diane and Caroline to pick up the other car later the next day. We were all going to Michael and Lynn's for Christmas dinner. Diane had the next few days off, and as usual I would be working lots of hours. The two girls could stay in Bridgeport for a while longer.

On the ride home Diane and I talked with more civility than we had in over a month. We didn't resolve any issues, but we talked and we listened. We used to have great conversations back in the days when we actually liked each other. Now, civility was an effort. She told me she was concerned about my drinking. I conceded the excess and told her that since Dad died, the holidays have been pretty rough. Rather than lecture or remind me that my drinking was hardly restricted to the holidays, Diane simply nodded. Soon the topic turned to what we should do when we arrived home. Caroline was already fast asleep in the back seat. It was agreed that Diane would bring her up to bed. I would don the costume and start making noise. When she woke up, Diane would bring her down to see Santa. I would be careful to keep my back turned so she couldn't see my face. Ho, ho, ho, this was going to be great!

I pulled into the driveway around 2am. Diane had started to nod off in the car. We were both so tired that she suggested we scrap the whole Santa gig, put the presents under the tree and just go to bed. I vetoed that idea. We had the outfit. If nothing else, we should get a picture or two out of it. She agreed. I quickly dressed, then grabbing an old pillow case, began loading up with presents. The suit felt even better than when I had tried it on in Bridgeport. I was suddenly reenergized. This is what it feels like to be Santa!

With loud and reckless abandon, I began stomping around the living room. "Ho Ho Ho", I shouted. Caroline didn't budge. "HO HO HO, MERRY CHRISTMAS! MERRY CHRISTMAS CAROLINE! MERRY CHRISTMAS EVERYBODY! HO HO HO MERRY CHRISTMAS. HO HO HO HO HO!" I paused to catch my breath. Silence. Try harder. STOMP, STOMP, STOMP. "HO HO HO HO HO! IT'S CHRISTMAS EVERYBODY. MERRY, MERRY CHRISTMAS! CAROLINE, WAKE UP AND SAY HELLO TO SANTA. I HAVE PRESENTS FOR YOU! MERRY CHRISTMAS EVERYBODY!" Frustration was setting in. Exhaustion was setting in. I grabbed a broom and began whacking the ceiling. Again, I stomped. Again, I shouted. Again, I grabbed the broom. Wrong end! Instead of whacking the ceiling with bristles, a small round hole from the handle punctured its way through the sheetrock.

Diane called downstairs to me. "It's okay. We did the best we could. She's not getting up. If you're done, just kill the lights and come on up. I'm going to bed."

Out of the corner of my eye I caught what appeared to be a flash of light that briefly flickered through the front window. I glanced over to see if it was an emergency vehicle or a neighbor getting up early or returning home late. Instead I saw my own reflection and a look of total despair. "Some Santa," I scoffed. "Merry fucking Christmas." Turning away, I stuffed the hat, wig and beard into the pillow case. Again, there was a flicker in the window. This time the reflection was not my own. It was a face I had not seen in a very long while.

"Dad?"

"Ho ho ho yourself. You know, it was thirty years ago today

that I did the exact same thing you are trying to do. We were living in the city. I slammed every door in the house but there was no way you and your sister were getting up. Finally, just like you I grabbed a broom and wound up with a hole in the ceiling. Unfortunately, you have a lot more patching up to do than just a ceiling."

"But..."

"Here's the 'but.' You are in a very good situation but you are making some very bad decisions. You know I made more than my fair share of stupid mistakes in life, but this wasn't one of them. You have a wonderful family. Don't throw that away."

For a moment I hung my head in reflective shame. Looking up again, he was gone.

"Babe, are you okay? Are you coming to bed?"

"No, yeah, everything's fine."

"I heard you talking. Who were you talking to?"

"No one. I'll be up in a minute. Something I ate didn't agree with me. That's probably what you heard. I'll be there as soon as I'm done in the bathroom."

Once again, I looked to the window. Nothing. I raced to the bathroom. As I sat atop the bowl, my neck went limp and my head fell into my hands. Sobbing uncontrollably, I paused only for a moment to reach over to the sink to turn the water on, hoping that the noise would drown out my muffled wails. Wave after wave of emotion swelled over me, cascading from my eyes. "I am sorry. I am sorry. I am so sorry." That was all I could say. I was begging for forgiveness from everyone I knew, both living and dead. I was begging for forgiveness from myself.

Forgiveness doesn't come easily. There was no sense of how I had come to this point. There was even less of a sense as to how it might be undone.

It may have been a minute or it may have been an hour.

Without a word I climbed into bed. Rolling to my left I reached over and wrapped my arm tightly around the woman that I once loved so dearly. "I love you," she whispered. "Everything is going to be okay. I promise."

"I love you too," I gasped. Then I squeezed her just a little bit tighter, hanging on to the hope that exists when there seems to be nothing else to hang on to.

I wish I could say that Christmas Eve was a turning point for us and that things quickly improved from there. They did not. After that night I became even more consumed with the grief that I could no longer hide. I continued to work late and drink more.

You can never tell if you have hit bottom until you are on your way back up. For me it came the following March. I arrived home late, around 8pm after a ten-hour workday and two hours at the bar. Instead of being greeted by my loving family, I found an empty house with just a short, handwritten note on the kitchen table.

Ralph,

I have taken Caroline to go stay with my parents for a while. I don't know if or when we will be coming home.

Diane.

Diane and Caroline arrived home around 10 o'clock that night. She got as far as Exit 46 on the Merritt Parkway then turned around. Instead of coming straight home she simply drove without direction for several hours while deciding what to do.

Caroline saw me first and started to cry. Diane quickly pulled her away and said "Daddy's sick." I was on the floor, slumped against the wall in the kitchen. There was a picture in one hand

and an empty bottle in the other. My clothes were covered in vomit. I wasn't trying to kill myself, I was just trying to kill the pain. I tried to speak but could not. Nor could I cry any more. Diane put a pillow beneath my head and a blanket over me, then let me sleep where I lay. We didn't speak more than a few words to each other for the next three days. I slept in our bed. She slept in Caroline's room.

On the fourth day we began to talk a little. We saw a couple's counselor. He was of no use. I began to see a therapist. Not much help there either. There are some things you just have to do on your own. Progress came slow, but it did come. I quit drinking for a year. Eventually we became a couple again. Eventually I learned how to be a good father and a better husband. I never made it to the person I wanted to be, but I never stopped trying.

CHAPTER FIFTEEN

Dear Caroline-Key West, Florida. This tourist town is two miles wide by four miles long, with a year-round population of around 22,000 residents. Crammed within those borders you will find a nearby Navy base, a large gay community, and a row of beach-side mansions that are owned by various celebrities and business tycoons. You will find poverty in a Caribbean village made up mostly of Cuban, Bahamian, and Haitian immigrants. It is a haven for writers, artists and musicians. There are several large churches and active religious organizations. What makes Key West unique, however, is its level of tolerance. The poor immigrant and wealthy celebrity are treated as equals. The war veteran and radical expatriate are both respected and valued. It is simply the most live-and-let-live place I know. In Key West the only thing not tolerated is intolerance.

It didn't take long before Key West was an annual destination for us. Why did we love it? There was just a natural connection. We made memories there. Over the years, each trip seemed to be marked by unique and defining moments that often bordered on the absurd.

*W*e took our first trip together to Key West three years after we got married. We were settling into our first home and couldn't afford much of a vacation. Martha was now living in Miami. She suggested we find a cheap flight and stay with her for a few days. She could loan us a car to use, and we would be free to come and go as we pleased. At some point, we decided to book a room in Key West for a night. It was September, the slowest time of year, so we talked our way into a half-price room at the Pier House Resort, in the heart of the island's night life.

It was a slow, relaxing drive and we stopped often, to stare at the scenery or walk along the water. A three-hour drive took us seven, but there was no need to hurry. As we arrived, the island was abruptly deluged by a large, slow moving thunderstorm that flooded the streets. Ten minutes after settling into the hotel, the entire island lost power. We dropped our bags and headed out to see what was happening on Duval Street. Key West is used to extreme weather, so a flash flood and a loss of power was a minor obstacle to the shop owners and year-round denizens. Restaurants and bars were quickly illuminated by the flickering glow of candlelight. Free drinks were indiscriminately handed to passing pedestrians in exchange for a promise to come back once power was restored. A half hour later, the lights returned. By that time, Diane and I were having dinner outside at the Half Shell Raw Bar. The Half Shell had a generator and some of the best conch fritters on the island.

We returned to Key West two years later. Stressed over our infertility issues, we just needed to get away. Everyone was telling us to relax and I knew of no better place. Three days at the Pier House. As usual, our long drive down U.S. 1 was made longer by side excursions. We spent a few hours on a side trip into the Everglades. We had hoped to see alligators but could do no better than a skunk and a raccoon. Just south of Key Largo we found a secluded dirt road that led to the Gulf of Mexico. There we went skinny dipping. Our nature frolic was abruptly interrupted when two kids with fishing poles wandered along. They giggled, we blushed, and both parties left with smiles.

We arrived at the Pier House fairly late and very hungry. Opting for convenience first, we dropped our bags and headed across the street for a nice dinner at the Jetty. We had eaten there before. Good food and not too pricey. We were seated upstairs and outside on a balcony facing the corner of Duval and Front Street. Mario, our extremely flamboyant waiter, began gushing about how we must try the oysters Rockefeller. "Simply delight-ful" he kept repeating as he kissed his fingertips. We had to laugh, not at our waiter, but at an inside joke about how oysters are sup-posed to be a fertility food. We ordered the appetizer and they were indeed delightful.

From our perch, we could hear the banter on the street as vendors hawked tee shirts and souvenirs. There was also the amal-gamated music of at least ten bar bands in a four-block radius. Above it all I heard a saxophone. Its sultry wail was emanating Two Friends Restaurant and Bar, on Front Street. Diane and I had eaten breakfast there the last time we came down. There was a talented little jazz quartet playing tonight. Our friend lamented that his shift would run too late, but we shouldn't miss it. We were exhausted, so a nightcap and a little music would be the perfect conclusion to a really good day.

The name Two Friends is only part of the logo. The bar carries the motto that there is "No greater love than the long enduring love of one drunken friend and another." How true. We arrived around midnight as the Dexter Knight Quartet began their sec-ond set. After a couple of drinks, we would head back to the room. That was the plan. By one-thirty I was on my sixth Scotch, while Diane was finishing off her fourth rum runner. The band was great, the liquor was smooth, the company was outstanding. There was no reason to leave.

Before taking their final break, Dexter stepped to the microphone. "That concludes our second set. We're going to step aside and be back in twenty minutes, but before we go we want to do a request for a very good friend." The group then rolled into a rollicking version of "New York. New York." As with every other song they played, it was musical perfection, but I was incredulous, annoyed, and drunk. Leaning across the table I yelled into Diane's ear. "Sad. A great band that can play any song in the world and they do a cheesy-ass song like New York, New York." I didn't think my comment was loud enough to be heard beyond the table, but for all I know the entire room heard me.

Dexter finished the song and announced "And that was for our good friend Mr. Tony Bennett." Heads quickly swirled. From the table directly behind us, a handsome, tanned man with sparkling eyes stood up, waved and smiled. Before disappearing through the kitchen, he reached over and tapped me on the elbow. "Not bad for a cheesy-ass song, eh?" We both laughed. From his glass, I surmised that he too was drinking Scotch. I raised mine and toasted the legend. Five years later Diane and I saw him at a sold-out show in Connecticut. His set did not include New York New York.

Fifteen years into our marriage, Diane and I had been to Key West seven times. Where we had once gone to escape the stresses of infertility, we were now heading there to escape the pressures of work and parenthood. It's not that parenthood was that rough. We were very fortunate. Caroline was healthy, well-adjusted and well behaved. Still, it is a full-time job, and like any full-time job you need to take a break.

My job was not going well. Fred Vaughn was still the editor in chief, but his health was failing. Six months later, he would be dead. The paper was teetering on insolvency. Fred was looking to step down and he was looking for me to step up. I didn't want to captain a sinking ship. At the same time, I was being courted by network television to write copy for a local affiliate. It paid fairly well, but the writing was restrictive and heavily censored by the corporate overlords. I had to make a decision soon but was starting to crack under the stress. Meanwhile, in South Florida, Martha had her own stresses to deal with. Her marriage was over and headed towards a bitter divorce. This left her with the female version of a mid-life crisis. It was time for everyone to run away.

I found a pretty good deal for four nights at the Casa Marina in Key West. We got an early morning non-stop to Miami where we picked up a ragtop Jeep as our rental car. With a little bit of luck, we could be sucking Margaritas at Two Friends by late afternoon. Diane's parents took care of Caroline while we were away.

Martha booked two nights at the La Concha. She was coming down with Jake, a guy she had met at work. He was a lawyer. He was also ten years younger, had a full beard, and drove a Harley. I thought I knew Martha better than anyone, but the last thing I ever expected to see was my sister with her hair tied up in a red bandana, clinging to the back of a low-rider. Despite all efforts to the contrary, we had both become boring middle-class suburbanites. Seeing her on that bike was one of the proudest moments of my life.

They rolled in on a Harley, while we putted around on a moped. It was quite the contrast, but it fit the Keys. Since Diane and I had arrived a day before them, we spent our first day just relaxing. Earlier, we drove up to Bahia Honda State Park about thirty miles north. Key West may be a paradise, but its beaches are nothing to brag about. Bahia Honda has white sand, warm, crystal clear water and long shallow flats leading into the Gulf of Mexico. During low tide you can walk over a hundred yards out to a sandbar and never be more than waist deep. I imagine during tourist season some of the beaches fill up, but this was off-time, so there were plenty of secluded spots to be had. We swam and baked in the sun before heading into town for a late lunch.

After grabbing a bite, it was decided it was best to stay out of the heat. That gave us choices. We could head back to the hotel and "play" or we could find a bar with a band. There would be plenty of playtime to be had, so we took a seat at Skipper's Saloon, a popular haunt that we knew quite well. The saloon is a dark and dingy place with enough stories and legends to fill a dozen books. It is said to be the oldest bar in Key West. It is said to be haunted. It is said to have been Hemmingway's favorite watering hole. At one time it was a mortuary. Glass bottles, once filled with holy water are still visible through the brick and mortar walls. The place has character, but I just wanted a beer. We were waved inside by a guitar player with a tip jar who was doing a horrible rendition of Bob Marley's "No Woman No Cry." His long scruffy hair and cigarette stained teeth gave the impression he had not performed any type of personal hygiene in over a year. No woman, no surprise. His next song, Neil Young's "Southern Man" wasn't much better. I dropped two bucks in the jar and we took a seat at the far end of the bar.

Diane ordered a rum and tonic and I got a Bud Light. Behind the guitar guy was a small room with two battle scarred pool tables and several warped sticks. We briefly debated as to whether we should get some quarters and knock a few balls around. As I reached for my glass, I caught a light whiff of gardenia and saw a long thin arm wrap around Diane's shoulder.

"Well aren't you the cutest thing. Hey sweetie, having a good time?" We both turned to see an attractive woman, somewhere in her late thirties or early forties, with straight, waist-length brown hair. Behind a pair of John Lennon sunglasses were seductive bedroom eyes. Key West has forever been known for its sexual permissiveness and I found the idea of this vixen making a pass at my wife strangely fascinating. Diane shot me a look that could best be described as confused.

"Is this your guy? I bet the three of us could have a lot of fun together." She told us her name was Linda and sat down beside Diane. Despite the odd introduction, we began a very pleasant but rather ordinary conversation. She asked where we were from and we talked a bit about our lives in Connecticut. Linda told us she had been in Key West for so long that she considered herself a native. Another ten minutes or so passed as we the three of us talked about everything from the weather to the crappy musician at the door. All the while, Linda neglected to share with us a fairly significant piece of information.

A short, thin, white haired man approached Linda from behind. His face was a ruddy roadmap of wrinkles, each one with its own story to tell. There was no need to guess who the old guy might be. His face was plastered throughout the bar. The legendary Garrison Malone, aka The Skipper, kissed his wife on the back of the neck and put his arm around her waist. "Who are your new friends Babe?"

I may have thrived on the accepting lifestyle that the Keys held, but that couldn't stop me from being star-struck at the chance to meet the ancient mariner. The stories of Skipper Malone are too numerous to tell, but the short bio goes something like this: Grew up in Northern New Jersey. Had to leave abruptly when he was almost killed after getting caught scamming the mob. Came to Key West in the late 1940's where he worked the shrimp boats. Bought and ran a charter boat in the 1950's. In the late 1950's and early 1960's Skip helped the CIA with several operations involving covert actions in Cuba. Somewhere along the way he bought the saloon that now bears his name. Twice he was elected mayor of Key West. A notorious womanizer, he had several wives and more than a dozen children. He was a friend of Tennessee Williams, and Shel Silverstein. He knew both Ernest Hemingway and Jimmy Buffett. Now his wife was flirting with my wife, while the legend was offering to buy us lunch.

"Why don't we all go to the Purple Mango and grab a bite." It wasn't a suggestion. The bartender disappeared for a second and in less than a minute an old Cadillac was waiting for us outside the back door. The Purple Mango is a dive, hidden behind a strip mall on the north end of the island. It is a local pub, seldom seen by tourists, but is extremely popular among fishermen and gay couples. Dining was mostly outside but we were shown to a secluded booth inside, where it was cooler and a bit more private. The Skipper, after all, was a celebrity, even to locals. His privacy was respected and guarded. I followed the old man's lead and ordered the jerk chicken. Diane and Linda both got salads.

The initial awe that had struck me from meeting Garrison Malone quickly abated. We were a couple of Jersey guys, and that gave us something in common. While I'm sure Linda had heard the old man spin his yarns a thousand times, she seemed to genuinely enjoy watching others delight in hearing them. She took even greater joy in hearing us tell stories of our own. At one point I couldn't resist sharing the tale of our encounter with Tony Bennett.

"Tony used to come down here a lot." Skipper offered. "He's a painter you know, not just a singer. He's done a few island scenes that have fetched a pretty good price. He's on tour now, but I'm sure he'll be back. A lot of people think Jimmy Buffett is the only big name in Key West but there are plenty of others who come here."

Skip pointed to a nearby table whose dishes had not yet been cleared. "Grab that paper." I got up and fetched a copy of the

Citizen, the island's daily newspaper. On the front page was an article about Tom Cruise's recent visit. The Skipper spoke of Tom as though he was an old friend. After lunch he and Linda both had to tend to errands, so they had the driver drop us off at the hotel. There were no plans to meet again, but I was sure we would.

The following morning, I awoke way too early for the Keys. Diane would have slept until noon if I let her, but there was no reason for me to be up at seven. I decided to grab a cup of coffee. Unfortunately, in the laid-back world of island life, a good cup of Joe is hard to find. Still, old habits are hard to break, so in my usual routine I woke at dawn and wanted a jolt. I was told there was a Starbucks just inside the La Concha Hotel, where Martha and Jake would be staying. I hopped on the moped and went for a ride.

While the Casa Marina was beautiful, I regret that we never got to stay at La Concha. It is the oldest large hotel on the island, as well as the tallest building. The hotel oozes with elegance and opulence I entered the marble and mahogany lobby wearing shorts, a tank top and flip flops, looking just like any other patron, minus the designer label. At the front desk I left a message for Martha and Jake to meet us at Two Friends around two. Twenty minutes and a double espresso later I was back at the Casa reading a newspaper by the pool.

We arrived at Two Friends a little after the appointed hour and parked our scooters next to what I correctly assumed was Jake's Harley. We found them at a table facing the street, working on a double order of greasy conch fritters while washing it down with Coors Light. Introductions were brief and informal. I ordered four shots of tequila. We toasted our escapes from reality. They were excited to hear of our lunch with the Skipper. We wanted to know all about the ride down on the bike. Our families were reunited and a new friend was made.

Two, (or was it three?) days of drunken insanity followed. Two blocks from Casa Marina we stumbled upon what looked like a pretty good party. Beach attire, cash bar and great appetizers. The band was only so-so but everyone was dancing. After about an hour or so, someone asked the unexpectedly obvious question "Are you with the bride or the groom?"

We had inadvertently crashed a wedding. I resorted to my old standby answer. Flashing my press pass I replied "Neither. I'm with the Miami Herald. I'm working on a series of articles about weddings, anniversaries and reunions in the Keys. Pretty cool huh? I get paid to go to parties. Can I get your name?"

An hour later we returned to Casa Marina, where a Jamaican style barbecue was set up on the beach, complete with jerk chicken and curried goat. The reggae band was good enough to make me believe that Bob Marley might still be alive. Jake and I got coerced into playing touch football with a group of twenty-somethings on the edge of the water. Slightly older, drunk guys should not play beach football, particularly after eating spicy Jamaican food. I didn't throw up, but I did fall down a lot. Jake proved to be a pretty good athlete, throwing a couple of touchdown passes, then taking the last play himself to win the game for our team. The barbecue was followed by a dance party which was followed by the four of us passing out for an hour or two in lounge chairs on the beach. When we awoke, somewhere around one o'clock, Marty and Jake wanted to go back to La Concha and call it a night. Diane and I had napped enough to want to party some more.

Off-season or not, the island was hopping. We piled into our rented Jeep, then after letting our comrades off at La Concha, Diane and I cruised the nearby streets for over twenty minutes in desperate search of a parking space. We were almost ready to give up when we found a small spot about a foot longer than our vehicle, near the corner of Simonton and Caroline Street. Three hours later, with all of the bars either closed or closing, we stumbled out in search of our car. We were in no condition to drive.

The Jeep proved easy to find. It was the one with the police car in front and the tow truck in back. The bright flashing lights hurt my head. We ran towards the vehicle waving our arms. "Wait, wait, wait. Stop. Officer, what's going on?"

"This your vehicle?"

"Yeah. I mean no. It's my rental."

"It's illegally parked."

"Well I'm here now. Just give me the ticket and we can both be on our way."

"Have you been drinking?" Key West cops have a keen grasp of the obvious.

"Uh, yeah. A little."

"Then the car gets towed."

At that point Diane stepped forward. "Wait a second. What do you mean it's illegally parked? It's in a parking space."

The officer led us around to the sidewalk side of the car and pointed to a sign that said No Parking Beyond This Point. The grill and bumper of the car extended beyond the sign by about eight inches.

Diane then showed the police officer how the curbside cutout had extended the room for parking to at least a foot or more beyond the sign. "How can we be illegally parked? We didn't even use up the full parking space."

"You parked past the sign. That means you are illegally parked."

"Bullshit. We are parked in a legal parking space. If the sign is in the wrong place, that's your problem. You have to move the sign." Diane was becoming belligerent and I was getting nervous.

"Did you just tell me to move the sign?"

"Yeah. the sign is in the wrong place, so move the fucking sign."

This was not going well, so I tried to intervene. The escalating tensions had infused me with enough adrenaline to offer the pretense of sobriety. "Officer, I'm very sorry. Please ignore my wife. She obviously has had too much to drink. We never intended to do anything wrong. I simply assumed that since the cutout for the parking space extended a bit further, that the parking space allowed for a foot or two beyond the sign. If I was mistaken, I apologize and will gladly pay the ticket."

The officer hesitated for a moment and assuming he might concede, I walked to the back of the car and unhooked the tow truck's chain from the bumper. This simple act proved to be the catalyst that turned a bad, but controllable situation into a major fiasco. The tow truck driver took firm hold of my arm. "We were called out here to tow. Now we are going to tow."

"Let go of me asshole." The driver held fast to my left arm, so with my right arm I punched him square in the jaw. This hurt my hand, but had no effect on the burly caveman. Meanwhile, Diane again went nose to nose with the cop. "So, are you going to move the fucking sign, or what?"

By 4a.m. two very drunk suburbanites from Connecticut, with a towed Jeep rental, were sitting in a jail cell in a back corner of the Key West Police Department. It probably wasn't the first time something like this had happened, but for Diane and me it was slightly out of character. I had a black eye and bruised wrist. The shiner was the return punch from the tow truck driver. The bruised wrist was a combination of the driver's grip on my arm, and a pair of handcuffs that were fitted extra tightly for my general discomfort. By 5a.m. we both had puked a couple of times and dozed off for a while. I woke up around 7, and jostled Diane until she too was awake.

Shortly after 8, we were visited by a new old friend. Key West's favorite citizen, Skipper Garrison Malone was out for his morning walk. Ever the politician, he would stop to chat with whomever he passed on the street. In the early morning hours, the island was abuzz with sanitation workers, delivery drivers, and shop owners.

Malone decided to wander into the police station and say hello to the men in blue. When he asked what was new, the officer at the desk told him of the two drunk tourists who got carried away last night and were now sitting in a cell out back. With the help of his walking stick, the Skipper swung open the waist high gate and strolled past the front desks to the cages in the rear. I don't know who was more surprised when I looked up and saw the kindly old man.

Since the Skipper had already heard the police version, he was curious to learn our story of what had transpired. There wasn't much variation, except I insisted I wouldn't have hit the tow truck driver if he hadn't been so rough in the first place. Diane quietly offered her only argument, which was that the sign is in the wrong place.

"What about the sign?" Skip asked. The officer again repeated what we had heard previously. The size of the cutout doesn't matter. If it says you can't park beyond the sign, you can't park beyond the sign. Skip put his arm around the officer and looked up at him in the most fatherly of ways. "Larry, I know these people. They are friends of mine. They may have overindulged a bit but I'm sure they meant no harm. Why don't we all take a look and see for ourselves."

It's hard to imagine that in any other town besides Key West, two tourists, both charged with assault, would be allowed to return to the scene of the crime with an arresting officer and an ex-mayor. But this was Key West, and things are done a little differently there. A few moments later the four of us were standing on the corner of Caroline and Simonton, reenacting the events that had taken place. There was no disagreement on the specifics. It was a matter of interpretation. The Skipper slowly walked around the now vacant spot that a few hours earlier had been the scene of so much excitement. He looked at the green and white sign. He looked at the markings on the street. He looked at officer Larry, and he looked at the two tourists with hangovers. Slowly he circled the sidewalk and pavement a second time, rubbing his white bearded chin. Once again, he put his arm around the tall, sturdy policeman. "I hate to say this Larry, but this thing is definitely in the wrong place. Let's move the fucking sign."

Two hours later Diane and I were free from incarceration, albeit four hundred dollars poorer. They wouldn't waive the towing fees. Ordinarily I'm inclined to hold a grudge. Yet, in the surreal world of this tropical paradise, I somehow found it in my heart to forgive the asshole wrecker driver who gave me a black eye. Picking a fight with him was not the right thing to do, especially since he was so much bigger and stronger than me. We laughed, apologized for the fracas, and shook hands. I then called Martha and she convinced us to meet them for brunch at the La Concha. This time we walked.

With less than two hours of sleep, a massive hangover, and my right eye swollen, we must have been quite the sight. Diane and I poured into one side of a booth and promptly ordered two Bloody Marys and coffee. Not to be outdone, Jake got a Bud Light and Martha a screwdriver. As our dying brain cells and inflamed livers again recovered from alcohol deprivation, we told our sordid tale. Martha suggested a quiet day by the pool to recover from our near-death experiences. That idea was overruled Jake's desire for more testosterone driven insanity.

Snorkeling was discussed as a possibility, but given our current physical state, that probably wasn't a good choice. Puking in the water might attract some interesting fish, but it wouldn't make for a very pleasant experience. A fishing trip offered the same promise of seasickness. Whatever we did it had to be edgy. A return to Bahia Honda was an idea with some merit. The girls could sun themselves, while we could snorkel close to shore, or rent a couple of kayaks. As ideas flew by, Martha shouted out "I know. Why don't we all get tattoos?" The suggestion might not have seemed so odd, had it not come from my sister. This was Martha, who is generally expected to be the lone voice of reason. We all immediately agreed.

Diane and I had considered this on a previous trip, so we knew where to go. There were two places just north of Key West on Stock Island. One was Blue Dolphin Tattoo, the other was called The Ink Spot. The Dolphin was cheaper but Ink Spot was known for doing better work. After further discussion, it was decided that we would all get the exact same tattoo in the exact same place. A lasting memento from our excellent adventure. A small conch shell would be inked just above our ankle on the inside of our left leg, with the letters KW below.

Diane and Martha decided to spend two hours shopping, which allowed Jake and me to go work out the deal. I hopped on the back of his Harley and we headed up the road. After a brief discussion outside The Ink, we walked through the door and asked to see the owner. Sitting behind a small, cluttered desk, in a cubicle at the far corner of the building was a large bald man, almost completely covered with artwork. I extended my hand and gave a falsely confident grin.

"I'm Ralph Campbell. I'm a reporter with the Associated Press. Jake Wilson here is an attorney for the State of Florida. Relax, you're not in any trouble. I'm working on a piece about the growing popularity of tattoos among older clientele. It's a story I'm hoping to go national with. Jake here is an old friend who is helping me out a little. Can you spare a few minutes to show us around and maybe talk a little?"

The big guy gave a nervous smile. "Sure. You got I.D.?"

I fumbled through my wallet and found my National Press pass. "Here you go." I handed him the card knowing that he wouldn't have a clue as to what it was. Bart gave us a tour, making sure he emphasized the extremely sanitary conditions and the attention to artistry. It was Bart who asked if I had ever been inked, suggesting that you can't really understand the appeal of getting a tattoo without experiencing it. Since he would likely get additional business from a favorable story, he offered to personally ink me for free.

I countered by telling him that since I was looking for various perspectives, there were four of us that had agreed to get the same tattoo. We would then share our thoughts. I told Bart that the plan was for all four of us go to different places, but since I trusted him a bit more than the two other establishments I had recently visited, getting all four at the same shop made more sense. There was no debate. Bart quickly agreed to ink all four of us, free of charge. An appointment was set for seven o'clock. As we were leaving Bart turned to me and asked, "Hey, what happened to your eye?"

"There's a guy in Key Largo that does freelance work. His studio was filthy and his work sucked. He didn't like it when I told him I was sending the Health Department after him. The bastard popped me. That's why I travel with a lawyer. You have no worries. I like your place. I can tell you do good work."

And that's pretty much how our vacation ended. No other incidents. Four permanent reminders of our temporary insanity. Four formerly boring, middle-class suburbanites returned to the real world, having experienced more in few days than they would during the rest of the year.

There is something wonderful about losing your mind if you can do it by choice and then return to your senses. For that, I found no better venue than Key West. There would be many more trips to the Keys. For several years, it was our routine to spend a week or more in a rented house or condo. My job would always be stressful, but an annual escape to the island could provide enough decompression to make it bearable.

Upon returning home from our vacation with Jake and Marta, I was given the news that the Hartford Examiner would be folding by the end of the year. Fred Vaughn was diagnosed with liver cancer, and the offer I had from the television station had been withdrawn. Fred died two weeks after Christmas. I got lucky and was offered the job of assistant editor at the Hartford Courant. I always despised that paper, but I had a family to feed. It too would suffer financial hardships, but somehow survive. While I probably didn't help them much financially, I do believe the quality of journalism improved while I was there.

CHAPTER SIXTEEN

Dear Caroline-I am not a perfect person. I have never been, nor have I ever claimed to be one. Sometimes the best you can hope for is to not repeat your past mistakes, but even that can be difficult. Everyone falters, but lapses of moral turpitude are more than just errors in judgment. They are hurts that never heal. Immorality is a sin of the soul.

𝒥 have never believed in standard clichés about a midlife crisis. It seems to me that it's too easy to make the title fit reality. Define midlife. Is it the median age of life expectancy or is it some nebulous point in time between the age of 35 and 55? It is safe to say that everyone will have some crisis of morality, faith or fidelity during that time. It is only natural. Those are the years when most of us realize, for better or worse, who we are. Chronologically, we are no longer young and never will be again. Worse yet, we are on a rapidly accelerating ride towards our ultimate demise. It's enough to rattle anyone. Is that a midlife crisis? If it is, I have had at least a half-dozen.

Maybe I'm wrong to associate the mid-life question with the very complex issue of infidelity. It has long been debated what fidelity specifically means and whether it is natural. Scientists like to point towards the animal world for examples. Infidelity is rampant there, but examples of monogamy also exist. A lot of weird things go on in the troubled world of animal relationships. Male sea horses get pregnant, some female insects kill and eat their spouses after mating, and certain types of monkeys practice mating rituals that include throwing feces at each other. Maybe it is a fair comparison.

My own take on this matter is that fidelity is the intention and the goal. This is not at all an unrealistic goal. Once committed to a relationship there is no reason to look elsewhere. If you are tempted, then the relationship is failing. It is my belief that infidelity does not exist as a polygamous instinct, but rather from the desire to fill a void when our lives are in turmoil. I suppose there are exceptions. Some people choose what we like to call "alternative lifestyles." I don't mean to be dismissive, but I haven't heard of too many "open relationships" that have lasted twenty or thirty years.

It takes two. Over the years there have been situations when I have been faced with the opportunity to break my vows with Diane but did not act upon it. Why? Because I had no reason to. I was happy with my marriage and I was happy with myself. Infidelity is more a result of failure and discontent than of weakness. Likewise, there were periods when our relationship was struggling, and I would have cheated but did not. This inaction came from lack of opportunity rather than a sense of morality. I have no reason to doubt that Diane faced similar dilemmas, opportunities and choices.

As I approached my forty-fifth year of life, I was not a happy person. I did not like who and what I had become. In many ways I was Fred Vaughn. I was a crass, arrogant workaholic bully. I was once again working sixty to ninety hours each week because the job gave me a sense of appreciation and satisfaction that I could no longer find at home. At home I spent most of my time watching television with a glass of whiskey in my hand and a ball game on TV. Caroline needed a father, but I was too busy, too tired, too drunk. Diane needed a husband and a lover, but I was uninterested and unresponsive. What made this situation even more pathetic was that I was fully aware of what was going on. I knew I had become an ass. I knew my life was on a fast-track to ruin, but I was so dark and unhappy that I just didn't care.

I started working in newspapers just as they began their final great decline. Cable television began the era when news had to be instantaneous. CNN led the way. Other news and sports channels soon followed. More importantly, the internet became part of our culture. By the early years of the 21st century, a vast majority of homes had at least one computer and almost all of these were connected to the web. The Hartford Courant was printing old information. The best we could offer was a hard document containing a variety of stories written from various angles, all neatly packaged in a cheap, lightweight, portable format. Eventually the electronic media would render this format obsolete.

Not long after joining the Courant, I was asked to speak at a four-day convention of news editors, to be held at the Mandalay Bay Resort in Las Vegas. Technology was the primary topic. How to use technology to our advantage. How to combat the information explosion that was reducing our readership and stealing our advertising revenue. How to open new markets. There would be seminars on web design; symposiums on new sources of advertising sponsorship; where and how to reduce expenses. It was a new era. The newspapers were no longer competing with each other, they were competing with every alternative to their form of media. We knew it was a battle we couldn't win. The best we could hope for was to postpone our inevitable death as long as possible.

Day one would be devoted to late arrivals, introductions and cocktail parties. Day two would be a trade show. Consulting firms, software companies, legal services, and subcontractors of every type would have booths and tables set up to attract our business. Day three would be roundtable discussions and debates. Day four would be networking, more cocktail parties, and some early departures. At 2pm on the third day I would be leading a group on the topic of "Sensationalism vs. Hard Facts. Making the Story Sell." Having been a disciple of Fred Vaughn, it was a subject I knew quite well.

Spouses were not encouraged to attend, but some did. In our case the decision was made for us. Caroline was in school and someone had to be there for her. Diane wanted to join me, so we tried to work things out. Once again, we had fallen into a rut. We weren't arguing, but we weren't communicating. We were just getting through the day. Maybe some time together would help.

There is a crazy romantic vibe to Vegas. The opportunity for a few days away from our daily routines offered the promise that we might rekindle some of whatever had been lost. We hoped her parents might consider staying at our house while we were gone. It was also my hope that if Diane could spend some time in my world she might better understand what I do and the pressures that go with the job. This might help us get back on track. It was not to be. Two weeks before the convention Diane's dad was rushed to the hospital for bypass surgery. It was an unfortunate but unavoidable turn of events. She stayed. I went. He recovered.

This was not my first trip to Vegas. Ten years earlier, Fred Vaughn had dragged me along to a similar conference. Back then, it wasn't so much a conference as a frat party. He drank, gambled and golfed. I basically acted as his valet, keeping his appointments and paperwork in order. Summer in Vegas is a bit on the warm side. I soon learned that the old adage about it not being the heat but the humidity was pure bullshit. Each day we reached the hellish temperature of 115 degrees. You couldn't stay outside for more than a few minutes without having your skin turn dry and crusty while at the same time having every mucus membrane in your body evaporate. From the moment we arrived I couldn't wait to get home.

This trip was different for a number of reasons. The convention was important, and I played an active role. Newspapers were in trouble and if we didn't devise a better survival strategy we would soon go the way of the telegraph. Both weather and accommodations were better than my previous visit. Vegas was in the midst of an unseasonably cool spell, with temps topping out in the low 80's. Mandalay Bay was one of the nicer resorts on the Strip. There would be time for leisure, but we were definitely there for business.

It was a very long first day. My flight left Bradley Airport at 6:45am on Sunday May 14th. That meant we had to leave the house by 5:15. Diane drove me to the curbside check-in. A quick, dispassionate kiss and I was on my way. There would be a three-hour layover in Chicago before continuing on to Vegas. Because of the three-hour time difference, and despite the long layover, I could expect to be arriving shortly after 1pm. That didn't happen. Thanks to some bad weather over Denver, my connecting flight was delayed ninety minutes. Waiting around airports can be dreadful, but this time it wasn't too bad. I found myself a friend.

Like myself, Missy Corrigan was a senior news editor. She worked for the Springfield Union Times, about a half an hour north of Hartford. We knew each other fairly well, in a casual way, having been in the business for about the same length of time, covering many of the same stories. We both still did a bit of writing for our respective papers, but mostly tended to administrative functions. That is the price of success. You get promoted away from doing what you love and are good at. I liked Missy.

She was a dedicated, professional who was passionate about getting the right story and getting the story right. Yet she was not all work and no play. At times her quirky sense of humor would emerge, usually accompanied by a sly, mischievous grin.

I thought I saw her walking into the terminal just as I was saying my good-byes at the check-in. We came face to face at the Starbucks near the gate. We talked over coffee. Same flights. Same basic itinerary. She would not be a speaker, but she did sign up for my discussion on sensationalism. Missy commented that the roundtable was the part of the conference she was most looking forward too, primarily because sensationalism was not part of her paper's format. She believed, for better or worse, the Union Times would now have to rely on it to survive.

The Courant leaned a little stronger on hyperbole than other New England papers. I suppose the Boston Globe did the same. It is not that we were deceptive or trying to force an agenda. We also avoided the brazen approach taken by the New York Post or the Daily News. We just wanted to catch people's attention. The Springfield Union Times was a straightforward "just the facts" publication. By using that format, they took some readers away from the Courant who felt we were biased, while we took some readers who felt they were bland. Both assertions were true.

It might be worth mentioning that Missy, Melissa was her real name, was no stunning beauty. I don't mean that to be cruel in any way. Likewise, I have never had any illusions about my own physical mediocrity. No one ever hired me for my looks. That is not to say that we were homely. There simply wasn't an immediate attraction based on looks. On this particular Sunday she was dressed in khakis and flats with a printed silk blouse. Business casual. A petit woman in her early 40's, she stood maybe five foot two and not more than one hundred pounds. Her sandy brown hair had a few curls that fell just above the collar. She looked more like your average housewife than a newspaper editor.

Just prior to boarding the flight we exchanged cell phone numbers and promised to keep in touch. Maybe even get together for a drink or a bite to eat during our stay. You don't want to cling to people during these conferences, but it is far worse to wander the hotel alone with no one to talk to and nothing much to do. In most towns that is pathetic. In Vegas it is expensive.

I dozed and listened to music for the trip to Chicago. Missy sat eight rows behind me. I caught up with her again as we prepared to change planes. When the departure board showed a lengthy delay on our connecting flight, we found an IHOP to have a late breakfast, followed by a couple of Bloody Mary's at a bar near our boarding gate. It was a pleasant way to keep ourselves occupied until it was time to get on the plane.

Mostly it was shop talk. That was what we had in common. I didn't care to burden anyone with the fact that my marriage, while not completely on the rocks, was precariously close to the reef. It is always easy for a parent to talk about their kids, but I avoided that subject as well. Missy had no kids so the conversation would be one-sided and boring. Shop talk is great for common ground, but even that gets old before long. The topic soon changed to other interests we shared. Food and dogs. Those subjects got us through the next hour.

We were running out of things to say. After a brief but awkward moment of silence I filled the empty airwaves with the first thing that came to mind. Glancing across the causeway, I noticed a small sushi place. I quipped that my nine-year-old daughter has been wanting to try sushi. "Do you like sushi? We have a few places by us that are okay, but nothing I would rush to recommend. Do you know of any places in your neck of the woods that might be suitable for a precocious kid?"

"There's the Mako on Boston Ave. Really good. I love sushi, but you're right, you have to be careful. I did a story a few years ago on a salmonella outbreak that we traced back to a place in Westfield. It was lucky that no one died. The place was filthy. The Mako can be trusted. You also have a place in East Hartford. Sapporo's. They're good, but Mako is better. So, your daughter wants to try sushi? Pretty adventurous for a nine-year-old. I thought you had twins?"

"Nope. Just one, along with a wife, two cats and a beagle named Truman. Caroline is nine going on thirty. Truman is the true free spirit in the family."

"Beagles always are. Up until two years ago I had a beagle. Mickey was a klutz. He used to hang his head low and trip over his ears when he walked. Great dog. My ex got him when we got divorced. He got to keep the dog and I got to keep my sanity."

"Sorry to hear that. Yeah, these aren't the best of times for my marriage either, but what can you do? Any kids?"

"No. That was the problem. We both have demanding careers. We couldn't make time for each other, much less a family."

Both of us understood that it was impolite to burden each other with tales of marital woes, so the subject turned back to food, pets and the print media. A few hours later we were picking our luggage off a carousel in Las Vegas.

The conference went well. At least as well as can be expected from any gathering of pretentious, self-indulgent, highly competitive journalists. Speeches were given. Topics were discussed. Contacts were made. Old acquaintances were reunited. My roundtable turned into a mild debate between the hard news reporters and those who contended that contemporary news is now information entertainment. I sided with the group that believes having your facts in order is completely meaningless if no one is interested in hearing what you have to say. A little sensationalism can be done without sacrificing accuracy. Given the dreadful financial situation of most papers, even the critics reluctantly agreed.

Afterwards I spent an hour or so at a cocktail reception. Several roundtable attendees tracked me down to further state their case or continue our discussion. I nodded politely, while desperately looking for a way out of there. There is only so much rehashing that one can take. It's like watching the news after the President makes a speech. He gives a fifteen-minute speech and for the next two hours a dozen reporters will tell you what you just heard him say.

Again, I saw Missy. She was across the room looking equally trapped and in need of an escape. She glanced my way with a pleading look. As politely as possible, I excused myself and hero-ically strode towards her, proclaiming that I had something im-portant to speak to her about in private. She smiled and stepped away from an old codger who would have her in a coma, had I not dragged her far away from his mindless drone.

"What's the urgency?" she asked.

"The urgency is that my head will explode if I have to spend another five minutes here. Can I talk you into joining me for a drink next door at the Luxor?"

"Bless your muckraking heart. Please tell me we are not this dreadful?"

"Speaking only for myself, I assure you that you are not."

Missy blushed. "Is that the investigative journalist talking or just bullshit?"

It shouldn't have happened but it did. In the course of two hours and several martinis we both found ourselves spilling our guts about how unhappy we were in our personal lives. Missy was lonely and lamented on how she had allowed her marriage to fail. I told her I was alone in a crowd, surrounded by people who I thought loved me, yet still left me feeling unloved. Around nine o'clock I walked her back to her room. She invited me in. I didn't leave until morning.

Adulterers will often say that it wasn't about sex. Of course, it was. My sex life at home was infrequent and unsatisfying. Good sex is important. When you are young it is all you think about and much of what you talk about. Why then, as your age advances and your body loses some luster should that change? Missy and I had great sex. At least it was as great as two middle-aged, not particularly attractive people could have under the circumstances.

Adulterers will sometimes say that they didn't mean for it to happen. More lies. If I didn't mean for it to happen it wouldn't have. There were choices to be made. Like many men my age, I had begun to wonder if it was possible for another person to be physically attracted to me. I wanted to feel desirable again. This was my opportunity. I wanted it to happen, if not with Missy, at least with someone a lot like her.

I didn't love her. Okay, that cliché was true, but I'm not sure that I loved Diane at that point either. It's hard to love others when you hate yourself. I was unhappy with almost every aspect of my life, but for a little while I was less unhappy when I was with Missy. I wanted to feel understood and I wanted to feel appreciated. She made me feel that way. I didn't have to love her and she didn't have to love me, just as long as we connected on some level.

We sat next to each other on the flights home, wondering what to do next. This was new for both of us. Was it a onetime moment of weakness, or a beginning? We chose to make it a beginning. We already had a friendship and a working relationship, so we chose to make it about sex. We also chose to keep it from everyone we knew, including friends and coworkers.

Maintaining secrecy and arranging our rendezvous was relatively easy. Every week we would exchange emails outlining schedules, meetings and locations. I could always disappear for at least two hours. On such "dates" I would call ahead to a hotel to see if they had vacancies. I never made a reservation and always paid cash. The hotels were quite forgettable. Most were among the dozens of small chains that dotted the state roads near Bradley Airport. On a few glorious occasions I was required to spend a weekend working in New York or Boston. Missy would join me. Nicer hotels. No assumed names.

For five months I lived what some might call a double life. Each day I went to work and each night I returned home to Diane and Caroline. I went to school plays and sporting events. We had dinner together, sharing conversations about the events of the day. The guilt I felt was no more than the guilt that someone on a diet might feel when they ate a candy bar. I was hungry. Missy satisfied that hunger.

Others have claimed that their infidelity helped to save their marriage. I make no such assertions. The affair happened, it ran its course, and then it ended. It did, however, have a positive effect on my relationship with Diane. In my efforts to maintain secrecy, I found myself paying more attention to her at home. We watched television together, went to movies, had conversations, ate out, and even made love. While conversation never centered around the struggles of our relationship, we both began to understand each other better, sharing the day to day stresses and anxieties that each of us routinely faced, but never spoke of. During that time, we did become closer.

The relationship with Missy ended abruptly and predictably. I was away for ten days. Diane, Caroline, and I went to San Diego for a weeklong vacation. It was a terrific time. We visited the zoo, went to the beach, drove to the mountains, and even went shopping twice in Tijuana, Mexico. If I had to pick any place other than Key West, San Diego would be my favorite destination.

Upon returning, I immediately contacted Missy. She was busy for a few days but we were both scheduled to be at a press luncheon in Worcester on Thursday. Afterwards we went out for drinks at a bar in nearby Shrewsbury. It was there that she told me she met a guy from her gym. I nodded, knowing full well what that meant. She was worried, but I was relieved. I knew we wouldn't last, but I had no idea how it would end. This was comfortable, and the timing was good. We would both be alright.

I got home around seven, handing Diane a small box which contained a pair of gold earrings. Surprised and excited, she asked "What's the occasion?"

"No occasion. The luncheon was at the Marriott. I stopped by the gift shop on the way out, to grab a cup of coffee. I saw the earrings and though of you."

Missy and I exchanged emails and phone calls for a while. Her relationship with the guy from the gym lasted three months, but there were other guys. As far as I know she never remarried. A year after we stopped seeing each other, she took a job with the Cleveland Plain Dealer. After that we lost contact.

Did Diane ever know of the affair? If she did she never said anything. I'm sure there were times when she suspected. Those suspicions were not necessarily during the five months with Missy. There have always been times when times are tough. It is then that you look for whatever comfort you may find, wherever you may find it. Likewise, I do not know if Diane was ever unfaithful in our marriage. If so, I wouldn't blame her. I'm quite certain she had opportunities and temptations. There were far too many times when I ignored her or pushed her away. Unhappiness knows no double standard.

It would be wrong to say that this was the low point in our marriage. It was one of several low points and it would be senseless to rank them. Every life has such times. We emerged from the darkness the way we always do, with time. Clouds lift. A clear sky gives way to warmer days. Gradually Diane and I began talking more. The more we talked, the more we fell back in love, again.

Both Richard and Caroline were stunned by what they had just read. Caroline began to pace the room. Grabbing a glass by the sink, she then reached for the pitcher of margaritas on the room service tray and poured herself a drink. She downed it in two gulps and laughed.

Richard looked confused. "Talk to me. Are you angry? Did you know about the affair? What's in your head?"

Again, Caroline laughed. "No and no. I didn't know about the affair and I'm not angry. That's why I'm laughing. The answer should be yes and yes, but it's not. I was old enough. If I had been closer to my dad, I might have seen the signs, but I didn't have a clue and I don't think Mom did either. I remember the Vegas trip. It seemed like no big deal. Mostly, I remember Dad stressing over his presentation. I'm not angry, because there were a number of times when I knew Mom and Dad were unhappy. That was one of those times. There were months when they acted more like roommates than as a married couple. Maybe every marriage goes through that. God, I hope not. But I kind of understand how it can happen. Am I making any sense?"

"You are," he replied. "Maybe that's the purpose of this whole thing—whatever this thing is. To make sense of things you could never otherwise understand."

CHAPTER SEVENTEEN

*W*hen the phone rings at 5am on a Sunday, it is never a good thing. As a newsman, my first thought would always be that there was some major event happening and I had to be there to report it. My second thought was that someone died. Neither choice was appealing, but that was my world. I glanced at the display before taking the call. It was Catherine. Shit. I hadn't heard from my younger sister since Christmas. Someone must have died. Maybe not. Maybe she was drunk. Drunk I could handle.

"Hey brother. Sorry to call so early but I got big news. The witch is dead."

"Huh? What witch? Speak English."

"Carmen. I've been working the overnight at Shoreline Medical. They wheeled her in around one o'clock. Heart attack. They did what they could but she was gone when she got here. It was bound to happen. Remember how slim she was at Dad's funeral? Her weight had ballooned back to up to about 350 pounds. I got word as soon as the ambulance arrived, but I didn't find out she was gone until just a few minutes ago. I tried calling Marty but no one answered."

While my relationship with Cat had never been strained, it was sporadic at best. I've never really stopped to figure out why, not that it really mattered. I knew she was working as a nurse.

Unbeknownst to me she was currently on third shift at Shoreline Medical Center, a small hospital in Long Branch, New Jersey. The hospital was just five blocks from the apartment where Carmen had been living since she divorced my father.

Diane, usually a sound sleeper, was now wide awake and sitting up. She kept nudging me, trying to find out who I was talking to and who had died. After covering the receiver and telling her it was Cat, I gruffly waved her off and resumed talking with my sister.

"I can track down Marty," I told her.

"I know this is awkward for you. Are you going to come down for the funeral?"

"It's busy as hell at work right now," I said. That's always an easy excuse when you don't want to do something. "Yeah, I guess I'll have to come down. I may just do a one day back and forth for the wake. I'm not going to the funeral. What do you figure? Wednesday and Thursday?"

"Yeah, probably."

"Let me know as soon as you know. I'll see you in a couple of days."

With that, I hung up the phone. Turning to a semi-agitated Diane I simply replied "Carmen is dead." The look on my wife's face changed as she struggled to grasp what those words meant to me. Was it a relief? A final exorcising of demons? Or was it a forced immersion into a painful and long discarded past? All of the above. My first thought was to shut down. I went downstairs and poured myself a double shot of Scotch, then ate a cheese sandwich so the booze wouldn't rot my stomach. Then I returned to bed. I never sleep past eight. On this day I didn't get up until noon.

It was midafternoon before I tried to contact Marty. By then she already knew. Sunday night we got word that the wake would be Wednesday from four to eight and the funeral at ten the following morning. Marty was flying up on Tuesday morning and staying until Friday. I would drive down Wednesday morning and drive home the same night.

At home my relationship with Diane was finally coming out of a dark period. There had been strains and challenges, but events like this always seemed to bring us closer together.

"I can get someone to stay with C. for a day or two. Do you want me to go with you?" School had just finished, so Caroline could have easily stayed with one of the neighbors. It seemed like she was always sleeping over somewhere.

"No Babe. I got to do this one myself. It will be a one day run. I never did see much sense in watching them put somebody in the ground. I'll go, stay for an hour or two, be seen, and come home. For me, Carmen died a long time ago. I'll try to put some closure to it but nothing much will change. It's better if I drive alone to spend some time in my own head."

"Are you going to stop and see Beverly?"

"Not this time. I just want to get in and out as quickly as I can."

As I drove down the Merritt Parkway towards the Tappan Zee, I sat in silence, trying not to think. It seemed best if I let whatever thoughts and emotions might be there come naturally. For a very long time, there was nothing. Intermittently, my thoughts were filled with the nervous twinge of curiosity. Who would be there? Would I be shunned or welcomed by her family? None of that really mattered. I was there because it was my duty. I had to pay my final respects to a person who I may not have looked kindly upon, but who was a part of my life for several years. I would be cordial and respectful, then leave.

The wake was being held at DeMuro's Funeral Home on South Street, in Long Branch. The drive had taken less time than

I expected, so I arrived shortly before three. Two blocks from the funeral home I pulled into the Cristo Diner, figuring I could grab a sandwich and a cup of coffee, then walk to the wake. After more than three hours on the road I was cramped and eager to stretch. As I emerged from the car I inhaled deeply. There is something wonderfully rancid about the smell of New Jersey's salty summer air. A quick glance around made me remember that it was the same old place I once knew and never loved. I chirped the lock and walked toward the diner.

Just four or five steps from the car I was struck by the unsettling sensation that someone was watching me. Eight steps later as I passed the curb and strode onto the walkway, that odd vibration was confirmed with the steady clipping of footsteps behind me. For a moment I paused, considering whether to turn or proceed. The choice became self-evident as a voice called out "Hey pal, mind if I join you?" I turned to be greeted by the smiling face of my father, now dead for more than ten years.

"I wasn't sure if you would come. I'm glad you did."

"What are you doing here?" I asked. It was a pretty stupid question.

"I figured if you came, you might want to talk."

"About what?"

"You tell me. Baseball? Your Yankees are looking good again this year. I still can't stand them, but I gotta be impressed."

I didn't respond, at least not with words. My puzzled look clearly told the apparition that his attempt to lightly break the ice wasn't working. He opened the door and we both stepped inside. There was a vacant booth in the far-right corner near the kitchen. As we took a seat, the apparition waved to the waitress as though he knew her. She gave a smile of recognition and waved back.

"You came for the funeral," he said, "but I think this may be an opportunity to bury more than just Carmen."

My confusion was apparent. I tilted my head in the manner of a curious beagle. "I have no idea what the hell you are talking about."

"Okay, let me get to the point," he said, with his steel blue eyes piercing directly through mine. "I put you through some shit when you were younger and we both know that Carmen was the biggest piece of shit I put you through. We also know that we were starting to get past all of that when I had to leave this world. Unfinished business. It's not a good thing. But unfinished business doesn't get resolved instantly. It takes some time. Like now. Maybe, just maybe, now might be a good time."

I looked down at my shoes. Yep. I still had feet. Then I rubbed my eyes and shook my head to wake up, in case I had been sleeping. Looking up I saw he was still there. A sudden shudder of fear came over me. "Am I dead?" I asked.

"Nah," he laughed. "I am, but you got a few more years."

Muttering to myself I began trying to logically piece it all together. "I'm not dead. I'm not sleeping. But I'm at a diner in New Jersey on my way to a funeral, and I'm talking to a fucking ghost."

"You ain't nuts either, so get that out of your head." Dad reached back and felt his pants pocket. "Shit. I forgot my wallet. Do you mind picking up the tab on this one? I could sure use a cup of their piss-weak coffee."

I didn't think ghosts were supposed to have substance, but this one did. I tried to somehow make sense of it. I knew he was dead. He had to be. I went to his funeral. I saw the body. Silently I asked myself if he had somehow faked his own death.

"Nope" he responded, while reading my mind. "I'm real and I'm real dead."

Beatrice, our waitress, brought us two coffees. He ordered us both a slice of cheesecake then suggested she put another pot of coffee on. "This may take a while." Then, without hesitation, the once familiar face leaned forward and began talking.

"I did some really stupid and selfish things over the years and you wound up paying the price. Some I can try to explain and some I can only apologize for, but I owe you that much. I can't undo what you went through, but maybe I can help you make fewer mistakes in your own life."

"Dad, you don't owe me anything."

"Yeah I do. Look, when your Mom got sick I didn't know what to do. That's normal. But rather than focusing on her, I thought more of myself. How am I going to deal with this? How are we going to pay the medical bills? I knew she was going to die and it scared the hell out of me, not because she was suffering but because I didn't know how to be a grown-up person and survive on my own. I couldn't care for myself, much less a sick wife and three kids. It terrified me. At a time when I should have been thinking about everyone else, I thought only of me."

I sat silently and listened. I knew he was right and I knew that facing the truth hurt him, but his pain wasn't mine. Rather than excusing his actions, I felt a burning anger rise from within. Instead of giving sympathy, I lashed out.

"Why the hell are you here?" I demanded. "Are you here for me, you, or her? I came to pay my respects because it's the right thing to do, then get the hell out of here and go back to my real life. It's too late for anything else. What do you hope to accomplish by being here?

"Listen to yourself. You're still mad as hell at me after all these years. As for your charmed life, I wouldn't be so sure. If it was so great you probably wouldn't have had that little fling last year."

His words stung, and still he continued. "You're still mad at me because you had a shitty childhood. I get that and believe me, I am sorry. You came here so you could bury the last vestige of that episode, but I don't think you can bury it until you come to terms with it. The only way you can come to terms with it is by confronting it and that means confronting me. Remember the movie A Few Good Men? Tom Cruise screams 'I want the truth!' and Jack Nicholson fires back 'You can't handle the truth!' It's time you got the truth."

"Since when did you become so damn enlightened?" It was a stupid comment, but I was on a roll.

He smiled. "You can learn a lot by being dead."

There was no retort to that. I looked at him for a moment, then realized the image I saw was the same one I last saw shortly before he died. I guess you don't age after you die. Unable to respond further in anger, I began to laugh. "Okay, let's talk. I do have questions. Do I have to ask them or are dead guys psychic, so you can just answer them?"

"Doesn't work that way. I think I know what's going on in your head, but I'm still not that smart. You're going to have to tell me. Besides, it has been a long time since I actually got to have a conversation with my son."

Beatrice returned with a carafe of coffee, and a handful of creamers. "Miss," I said. "We're going to do this backwards. Can you put me in for a pastrami Reuben on rye? No fries. Just the sandwich. You want one too?"

"No thanks. I'll stay with the cheesecake."

"Okay," I began. "First big question. Mom got sick and died. A few days later, Grandpa moves out. A month later you allegedly start dating again. Six months later you're married. Sounds a little suspicious. You were screwing around while Mom was in the hospital, weren't you?"

"Believe it or not, the answer is no." He looked down at his coffee. There was shame on his face as he saw his reflection in the cup. He spoke calmly and clearly, but there was a quiver in his voice. "This isn't easy for me either, but I'll do the best I can. Your mom died in December, but by late Summer we knew she wasn't going to make it. She knew I was barely able to care for myself much less three kids, but she made me promise that I would never split up you three. Both my sisters and her family didn't agree with that. They each felt I wasn't up to the task so they offered to help raise you. I made it clear that I was going to honor Camille's wishes no matter what. Discussions on this subject sometimes got a little heated, and on the night before the funeral an argument broke out between me and your grandfather. I insisted he leave. That's why he moved out. "

Dumping two sugars and three creamers into his cup he swirled his spoon and drew a long slurp. "Weak," he said.

"Of course, it's weak. You're drinking sugar and milk for Christ's sake. You don't leave any room in the cup for the coffee."

Dad smiled. "Your mother used to drink it the way you do. Strong and black. She used to give me a hard time about it too."

"It's a Navy thing. Guys got beat up for drinking it the way you do."

"Anyway," he continued, "I knew I was in over my head. I probably could have handled taking care of you, but what the hell did I know about raising two girls? The truth is I was spoiled and selfish. I wanted someone to take care of me and I didn't want the job of taking care of someone else. From the day your mother died I set myself out on the task of finding another wife and mother. I wasn't looking for love or sex. I was looking for a maid and a nanny. Carmen was the first person to come along."

"You didn't love her?"

"I didn't even like her. I'm ashamed to admit that, but it's the truth. I'm pretty sure she didn't care all that much for me either, but we each got what we were looking for. I got what I wanted and she got a ring. At that time, a woman who was in her thirties and never married was considered a spinster. She had younger sisters who were married. She wanted to be a married sister too.

That part might have been okay, but she should have never been a mother."

"But when you saw that she was a psycho, you could have done something about it. Instead you did nothing."

"I tried. But really, what could I do? After a while I began to kid myself that it wasn't that bad. You were fed, groomed and clothed. We did some fun stuff together. It was bad, but it wasn't all bad."

"Even now you're trying to convince yourself of that, aren't you? Who can't handle the truth? What do you mean you tried?"

The words stung. "I know you heard us argue about money and the house, but there were other arguments that you didn't hear. I went to bat for you kids plenty of times, but usually I was too weak to hold my ground. One time she threatened to kill herself because I told her I was going to take you kids and leave. Another time she threatened to divorce me for adultery."

"Did you cheat on her?"

"Damn right, I did. Kids in your era talked about sex and drugs and rock and roll. For my generation it was sex and booze and jazz. I didn't drink, but maybe I should have. A year after we got married, my cousin Mickey introduced me to a few of his friends. Mickey was always something of a playboy. I got caught once because she got suspicious and checked the phone bill. There was a number she didn't recognize, so she called it. When she did, I answered the phone. We didn't have caller I.D. back then."

"Did she ever cheat on you?"

"Nah. At least I don't think so. I was probably the only person stupid enough to put up with her bullshit. There were at least a dozen times I should have taken you kids and left. I was miserable. I knew you kids were being treated badly. But I just didn't have the balls to do something about it; even after that incident when you went to the police chief's house.

It wasn't until you joined the Navy that the shit finally hit the fan. I knew you joined to get away from us. She thought it was great. I hated it. I wanted you to go to college. We could have figured out a way to do it. Instead you ran away from home. She wanted you out of the picture and was hoping your sisters would follow. When I finally snapped it was too late. It was too god-damn late."

A lone tear streamed down from his left eye. Another person might have backed off, showing compassion for a man who was now bearing his departed soul, but another person hadn't endured my childhood.

"No shit it was too late. I just don't understand how you could sit back and do nothing while you were treated like dirt and we were deprived of basic human decency. Can you at least understand why you're not exactly my favorite person in the world?"

"Yeah, I understand, but that's why we're talking. It may not change how you feel, but at least I get to give you my side of things. There was a lot to it. I was a selfish coward, pure and simple. I wish there was some way I could change that, but I can't. When it became obvious that Carmen was a huge mistake I was afraid to do anything about it because I figured she was still doing a better job than I could."

"Yeah, you said that already. So that's it? You came here to tell me that you wanted to be a good father but you're sorry things turned out so shitty? Seems to me you could have popped into a dream or sent an email or something."

He looked up then pointing to his cup he waved Beatrice over to warm it up. Waiting until she left, he again sat up straight, then leaned forward. "I didn't come here for me. I came here for you."

"What do you mean?"

"I mean, you are more like me than you realize or want to admit."

"Bullshit. How?"

"Let's start with parenting. I know I was shitty at it but how good are you? How many hours a week do you work? Sixty or so, right? On most days you leave the house before your kid is awake, then you get home at seven, eight or nine. That doesn't leave much time. You're exhausted or stressed when you get home. How often do you bark at her for making too much noise or leaving a mess or just because you are tired and frustrated? How often do you hug her or tell her you love her or just sit with her and talk for a while?"

"Are you saying I'm a lousy father?"

"I'm just saying you need to do better."

"But I have to work and you know my job is demanding. Diane and I figured out long ago that one of us needs to be the breadwinner and the other has to be there for Caroline."

"You're an excellent breadwinner and I'm proud of what you have accomplished. Now put that same effort into what you accomplish at home. You can do both." He paused for a second and let out a sigh. "Then there's the issue of your marriage…"

"What issue is that?"

"I made a huge mistake when I married Carmen. You found a much better match in Diane. Not perfect mind you, but pretty damn close. Her strengths are your weaknesses and your strengths are hers. You complement each other very well, but you don't see it and you are in danger of losing everything."

"Losing everything? What do you mean?"

"I mean she really loves you but she feels unloved and alone. It's one thing for her to take care of Caroline while you work. She loves doing that and Caroline shows her love in return, but she also needs some attention from you. The kind of attention that only you can give."

"Our sex life isn't awful. We've had our problems over the past couple of years but we'll be okay."

"I'm not talking about sex. When was the last time you went for a walk together and just talked? Have you ever cooked a meal together, or worked on a project around the house? You do stuff separately so as to not get in each other's way. You need to get in each other's way. You need to reconnect. You guys do that once a year in Key West, then ignore each other for the remaining fifty-one weeks. She's not happy right now. Don't blow the best thing you've got going for you."

"And how do you know this?"

He just stared into my eyes. I knew he spoke the truth. The stare was not frightening, but it burned a hole into my soul. For a long time, we sat there, drinking our coffee, not saying a word. Finally, I just said "Thanks. I guess we did need to have this conversation."

For a moment I thought about asking him to tell me about eternity and the afterlife. How often do you get to have a conversation with a dead guy? There was so much to ask. Was there heaven and hell? What was dying like? Does everyone get life after death or do you have to be selected? I thought about it, but not for long. I figured he would pop up again sometime and we could talk some more.

I waved for the check. "I guess we ought to go." Then, glancing at my watch, I realized the wake was already over. "Shit, now what?"

"There was a big accident on the parkway about five minutes behind you. You can always say you were stuck in that. There's still the funeral tomorrow."

"Nah. I think I've had enough of New Jersey for one day. They need me at home."

"Good idea," he smiled. "What are you going to tell them?"

"I'll tell them the truth. I got all the way down here, then realized that I didn't want to do this. I only came down for appearance sake and once I got here decided that wasn't a good enough reason."

There was no long good bye. As we got up from the table we hugged. "I'm really proud of you," he said. "Take care of your family and I'll be even prouder." Ghost or not, the hug was real. As we departed the diner, I reached back to hold the door but when I turned around, he was gone.

The drive back to Connecticut was a blur. I arrived home shortly after midnight. Diane was asleep on the sofa with the television still on and a cat asleep on her feet. Startled to see me, she looked up as if to ask if I was real or a dream. Rather than answering, I coaxed her up to bed promising that I would tell her all about it in the morning. Checking on Caroline I was surprised to see that her bed was empty. Diane murmured that she was sleeping over Jessica's house. They were going to the beach in the morning. It disappointed me that she wasn't home, but that also meant I had an opportunity.

Still wired and awake from all that coffee, I poured myself a glass of bourbon and sat down at the dining room table with a pad and paper. I collected my thoughts, then began doing what any good reporter does. I took notes. By 3am I was tired enough to sleep.

I woke refreshed around 9am. After a quick shower and a glance at the morning paper, I woke Diane and asked her if she wanted to go out for breakfast. She liked the idea.

"Where do you want to go?"

"How about Vernon Diner?" I suggested.

As we walked into the diner, I found myself looking for Beatrice. She wasn't there.

CHAPTER EIGHTEEN

*J*ohn "Howard" Simmons was born as Jan Symkowicz, during the early part of the twentieth century, in a small village in southeastern Poland that is now part of the Ukraine. The family settled in Brooklyn, but after two years moved east to Bridgeport, Connecticut, escaping the perils of the big city. It was appropriate that John was born on February 14th, Valentine's Day, because a sweeter man I have never met.

John was the oldest of eleven children, although two would not live past infancy. That left John with four brothers and four sisters. Two would become priests. Two would become nuns. The other four would all go on to college, becoming a doctor, a nurse, a teacher, and an engineer. John quit school when he was twelve years old, having just completed the eighth grade. He was smart enough for college, but as the eldest male, he was expected to do his part to support the others. His sense of duty was too great for regret. Family came first. It always would.

John worked many jobs but eventually found himself do- ing assembly work for Bullard, a machine tool company in Bridgeport. Forty-two years later he would retire from that same company. Shortly after going to work for Bullard, John began singing in the choir for Saint Michael's Catholic church. It was there he met Mary Kowlaczyk, a switchboard operator for the phone company. They courted for over a year. Stubborn and independent, Mary would repeatedly shun her suitor's request for marriage, but John would not be deterred. He finally wore her down. The two were wed at the church where they sang. Between the two families there were five other men named John. Family gatherings could get quite confusing so she began calling her husband Howard, after Howard Avenue, the Bridgeport street on which they lived.

Both John and Mary were loyal Democrats, and so their first child, Frank, was named after President Franklin Roosevelt. Over the years, six more children would follow; John, Diane, Michael, Ella, Sophie and Nicolas. Nicholas was the youngest, born on Christmas Day.

A proud and patriotic man, Howard Simmons tried to join the Army during World War II, despite having a wife, a son, and another son on the way. Americans were fighting in Europe for the liberation of his native Poland. Howard never got past the physical. A rather pronounced heart murmur was noted, and his attempt to enlist was nullified. He took solace in noting that Bullard was instrumental in providing machine tools that helped build the ships and planes that won the war.

John was sixty-nine years old and already retired when I first met him. Diane came up to the campus with her parents to meet me, see the apartment, and check out the school. To reassure them, I made a point of having my girlfriend Jennifer there when they arrived. It probably wasn't necessary. I could tell they liked me. We had similar immigrant cultures in common. I understood the struggles of lower middle class, blue collar, ethnic families. It also helped that I wasn't black, Jewish or Russian.

A few months later when we announced that Diane and I were a couple, Mary urged Diane not to cheapen herself and to move out rather than cohabitate. John, who seldom disagreed with his wife, felt otherwise. "Let them figure it out," he would say. "They're not kids anymore. When we were their age we were already married and had kids."

"But that's not how we raised her. You don't live with your boyfriend until you are married. We were married." She argued. "What about the church?"

"What about it? How often does she go to church now? Besides," he continued, "we taught her to think for herself and to make her own decisions. That's what she's doing. If it turns out to be a mistake, she'll learn from it. She's done pretty well so far."

Eventually, I interjected my way into the discussion. "Look, I can really appreciate where you are coming from. We wrestled with similar questions. We didn't want to make you uncomfortable, and there is some concern that living together could be a distraction from school. On the other hand, we already know that we get along as roommates, and good roommates are hard to find. Besides, it's a two-bedroom apartment. There is plenty of space for us to stay away from each other."

Mary laughed. "I think you're trying to snow me."

With a mischievous smile, I replied, "Guilty as charged."

"See." John said. "Leave them alone. They'll be fine."

With that I poured us each a shot of cheap vodka. "Thanks Dad." I toasted.

"Not so fast," he cautioned. "Just because I like you doesn't mean I trust you."

In the years that followed we did indeed like, trust and respect each other. There wasn't much for anyone to dislike about Howard Simmons. He was calm, kind and seldom confrontational. In his retirement years, he took great pride in rising early each day and, over a cup of coffee, read the daily newspaper from cover to cover. Prior to our wedding, it was the Bridgeport Post. Before long, he switched allegiance to his son-in-law's paper.

I could always tell when he disagreed with something I had

written. He would never directly challenge my position, but he would question it further. When I wrote that the scandals of the Reagan administration were more a matter of politics than substance, he asked if my views were softened by Reagan's charisma. Would I have been so tolerant if the President was Nixon or Carter? Howard loved to talk politics. Our debates could be lively, but they were never hostile.

On the home front, however, there was never any debate. As long as I treated his daughter and granddaughter well, he left us alone. In his own family life, he had been tormented by an assertive mother who would often impose her will on what he and his wife should or should not be doing. He swore never to interfere and he meant it. On more than one occasion Diane and I would be arguing in front of him. Howard would quietly leave the room. Mary would admonish him. "Aren't you going to say something?"

"Why should I? They'll work it out. If they want me to say something, they'll ask. Leave them alone. They'll be fine."

I've met thousands of men who were smarter. None were wiser.

It was with modest fanfare that Howard Simmons celebrated his ninetieth birthday. Franklin rented the VFW hall in Bridgeport. Diane and I paid to have it catered. Others paid for the bar tab, decorations, a DJ, deserts and gifts. Sixty assorted friends and family showed up to pay tribute. The party itself ran from noon until five, allowing plenty of time for the veterans to redecorate the hall for that evening's Valentine's Day dance.

As with most parties, it started slowly as people trickled in. Once the room began to fill, Franklin took over as emcee, encouraging others to step up to the microphone and tell their favorite Howard Simmons story. Most stories were of some random act of kindness that Howard had shown toward them. Other's told of the wisdom of the man.

As one might expect, on the event of his ninetieth birthday Howard was lavished with gifts from his well-wishers. There were seven different ninety-dollar gift certificates from some of Fairfield County's finest restaurants. There was cash, clothes and liquor. There were tickets to see a Broadway show. Mary, ever the practical wife, got him a new suit to wear to church on Sunday. The beloved old man accepted each gift with a kiss on the cheek and an embarrassed sense of humility. As the party concluded, Howard shuffled to the microphone to softly utter a few words of appreciation.

"I want to thank you all for coming today. While I don't understand why another day off the calendar should entitle me to such a celebration, I am very grateful to you all. I have been blessed with a wonderful family and many wonderful friends. I love you all. Thank you."

A few hours later, shortly after watching the ten o'clock evening news, Howard rose from his recliner and began to head upstairs to bed. Mary shut the television off and got up from the sofa. She would go into the kitchen for a cup of tea before joining her husband in bed. Howard took two steps towards the doorway, turned to face his wife, then collapsed.

We arrived at the Saint Vincent's Hospital around 6am. Mary had not slept. Howard was still unconscious. Diane quickly grabbed a nurse and asked of her father's condition. The nurse was unsure, so she found the attending physician. Slowly the doctor began to explain, but she was in no mood for slow explanations. "I'm a damn pharmacist," she blurted. "Talk to me in medical terms. I need to know what is going on. I'm the one who has to explain it to the others."

"Congestive heart failure. The damage seems to be in the atrioventricular valves, most likely the tricuspid. It's too early to be sure, but that seems likely. Your mother said something about him having a murmur, so that diagnosis fits. If he makes it through the next few hours we'll have a more precise answer and a course of action. Meanwhile both hypoxia and pneumonia are secondary risks. He is in a coma but we have been able to stabilize his vitals."

"Can we see him?"

"Not until he is stable. The next few hours are critical."

"What are his chances?"

"I can't honestly say. It's particularly tough with someone that age."

"Don't patronize me. I know my father's old. You must have some idea. Is he going to die today?"

"Probably not, but I don't want to offer false hope. He may not come out of the coma, but he will most likely hang on for at least a few days, then take a turn, either better or worse."

Three days later Howard Simmons awoke from his coma. Mary was by his side, holding his hand while she dozed in the chair. Diane and I were sitting on folding chairs watching television. Sophie and her husband Rick had stopped in, mostly to see Mary and to ask Diane if there was anything new from the doctors. He was stable and on life support. Nothing had changed. Nothing was expected to change any time soon, but it did. From beneath his oxygen mask, Howard began to make a moaning sound. Then his eyes opened. At once we began screaming for a nurse. Howard leaned forward and tried to sit up but was abruptly pushed back by two large male nurses, as a doctor rushed into the room.

For a while a team of two men and two women, dressed in lab coats, worked feverishly on him, taking blood, checking vitals, changing his IV and catheter. They were too busy to explain what was happening. Howard grew impatient as he tried to speak. One doctor said he would give him a mild sedative, but it wouldn't knock him out. The hope was that he would remain alert, but not agitated. "Ativan?" Diane asked. The doctor nodded.

Finally, after wrestling with his voice and his weakened muscles, Howard demanded to know what was going on. Doctor Wilcox calmly explained to the old man where he was, how he got there and that he would be hospitalized a while longer. He responded by turning to his wife with sad eyes, "I'm sorry Mary. Don't worry. Everything is going to be alright."

"Just be still and get better you old fool" she smiled. "You gave us quite a scare."

Doctor Wilcox then called the family out into the hallway. He wanted to explain to everyone the need to avoid false hope. A brief and sudden emergence from a coma was not uncommon, but it didn't lessen the severity of the situation. I was leaving to join them, but the old man began tugging at my sleeve. He had something important to tell me.

"Go back to the house," he whispered. "Pull the sofa in the family room away from the wall. At the far-right corner, pull up the rug. There is something there. Bring it to me."

"Bring what back? What am I looking for?"

"Just go. When you come back I will try to explain. Don't say anything to the others. Just do it."

There was a look of desperation in his eyes. What could it possibly be? I pulled out my phone and pretended to listen. I then turned to Diane and said that the Courant just called. I needed to run a quick errand. I would be gone an hour at most. She was used to me getting such calls so the lie went unquestioned. Now that Howard was awake, no one wanted to leave. I slipped out quietly and headed towards the Simmons residence.

The building on Howard Avenue was a typical city row house, built in 1908. I found the spare key they kept hidden behind the mailbox. Entering through the front door I went straight for the

RALPH YOURIE

sofa. After dragging it away from the wall I immediately noticed something small and shiny, glimmering from the corner where Howard instructed me to look. By dragging the sofa, the rug curled up away from the wall, revealing a small gold and diamond wedding ring. It had been missing for seventeen years. I wrapped the ring in a paper towel and put it in my pocket.

Howard looked up when I returned to the room. He appeared to be alert and comfortable. Sophie, Diane and Rick were still there. Mary turned and asked if everything was okay at work. Everything was fine. Reaching into my pocket, I took the small package and pressed it into Howard's hand.

"It was right where you said."

Mary and the other's looked confused. "What did you just give him? What are you talking about?"

Howard opened his hand and extended a frail arm towards his wife, revealing the paper towel. Taking the small object from his hand she slowly peeled away the paper, revealing its hidden treasure. At once she recognized the ring.

One day while cleaning house, Mary had taken the ring off and left it on a coffee table. Her chores were tragically interrupted by one of those phone calls that you hope to never get. Her sister Delores, Dee for short, had been killed in a car accident. Mary dropped everything and raced to her sister's home. Meanwhile, the ring was never seen again. It wasn't until late that night when she returned home, that she even thought of the ring. It was no longer on the table.

I glanced over to see Howard's expression. His face was alight with a proud and peaceful smile.

"How can this be?"

Despite being very weak and short of breath Howard managed to lift himself to an upright position so he could speak to everyone in the room. We all closed in to listen.

"Maybe it was a dream, but I don't think so," he began. "Last night I met Dee for coffee. I don't know where we were, but it looked like an old diner. The place was called Cristo's. Dee told me she was sorry about your ring. It was her fault that you had lost it. She then told me where to look. I sent Ralph to get it."

"But that's impossible," Mary shook her head. "Dee has been dead for years."

"Then maybe I was dead last night. Who can say? I only know what I saw and now you see what she told me. When you got the phone call about her accident you hurried to go see her. In your rush you knocked the ring from the coffee table and it fell behind the couch. There it stayed until today."

Diane turned to me. "So, there was no call from work?"

"No." I let out a nervous laugh. "This call came from a higher authority."

"Did you see anyone else?" Mary asked.

"No, but I think I will be joining them soon."

"Don't say that. Now that you're awake you'll be back on your feet in no time."

"Maybe, but I don't think so. I don't know why. It's just a feeling I have. Don't be afraid. I'm not."

Mary's face turned stern and almost angry. "Don't talk that way, you old fool. You're not going anywhere except for home with me."

Rick tried to cut the tension. "Ma's afraid you're gonna cheat on her in the next life. Dee always was an attractive woman."

No one laughed.

"A joke," he said. "I was making a damn joke."

"Rick's right" Diane offered. "We've all gotten too serious. Look, Dad's awake and Ma has her ring back. Finally, we're all having a good day."

With that the conversation quickly changed. Diane and

Sophie began talking about the kids, Rick and I talked about the Yankees, and Mary sat holding Howard's hand, all the while looking at the ring that once again adorned her finger. Doctors and nurses came and went. His vitals were stable. Diane and I left around 6pm, giving way to Franklin and Wendy. Rick and Sophie would be leaving shortly.

At 5am the home phone rang. This time I thought it was work. It was not. John "Howard" Simmons was gone. At 11pm he fell asleep. At 3am the lines on the monitors went flat. Alarms went off. Doctors and nurses rushed in, but there was nothing to do.

The pain of his departure was lessened by the excitement of the previous day. Was he really gone? Perhaps he was back at Cristo's having breakfast with Dee.

I spent almost my entire adult life as a writer. It was my good fortune to be paid to do something I love. For that I have received accolades and monetary rewards. Nothing I have ever written has given me the pride and satisfaction that went into writing and delivering the eulogy for this man. Sometimes words come easy. This did not. It had to be perfect. Every word, every sentence, every extended pause or punctuation had to be full of meaning. It took me twelve hours to write two pages. I then gave it to Mary for approval. Her tears stained the pages. Diane read it next. Both approved.

Did Howard really talk with Dee the night before he emerged from his coma? Did he actually foresee his own death? The answer is yes. I believed it then, and I know it to be true now. We all are given the opportunity to talk with the departed. You have to see with your heart and listen with your soul. It is an opportunity that no one should miss.

CHAPTER NINETEEN

Dear Caroline-We are all, at times, hypocrites. I was probably worse than most.

J have often heard tales from other parents of the horror that goes with raising teenagers. I beg to differ. Babies terrify me. Teenagers are easy. Babies demand constant attention. Teenagers can be ignored. Babies cry, fill diapers, and do not sleep when others do. They must be carried everywhere, along with fifty pounds of gear. Teenagers ask for little more than twenty bucks and the keys to the car.

Raising Caroline was easy because I had very little to do with it. Diane did all the heavy lifting. She was the one who got her dressed, fed and on the bus each morning. She was the one who took her to dance class, Girl Scouts and field hockey. It was Diane who mended bruised knees and broken hearts. I knew nothing of how to raise a little girl into a young woman. Diane had been through it all, in her own childhood rites of passage. I stayed in the background, providing structure, discipline and a paycheck.

That is not to say that I didn't try to do my part. I was clumsy at it, to be sure, but I tried. We went to amusement parks and rode the scariest roller coasters together, laughing and screaming the whole time. We snorkeled side by side off Key West, nudging each other and pointing with wonder as stingrays, parrotfish and an occasional shark glided past. And I was the one who got to chaperone her on her first dates, where I took great joy in intimidating her would-be suitors.

Father-daughter conversations about life and its many perils were not usually part of the relationship. There was an occasional warning to "do this" or "don't do that" but detailing the facts of life was left up to Diane. She explained to Caroline what her period was and they went shopping together to buy her first bra. I was kept informed, but said and did little.

I would be lying if I didn't admit to being a bit jealous of Diane's relationship with Caroline. They were mother and daughter, but they were also best friends. I was unwilling or incapable of sharing in that affection. I did what I could and watched from afar. At times I felt Diane lavished too much affection on our daughter and not enough on me. And yet I did little to deserve or invite such an emotional exchange. I tried, but that's not who I was.

On a snowy Saturday morning in mid-January, Caroline, along with her friend Roy and our neighbor Christina, were in the family room, eating Coco-Puffs without milk and watching cartoons. The room was relatively quiet, other than the sounds coming from the television and the percussive noises that go with three kids munching away with all of the social graces of farm animals. They looked bored but content. I really cannot say why, but I suddenly felt consumed by a burst of fatherhood. It seemed like a good time to be a Dad. It was time for the Big Talk.

I asked the kids to come into the living room for a minute. "I want to discuss something," They looked at each other with confusion, but dutifully complied. They shuffled off to the next room and huddled together on the sofa, with Roy in the middle, holding cereal box. And so, The Talk began.

"You may find this hard to believe," I told them, "but I wasn't born old. Diane and I were once your age and understand what it is like to make that journey from being a kid to being an adult. It's fun, exciting, confusing, scary, joyous and painful. Sometimes it's all of those things at the exact same time. It is a time to experience new things. Some are good, some not so good, some are both. Mostly I'm talking about sex and drugs, but there are other considerations."

Roy blushed and looked down at the box of cereal at the mention of sex, while Caroline and Christine looked at each other as if to say "did he just say what I heard him say?" Nevertheless, I continued.

"You are now at a point in your life when you will be given the opportunity to take part in a variety of adult experiences. I would be a liar, a fool and a hypocrite if I stood here and gave you a long list of what not to do. I would be a fool, because I could talk all day about what not to do, but you will probably do them anyway. I would be a hypocrite because almost anything that I would warn you not to do, Diane and I have done. That doesn't make it good or okay. We would hope that the three of you are smarter than we were and will make better decisions. I just want you to be aware that when you take part in an adult activity, your actions have consequences.

I said I wasn't going to give you a long list of what not to do, but I am going to give you a short one. Three to be exact. Three completely unbreakable rules. Break any one of these three and it can ruin your life. Got it? Okay, here we go-

Rule number one: Don't get pregnant. To be more specific, don't get pregnant until you are done with high school and college. It may not kill you, like drugs and alcohol can, but it will end your life as you know it. Let's talk about choices and consequences. Let's say you get pregnant when you are sixteen. You have a lot of options, but none of them are good.

One option is to get an abortion. I don't know how you feel about it, but the fact is you are killing a potential life. That's a heavy burden. Another option is to have the kid and put it up for adoption. Do you drop out of school for nine months or continue going to school only to face teachers and classmates while carrying a kid you have no intention of keeping. When the time comes, how will you feel about giving birth to a beautiful newborn then having him or her forever taken away? Most women I know who gave a child up for adoption spent the rest of their lives wondering how their baby turned out. What kind of childhood did they have? What kind of person did they grow up to be? How do you react if one day they show up at your door and ask why you didn't want them?"

I paused for a moment, in search of a reaction. Much to my surprise, what I saw was their captivated stares. And so, I continued.

"A third option is to keep the baby. This usually means dropping out of school never getting a high school or college diploma. It also means missing out on proms, parties and socializing with all of your friends. You no longer have time for that because you have a baby to take care of. And since you never got to complete your education, you will most likely spend the rest of your life stuck in a dead-end minimum wage job. No nice house, new car, or Disney vacations. You are trapped. Get pregnant before you finish your education and your life as you know it is essentially over.

The cereal munching had stopped. The three adolescents were now staring at me with all the rapt attention that might normally be associated with cell phones. I knew I had them.

Rule number two: Never allow anyone to drive while under the influence. In some cases, the penalty for this is death. Since I'm in the newspaper business, I know the numbers. Last year, there were more than 5,000 traffic fatalities involving persons under the influence, who were under the age of 21. In some cases, dying is the easy part. Suppose you wind up as a quadriplegic, confined to a chair and a breathing tube for the rest of your life? Suppose you are the driver and you kill a young family, a child, or your best friend? Can you live with that? Can you deal with standing up in court to explain why you allowed yourself or someone else to drive in an impaired condition and killed someone? Are you willing to go to jail for such stupidity?

It is my hope that you three will be smart enough to avoid drugs and wait until you are of legal age and then use alcohol responsibly. That is my hope, but I'm not naive. So here is a safety net. This goes for all three of you. If you ever find yourself in a situation where you or the person you are with, should not be driving, call me. I don't care if it is four in the morning and you are a thousand miles away. Call me. I will get you safe passage home. No lectures. No unpleasant consequences. No questions asked. I will respect you for turning a bad situation into a good one. The rule is unbreakable. So is the safety net.

The third and final unbreakable rule might be the easiest. Don't get arrested. I'm not saying don't drink. But if you do drink, drink responsibly. Don't get busted for underage drinking. Or smoking pot, or DUI, or shoplifting, or vandalism, or anything else. A conviction will follow you around for the rest of your life. It will stand in the way of you getting a good job and it will forever label you as a bad person. I know the three of you are not bad people but being a convicted felon will convince a lot of people that you are.

That's it. Three unbreakable rules. If I can teach you anything, it is that actions have consequences. Getting pregnant, driving or riding with someone who is under the influence and getting arrested, each have the most severe long-term consequences I can think of. Any of the three will completely alter your lives in ways that you are not prepared to deal with. That still leaves a whole lot of other stupid ways to ruin your life, just not as profoundly. I hope you will make good decisions, but if you at least stick to these three unbreakable rules, you should be okay. Any questions?"

At first, I was greeted with blank stares and silence. Finally, Roy spoke up. "So, what's the worst thing you ever did that wasn't one of the three?"

"Roy," I replied, "A bad decision is something to be ashamed of, not bragged about. But here is something else to consider. All bad decisions fall into one of two categories: Things you should have said or done, and things you should not have said or done." In retrospect, it was a pretty stupid comment.

Caroline didn't think so. "Wow, Dad, that's really profound."

"Just stick to the big three. Do you think you can do that?" I asked. The three all nodded in unison. "Good. Now, while I still have your attention, I want to teach you one more thing that may come in handy some day. Roy, stand up."

He did as I asked. "It's an old trick I learned in the Navy. You should never pick a fight, but there may come a time when you will have to defend yourself. Just like with the three rules, we can keep it simple." I reached over and grabbed the bone between his neck and shoulder. He let out a little nervous whimper. I then invited the two girls over to feel where I had clasped.

"That's his collarbone," I explained. "You can feel your own to get a better idea. It is usually exposed and vulnerable. If you ever find yourself in a situation where you have to fight back, look for a chance to throw a direct punch to the collarbone. If you hit it straight on, it will snap, causing excruciating pain, but no life-threatening injuries." I then maneuvered Roy into several stances and play-acted a few situations to demonstrate. Naturally, the three all wanted to know if I had ever actually employed these moves on a real person. I thought for a moment, then lied, "Luckily, no."

It was one of my proudest moments as a dad. The following weekend, Caroline brought four other friends over to the house and asked me to have the same talk. I was happy to do so. Everyone wants to be the "cool dad," and for at least this one time, I got to be that guy. Over time, the three unbreakable rules became part of our family legend and lexicon. Whenever Caroline would go with friends, or stay over someone's house, I would simply call out, "Remember the three unbreakables!" Each time, she would laugh and renew her vow. Before long, whenever Diane and I would go somewhere without her, she would invoke the same warning to us. Did Caroline ever break any of the three? Maybe, but in my heart, I believe she didn't.

A few weeks after laying down the three rules, I was working at my desk when a call came in from an old friend in Key West. Through our many visits there, Diane and I became acquainted with a number of local residents. This call came from Robbie Wilcox, editor of the Key West Citizen. As a fellow newspaper-man, he wanted me to be among the first to learn that my friend, Skipper Garrison Malone, had passed away at the age of 94. The official cause of death was a heart attack, but the real reason was that he had lived his life to the fullest and it was simply time to move on.

The news hit me hard. We had just seen Skipper six weeks ago, when Diane and I made our yearly pilgrimage to the island. Twice we had lunch with Skipper and Linda. Once, Tommy, a son from one of his many past relationships, stopped by to join us. Tommy had taken over the daily operations at the bar. Privately,

Skipper told me that he was concerned that Tommy had neither the brains nor the balls for the job. Unfortunately, among family members, he was considered the most qualified. Diane and I had met Tommy several times before but had yet to form any strong opinions about him.

The call came in shortly before 5pm. I called Diane to tell her I would be late, without telling her why. I then spent the next two hours at my desk, with tears in my eyes, as I scribbled whatever notes came to mind about my friend, the ancient mariner. I left the paper around eight o'clock, emotionally exhausted. For six months prior, at Diane's constant urgings, I had sworn off drinking. I was a functional alcoholic, and I knew it. Now I really needed one. I turned into the parking lot of the Main Street Pub and awoke six days later in a hospital bed.

When I opened my eyes, the first person I saw was Fred Vaughn. Before I even saw the old bastard, I could smell his cigar. He was wearing that ugly tweed jacket that he always wore, with his tie loose and the collar undone. Leaning forward in the chair next to my bed, he grinned smugly. It was more of a sneer than a smile. This was not a reassuring sight. "Oh fuck," I said. "I'm dead."

"Nah, you ain't so lucky, you stupid jackass," the old man said. "My guess is that pretty soon you are going to wish you were dead. You really screwed up this time."

Fred leaned back and took a long draw on his cigar, oblivious to the countless signs that prohibited such an action. He exhaled slowly, with a long sigh, whistling through his gapped front teeth. "Hey Camby," he began. "Do you remember how we met?" I could not respond. There was nothing physical to stop me from speaking. The words simply would not come. The old man continued. "Let me refresh your memory. On this day, twenty-something years ago, a scared and desperate college kid showed up late in my office, begging for a job. As you may recall, I threw the little shit out on his ear. I'm pretty sure he cried all the way home."

"A few hours later, we had the good fortune of being reunited outside a certain Manchester bar, when my Lincoln smashed into whatever piece of shit you were driving. Rather than me going to jail, we negotiated. You got your dream job and I got one of the best newsmen I ever saw. You know, it would have been great if this story ended right there, but it didn't. You've gone on to become a real prick, just like me. That doesn't exactly sound like a storybook ending, if you know what I mean."

I responded with the only clear thought I had in my head. "Why are you here?"

"Good question," he responded. "That's one of the things that makes you so good in the newsroom. You ask good questions. Why do you think I'm here? Maybe I got bored sitting around in the afterlife and figured I could use a little excitement. Watching you sideswipe a minivan on I-84, flipping both vehicles was pretty exciting but not exactly what I was hoping for. The three kids are okay. The mother I'm not so sure about. Last I heard was she had a shattered pelvis and lost a lot of blood. All your injuries are in your head, both literally and figuratively."

"But how?"

"There's an even better question," Fred chortled. "It's a pretty short story and you are luckier than you may ever know. It goes like this. You were upset over the death of your friend from Key West. Instead of going home and sharing your sorrows with your lovely wife, you drown them in a bottle at the pub. About ten-o'clock you stumble out of there, totally shitfaced and head for home. Near Exit 67 you pass out, then cross three lanes, taking out a single mother and her kids as they are heading home from Walmart."

Fred began laughing to himself again. "Boy, you are one lucky sonofabitch."

"Lucky? I'm half dead and I almost killed three people. That's lucky?"

"Four people, and yourself. That makes five. Anyway, remember a few years ago, there was a story about a cop who was facing internal investigation charges for roughing up some scumbag he arrested?"

"Yeah. Ricky Schroeder. I remember. We looked into it, then buried that story. I remember we talked about it. We both felt that the dirtbag he was kicking around deserved it. We didn't want to see a good cop get a bad rap."

"Exactly. Guess who was the first cop on the scene at your accident? Our boy Ricky. He knew you reeked of booze, but he figured he owed you one. He got you out of there before anyone could question your sobriety. The report said you fell asleep at the wheel. It was sort of true, but not the whole story. By the time they got around to doing blood tests, your alcohol level was borderline and probably inadmissible. For the past six days you have been in a coma. You still are. Don't worry, you will come out of it tomorrow. You know, Camby, you were pretty convincing when you gave the kids those three unbreakable rules. Too bad you weren't smart enough to follow them yourself."

The following day I opened both eyes as someone in a with a white coat and a flashlight, pulled on my left eyelid and tried to blind me. He was about half my age, wore thick black glasses, hadn't shaved in a week, and reeked of too much cologne. I jerked my head to the right and puked.

"Welcome back," he replied, in what I'm guessing was an Iranian accent.

My head was pounding and my mouth was dry and tasted of bile. A few seconds later Diane burst into the room. The Iranian in the white coat pushed her away but allowed her to stand bedside. She touched my hand and a flood of tears came to both our eyes. Hers were tears of joy. Mine were of shame. "I'm tired, I said," and again drifted off.

Three hours later, I again awoke with Diane by my side. She called for the nurse, who quickly retrieved a doctor. This was not the Iranian, but a short thin woman with wavy gray hair.

The first words I spoke should have been to Diane. I should have squeezed her hand and told her that I love her. Instead I asked about the woman whose car I hit. This startled everyone. If I had fallen asleep at the wheel and been in a coma for a week, then how could I know about the woman? "You hear things when you are in a coma," was all I said.

I was told that the woman was stable. Since the accident, she had two hip surgeries. More would follow. Although it was too early to tell, the doctors believed that she would probably walk again, but not without a cane or a limp. I swallowed hard, knowing that my stupidity could easily have ended both her life and mine.

"And the kids?" I asked.

The doctor sighed. "Aside from the emotional trauma, they should be fine."

Within a week I was able to work a few hours a day from my hospital bed. After two weeks they let me go home. A week later I returned to work full-time. It is hard for most people to understand it, but that job is what gave me my personal identity and in doing so gave my life meaning. I know it sounds like misplaced priorities, and it is, but I also know it to be the truth.

I thought that by making a name for myself in the industry and by pulling in a decent paycheck, I was providing well for my family. Providing for them is very different from providing them with what they need. They needed my time, but I gave them a paycheck. They needed comfort and I gave them my name and my reputation. Anyone can make a good living. It takes much more to make a good life.

We have all heard tales of deathbed epiphanies. It was almost miraculous that I was not on my deathbed, but I did indeed have an epiphany. I cannot claim to have lived a perfect life after the accident, but I never drank again. Work would continue to be a driving force in my life, but the patience and love from my family became a strong enough magnet to sometimes pull me away from the job, and back to where I was truly needed.

The woman whose car I hit would have to endure five more surgeries and one life-threatening infection. It took two years of excruciating pain and superhuman effort, but over time she was able to walk without canes or crutches. During that time, her insurance company sued my insurance company for my stupidity. The suit was settled out of court for just under a million dollars.

The accident never made the papers or the news. Journalists protect journalists. A year later, I repaid Ricky Schroeder, after the officer diffused a hostage situation, stemming from a botched bank robbery. It was basic "in the line of duty" stuff, but we glorified him in a front-page headline. A few months later, he made detective. Fred Vaughn was right. It's all about who you know.

I never told Diane the truth about what happened that night, but I'm sure she knew. Except for occasional vertigo, my head injuries healed. At least that's what the doctors told me at the time. There was no cure, however, for the guilt. I condemned myself for being a phony, a liar and a hypocrite. After the accident I tried harder than ever before to be a good person, but I would fail as often as succeed. My sole consolation is that from that point forward, I never stopped trying.

There was a look of both shock and horror on Caroline's face. "I never knew any of this. I mean, of course I knew of the accident, but none of the circumstances. I'm not sure Mom knew either. She probably suspected, but I'm sure she didn't want to know."

Richard hesitated before saying anything, and even then, he measured his words carefully. "You seemed willing to give your father a pass on the affair. What about now?"

After a long silence, she muttered, "hate the sin, love the sinner." As she spoke, she seemed to be chewing on that thought. "Of course, I'm angry at him for nearly killing that family and himself. But, although we never really acknowledged it, he was an alcoholic who couldn't always control himself. That doesn't make him blameless, but it does make him worthy of forgiveness."

"How about you? Did you ever break any of the three unbreakable rules?"

"Nope. But I did come close. I almost got arrested. Once, while in high school, I was at a party with lots of underage drinking. One of the neighbors called the cops, complaining about the noise. When the police arrived, they found two dozen marijuana plants growing in the basement. I didn't get busted, but the cops called my parents and made them come get me. They didn't seem upset, but I was totally freaked out. Both Mom and Dad had their faults, but I never wanted to disappoint them."

CHAPTER TWENTY

Dear Caroline-Everyone knows they are going to die. What we choose to do with that knowledge goes a long way in determining how we live our lives. Some opt for a life of safety, attempting to prolong the inevitable by reducing the risk factors. Others live on the edge of danger, savoring every adrenaline induced moment. There are those for whom religious devotion is both a comfort and a lifestyle. Death is not so bad if you know that life here on earth is preparation for an even better life beyond. For agnostics and atheists there is no such comfort and yet they find a way to make the best of what they believe to be a short and finite period of consciousness. It all comes down to beliefs and choices.

What happens when choice is taken away? While others would profess a desire to pass away in peace, I always said I wanted a very slow and extremely painful death. This makes people uncomfortable. Slow and painful deaths are certainly a possibility, but why would anyone ask for one? In my own warped perspective, there was comfort in pain. Despite having had several experiences that might be termed "paranormal", my views on life after death were, at best, agnostic. The thought of dying and disappearing into eternal nothingness terrified me. It was my hope that a slow and painful death would make continued living so unbearable that I would welcome the end regardless of whether or not there was anything for me in the great beyond. Thankfully, I did not get my wish.

I didn't know it at the time, but the accident was the beginning of the end. After my initial recuperation, my overall health, pretty much, went back to normal. In some ways it was better than normal. I had stopped drinking and began exercising. I was at a healthy weight and in many ways, never felt better. It wasn't until a few years after the accident that I sensed something might be amiss.

Stress. It had to be stress. Frequent headaches were my primary symptoms. I shrugged it off. It was nothing. I've been working too hard. A couple of Excedrine and I'll be fine. If it gets worse, I'll see a doctor. Fear and guilt would not permit me to drink, so I began seeing a psychiatrist. We would make small-talk for about twenty minutes, then spend another twenty discussing how work and financial worries were tearing into me. The session ended with a prescription that made me feel like a zombie and a bill for one-hundred forty-six dollars.

The paper was faltering, I had Caroline's college tuitions to pay, and many of our investments had crumbled during a recent economic meltdown. Still, things really weren't so bad. We were hardly poor. Diane was working full time at the hospital and the house was finally paid off. Money was something I always worried about, but it never consumed me. If the paper went under, I could always find work. Fred Vaughn taught me the importance of contacts and I had made plenty of them over the years.

Caroline was no stress at all. She was a nursing student at Boston College, who handled both the rigors of her studies and an active social life with ease and balance. The hefty cost of her tuition was offset by scholarships and a modest trust fund that

I started shortly after she was born. While in Boston, she didn't have a car, but was just a two-hour train ride from home.

Likewise, my marriage was no longer stressful. Over the years we had been through some struggles, but somehow managed to weather the storms. When Caroline left for school there was some concern that Diane wouldn't be able to handle the empty nest, but we both adapted well. That's not to say it wasn't an adjustment. Going from a house full of teenagers, to the quiet of a cat and dog took a bit of getting used to, but we managed. I was working less hours, while Diane began working more. This somehow landed us together at home more frequently. It was a good thing. We talked a lot. As a result, we became better friends and better lovers.

If it wasn't money or marriage or children that was stressing me, then what was it? Simply put, it was my fear of death. I had somehow survived a near-fatal car crash. I had passed my fiftieth birthday. I had outlived my mother by more than a decade and was rapidly closing in on my father's age at the time of his death. Diane's family seemed to live forever. In mine, fifty was ancient.

The specter of short longevity weighed heavily upon me. I recall thinking at my father's funeral how appropriate and at the same time how unfair things were. His life had been a litany of mistakes and misfortune. It took him nearly sixty years to get things right, and when he finally did, the poor guy dropped dead. Was it justice or serendipity? I had concluded that this was God's way of making sure he didn't screw things up again. Now, at a slightly younger age, I too had finally gotten my affairs in order. If past is prologue, my days might be numbered. Unfortunately, I was right.

I never discussed my self-torment with Diane. Sharing joy is wonderful. Sharing pain leaves two people in pain instead of one. Instead, I medicated. Since alcohol was off-limits, Xanax and marijuana became my drugs of choice. Neither were addictions, but both were habitual. A pill here; a pill there. A joint after dinner. Almost always with Diane. For her, weed was a mood enhancer. For me, it quieted my mind. It buried the pain but not the problem. The headaches persisted on an almost daily basis until I finally opted to see a real doctor.

Milt Greenberg was my regular physician. He went through all of the usual paces. Blood pressure, sinus problems, glaucoma. Everything checked out. The next step was a CAT scan. That would provide a detailed image of the brain, hopefully giving an indication of where and what the problem was. Meanwhile, I was told to eliminate sodium and caffeine from my diet. Easier said than done. As with so many other things in my life, I succumbed to temptation, at first cheating a little, then a lot. By the time I had the scan done on March 9th, I was back to my old habits of drinking four or five cups of coffee a day and pouring salt on almost everything I ate.

The call from Greenberg's office was not what I expected. I expected everything to be normal. At worst they might tell me that they wanted to run more tests. That's what I expected. What I got was a rather somber call on Friday afternoon from the doctor, saying that he and the neurologist, Dr. Bernard Kingman, wanted to meet with the two of us as soon as possible.

"Why do you want both of us there? It's bad, isn't it?"

"Well, there are some problems that we need to discuss."

"Cancer. I have brain cancer. Is that it?"

"No, but I don't really think we should have this discussion over the phone. It's always better if we can show you the actual scan and explain what we found. Can you and Diane be here at eleven on Tuesday?"

"Yeah, sure I can be there. But I don't see why Diane has to be there. Look doc, I know she's the medical person in the family and would probably have the right questions to ask, but if it's bad news then I prefer to go by myself. Let me soften the blow for her. Then she can call with any questions she might have. For now, let me be the one to stress over things."

"I really would prefer if you both came, but if that's the way you want it, I guess I'm okay with that."

I hung up the phone and paused for several moments. My mind was racing. I immediately pounced on the internet. The Mayo Clinic website had an entire section devoted to diseases of the brain. If it wasn't cancer, what could it be? There were far too many possibilities to even have a clue. Blood clots, aneurisms, viral infections, meningitis, encephalitis, not to mention at least thirty other maladies that I had never heard of. This was getting me nowhere. I would just have to wait until Tuesday.

My mood changed and Diane took notice. Reluctantly I told her that I was nervous. Greenberg called and I would be meeting him on Tuesday to go over the results.

"Well, what did he say?"

"Nothing really. It was actually his secretary who called to set up the appointment." It was a lie but a good one.

"Want me to go with you?"

"No, no. You're working and this could take a while. You know how he is. He wants to show me the scan and explain all the little details. I'll call you when I get done so you can translate his medical gibberish."

"Okay. You sure?"

"Sure, I'm sure."

"Well don't get all worried about it. I'm sure if it was anything bad, he would have called sooner."

With that I retreated to the bathroom, locked the door, sat on the toilet and cried.

There is a line from the classic movie "Pride of the Yankees" where baseball great Lou Gehrig is meeting with his doctors, knowing full well that they have bad news. "Give it to me straight, Doc," the slugger says. "Is it strike three?" The doctor hangs his head, then nods. "I'm afraid it is, Lou." It was then that he learned he had amyotrophic lateral sclerosis, a rare neurological disease that would soon claim his life and bear his name.

When I arrived at Doctor Greenberg's office the waiting room was full. The receptionist recognized me at once and I was quickly led past all waiters and into his office, where he and Doc Kingman were waiting. A number of charts and folders were spread across his desk. After exchanging pleasantries, I attempted my best Gary Cooper. "Give it to me straight Doc. Is it strike three?" I don't think they understood the parody. Dr. Kingman reached forward, took one of the envelopes, leaned back and replied "Yes and no."

"Yes and no? What the hell kind of answer is that?"

"An honest one," Greenberg replied. "You have a brain aneurism. Probably the result of your car accident. Because of its size and location, it is inoperable and pretty much untreatable. Do you know what an aneurism is?"

A deep breath was followed by a heavy sigh. "I have some idea but go on…."

"An aneurism" he continued, "is what we call it when a blood vessel balloons. This is not simple swelling. It often looks like a berry hanging from a stem. If that balloon breaks, in all probability, you will have a massive stroke and die."

"So, when is it going to break?" I shot back. "Today? Tomorrow? Six years from now?"

"That's the problem. We just don't know. In your case it is not very large, but it is deeply embedded near the base of the occipital lobe." Dr. Kingman began pointing to blurred lines and red and black splotches on several charts.

"Here it is." Doctor Kingman pointed. I didn't see anything

but took his word for it and nodded. "It is too deep to safely get to. As for your question, you are right on all counts. It could burst today or it could be twenty years from now. In a few rare instances they have receded and gone away on their own. I don't mean to be negative, but don't count on that. There is no sure way to predict it, but in all likelihood at some point it will rupture. When it does it is called a subarachnoid hemorrhage. A massive stroke."

"Then you'll just have to operate," I interrupted.

"Operating is out of the question. Chemo and radiation are equally unadvisable because the dose required would cause residual harm that would exceed any possible benefit."

"So, we have no plan of attack? I just live knowing that with no advance notice I might suddenly die?"

"There are a few basic lifestyle changes that will reduce the chance of a rupture," Greenberg offered. "Nothing is likely to shrink or remove the aneurism, but you can decrease the likelihood of a rupture. Have you been avoiding salt and caffeine like I recommended?"

"Not really."

"The next cup of coffee you have could be your last. There are risk factors. Avoid them. Run from them. Next, we have to keep your blood pressure in check. I'll up your dose of amlodipine. If you don't already have one, go out and get one of those home blood pressure kits. I want you to check your blood pressure three times a day. If the top number is over 130 or the bottom number is over 80, sit down, take ten deep slow breaths and take a Klonopin. I'll give you a prescription for that. Next comes diet. Chicken and fish. No red meat. Last thing. No heavy lifting or straining. Nothing more than ten or fifteen pounds."

"What about sex? Does that count as straining?"

Greenberg smiled, but I was serious. "Sex is fine as long as you don't try to carry her upstairs to do it."

The meeting went on for another twenty minutes. A schedule was set for follow-up appointments and further testing. Remission was very unlikely but not completely out of the question, so I tried to cling to false hope. The aneurism was the size of a small blueberry and it wasn't hanging on by much.

It was agreed that I would be the one to tell Diane. Both Greenberg and Kingman assured me that my wishes and my privacy would be respected. Both of them lied. They had spoken with Diane the day before my appointment. They wanted to be sure that she understood the gravity of my situation and that she assisted in my care. She agreed to go along with my charade and feign no knowledge of my diagnosis unless I mentioned it to her first.

I did not return home right after my appointment. Instead I called Diane on my cell and told her everything went fine and I was going to work. I could give her the details when I got home. This was not what she wanted to hear, but she understood. The paper was always my sanctuary. It demanded so much focus that there was no room for personal woes. When I got home around seven she was ready with dinner and a litany of vague and probing questions. I had anticipated this. I thought my answers were properly prepared. I was wrong.

"So, what did Greenberg say?"

"Not much. My blood pressure is back up and he thinks I have too much stress. Like all doctors his answer is more pills. Amlodipine and Klonopin. I don't like the idea, but if it takes care of the headaches, I'll go along with it. You know how I feel about this. All doctors are drug peddlers, treating symptoms not patients. For now, I'll play along. You had a dentist appointment this morning. How did that go?"

"Good. Just a cleaning. What did the CAT scan show?"

"Not much. I'm not sure they knew exactly what they were

looking at. When they pointed to something on the chart it just looked like a blur or a blob. They would show me one or two things and say these are fine, then point to something else and say that we have to watch this or monitor that. If the headaches aren't gone in a week or so they want to do another scan."

"If you have to go back, I'm going too. I want to hear what they say."

"No way. You get too worked up over everything."

"I want to make sure you're going to follow doctor's orders."

"Okay Mom." I smiled sadly.

In the days and weeks that followed not a word was spoken about my condition. Perhaps more important, not a word was spoken to Caroline. We went about our daily lives, pretending that all was as it ever was. Things were different, but the differences were subtle. Moments of melancholy and quiet introspection were interwoven with a desire to squeeze as much living as possible out of whatever time we had left. This wasn't "Live like you were dying." It was live as you should have been living all along. Take nothing for granted. Enjoy the moment.

Diane proved to be a wonderful actress in concealing her worry and her grief. Occasionally she would peek over my shoulder as I tested myself, to see how my blood pressure was doing. Other times she would steer me away from a burger joint or from ordering steak at a restaurant. She was the master thespian, pretending that our lives had not been dramatically changed by an impending tragedy.

Circumstances were rapidly changing around us. The ever-crumbling finances of the paper had finally reached a crisis point, as the Courant embarked on a massive restructuring and consolidation. They offered me early retirement. The severance package was a good one. One year of full pay and two years of medical benefits. The healthcare benefits were key, since my medical bills could be daunting. There was a small going away party, then without fanfare, I was suddenly among the ranks of the unemployed. No more eighteen-hour days. No longer did I have to balance political correctness with a desire to report the truth. No longer was I part of the profession that in every way defined my life. It was awkward, but the timing was perfect. The most stressful part was learning to live without stress.

Maybe it was the medication or the diet or the premature retirement, but the headaches were gone. Follow-up exams showed no change in my condition but I felt better than I had in years. I took a job at a local Barnes and Nobel. Let someone else have the headaches. I sold and read books.

Diane's professional life had also changed. Long ago we forged an unspoken pact that for at least one of us, Caroline would come first. One of us had to be the breadwinner while the other would contribute financially when possible, but would be the primary caregiver to our daughter. It was very fortunate that we could do this. I had a demanding job, but it paid well enough to carry the weight of our bills. Diane got decent pay for part-time work. She had flexible schedule that allowed her to get Caroline on and off the bus and to dance or basketball or whatever activity might be happening at that moment. I was there for most of it. Diane was there for all of it.

A few days after I sealed my fate with the paper, the two of us went out to dinner. Diane had big news to discuss. After twenty years of part-time work, she was returning to full-time. Several resumes went out. Almost immediately, one came back. She was being offered a position as a staff pharmacist at the Mount Sinai Geriatric Hospital in West Hartford. Fifteen years ago, she had done a temporary stint there. She loved the staff and patients but the hospital couldn't offer her a sufficiently flexible schedule.

They now offered her a permanent, full-time position. In her own tactful but outspoken way, she expressed her concerns, recounting every reason she could think of as to why this might not be the place for her. Director Mike Hartmann, informed her that in the past year there had been considerable turnover among pharmacy personnel. He was building a new staff from scratch and he wanted her to be a part of it. I could tell she was excited.

"Think I should take it?" she asked.

"What do you think? It sounds to me like you've already made up your mind."

"Maybe. Not really. I mean it does sound good and I do like the place. Now with Caroline away at college, I have plenty of time."

"Do you know this guy, Mike Hartmann?"

"I know of him. He was an inspector for the state. Smart guy. He always seemed pretty decent, but I guess you never know until you actually work with someone."

"True. Pros and cons?"

"Pros are money, benefits, location, a steady paycheck, decent hours. Cons are that I'll be locked in with a rigid work schedule, so if Caroline has something going on at school I may not be able to go."

"My turn for that."

"That's what I've been thinking. We've worked these things out over the years, but when you get down to it, I've had jobs but you had a career. I worked hard to become a pharmacist and I like being one. It may be a little late, but I want a career too."

And so it was. The job could not have come at a better time. The unspoken thought was that if she had a full-time job, she and Caroline would be fine after I was gone. Her days would be full and the bills would get paid. Diane began her career on Monday, July 5th. I was beginning to wrap up my life and she was starting a new one, not knowing if I would be there or not. As crazy as this sounds, those were some of the happiest days of my life.

CHAPTER TWENTY-ONE

*L*ife as we knew it was in a state of constant change. I said goodbye to my career and Diane said hello to hers. And while health issues weighed extremely heavily on our minds they were never discussed. As each day passed, concerns lessened. I felt fine. A couple of years passed. My vitals were good, the headaches had eased, and often I went for days without being reminded of my condition. Our lives were changing, but at least I felt normal.

Many of the changes had to do with Caroline. That little girl, whose childhood I missed so much of, had grown into a beautiful adult woman. We had grown accustomed to her coming home for a long weekend during the school year, visiting her at Boston College, or meeting her for dinner near Quincy Market. Then, following spring break during her junior year, she began spending a lot of time with her new boyfriend, Richard Smythe. Not Rick, or Richie or Ricky; he was Richard.

Caroline had no shortage of male suitors, but this was different. Everything about the relationship seemed natural and uncomplicated. They complemented each other well. I knew the signs because it rekindled the feelings I originally had when I first met Diane. If neither of them screwed things up, this could be a long-term situation.

Things got a bit more real, when for her senior year, Caroline did not return to the dorm, but instead moved in with Richard.

Diane and I have lived together before marriage, but the idea of Caroline and Richard living together took some getting used to. Let's be honest; no parent wants to think about their child having sex, just as that child would rather not imagine their parents doing it. Yet, if we choose our relationships wisely, both will happen with some degree of regularity. Cohabitation implied sex. We got used to the idea by not thinking about it.

The same could be said of my aneurism. The less we talked about it, the less we thought about it. The less we thought about it, the less real it became. Fortunately, I was feeling good, so we clung to the hope that things just might work out after-all.

Caroline and Richard's relationship continued to flourish. Soon there were wedding plans. It would be a November wedding in Boston, six months after Caroline's graduation. For their honeymoon, I booked them a week at the La Concha, in Key West.

With no signs of health issues, it was decided Diane and I deserved a vacation getaway of our own. Montego Bay, Jamaica. We had gone there years ago and hoped to return there for our twenty-fifth wedding anniversary, but my accident intervened. Now, as we approached our thirtieth anniversary, it occurred to us that a tropical escape might be the best medicine of all.

Although we had only been there that one time, we always yearned to go back. Jamaica has high crime and abject poverty, but we really enjoyed the island, the food, the music and the people. On our previous trip, we had been there for the Reggae festivals. Aside from Bob Marley, we knew nothing of the music other than that we liked it. Unbeknownst to us, we had the rare opportunity to see Peter Tosh and Jimmy Cliff, both legends of the genre, together on stage. Tosh was now dead, and Cliff no longer lived on the island.

We rented a condo on the beach. For eight glorious days we divided our time between doing what tourists do and just doing nothing. We took a sunset cruise. We listened to live music. We went fishing and snorkeling. We slept late and then sat on the beach all day. We even got our hands on a little ganja and smoked ourselves silly. I remember thinking, 'If I have to die soon, this isn't a bad way to go.'

We returned home from Jamaica shortly after midnight on August 19th. The next two weeks were likely to be hectic. Unbeknownst to us, Caroline and Richard had planned an early surprise birthday party for Diane on Labor Day weekend. After that they would be completely absorbed in careers and wedding plans. We might not see them again before the big day.

The birthday party was to be at Diane's brother's house. Nick had a large house with a fenced-in yard and a pool. There was no need to have it catered. Everyone involved in the planning, except for Caroline and Richard would bring food. They were responsible for getting us to the party. Friends, siblings, nieces, nephews, cousins and assorted others would all be there. All told, ninety people were invited. It was requested that there be no gifts, although Franklin had made a point of buying a fifth of Balvenie. It was expected that Frank and I would quietly go about killing the bottle, while sharing it with no one. I knew I wasn't supposed to drink, but maybe just this one time it would be okay. As an added surprise, the celebration was also going to be a wedding shower. It was going to be a great time.

The end came suddenly and without pain. At precisely 1:09am, less than an hour after returning home from our week in Jamaica, I grabbed the largest of our four suitcases and headed upstairs. In yanking the handle with an abrupt jerking motion, a little voice screamed in my head as I recalled what the doctors had warned. No straining. No sudden moves. No heavy lifting. It was too late. Halfway up the steps I felt my face grow warm and flushed. Two steps later I was blinded as a white light began as a small star in the upper right-hand corner of my field of vision, but rapidly expanded to consume all that I could see. One more step. I tried to call out but no words came. My grip released, the suitcase fell, and I tumbled backwards down the stairs.

The doctors would say that I was dead before I hit the last step, but I don't recall it happening that way. There was no pain, no sound. Only the explosion of white light. I knew what was happening but I was not in control. Disembodied with nothing to see, hear or feel I was simply surrounded by light; or was it I who was becoming the light? Suspended in space? Falling? Traveling at the speed of light? It happened so quickly and so slowly. My thoughts raced but there was nowhere for them to go. There was a moment of panic. Would everything suddenly go black and I would cease to exist? Was I to be forever suspended in this illumination? Either of those two possibilities would surely be hell. Is there a hell or a heaven?

I never really did believe in heaven or hell as a destination, such as it is taught in religious doctrine. I tended to subscribe more to the belief that life on earth was both heaven and hell. My best days at the paper were heaven. Key West was heaven. Happy times spent with Diane and Caroline were heaven. The years I spent tormented by Carmen were hell. As for what came next, I didn't know. Now that I was about to be among the dead, I had to wonder. Good or bad, I just wanted it to be something. Eternal nothing would be worse than hell.

There was no crossing over. No tunnel. No harps, no angels, no visit from Saint Peter or Jesus. Those things belong in the movies, or in someone else's experience of death. None of it happened to me.

Time no longer had meaning, but gradually the piercing

brightness faded. At the time, I was so absorbed in the experience that I was unaware of this change. It became first apparent when I saw what I thought to be a shadow and a silhouette. Forms began to take shape. Perhaps I wasn't dead after all. There was a faint sound, like the clattering of stainless steel utensils or instruments. Was I alive and in the hospital? There were muffled conversations. The shadows grew darker, sharper, clearer. I began to feel again. No pain, just ordinary sensation. I felt myself returning to my own skin. My own clothes. It felt as though my bottom was comfortably pressed into the seat of a cushioned chair. Finally, a voice rang out as clear as day. It was a voice that I had only heard once before.

"You ready for some coffee Hon?"

It was Beatrice, the waitress from the Cristo Diner. The last time I was in there I had lunch with my father's ghost. This was all too damn weird, but there I was in that same corner booth looking up at Beatrice and across from my father. Everything was the same as before and yet it seemed different. "Black, no sugar," I smiled and answered. At last I knew what was going on. This was a dream.

I didn't say it was a dream, I only thought it. That didn't matter, because my father had obviously heard it. "No, it aint," he said. "Not this time. This time it's for real."

"What's for real?"

"Remember when you were a kid and I used to play those old Louis Jordan records for you?"

"Yeah, sure."

"Do you remember what your favorite song was of his?"

"Sure. Saturday Night Fish Fry."

"No it wasn't."

"Yes it was."

"It wasn't."

"It wasn't? Okay, I guess I don't remember. You tell me."

"Jack You're Dead."

"Yeah, that's right. Good song. We didn't like much of the same music, but that stuff we could agree on. Louis Armstrong and Louis Jordan. Jack You're Dead. Great song. But what's your point?"

"Think about it."

"C'mon. Let's not play games. What does Louis Jordan and Jack You're Dead have to do with…." It had taken a moment, but now I understood. "You mean…?"

He nodded. Beatrice smiled.

"Would you like the deviled eggs or the angel food cake?" she laughed.

I didn't think it was funny. "Relax," she smiled, resting her hand on my shoulder. "You're going to be fine. You guys talk. Just wave if you need more coffee."

"So, I'm…"

"Dead. Croaked. Kicked the bucket. Bit the dust."

"And this place is…?"

"A good place to start."

"No out of body experience? I don't get to see people crying around me as they cover my face with a sheet?"

"Is that what you want?"

"Hell, no. I just thought…"

"If you don't want it then don't ask for it. The people you left behind, they will be fine. There will be mourning and grief, but that's part of that life. It's not part of this one."

"But I never got to say good bye."

"Is that so important?"

"Kind of. Yeah, I think it is."

"I'm not sure that there is anything we can do about that."

"You just said 'if I don't want it, don't ask for it.' What about things that I want and want to ask for?"

"Same as before. You can't always get what you want, but you get what you need."

"Since when did you start quoting the Rolling Stones?"

"What difference does it make as long as it's true?"

"But I need to say good-bye. I need to let them know that I'm okay."

"I'm sure at some point you will get that chance, but not now. I didn't get to say good-bye to you, did I? Don't you think I felt the same way when I died? Look...I understand this is all very sudden and confusing, but like life itself, this is a process. There is an order and a reason to things. You may not understand it and most of the time I don't either, but it's going to be okay.

Let's start with the good news. You are about to embark on another long and wonderful life. There will be some old departed friends that you will be reunited with, and some new people to meet. The bad news is that you won't be seeing Diane and Caroline for a while, but they'll get here eventually. Trust me. Everything is going to be okay. Not perfect, but very good and as it should be."

I clung to his last words. "Not perfect. What do you mean not perfect? I thought this was heaven. Isn't heaven supposed to be perfect?"

"Nah, that's a bunch of bullshit," he chortled with an unsettling laugh. "Heaven is a made-up place because there is no better way to explain what you don't know." He waved Beatrice over. "More coffee please." Looking up at her he asked, "Bea, is this place heaven?"

"For me it is," she replied. "But that's just me. It's where I want to be and where I need to be right now. For you it's probably some place different. For some people this might even be considered hell. That is, if there was such a thing as heaven or hell."

The harder I tried to wrap my head around things, the more

confused I became. There is an afterlife and apparently, I'm in it, but there is no heaven or hell. I'm with my father in a diner in New Jersey, a place I have been to before, but the first time it was in real life and now it's in the afterlife. I began to talk aloud, slowly and deliberately, in an attempt to fit the pieces together.

"Physically I'm here. It all feels very real. It must be real because I can taste that the coffee is too weak and you still smell like cigarettes. But I'm dead and so is everyone around me." I looked up at him. "Is that right? Is everyone here dead too?" Dad nodded in assent. So far, I had it right. "There really is no heaven or hell," I continued, "but life goes on in this different place and time. It's not perfect but it is good. I know this to be a place I've been to before, but when I asked where or what it was, you replied that it is a good place to start. That must mean that this is just a temporary illusion before I get whisked off to someplace else."

"Damn! You were doing so well and then you got off track. Try to forget about time and space. They don't matter right now. This place is real and it is here and now. This is where you start your new life. And it is a good place to start. That's what it is all about. Getting you started on your new life. It's not like before when you pop out as a slimy and sniveling newborn with nothing but your future experiences to work with. That was your first beginning. We all had to start somewhere. This is your second beginning, but in this life there is no denying the past. The past is what you build on, whether it was from your first life, or this one or the next one."

"Whoa. Stop right there. The next one? You mean we'll all die again and move on again after this…whatever this is?"

"I don't know. I have only been dead once, so far. I'm just guessing at the next part. Regardless of what we believed the first time around, none of us really knew for sure that there was life after death, but now that we are here, we know that there is. Why wouldn't there be life after a second death? It's just a guess, but it makes sense."

For a moment I looked away, staring across the room and out of the tinted windows at the front of the building. Cars were filing in and out of the parking lot. The street beyond was jammed with what appeared to be early morning commuter traffic. The sun was rising just beyond the trees, houses, and businesses that lined the avenue. I pointed towards the window. "Out there. Is that real?"

"As real as you and I." Dad smiled, and I returned the grin. The word "real" no longer meant much to me.

"So, what happens now? What happens when we walk out that door? I assume we will be walking out that door at some point. Am I right?"

"Now we're getting somewhere." A big grin. "Bea. Two coffees to go and the check please." Reaching into his wallet, he pulled out a twenty and dropped it on the table. "Always tip big when you are a regular somewhere. I taught you that, remember? If you're only going to be somewhere once it doesn't matter, but if you plan to keep coming back, it's best to give them a good reason to remember you." With that, he stood up. Instinctively, I stood up too.

"Where are we going?"

"Oops. Sorry. Sit down. I didn't explain that part yet, did I? We're going to my place. I'm renting a little house in Sea Bright just a block off the beach. You will be staying with me for a while until you get comfortable with your new situation. Everything is set for you. Clothes, a car, credit cards. It's sort of like joining the Witness Protection Program. You get to start over with all new stuff. Not bad, eh? After that, who knows? I've got my own life to live and so do you. The way I see it, our job here is to avoid repeating the mistakes of our past. We will make new mistakes and that's okay."

"Once I get settled, then what?"

"Same as before. You meet people and make friends. I know it's soon but eventually you might even start dating. It's a complete do-over, except you are hopefully smarter, having learned from all the dumb shit you did the first time around. You get a job and go to work just like before. The bad news is that your new life will be a lot like your old one. There will be good times and bad. You will still feel pain. The good news is that it is a pretty easy adjustment, because everything feels so familiar. One really good thing about it is that you don't age. I hope you like the way you look and feel right now because it aint going to change very much."

"What kind of job? Am I still a writer?"

"You'll always be a writer. That's who you are. But that's not what your job is going to be. I think there is already something lined up for you. There's a new guy, Gary, who just moved into the big house across the street from me. A crusty old sailor type. Says he knows you from when he owned a saloon in Key West. Gary. Garrison Malone. I think that's his name."

"Skipper? You're kidding me. Skipper Malone is your neighbor?"

"Yeah, that's the guy. A real character. The guy's got so many stories, I can't even begin to guess if any of them are true. He just bought a rundown little bar and pool hall across from the boardwalk. He says he'll be sticking around for a year or two, then head back to Key West. He wants you to help him run the place. I guess you made quite the impression on him a few years ago. He's been dead for a while, but he came here just for you."

It was all so sudden and yet, oddly enough it felt comfortable. There was great relief to know that I was not sentenced to a hereafter of eternal nothingness. I didn't disappear. I crossed over, to who knows what, but it seemed as though it just might be okay.

I had one final flash of panic. I read somewhere that near-death experiences, in which people were reunited with lost loved ones, were actually the finally spark of life before the flame goes out. For a moment I was paralyzed. Then, a reassuring hand touched my shoulder. Again, it was Beatrice.

"It's okay to be afraid. We all were. But the light doesn't go out. Quite the opposite. The flame gets stronger."

The two of us rose and headed for the door. I didn't know or understand anything about what had happened or what was to come, but it was time to move on and find out. There was comfort in knowing that I once again had my Dad and an old friend to help guide the way. Beatrice held the door as we stepped outside into the light of the morning sun. Somehow, it was going to be okay.

CHAPTER TWENTY-TWO

*E*ven in the afterlife, Skipper Malone has connections and clout. Diane and I had returned to Key West at least a dozen times since the infamous escapade that landed us in jail. Over time, we had become true friends of the legendary mariner. Why he took such a liking to us, I cannot say. Gary liked almost everybody, but at some higher level we connected. He felt that I was not your typical journalist or tourist, and he certainly was not your typical anything. With each visit to the island we spent time with our friend, sharing old stories and creating new ones.

I've been exposed to death all my life, but the Skipper's passing hit me unexpectedly hard. He was well past ninety years old and in failing health, so it should have surprised no one. I always assumed he was immortal. With the possible exception of Fred Vaughn, he was the most memorable character of my first life. Unlike Fred, however, Skipper was lovable, as well as charismatic.

Upon my own death I reunited with my friend, and promptly went to work for him, helping to transform an old billiard room into a popular beachfront night spot. Garrison was easy to work with, and we again found plenty of time for conversations and camaraderie. Late one night, after closing the bar, we sat down for a long talk. I expressed deep remorse that I had not been given the opportunity to say good-bye to my family. More so and perhaps as part of my penance, I expressed a deeper regret that Caroline did not get to know me as well as I would have liked. There were so many stories to tell. So many lessons learned that I did not share. So many mistakes that I had made. I always assumed I would be there to teach them at a later time, but fate intervened. I was gone and now it was too late.

The Skipper listened with a sympathetic ear. This was his penance too. Garrison the legend was not Gary Malone the person. He loved his own children but they hardly knew him. We sat down and opened a bottle of Wild Turkey. Skipper then produced an old cassette recorder, inserted a tape and hit record. He asked me to tell him all of the stories that I could not or did not tell my daughter. Six hours, four cassettes and an empty bottle later, we made our way home. I went to sleep. Skipper went to work.

Three days later he handed me a copy of the manuscript that you are now reading. I say it is a copy, because I must assume that you have the original. My friend assured me that the original had been properly delivered to my family with all of the care and love that could be given. I didn't ask him how, where or why. Those are questions he would not answer. My only reply was a simple "Thanks." Good deeds and gratitude. That is mostly what the Skipper and I are striving for these days.

Perhaps it was my father that reunited me with Garrison. Perhaps it was Garrison who brought me to my father. Maybe Beatrice had something to do with it all. I just don't know. Here among the newly dead, it's hard to figure that stuff out. All three are good friends, but none more than Skipper. I believe it was fate and good fortune that brought us together. Maybe someday I can repay him, by helping him to reconnect with his own family and former self. For now, I am satisfied with the knowledge that in this life, I again have family, friends and the opportunity to try to do good.

Dear Caroline-None of us is perfect, and I'm not yet convinced that we are evolving on any path towards perfection. We are constantly asked to do the right thing and yet we routinely make bad decisions. We are all sinners and saints and yet, deep down, I know it is in our nature to do good.

These stories that I have recounted, are the story of my life. There is a line from an old Jimmy Buffett song that goes "Some of it's magic and some of it's tragic, but I've had a good life all the way." That about sums it up. It took my own father two lifetimes to tell me his story. These are the stories that I have never told you. But they are stories that you need to know. It will not be long before you have children of your own. Do not deprive them of the opportunity to love you for who you are. It is important to know each other and understand who we are and where we came from. It is that truth which will guide us along our path and take us to wherever it is that we may be going.

EPILOGUE

*A*fter three pitchers of margaritas and one pot of coffee, Caroline and Richard were both awake and exhausted. From the window of their room at the La Concha, they could see the first glimmer of a new day dawning. For hours they had taken turns reading. There were gasps of horror, exclamations of joy and fits of laughter. There was so much she never knew about her father and yet so many questions still to ask. Questions that, for now, must go unanswered.

Finally, without another word, Caroline gathered up the pages and neatly returned them to the envelope, which she set gently on the nightstand. After washing her face and running a brush through her hair, she and Richard poured the last of the coffee into paper cups and took the stairs to the rooftop observation deck. From there, arm in arm, they watched the sun slowly rise across the horizon, beyond the White Street Pier. She envisioned her father's soul rising in the midst of that fiery ball. This was Key West and she knew that her father would always be here.

Nine months later, Caroline gave birth to a son. They named him Garrison Richard Smythe. In time, she would tell the boy many stories. Stories of her own life, but also of his grandmother and grandfather. Often, she would think back with wistful wonder and remember that La Concha sunrise. And with each memory she would smile. As long as her father's spirit was alive, the sun would continue to rise and there would always be stories to tell. Oh, so many stories to tell.